THE SHARING KNIFE

❧

PASSAGE

ALSO BY LOIS MCMASTER BUJOLD

The Spirit Ring

Falling Free

Shards of Honor

Barrayar

The Warrior's Apprentice

The Vor Game

Cetaganda

Ethan of Athos

Borders of Infinity

Brothers in Arms

Mirror Dance

Memory

Komarr

A Civil Campaign

Diplomatic Immunity

The Curse of Chalion

Paladin of Souls

The Hallowed Hunt

The Sharing Knife: Beguilement

The Sharing Knife: Legacy

THE SHARING KNIFE

Volume Three
PASSAGE

Lois McMaster Bujold

An Imprint of HarperCollins*Publishers*

THE SHARING KNIFE, VOLUME THREE: PASSAGE. Copyright © 2008 by Lois McMaster Bujold. All rights reserved. Printed in the United States of America. No part of this book may be used or reproduced in any manner whatsoever without written permission except in the case of brief quotations embodied in critical articles and reviews. For information address HarperCollins Publishers, 10 East 53rd Street, New York, NY 10022.

Eos is a federally registered trademark of HarperCollins Publishers.

Designed by Susan Walsh

ISBN 978-0-06-137533-0

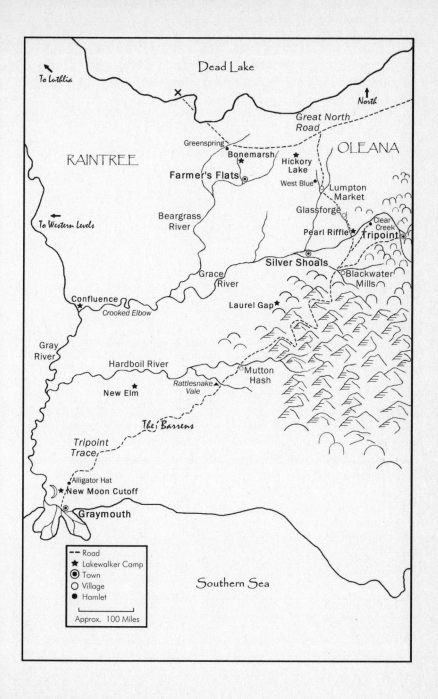

THE SHARING KNIFE

PASSAGE

1

Dag was riding up the lane thinking only of the chances of a Bluefield farm lunch, and his likelihood of needing a nap afterwards, when the arrow hissed past his face.

Panic washing through him, he reached out his right arm and snatched his wife from her saddle. He fell left, dragging them both off and behind the shield of their horses, snapping his sputtering ground-sense open wide—range still barely a hundred paces, *blight* it—torn between thoughts of Fawn, of the knife at his belt, of the unstrung bow at his back, of *how many, where?* All of it was blotted out in the lightning flash of pain as he landed with both their weights on his healing left leg. His cry of "Spark, get behind me!" transmuted to "Agh! Blight it!" as his leg folded under him. Fawn's mare bolted. His horse Copperhead shied and jerked at the reins still wrapped around the hook that served in place of Dag's left hand; only that, and Fawn's support under his arm as she found her feet, kept him upright.

"Dag!" Fawn yelped as his weight bent her.

Dag straightened, abandoning his twisting reach for his bow, as he at last identified the source of the attack—not with his groundsense, but with his eyes and ears. His brother-in-law Whit Bluefield came running across the yard below the old barn, waving a bow in the air and calling, "Oh, sorry! Sorry!"

Only then did Dag's eye take in the rag target tacked to a red oak tree on the other side of the lane. Well . . . he assumed it was a target, though the only arrow nearby was stuck in the bark about two feet below it. Other spent arrows lay loose on the ground well beyond. The one that had nearly clipped off his nose had plowed into the soil a good twenty paces downslope. Dag let out his pent breath in exasperation, then inhaled deeply, willing his hammering heart to slow.

"Whit, you ham-fisted fool!" cried Fawn, rising on tiptoe to peer over her restive horse-fort. "You nearly shot my husband!"

Whit arrived breathless, repeating, "Sorry! I was so surprised to see you, my hand slipped."

Fawn's mare Grace, who had skittered only a few steps before getting over her alarm at this unusual dismount, put her head down and began tearing at the grass clumps. Whit, familiar with Copperhead's unsociable character, made a wide circle around the horse to his sister's side. Dag let the reins unwrap from his hook and allowed Copperhead to go join Grace, which the chestnut gelding did after a few desultory bucks and cow-kicks, just to register his opinion of the proceedings. Dag sympathized.

"I wasn't aiming at you!" Whit declared anxiously.

"I'm right glad to hear that," drawled Dag. "I know I annoyed a few people around here when I married your sister, but I didn't think you were one of 'em." His lips compressed in a grimmer line. Whit might well have hit *Fawn*.

Whit flushed. A head shorter than Dag, he was still a head taller than Fawn, whom, after an awkward hesitation, he now embraced. Fawn grimaced, but hugged him back. Both Bluefield heads were crowned with loosely curling black hair, both faces fair-skinned, but while Fawn was nicely rounded, with a captivating sometimes-dimple when she smirked, Whit was skinny and angular, his hands and feet a trifle too big for his body. Still growing into himself even past age twenty, as the length of wrist sticking from the sleeve of his homespun shirt testified. Or perhaps, with no younger brother to hand them down to, he was just condemned to wear out his older clothes.

Dag took a step forward, then hissed, hook-hand clapping to his buckling left thigh. He straightened again with an effort. "Maybe I want my stick after all, Spark."

"Of course," said Fawn, and darted across the lane to retrieve the hickory staff from under Copperhead's saddle flap.

"Are you all right? I know I didn't hit you," Whit protested. His mouth bent down. "I don't hit anything, much."

Dag smiled tightly. "I'm fine. Don't worry about it."

"He is not fine," Fawn amended sternly, returning with the stick. "He got knocked around something fearsome last month when his company rode to put down that awful malice over in Raintree. He hasn't nearly healed up yet."

"Oh, was that your folks, Dag? Was it really a blight bogle—malice," Whit corrected himself to the Lakewalker term, with a duck of his head at Dag. "We heard some pretty wild rumors about a ruckus up by Farmer's Flats—"

Fawn overrode this in concern. "That scar didn't break open when you landed so hard, did it, Dag?"

Dag glanced down at the tan fabric of his riding trousers. No blood leaked through, and the flashes of pain were fading out. "No." He took the stick and leaned on it gratefully. "It'll be fine," he added to allay Whit's wide-eyed look. He squinted in new curiosity at the bow still clutched in Whit's left hand. "What's this? I didn't think you were an archer."

Whit shrugged. "I'm not, yet. But you said you would teach me when—if—you came back. So I was getting ready, getting in some practice and all. Just in case." He held out his bow as if in evidence.

Dag blinked. He had quite forgotten that casual comment from his first visit to West Blue, and was astonished that the boy had apparently taken it so to heart. Dag stared closely, but not a trace of Whit's usual annoying foolery appeared in his face. *Huh. Guess I made more of an impression on him than I'd thought.*

Whit shook off his embarrassment over his straying shaft, and asked cheerfully, "So, why are you two back so soon? Is your patrol nearby? They could all come up too, you know. Papa wouldn't mind. Or are you on a mission for your Lakewalkers, like that courier fellow who brought your letters and the horses and presents?"

"My bride-gifts made it? Oh, good," said Dag.

"Yep, they sure did. Surprised us all. Mama wanted to write a letter back to you, but the courier had gone off already, and we didn't know how to get in touch with your people to send it on."

"Ah," said Dag. *There's a problem.* There was *the* problem, or one aspect of it: farmers and Lakewalkers who couldn't talk to each other. *Like now?* For all his mental rehearsal, Dag found it suddenly difficult to spit out the tale of his exile, just off the cuff like this.

Fortunately, Fawn filled in. "We're just visitin'. Dag's sort of off-duty for a time, till his hurts heal up."

True in a sense—well, no, not really. But there would be time to explain further—maybe when everyone was together, so he wouldn't have to repeat it all over and over, a prospect that made him wince even more than the vision of explaining it to a crowd.

They strolled to recapture the horses, and Whit waved toward the old barn. "The stalls you used before are empty. You still got that man-eating red nag, I see." He skirted Copperhead to gather up Grace's reins; from the way the bay mare resisted his tugging to snatch a few last mouthfuls of grass, one would take her for starved—clearly not the case.

"Yep," said Dag, stooping with a grunt to scoop up the gelding's reins in turn. "I still haven't met anyone I disliked enough to give him to."

"And he's been ridin' Copperhead for eight straight years. It's a wonder, that." Fawn dimpled. "Admit it, Dag, you like that dreadful horse." She went on to her brother, in a tone of bright diversion, "So, what's been happening here at West Blue since I left?"

"Well, Fletch and Clover was married a good six weeks ago. Mama was sorry you two couldn't be here for the wedding." Whit cast a nod at the solid stone farmhouse, sited on the ridge overlooking the wooded valley of the rocky river. The newlyweds' addition of two rooms off the near end, still in progress when Dag had last seen it, seemed entirely complete, with glass windows, a wood-shingle roof, and even some early-autumn flowers planted around the foundation, softening the fresh scars in the soil. "Clover's all moved in, now. Ha! It didn't take *her* long to shift the twins. They lit out about twenty miles west to break land with a friend of theirs, only last week. You just missed 'em."

Dag couldn't help reflecting that of all his Bluefield in-laws, the inimical twins Reed and Rush were probably the ones he'd miss the least; judging from the sudden smile on Fawn's face, she shared the sentiment. He said affably, "I know they'd been talking about it for a long time."

"Yeah, Papa and Mama wasn't too pleased that they picked just before harvest to finally take themselves off, but everyone was so glad of it they didn't hardly complain. Fletch came in on Clover's side whenever they clashed, naturally, which was pretty much every day, and they didn't take any better to him telling them what to do than to her. So it's a lot more peaceable in the house, now." He added after a reflective moment, "Dull, really."

Whit continued an amiable account of the small doings of various cousins, uncles, and aunts as they unsaddled the horses and turned them into the box stalls in the cool old barn. With a glance at Dag's stick,

Whit actually helped them put up their gear without being asked and hoisted Dag's saddlebags over his shoulder. Feeling that such an apologetic impulse should be encouraged, Dag let him take them. As they made their way back out to climb the hill to the house, Fawn refused to give up her own bags to Dag, telling him to *mind himself,* and thumped along under the weight with her usual air of determination. Despite their late difficulties, she seemed far less troubled than at her previous homecoming, judging from the smile she cast over her shoulder at him, and he couldn't help smiling back. *Yeah, we'll get through this somehow, Spark. Together.*

❧

The farmhouse kitchen was fragrant with cooking—ham and beans, cornbread, squash, biscuits, applesauce, pumpkin pie, and a dozen familiar go-withs—and the moist perfume of it all made Fawn weirdly homesick even though she *was* home. Mama and Clover, both be-aproned, were bustling around the kitchen as they stepped through the back door, and Mama, at least, fell on Fawn with shrieks of delighted surprise. Blind Aunt Nattie lumbered up from her spinning wheel just beyond the doorway to her weaving room, hugged Fawn hard, and spared an embrace for Dag as well. Her hand lingered a moment on the wedding cord circling Dag's left arm, below his rolled-up shirt sleeve and above the arm harness for his hook, and her smile softened. "Glad to see this is still holdin'," she murmured, and "Aye," Dag murmured back, giving her in return a squeeze that lifted her off her feet and made her grin outright.

Papa and Fletch clumped in from wherever they'd been working—with the sheep, from the smell—when the greetings were all still at the babbling stage. Plump Clover, announcing that the food wouldn't wait, sent Fawn and Dag off to put down their bags and wash up. She hurried to set extra places, and wouldn't let Fawn help serve—"Sit, sit! You two must be tired from all that ridin'. You're a guest now, Fawn!" *Aren't you?* her worried eyes added silently. Fletch looked as if he were wondering the same thing, though he greeted his sister and her unlikely husband affably enough.

They sat eight around the long kitchen table, filled with the variety and abundance of farm fare that Fawn had always taken for granted but that still seemed to take Dag aback; having seen the austerity of life in a Lakewalker camp, Fawn now understood why. Dag certainly did not disapprove, praising the cooks and filling his plate in a way that demonstrated the ultimate compliment of a good appetite.

Fawn was glad for his returning appetite, worn thin as he'd been by this past summer's gruesome campaign. And he'd been pretty lean to start with. With his height, coppery skin, striking bony face, tousled dark hair, and strange metallic-gold eyes, Dag looked as out of place at a table full of farmers as a heron chick set down in a hen's nest, even without the faint air of menace and danger from his missing hand and the enigmatic fact of his being *a Lakewalker sorcerer.* Or *Lakewalker necromancer* as the bigoted—or frightened—would have it. *Not without cause,* she admitted to herself.

Fletch, possibly in response to the penetrating looks he was getting from his bride, was the first to ask the question, "I'm surprised to see you two back so soon. You're not, um . . . planning to stay, are you?"

Fawn chose to ignore the wary tone. "Just a visit. We're traveling through. Though I admit, it would be good to rest up for a few days."

"Oh, of course you can," cried Clover, brightening with relief. "That'll be a treat. I'd love to hear all about your new place." She added in an arch voice, "So do you two have any good news yet?"

"Beg pardon?" said Dag blankly.

Fawn, who decoded this without effort as *Aren't you pregnant yet?*, returned the correct response: "No, not yet. How about you and Fletch?"

Clover smirked, touching her belly. "Well, it's early days yet. But we're sure tryin'. Our betrothal ran so long, what with one thing and another, there seemed no reason not to start a family right away."

Fletch gave his bride a fond, possessive smile, as a farmer might regard his prize broodmare, and Clover looked smug. Fawn didn't always hit it off with Clover, but she had to admit that the girl was the perfect wife for stodgy Fletch, even without her dowry of a forty-acre field and large woodlot, linked to Bluefield land by a quite short footpath. Fletch put in, "We hope for news by winter, anyhow."

Fawn glanced at Dag. Despite the unhealed damage to his ground-sense, at this range he would surely know if Clover were pregnant already. He gave Fawn a wry smile and a short headshake. Fawn touched the malice scars on her neck, darkening now to carmine, and thought, *Leave it be.*

Mama asked, in a more cautious tone, "So . . . how did things go with your new people at Hickory Lake, Fawn? With your new family?"

Dag's family. After a perhaps too-revealing hesitation, Fawn chose, "Mixed."

Dag glanced down at her and swallowed, not only to clear his mouth of his last bite, but said plainly enough: "Truth to tell, not well, ma'am. But that's not why we're on this road."

Nattie said anxiously, "Those Lakewalker wedding cords we made up—didn't they work?"

"They worked just fine, Aunt Nattie," Dag assured her. He glanced up and down the table. "I should likely explain to the rest of you something that only Nattie knew when Fawn and I were wed here. Our binding strings"—he touched the dark braid above his left elbow and nodded to

Fawn's, wrapping her left wrist—"aren't just fancy cords. Lakewalkers weave our grounds into them."

Five blank stares greeted this statement, and Fawn wondered how he was going to explain ground and groundsense in a way that would make them all understand when they hadn't *seen* what she'd seen. When he also had to overcome a lifetime of deep reserve and the habit—no, imperative—of secrecy. It seemed by his long intake of breath that he was about to try.

"Only you farmers use the term *magic*. Lakewalkers just call it ground-work. Or making. We don't think it's any more magic than, than planting seed to get pumpkins or spinning thread to get shirts. Ground is . . . it's in everything, underlies everything. Live or un-live, but live ground is brightest, all knotty and shifting. Un-live sits and hums, mainly. You all have ground in you, but you don't sense it. Lakewalkers perceive it direct. You can think of groundsense as like seeing double, except that seeing doesn't quite cover—no." He muttered to his lap, "Keep it simple, Dag." His eyes and voice rose again. "Just think of it as like seeing double, all right?" He stared hopefully around.

Taking the uncharacteristic quiet that had fallen for encouragement, he went on, "So, just as we can sense ground in things, we can, most of us—sometimes—move things through their grounds. Change them, augment them. That's groundwork."

Mama wet her lips. "So . . . when you mended that glass bowl the twins broke, whistled it back together, was that what you'd call ground-work?"

Stunning the entire Bluefield clan to silence at that time, too, as Fawn vividly recalled—now *that* had been magic.

Dag, beaming, shot Mama a look of gratitude. "Yes, ma'am. Exactly! Well, it wasn't the whistling that—well, close enough. That was probably the best groundwork I'd ever done."

Second best, now, thought Fawn, remembering Raintree. But Raintree had come later, and cost more: very nearly Dag's life. Did they understand that this wasn't trivial trickery?

"Lakewalkers like to think that only we have groundsense, but I've met a lot of farmers with a trace. Sometimes more than a trace. Nattie's one." Dag nodded across the table at Nattie, who grinned in his general direction, though her pearl-colored eyes could not see him. Fletch and Clover and Whit looked startled; Mama, less so. "I don't know if her blindness sharpened it, or what. But with Nattie's helping, Fawn and I wove our grounds into our wedding cords as sound as any Lakewalker's."

He left out the alarming part about the blood, Fawn noted. He was picking his way through the truth as cautiously as a blindfolded man crossing a floor studded with knives.

Dag went on, "So when we got up to camp, every Lakewalker there could *see* that they were valid cords. Which threw everyone into a puzzle. Folks had been relying on the cord-weaving to make Lakewalker marriages to farmers impossible, d'you see. To keep bloodlines pure and our groundsense strong. They were still arguin' about what it meant when we left."

Papa had been staring at Nattie, but this last drew his frown back to Dag. "Then did your people throw you out for marrying Fawn, patroller?"

"Not exactly, sir."

"So . . . what? Exactly?"

Dag hesitated. "I hardly know where to start." A longer pause. "What all have you folks here in Oleana heard about the malice that emerged over in Raintree?"

Papa said, "There was supposed to have been a blight bogle pop up somewheres north of Farmer's Flats, that killed a lot of folks, or drove them mad."

Whit put in, "Or that it was a nerve-ague or brain-worms, that made folks there run around attacking one another. It's bog country up that way, they say, bad for strange fevers."

Fletch added, "Down at Millerson's alehouse, I heard someone say it was an excuse got up by the Lakewalkers to drive farmers back south out of their hunting country. That there never was any blight bogle, and it wasn't bogle-maddened farmers attacking Lakewalkers, but the other way around."

Dag squeezed his eyes shut and rubbed his mouth. "No," he said into his hand, and lowered it.

Clover sat back with a sort of flounce; she didn't voice it, but her face said it for her: *Well, you'd naturally say that, wouldn't you?* Mama and Nattie said nothing, but they seemed to be listening hard.

Dag said, "There was a real malice. We first heard about it when the Raintree Lakewalkers, who were being overwhelmed, sent a courier to Hickory Lake Camp for help. My company was dispatched. We circled, managed to come up on the malice from behind while it was driving its mind-slaves and mud-men south to attack Farmer's Flats. One of my patrol got a sharing knife into it—killed it. I saw it"—he held out his left arm—"that close. It was very advanced, very, um . . . advanced." He paused, glanced around, and tried, "Strong, smart. Almost human-looking."

Leaving out how the malice had nearly slain him, or that he'd been captain of that company and source of its successful plan . . . Fawn bit her lip in impatience.

"Here's the thing, the important thing. No . . . back up a step, Dag." He pinched the bridge of his nose. "I'm sorry. There's too much all at once, and I'm explaining this all backwards, I'm sorry. Try this. Malices have groundsense too, only very much stronger than any human's. They're *made* of ground. They *consume* ground, to live, to make their—

their magery, their mud-men, their own bodies, everything they do. They're quite mad, in their way." His face looked suddenly drawn in some memory Fawn did not share and could not guess at. "But that's what blight *is*. It's where some emergent malice has drawn all the ground out of the world, leaving, well, blight. It's very distinctive."

"Well, what does it look like?" asked Whit reasonably.

"It doesn't look like anything else," said Dag, which netted him some pretty dry looks from around the table.

Fawn pitched in: "It's not like burnt fields, or rust, or rot, or a killing frost, though it reminds you of all those things. It has a funny gray tinge, like all the color has been sucked out of things. First things die, if they're alive, and then they fall apart at the seams, and then they dissolve all through. Once you've seen that drained-out gray, you can't ever mistake it. It looks even worse to someone with groundsense, I gather."

"Yes," said Dag gratefully.

Mama said faintly, "You've seen it, then, Fawn?"

"Yes, twice. Once at that malice's lair near Glassforge, when Dag and I first met, and once in Raintree. I rode over, after. Dag was hurt on his patrol, which part he didn't tell you, I notice." She glowered at him in reproof. "He'd still be on sick leave if we were back at Hickory Lake."

"*You* got to go to Raintree?" said Whit, sounding indignantly envious.

Fawn tossed her head. "I saw all that country the malice had torn through. I saw where it got started." She glanced back to Dag, to check if he was ready to go on.

He nodded at her and picked up his tangled thread again. "Here's the thing. For the past twenty or thirty years, farmers have been breaking land in Raintree north of the old cleared line—that is, north of where the local Lakewalkers had deemed it safe. Or less unsafe, leastways. Lakewalker patrol records show malice emergences get thicker—more frequent—north toward the Dead Lake, see, and thinner south and away. South of the Grace River, they're very rare. Although unfortunately not all gone, so we can't stop patrolling those regions. It was at a north Raintree squatter town named Greenspring that this latest malice emerged. Practically under it."

Fawn nodded. "It hatched out down in a ravine in the town woodlot, by the signs."

Dag went on, "See, there was a lot of bad blood between the local Lakewalkers and the Greenspring settlers, on account of the arguments about the old cleared line. So when the malice started, none of the squatters knew how to recognize the early signs, or to pick up and run, or how or where to ride for help. Or they'd been told but didn't believe. Not that they wouldn't have needed to be lucky as well, because by the time a farmer can see the blight near a lair, there's a good chance he's just about to be ground-ripped or mind-slaved anyway. Like stumbling into a spider web. But with that many folks, if they'd all known, someone might have got out to spread the warning. Instead, the malice pretty much ate them. And grew strong way too fast. I think that a whole lot more people died in north Raintree than needed to this summer just because Lakewalkers and farmers weren't talking to each other."

"I hadn't ever seen a mass grave before," said Fawn quietly. "I don't ever want to again."

Papa gave her a sharp glance from under his gray brows. "I did, once, long time ago," he said unexpectedly. "It was after a flood."

Fawn looked at him in surprise. "I never knew that."

"I never talked about it."

"Hm," said Aunt Nattie.

Papa sat back and looked at Dag. "Your people aren't exactly forthcomin' about these things, you know. In Raintree *or* Oleana."

"I know." Dag ducked his head. "Back when there were few farmers north of the Grace, it scarcely mattered. To the Lakewalkers in the hinterlands north of the Dead Lake—I've walked up that way, twice— there's still no need to do anything differently, because there are no farmers there. Where it matters is in the border country, where things are changing out from under us—like Greenspring. And like West Blue." He glanced around the table. The food on his plate had all gone cold, Fawn noticed.

Fletch said, "I never got the sense Lakewalkers wanted farmer help."

"They don't, mostly," Dag admitted. "No farmer can fight a malice directly. You can't close your grounds in defense, for one, you can't make . . . certain tools." He blinked, frowned, seemed to take aim like a rider trying to clear a fence on a balky horse, and blurted out, "Sharing knives. You can't make sharing knives to kill malices." Swallowing, he went on, "But even if you can't be fighters, you might find better ways to avoid being fodder. Everyone alive should be taught how to recognize blight- sign, for one—as routinely as how to identify poison ivy or rattlesnakes or, or how not to stand on the wrong side of the tree you're felling."

"How would you go about teaching everyone alive, patroller?" asked Aunt Nattie, in a curious voice.

"I don't know," sighed Dag. "Laid out like that, it sounds pretty crazy. We came upon the Glassforge malice early, this past spring, only because of the chance of Chato's patrol stopping there and gossiping with the local folks about their bandit problem enough for Chato to realize there was something strange going on. If I could only *show* folks, somehow . . . I wouldn't have to talk." Dag smiled wanly. "I never was much of a talkin' man."

"Eat, Dag," Fawn put in, and pointed to his plate. Everyone else's was empty. He took an obedient bite.

"Folks could show off that patch of blight you say is by Glassforge," Whit suggested. "Then they'd all know what it looks like."

Clover eyed him. "Why would anybody want to go look at a thing like that? It just sounds ugly."

Whit sat back and rubbed his nose, then brightened. "Then you should charge 'em money."

Dag stopped chewing and stared. "What?"

"Sure!" Whit sat up. "If they had to pay, they'd think it was something special. You could get up wagon excursions from Glassforge. Charge five copper crays for the ride, and ten for the box lunch. And the lecture for free. It would get folks talking when they got home, too—*What did you see in Glassforge, dear?* It could be a nice little business, driving the wagon, making the lunches—it would sure beat pulling stumps, anyways. If I had the cash I'd buy that blight, I would. It'd be better 'n a forty-acre field."

Fawn didn't think she'd ever seen Dag look so flummoxed. It was all she could do not to giggle, though she mainly wanted to hit Whit.

"Well, you don't have any cash," Fletch pointed out dauntingly.

"Thank the stars," added Clover, fanning herself with her hand. "You'd likely throw it down a well."

"Quit your fooling, Whit," said Papa impatiently. "Nobody thinks it's amusin'."

Whit shrugged, kicked back his chair, and rose to carry off his plate to the sink. Dag, slowly, started chewing again. His eyes, following Whit, had an odd look in them—not angry, though, which surprised Fawn, knowing how seriously Dag took all this. With afternoon chores looming, lunch broke up.

❧

Later, putting their things away in the twins' old bedroom upstairs, Dag folded Fawn to him and sighed.

"Well, I sure made a hash of that. Absent gods. If I can't talk to my own tent-family and make them understand, how am I ever going to talk to strangers?"

"I didn't think you did so badly. It was a lot for them to get around, all at once like that."

"It was all out of order, I never explained sharing knives, they didn't half believe me—or else half of 'em didn't believe me, I wasn't sure which—it was all—oh, Spark, I don't know what I'm doing on this road. I'm just an old patroller. I'm surely not the man for this."

"It was your first try. Who gets everything right the first try?"

"Anyone who wants to live for a second try."

"That's for things that'll kill you if you miss, like . . . like slaying malices, I suppose. People don't die of stumbling over a few words."

"I thought I was going to strangle on my tongue."

About to hug him around the waist, she pushed off and looked up instead. She said shrewdly, "This isn't just hard because it's complicated, or new, is it? Lakewalkers aren't supposed to talk about these secrets to farmers—are they?"

"Indeed, we are not."

"How much trouble would you be in with your own folks, if they knew?"

He shrugged. "Hard to say."

That wasn't too helpful. Fawn narrowed her eyes in worry, but then just gave up and hugged him tight, because he'd never looked like he needed it more. The breath of his laugh stirred her curls as he dropped a kiss atop her head.

2

In the pressure of a short-handed harvest and a run of dry weather, Fawn and Dag lost their sitting-guest status almost immediately. Dag didn't seem to mind, showing both willing and a keen and practical interest in the farm and all its doings. It was all as strange and new to him, Fawn realized, as the very different rhythms of a Lakewalker camp had been to her. She wondered if he was homesick yet.

As usual, the Bluefields combined forces for the ingathering with the Ropers, Aunt Roper being Papa's sister. The Ropers' place lay just northwest of their own. Two of their sons and Fawn's closest cousin, Ginger, were still at home to help out, and amongst them all, they cleared Uncle Roper's big cornfield in three days. Next was the Bluefield late wheat. Dag proved unexpectedly adept with the long scythe. His arm harness held a wooden wrist-cap over his stump, and besides the hook he possessed an array of clever tools on bolts that he swapped in and out of it, including his specially adapted bow. The tool he usually used for clasping the paddle of a narrow boat on the lake also served to aid his grip on the scythe, and after a little experimentation he seemed to find his way into the swing of the task quite contentedly, so Papa left him to it.

Gleaning had been one of the first chores little hands had been put to, back when Fawn and Ginger and Whit had been only hip-high. They were all bigger now, but the gleaning still had to be done. Fawn crouched and shuffled her way across the bright gold stubble, and thought Clover and Fletch could well stand to be prompt in producing the next generation of shorter harvesters. Along the split-rail fence of the pasture, the farm's horses lined up in mild-eyed curiosity to watch the strange behavior of their people.

At the end of her row, Fawn stood up to stretch her back and check on Dag, working at the far end of the field with Papa, Uncle Roper and his boys, and Fletch to scythe and bundle sheaves and load them into a waiting cart. Dag looked very tall beside the others, though the sleeves of his homespun shirt were rolled up over a coppery suntan not that much deeper than the men's, and the hat shading his head, woven of lake reeds, was fringed around the rim just like their straw ones. Whit rose beside her, adjusted the strap of the cloth bag across his shoulder, and followed her gaze.

"I must warn Papa to watch and not let Dag overdo," said Fawn in worry. "He won't stop on his own."

"Just exactly how was he hurt, again?" said Whit. "'Cause when we went down to wash up in the river last night, all I saw new was that little bitty cut on his left thigh."

"It's not long, but it's deep," said Fawn. "The knife blade that did it went straight to the bone and shattered. The Lakewalker medicine maker had an awful time getting all the pieces fished back out. But that's not what's dragging him down so." Taking her lead from Dag, Fawn decided to stick with a much-simplified version of the truth. "The Raintree malice halfway ground-ripped him in the fight, tore up his ground all down his left arm and side. It nearly killed him. It's like he's walking around recovering from his own personal blight."

"Well, how long does that take?"

"I'm not sure. I'm not sure he's sure. Most folks who get ground-ripped just die on the spot. But Dag says when the Glassforge malice put these marks on my neck"—she rubbed at the ugly red dimples, one on the right side, four on the left—"it injured both flesh and ground. If the bruises had been just from a man's hand, they'd have cleared up two or three months back, with nothing to show. Ground damage is nasty stuff." Her hand crept to rub her belly as well, but she halted it, burying it in her skirt instead. Dag wasn't the only one to carry the worst damage hidden inside.

"Huh," said Whit, squinting at her neck. "I guess so!"

"The weakness and pain in his body don't bother him near as much as the harm the ripping did to his groundsense, though."

"That seeing-double thing he talks about?"

"Yes. Usually he can sense things out for near a mile away, which I gather is pretty amazing even for a Lakewalker. He says it's down to less 'n a hundred paces right now. The medicine maker said that's how he'll know when his ground is better, when he can sense out far again."

Whit blinked. "So . . . can he still do his groundwork? Like that bowl?"

Whit had been impressed by the bowl. Rightfully, Fawn thought. "Not yet. Not real well." She thought of some of Dag's other marvelous ground-tricks, still not regained, and sighed. When Lakewalkers made love they did it body and ground, with an ingenuity farmers never dreamed of, but she wasn't about to explain *that* part to Whit.

Whit shook his head, frowning again at the reapers. "He looks so wrong."

Fawn shaded her eyes with the edge of her hand. "Why? I think he's doing pretty good with that scythe."

"There's that hat, for one."

"I wove him that hat! Same as yours."

"Ah, that explains why he won't be parted from it. What that man does for you . . . ! But—" Whit gestured inarticulately. "Dag looks all right up on his evil horse. He looks right with that bow of his, anyone can see—you'd think it grew there on his arm, even without how his arrows fly just where he wants. I've never seen him draw that big knife of his, but I sure wouldn't want to be on the other side when he does."

"No. You wouldn't," Fawn agreed.

"But stick him with a scythe or a pitchfork or a bucket, he looks as out of place as—as if you'd hitched that leggy silver mare to a plow." He jerked his head toward the pasture fence.

Swallow, the dappled gray mare Dag had sent to West Blue as his Lakewalker-style bride-gift, pricked her curving ears alertly. She looked as elegant as moonlight on water, and as swift as a rippling stream even when she was standing still. Beyond, her black colt Darkling, as if proudly aware of collecting his due-share of admiration, kicked up his heels and danced past, tail flicking.

Grace was standing hipshot and bored along the fence line, dark bay coat looking warm and shiny in the sun. Copperhead of the uncertain temper had been left in exile in the small paddock below the old barn, but the two young plow horses Whit was bringing along, and known therefore as *Whit's team*, cropped grass placidly a few paces off. Warp and Weft were nice, sturdy, useful-looking beasts, but . . . you would never imagine them with wings.

"Swallow was supposed to be a gift to Mama." Fawn sighed. "I don't suppose Mama rides her."

Whit snorted. "Not hardly! She's too terrified. Me, I've only taken that mare a few turns around the pasture, but the way she moves sure does make it look a long way to the ground."

"Dag didn't mean her to be idle. I thought you might train her to the cart."

"Well, maybe. Papa means to breed her again, for sure. If we can find a stud around here worthy of her. He was talkin' about Uncle Hawk's Trustful, or maybe that flashy stallion of Sunny Sawman's."

Fawn said neutrally, "Trustful would be good." She added, "Papa and Mama aren't planning to cut Darkling, are they? Dag's tent-sister Omba was worried about that."

"Geld that colt? You'd have to be mad!" said Whit. "Just think of the stud fees, in a couple of years! He'll support his mama in her old age, sure enough—and our mama, too."

Fawn nodded in satisfaction on Omba's behalf. "That's all right, then." She added, "Grace was bred to a real fine Lakewalker stallion named Shadow before we left." Somewhat by accident, but that was another tale. "Dag expects her to throw a right lovely foal next spring, with his lines and her temper."

Whit grinned. "As long as it's not the other way around."

"Hey! Grace is a very pretty horse, too, in her own way!"

"If you like 'em short and plump, which I admit is a popular style around here."

Fawn gave him a suspicious scowl, but deciding he was referring to Clover and not herself, let the dig pass.

Whit lifted his brows and sniggered. "We'll have to tell Clover your mare is going to beat her to the finish line in the baby race. I want to see the look on her face."

I'm not in any baby race! Fawn was about to snap, but a loud, sharp whistle from the other end of the wheat field interrupted her. Papa took his hand from his mouth and jerked his thumb firmly toward the ground. His children, interpreting this without difficulty, shrugged in reply and crouched to their gleaning again.

∿

When Mama, Clover, and Aunt Roper lugged lunch up to the wheat field, everyone took a break under the nearby apple trees. Fawn collected a skirt-load of the wormier groundfalls and carried them across to the pasture fence as a treat for the horses. They all clustered up, making the fence creak as they leaned over it, and nuzzled the aromatic fruit out of her hands, their thick, mobile lips tickling her palms. She liked watching the happy way their jaws moved beneath their sliding skins as they munched and crunched and sighed in appreciation, and how they rounded their big nostrils and blinked their deep brown eyes.

She wiped the mess of apple bits and horse slobber from her hands onto her skirt, and started back toward the orchard. Dag was sitting with Uncle and Aunt Roper and Fawn's cousins, talking and gesturing. Trying to explain ground and groundsense to them, she guessed, partly from the way his hand touched the cord circling his left arm, and waved and closed and opened, but mostly by the way his desperately smiling listeners leaned back as if wishful to edge away, even while sitting cross-legged. Aunt Roper spotted Fawn, waved, and patted the ground beside her invitingly—*come protect us from your wild patroller!* Fawn sighed and trudged toward them.

The planned few days of rest in West Blue had slid instead into a few weeks of hard work, but Dag found himself oddly at ease despite the delay. The long days outdoors with the harvest-patrol had been laborious—that bean field, for one, had turned out to be much bigger than it looked, and before it was cleared Dag had started seeing cascades of beans in his sleep—but he *was* sleeping, and well, too. Indoors, every night, in a real bed, wrapped around Fawn. The food was not all dried-out to carry light, painstakingly rationed to the length of a pattern-walk, but gloriously, weightily abundant. There was no worse source of tension than an occasional clash of tempers, no deeper fear than of a splash of untimely rain.

This break in their journey had been good for him. The dark, sick pain in his bones from the blight was giving way to mere clean fatigue from well-used muscles. His left leg was not as weak—he hadn't needed his stick for days. He felt less . . . unbalanced. He had not, admittedly, attempted to stray off the Bluefield acres to the village, where he might risk encountering certain young men who had reason to remember his last visit with disfavor. But however Dag was now discussed in village gossip, the bad boys dared not stray up here, either, and Dag was content to be surrounded wholly by farmers who wished him well for Fawn's sake.

"So, patroller."

Sorrel's voice broke into Dag's drift of thought, and he tilted his head forward, closed his mouth, and opened his eyes, hoping he hadn't started to snore in his chair. As was their custom, the Bluefield clan had gathered in the parlor after dinner to share the working lights. Clover and Fletch had gone off to her folks this evening, but Tril sat in her usual place sewing; Nattie, though not needing the oil lamp, kept company plying her drop spindle; and Fawn and Whit had set up a table to make arrows, a skill Fawn had mastered this past summer.

Whit's awful marksmanship had turned out not to be merely from his complete lack of training; his little hoard of arrows, picked up for free somewhere, was ill-made and ill-balanced. When Whit had asked plaintively if Dag couldn't fix them the way a Lakewalker would, Dag had thought about it, nodded, and, to Whit's temporary horror, broken them over his knee. He'd then donated Fawn and a dozen old flint points to their replacement, being wishful to conserve his best steel-tipped shafts for more urgent uses than target practice. Besides, it was good for Whit to suffer some instruction from his younger sister. He was still, in Dag's view, too inclined to discount Fawn.

Now Dag raised his brows, tried to look awake, and answered Fawn's papa—*my tent-father?*—"Sir?"

Sorrel was studying him. "I don't believe I've said thank you for staying on through the harvest. You do more work with one hand than most men do with two."

Fawn, squinting to wrap a carefully cut trio of feathers to a shaft with fine thread, dimpled in an *I-told-you-so* sort of way.

Sorrel continued, "I never thought much before about what Lakewalker patrollers do, but I suppose it is hard work, in its way. Harder than I rightly imagined, maybe, and not much comfort in it."

Dag tilted his head in acknowledgment. Sorrel seemed clumsy but sincere, sorting through these new notions.

"But the thing is . . . I can't help but wonder . . . have you ever worked for a living?"

Fawn sat up indignantly, but Dag waved her back down. "It's not an insult, love. I know what he means. Because in a sense, the answer's no. Out on patrol, we might hunt, cure skins, collect medicines, trade a little, keep the trails clear, but that's all second place to hunting malice. Patrollers don't make and save like farmers do. My camp kin did that part. At home, my bed was always made for me. Not that I ever spent long in it."

Sorrel nodded. "But you don't have your camp anymore."

". . . No."

"So . . . how are you and Fawn planning to go on, then? Do you think to farm? Or something else?"

"I'm not sure," said Dag slowly—honestly. "I figured I was too old to learn a whole new way of life, but I will say, these past weeks have given me more to chew on than Tril's good cooking. I guess I never pictured having friendly folks to show me the trail."

"A farmer Lakewalker?" murmured Tril, raising her brows. Whit made a face, though Dag was not sure why.

"By myself, no, but Fawn knows her part. Maybe together, it wouldn't be so unlikely as it once seemed." His other potential skill, medicine maker, was far too dangerous to attempt in farmer country, he'd been told. Repeatedly. In any case, his weakened ground made the notion futile, for now.

Sorrel said cautiously, "Would you be thinking to take up land here in West Blue?"

Dag glanced at Fawn, who gave him a slight, urgent headshake. No, she had no desire to settle a mere three miles up the road from her disastrous first love, and first hate. Dag wasn't the only one of them who had been avoiding the village. "It's too early to say."

Tril looked up from her sewing, and said, "So what do you plan to do when a child comes along? They don't keep to schedule, in my experience." Her penetrating maternal look plainly wondered if he was simply being a male idiot, or if there was something he wasn't saying.

He wasn't about to go into the variety of methods available to Lakewalkers for not having children till wanted, some of which he was fairly sure—make that, entirely certain—Fawn's parents would not approve of. The secret of the malice-damage to Fawn's womb, as slowly healing as his own inner blight, she had elected to keep to herself, a choice he respected, and—what was that farmer phrase for letting go of a regretted past? *Water over the dam.* He offered instead, weakly, "Lakewalker women have children on the move."

Tril gave that the fishy stare it deserved. "But it seems Fawn is not to be a Lakewalker woman, after all. And from what you say, Lakewalker mamas have kin and clan and camp to back 'em, in their need, even if their men are off chasing bogles."

He wanted to declaim indignantly, *I will take care of her!* But even he wasn't that much of a fool. His eyelids lowered, opened; he said instead, merely, "That's so, ma'am."

"We plan to travel, before we decide where to settle," Fawn put in firmly. "Dag promised to show me the sea, and I mean to hold him to his word."

"The sea!" said Tril, sounding shocked. "You didn't say you were fixing to go all *that* way! I thought you were just going to the Grace Valley. Lovie, it's dangerous!"

"The sea?" said Whit in an equally shocked but very different tone. "*Fawn* gets to go to the sea? *And* Raintree? I've never been past Lumpton Market!"

Dag regarded him, trying to imagine a whole life confined to a space scarcely larger than a single day's patrol-pattern. "By your age, I'd quartered two hinterlands, killed my first malice, and been down the Grace and the Gray both." He added after a moment, "Didn't see the sea for the first time till a couple years later, though."

Whit said eagerly, "Can I go with you?"

"Certainly not!" Fawn cried.

Whit looked taken aback. Dag muffled a heartless smile. In a lifetime of relentlessly heckling his sister, Whit had clearly never once imagined needing her goodwill for any aim of his own. *So do our sins bite us, boy.*

"We're not done harvest," said Sorrel sternly. "You have work here, Whit."

"Yes, but they're not leaving tomorrow. Are you?" He looked wildly at Dag.

Dag did some rapid mental calculating. Fawn's monthly would be coming on shortly, bloodily debilitating since her injuries, though slowly improving as she healed inside. They must certainly wait that out in the most comfortable refuge possible. "We'll linger and help out for another week, maybe. But we can't stay much longer. It'll be near a week's ride down to the Grace. If we want any choice of boats we have to get there in time to catch the fall rise, and not so late as to be caught by the winter freeze-up. Or just by the cold and wet and misery."

A daunted silence fell, for a while. Nattie's spindle whirred, Whit went back to sanding a shaft smooth, and Dag considered the attractions of his bed upstairs, compared to dozing off and falling out of his chair onto his chin.

Whit said suddenly, "What are you planning to do with your horses?"

"Take 'em along," said Dag.

"On a keelboat? There's hardly room."

"No, on a flatboat."

"Oh."

More busy silence. Whit set down the shaft with a click, and Dag opened one wary eye.

Whit said, "But Fawn's mare's in foal. You wouldn't want her to drop her foal along the trail somewheres. I mean . . . wolves. Catamounts. Delay. Wouldn't it be better to leave her here all comfy at West Blue and pick her up when you got back?"

"And what am I supposed to do, walk?" said Fawn in scorn.

"No, but see . . . suppose you left her here for Mama to ride, since she can't ride Swallow. And suppose we each rode one of my team, instead. I'd been meaning to sell them in Lumpton next spring, but I bet down by those rivertowns I'd get a better price. Also Papa and Fletch wouldn't be put to the trouble of feedin' them all winter. And you'd save the cost of taking your pregnant horse on a boat ride she wouldn't hardly appreciate anyhow."

"How would I get back? Copper can't carry us double, and my bags!"

"You could pick up another horse when you get down there to Graymouth."

"Oh, so Dag's supposed to pay for this, is he?"

"You could sell it again when you got back. That, plus the savings for not shipping your mare, you'd likely come out pretty near even. Or even ahead!"

Fawn huffed in exasperation. "Whit, you can't come with us."

"Only as far as the river!" His voice went wheedling. "And see, Mama, I wouldn't be going off by myself—I'd be with Dag and all. Going out, anyhow, and coming back I'd know how to find my way home again."

"With money burning a hole in your pocket till it dropped through onto the road, I suppose," said Sorrel.

"Unless you met up with bandits like Fawn did," said Tril. "Then you'd lose your money *and* your life."

"*Fawn's* going. No, worse—Fawn's going *again*."

Sorrel looked as if he wanted to say something like *Fawn's her husband's business, now,* but in light of his prior prying, couldn't quite work up to it.

His drowsy brain forced into motion, Dag found himself considering not money matters, but safety. A Lakewalker husband and his farmer wife, alone in farmer country, made an odd couple indeed, and they'd already met more than one offended observer who might, had there been time, have taken stronger exception to the pairing. But suppose it were a Lakewalker husband, a farmer wife, and her farmer brother? Might Whit be a buffer for Dag, as well as another pair of eyes to watch out for Fawn? Because absent gods knew Dag couldn't stay awake all the time. *Or even another half-hour.* He swallowed a yawn.

"You could fall into bad company, down on that big river," Tril worried.

"Worse 'n Dag?" Whit inquired brightly.

Tactless, but telling. Sorrel and Tril gave Dag an appraising look; Dag shifted uncomfortably.

He had been brooding about the problems of Lakewalker-farmer divisions for months, without results that he could see, and here was Whit practically volunteering to be a patrol partner and tent-brother. If Dag turned the boy down, would he ever get another such offer? *Whit hasn't the first idea what it would entail.*

Of course, neither do I.

"Dag . . ." said Fawn uneasily.

"Fawn and I will talk about it. As you say, we're not leaving tomorrow."

"Dag could show me his blight patch, on the way past Glassforge," Whit offered eagerly. "I could be—"

Dag raised and firmed his voice. "*Fawn and I* will talk it over. We'll talk to you after."

Whit subsided, with difficulty.

Fawn eyed Dag in deepening curiosity. When he rose to go upstairs, she set aside her arrow-making and followed.

She closed the door of their room behind her, and he took her hand and swung her to a seat on the edge of the twins' beds, now pushed together. There was still a sort of padded ridge down the middle, but on the soft, clean linens, it wasn't at all hard to slide over in the night. Rather like a miniature snowbank, but warmer. Much warmer.

"Dag," Fawn began in dismay, "what in the world were you thinking? You give Whit the least encouragement, and he'll be badgering us to death to be let tail along."

He put his arm around her and hugged her up close to his right side. "I'm thinking . . . I took this road to learn how to talk to farmers. To try some other way of being than lords and servants—or malices and slaves—or kept apart. *Tent-brother* is sure another way."

Her fair brow furrowed. "You're doing that Lakewalker thing again. Trying to join your bride's tent, be a new brother to her kin."

He tilted his head. "I suppose I am. You know I mean to style myself Dag Blucfield."

She nodded. "Your family at Hickory Lake—what's left of 'em—I didn't get the sense they exactly nourished your heart even before you sprung me on 'em. Your brother acted like giving you one good word would cost him cash money. And you acted like it was normal."

"Hm." He half-lidded his eyes and lowered his head to nibble at her hair. He pressed a stray strand between his lips, rubbing its fine grain.

"Are you that family-hungry, Dag? 'Cause I admit I'm close to full-up, just now."

He pulled her down so that they lay face-to-face, smiling seriously. "Then you shouldn't mind sharing."

"Oh, many's the time I *wished* I could give Half-Whit away!"

His lips twitched. He brushed the dark curls from her forehead and kissed along her eyebrows.

"And there's another thing," she added severely, although her hand strayed to map his jaw. "Camping in the evening, have you thought how fast it would blight the mood to have him sitting there on the other side of the fire, leering and cracking jokes?"

Dag shrugged. "Camp privacy's not a new problem for patrollers."

"Collecting firewood, bathing in the river, scouting for squirrels? So you told me. There's a whole code, but Whit doesn't know it."

"Then I'll just have to teach him Lakewalker."

"Yeah? Best bring your hickory stick, for rapping on his skull."

"I've trained denser young patrollers."

"There are denser young patrollers?" She leaned back, so her eyes would bring his face into focus, likely. "How do they walk upright?"

He sniggered, but answered, "Their partners help 'em along. Feels sort of like a three-legged race some days, I admit. The idea is to keep 'em alive long enough to learn better. It works." His smile faded a little. "Mostly."

Her slim fingers combed back his hair, side and side, and pressed his head between them in a little shake. "You're still thinking Lakewalker. Not farmer."

"This walk we're on is for changing that, though. I figure if I can practice on Whit . . . I might have more margin for mistakes."

"We say two's company, three's a crowd. I swear with you it's two's partners, three's a patrol."

The fingers moved down to his shirt buttons; he aimed kisses at them in passing, and said, "I've been watching and listening, these past weeks, and not just all about how to herd beans. There's no more head-space for Whit in this house than there was for you. It's all for Fletch and Clover, and their children. Maybe if he was let out under a higher ceiling, he could straighten up a bit. With help, even grow—less wrenchingly than you had to."

She shivered. "I wouldn't wish that even on Whit." Her smile crept back. "So are you picturing yourself as a tent-brother—or a tent-father? Old patroller."

"Behave, child," he returned, mock-sternly. He tried to pay back the favor with the buttons, one-handed, and, benefiting from much recent practice, succeeded.

"With your hand *there?*"

His only hand was gifting him the most lovely sensations, as his fingers slid and stretched. Silk was a poor weak comparison, for skin so breathing-soft. "I didn't say what . . ." He groped for some wordplay on *behave,* but he was losing language as their bodies warmed each other.

The scent of her hair filled his mouth as she shook her head, and he breathed her in. She murmured muzzily, "Trust me. He will be the most awful pain."

He drew his head back a little, to be sure of her expression. "Will be? Not would be? Was that a decision, slipped past there?"

She sighed. "I suppose so."

"Well, he'll not pain you, or he'll be answering to me."

Her eyebrows drew in. "He sneaks it in as jokes. Makes it hard to fight. Especially infuriating when he makes you laugh."

"If I can run a company of pig-headed patrollers, I can run your brother. Trust me, too."

"I'd pay money to watch that."

"For you, the show is free."

Her lips curved; her great brown eyes were dark and wide. The little hands descended to the next set of buttons. All farmers but one faded from his concern. At this range, opening his ground to her ground was no effort at all. It was like nocking star fire in the bow of his body. She whispered, "Show me . . . everything."

Igniting, he rolled her over him, and did.

3

While Sorrel and Tril might have been dubious about letting their youngest son out on the roads of Oleana even under the escort of their alarming Lakewalker son-in-law, Fletch and Clover, once the idea was broached, were very amenable. Sorrel and Fletch did unite in extracting the most possible labor from Whit during the next week. With his precious permission hanging in the balance, Whit worked if not willingly then without audible protest. In any remaining spare moments, his bow lessons with Dag were set aside in favor of chopping cordwood for winter, a chore normally not due for another month. Though not discussed, the permission became tacit in the face of the mounting woodpile, as, Dag thought, not even Fletch would be capable of such a cruel betrayal.

Fawn's parents were unexpectedly favorable to the idea of housing Grace. Dag eventually realized it wasn't just because the mare was a sweet-tempered mount that not only Tril but even Nattie might ride—though Nattie, when this was pointed out, snorted and muttered something about *The cart will do for me, thanks*—but because she was a sort of equine hostage. That Fawn would need to return to collect her horse—or, by that time, possibly horses—seemed to give Tril some comfort. Though over the next several evening meals Tril did recall and recount every drowning accident that had occurred within a hundred miles of West Blue within living memory. Recognizing maternal nerves, Dag nonetheless quietly resolved to take Whit aside at some less ruffled moment and find out if he could swim any less like a rock than Fawn had, before Dag had done his best to drown-proof her. Even if it was growing a bit chilly for swimming lessons.

A light rain the night before their departure turned the dawn air gray and cool, muting the blush of autumn colors. As the three rode down the farm lane a few damp yellow leaves eddied past, along with farewells, blessings, and a deal of unsolicited advice ignored by both Bluefield siblings with much the same shoulder hunchings. Dag found it pleasant enough to be back aboard Copperhead and moving once more. Along the river road south, Dag tested his groundsense range and fancied it improved. A hundred and fifty paces now, maybe? Whit was temporarily too exhausted to squabble with his sister, so the day's ride was largely peaceful. And Dag would have his wife to himself tonight, in a cozy inn chamber in Lumpton Market; a touch, an exchange of smiles, a promissory gleam, that furtive dimple, left him riding in a warm glow of expectation as the afternoon drew to a close.

At the shabby little inn off the old straight road north of town, these comfortable plans received an unexpected check. A chance crowd of drivers, drovers, and traveling farm families had nearly filled the place, and Dag's party was lucky to secure a single small chamber up under the eaves. Looking it over with disfavor, Dag was inclined to think a bedroll in the stable loft would be better, except that the loft had been let out already. But the falling dark, the threat of renewed rain, the fatigue of a twenty-mile ride, and the smells of good cooking from the inn's kitchen cured them all of ambition to seek farther tonight, and the debate devolved merely as to who was going to get the bed and who was going to put their bedrolls on the floor. It ended with Fawn in the bed, which was too short for Dag as well as too narrow for a couple, Dag down beside it, and Whit crosswise beyond the foot. Even a chaste cuddle was denied, though Fawn did hang her arm over the side and interlace her fingers with Dag's for a while after she'd turned down the bedside lamp.

Peace did not descend. Before they'd gone down to supper Whit had forced open the window to combat the room's mustiness; unfortunately, he had thus admitted a patrol of late mosquitoes, roused by the afternoon's unseasonably warm damp. Every time anyone began to doze off, the thin, threatening whines induced more arm-waving, blanket-ducking, and irate mutters from one of the others, thwarting sleep for all. Dag instinctively bounced the pests away from himself and Fawn through their tiny grounds. Unfortunately, that concentrated the attack on Whit.

Some more rustling, scratching, and swearing, and Whit rose in the dark to try to hunt the bloodthirsty marauders by sound. After he bumped into the bed frame twice and stepped on Dag, Fawn sat up, turned up the oil lamp, and snapped, "Whit, will you *settle*? You're worse 'n they are!"

"The buggers have bit me three times already. Wait, there——" Whit's eyes narrowed to a gray gleam, and his hands rose in an attempt to cup a flying speck. Two quick claps missed, and he lurched over Dag again in pursuit, peering and trying to corner the insect against the whitewashed walls. His hands rose again, wavering with the target's erratic flight. Muzzy with annoyance and the first confusion of dream sleep, Dag sat up, reached out his left arm, extended his ghost hand like a strand of smoke, and ripped the ground from the mosquito.

The whine abruptly stopped. A puff of gray powder sifted down into Whit's outstretched palm. His eyes widened as he stared down at Dag. He gulped. "Did you just do that?"

Dag supposed he should say something useful like, *Yes, and if you don't go lie down and hush, you're next,* but he had shocked himself rather worse than he'd shocked Whit.

It's coming back, like my groundsense range!

And—gone again. He folded his left arm, freed of the hook harness for the night, protectively against his chest, and twitched the blanket over his stump, for all that Whit had seen it several times before. And tried to breathe normally.

Dag's ghost hand had first appeared to him back when he'd mended that glass bowl so spectacularly last summer, and had been intermittently useful thereafter. It was just a ground projection, the medicine maker had assured him, if an unusually strong and erratic one. Not some uncanny blessing or curse. A ground projection such as powerful makers sometimes used, but haunting his wrist in that unsettling form like a memory of pain and loss, hence the name he'd given it back when he hadn't yet understood what it was. Invisible to ordinary eyes, dense and palpable to groundsense. And then it had been destroyed, he'd thought—sacrificed in the complex aftermath of the fight with the malice in Raintree.

Where, in an utter extremity of panic and need, he'd ground-ripped the malice, and nearly killed himself doing so.

"Whit, just go lie down." Fawn's voice had an edge distinct enough from her earlier grumbling that even Whit heard it.

"Um, yeah. Sure." He picked his way much more carefully back over Dag, and grunted down to his bedroll once more.

Dag looked up to find Fawn propped on her elbow, frowning over the side of the bed at him. She lowered her voice. "Are you all right, Dag?"

He opened his mouth, paused, and settled on, "Yeah."

Her eyes narrowed in suspicion. "You have a funny look on your face."

He didn't doubt it. He tried to substitute a smile, which didn't seem to reassure her much. He felt a peculiar sharp throbbing in the ground of his left arm, as if a campfire spark had landed on his skin, or under it—a spark he could not brush away, though his fleshly fingers made a futile effort to, rubbing under his blanket.

She started to settle back, but added, "What did you do to that poor mosquito?"

"Ground-ripped it. I guess." Except it was no guess. He could feel the creature's lost ground stuck in his own, as those deadly malice-spatters had once been. Tinier, less toxic, not blighted, not a spreading death—but also not anything like a medicine maker's gift of ground reinforcement, warm and welcome and healing. This felt uncomfortable and sticky, like a spot of hot tar. Painful. Wrong?

Fawn rolled up on her elbow again. She knew, if Whit clearly did not, just how far outside the usual range of Dag-doings this was. "Really?"

"I probably shouldn't have," he muttered.

Her eyes pinched in doubt. "But—it was only a mosquito. You must have killed hundreds by hand, in your time."

"Thousands, likely," he agreed. "But . . . it *itches.* In my ground." He rubbed again.

Her brows flew up; her face relaxed in amused relief. "Oh, dear."

He made no attempt to correct that relief. He captured her trailing hand, kissed it, and nodded to the oil lamp; she stretched up and doused it once again. As the bed creaked, he murmured, "Good night, Spark."

"G'night, Dag," she returned, already muffled by her pillow. "Try'n sleep." A slight snicker. "Don't scratch."

He listened to her breathing till it slowed and eased, then, his arms crossed on his chest, turned his groundsense in upon himself.

The tiny coal of alien ground still throbbed within his own. He tried to divest it, to lay it as a ground reinforcement in the floor, or his sheet, or even his own hair. It remained stubbornly stuck. Neither did it seem to be starting to melt into his own ground, converted from mosquito-ground to Dag-ground as a man might digest food—or at least, not yet. He wondered if he had, in that moment of sleepy irritation, planted a permanent infliction upon himself.

Careless irritation. Not mortal panic. Not an overstretched, once-in-a-lifetime heroic reach, out of a heart, body, and ground pushed for an instant beyond human limits. Ground-ripping a mosquito was hardly a great act, nor of grave moral weight.

Except that ground-ripping anything wasn't a human act at all. It was malice magic, the very heart of malice magic. Wasn't it?

Lakewalker makers used two kinds of groundwork, in a thousand variations. They might persuade, push, or reorder ground within an object, to subtly alter or augment its nature. And so produce cloth that scarcely frayed, or steel that did not rust, or rope that was nearly impossible to break, or leather that repelled rain—or turned arrows. Or they might gift ground out of their own bodies; most commonly, into their wedding cords, but also as shaped or unshaped reinforcements laid in the matching region of another person's ground, to speed healing, slow blood loss, fight shock or infection. But always, the limits of the groundwork were in the limits of the maker doing it.

A malice stole ground from the world around it—limited, Dag swore, by nothing but its attention. And its attention ranged somewhere well beyond human, too. But while a person altered gifted ground into their own as slowly as a healing wound, malices seemed to do so almost instantaneously, not by persuasion but by simple, brute, and overwhelming force. Powered by yet more ground-ripping, in a widening spiral.

Perhaps such transformative power was not a human capacity. Even from the malice, Dag had only snatched deadly fragments. Anyone trying to ground-rip something whole the way a malice did might simply burst, like a man trying to drink a lake.

But a man might drink a cup of lake water . . .

Was a mosquito like a cup of water?

Dag considered the question, and then considered, more dubiously, the sanity of the mind that could even frame it. Or maybe he was coming down with brain-worms, like Whit's fabulous rumor. Maybe he simply needed to sleep it off. Surely the splotch would go down overnight like any other mosquito bite, absorbed by Dag's ground just as his body healed more purely physical welts. He snorted and rolled over, firmly shutting his eyes.

It still itched, though.

～

By the next morning Dag's whole left arm was so swollen he couldn't get his arm harness on.

Fawn was inclined to declare a day of rest in Lumpton Market, but Dag insisted he could ride one-handed, and Whit, anxious to pass at last beyond the places he knew, was not much help on the side of reason. By mid-afternoon Fawn was not happy to have her judgment confirmed when Dag fell into a fever. As if she needed any more evidence, he settled on a blanket and watched without protest as she and Whit set up their camp just off the old straight road south. A chill mist rose from the damp ground in the gathering dusk, but at least no more rain threatened.

"All this from a mosquito bite?" she murmured, sliding in beside him as he drew up his knees and hunched around the swollen arm.

He shrugged. "I don't think it's going to kill me. That spot in my ground is already starting to feel less hot."

She felt his forehead in doubt. But his skin was merely over-warm, not burning-dry, and he ate and drank, if with an indifferent appetite. When they rolled up to sleep she filched her brother's spare blanket away from him to drape on Dag, ruthlessly ignoring Whit's yelp of protest.

But by the following day, the swelling had gone down, and Dag claimed the ground-welt was being absorbed much like a normal ground reinforcement, if more slowly. He nevertheless grew flushed and silent in the afternoon; by his pinched brows and glazed eyes Fawn suspected a thumping headache.

As unshakable as Fawn felt in the lee-side of Dag's full strength, she hated her sense of helplessness when he was laid up. He had a store of uncanny Lakewalker healing knowledge in his head and a host of patroller tricks at his fingertips, impressive enough that Hickory Lake's chief medicine maker had tried to recruit him into her craft. But who cured the medicine maker? A farmer midwife or bonesetter would not be much help in some strange ground-illness, and Fawn realized that despite all this summer's experiences, she didn't actually know how to find a Lakewalker at need. It was too far back to Hickory Lake, and still several days ride to the Lakewalker ferry camp on the Grace River. Patrols or couriers did stop now and then at the inn at Lumpton Market or that hotel in Glassforge, but it could be days or even weeks till any chanced along.

The camp that Chato's patrol had hailed from was closer, she was fairly sure, but she didn't even know how to find that. That at least had a cure; she asked Dag that night where it was to be found, and he described it to her. For the first time, she began to see the point of their little patrol of three: not only because it would take two Bluefields to even lift Dag, but because one of them could stay with him while the other rode for help.

If strange Lakewalkers would even give help to Dag, half-exiled as he was. Which was a new and ugly thought.

But by the next day, Dag seemed much recovered. At noon they stopped at the roadside farm with the public well where they had first encountered each other, and reminisced happily over small details of shared memory while stocking up on the farmwife's good provender. That evening found them quite near to Glassforge. Dag opined they could detour off the straight road tomorrow to show Whit the blight and still make town before dark.

∾

They could not have chanced on a prettier day for a ride up into the un-peopled hills east of the old straight road. The sky was the dry deep blue that only the northwest winds brought to Oleana, the air as cool and tangy as apple cider. The trees here were mostly holding their leaves, and the brilliant sun turned their colors blinding: bright crimson edged with blood maroon, yellow gold, a startling flash of nightshade-purple here and there in the drying weeds. Dag's eyes grew coin-gold in this light, like autumn distilled. Fawn was glad it was Dag leading them up into these game-tracked humps and hollows, because she'd have lost her way as soon as their turn-off was out of sight. If not really been lost; she'd only to strike west to find the road again. But the blight was a smaller target—thankfully—some ten or twelve miles in.

The sun was climbing toward noon when Dag halted Copperhead on the beaten trail they'd been following. A frown tensed his mouth. Fawn kicked her mount Weft alongside, though Copperhead laid his ears back for show.

"Are we close?"

"Yes."

Her own recall of the place was too dizzied to permit recognition. She'd been carried in head-down and ears ringing, a prisoner, retching from blows and terror. And carried out . . . her memory shied from that.

Dag pointed up the trail. "This path goes to the ravine on the same side I came down. The visible blight should start about two hundred paces along."

"And the blight you can't see?"

He shrugged, though his face stayed strained. "I've been feeling the outer shadow for the past half-mile."

"Healing as you still are, should you go any closer?"

He grimaced. "Likely not."

"Suppose you wait here, then. Or better, back down the trail a ways. And I'll just take Whit in for a quick peek."

He couldn't argue with the logic of that. A hesitation, a short nod. "Don't linger, Spark."

She nodded and waved Whit on in her wake. He looked a trifle confused as he pressed his sturdy horse up next to hers. As Warp and Weft fell into a well-matched pace, he asked, "What was that all about?"

"Being on blight makes Lakewalkers sick. Well, it makes anybody sick, but I was afraid it would send Dag into an awful relapse like after Greenspring. Glory be that he saw the sense of waiting for us."

Whit glanced around. "But everything is drying up and dying back right now. How do you spot blight in winter? How is it that you're supposed to tell this here blight from . . . oh."

They reined in at the lip of the ravine. They must be very near to what had been Dag's vantage, that day. The cave was a deep hollow halfway up the ravine's far side, with a long outcrop of rock shielding the opening almost like a wall. The ravine itself was a dusty gray, devoid of vegetation but for a few skeletal tree trunks. The glimmering creek flowing through in an S-curve was the only movement, the only source of sound. No birds, no insects, no small rustles in the dead weeds. Even the breeze seemed stilled. The peculiar dry cellar-odor of malice habitation wafted faintly up to Fawn, and she swallowed, feeling sickened despite the sun on her back.

"That is the weirdest color I ever did see," Whit allowed slowly. "It's not hardly a color at all. Dag was right. It doesn't look like . . . anything."

Fawn nodded, glad Whit seemed to have his wits with him today, because she didn't think she could have borne stupid jokes right now. "Dag thinks that malice came up from the ground and hatched out right here. Malices all seem to start out pretty much the same, but then they change depending on what they eat. Ground-snatch, that is. If they catch a lot of people, they get to looking more human, but there was one up in Luthlia that mostly ate wolves, that they say grew pretty strange. Dag thinks the first human this one caught must have been a road bandit, hiding out up here, because after it grew its mud-men and caught more folks, it made them all be its bandit gang, at first." Though some of the men might not have been as mind-slaved as all that, which was in its way an even more disturbing notion. "The bandits who kidnapped me off the road brought me here. Dag was tracking them, and saw." From here, Dag would certainly have had a clear view of the mud-men carting her in like a sack of stolen grain. "He went in after them—after me—all by himself. No time to wait for his patrol. It wasn't good odds. But he tossed me his sharing knife, and I managed to get it in the malice. And the malice . . ." She swallowed again. "Melted. I guess you could say. Malices are immortal, the Lakewalkers claim, but the sharing knives kill them. Kill them in their ground."

"What are sharing knives, anyhow? Dag keeps mentioning them and then stopping."

"Yes, well. There are reasons. Lakewalkers make them. Out of Lakewalker bones."

"So it's true they rob graves!"

"No! They're not stolen. Dag—any Lakewalker would get mighty offended to hear you say that. People will their thighbones to their kin to be, be, like, harvested after they die. It's part of the funeral. Then a Lakewalker knife maker—Dag's brother Dar is one—cleans and carves and shapes the bone into a knife. They don't use sharing knives for any other purpose than killing malices."

"So that's what you stuck in the malice? Whose thighbone was it, d'you know? Does Dag?"

Fawn supposed gruesome interest was better than none. "Yes, but it's more complicated than that. Carving the bone itself is only the first step. Then the knife has to be primed. With . . . with a heart's death." She took a breath, not looking at Whit. "That's the hardest part. Each knife, when it's made, is bonded to its Lakewalker owner. Someone who has volunteered to share—to donate his or her own death to the knife. When such Lakewalkers think they're dying, either old and sick or hurt mortal bad, they, they put the knife through their own hearts and capture their deaths. Which are trapped in the knives. So every primed knife costs two Lakewalker lives, one for the bone and the other for the heart's priming. Ownership is . . . you can't buy such a knife. It can only be given to you."

She glanced up to see Whit squinting and frowning. He said slowly, "So, it's sort of like . . . a human sacrifice stuck in a canning jar and preserved, to take out and use later?"

Fawn thought of the long rows of wax-sealed glass jars she and Mama had filled and sealed and set in the pantry only last week. The domestic comparison was apt, but, oh dear. "Pretty much. But I'm not sure you should say that to Dag. Lakewalkers keep their knives private and treat 'em as sacred. It's their kin, you see. And their grief. But that's what sharing knives share. Deaths."

Whit blinked some more, then frowned across the ravine and said, "How far back does that cave go?"

"It's not deep."

"Can we go in?"

Fawn wrinkled her nose. "I guess so, if we don't stay long."

Whit glanced down the steep drop, nodded, and slid off and tied his horse to a tree. Fawn did the same and followed him in a scramble down the slope. Black shale cracked and slid under her feet. Even the clay dirt in the gully-washes, which should have been dull brown, had that same drained gray tinge. Whit picked his way across the stream on stones, not looking back till he reached the cave mouth, when he turned around to watch her puffing and lagging after him. "Keep up, Runt."

She was shivering inside too much to growl at the old taunt. She labored up beside him, and the dry, sour malice-smell of the cave hit her full-face. *How long till the rains and snows wash this clean?* Horridly blithe, he strolled into the shadow of the overhang.

"What a great place to camp this would be! It really looks like it should be a bandit hideout." He kicked at a broken old keg, part of a scattering of trash no one had bothered to cart away. "So where were you two, exactly? Where was this malice? How far did Dag have to throw his knife? He must not have known you then. It was a wonder you caught it."

"Here . . ." *Simplify.* "The malice picked me up by my neck." She fingered the dented scars. *Here. Here, right here, the malice ripped the ground from my unborn child, poor half-wanted waif, here she died, here Dag was nearly torn apart by howling man-beasts, here I struck, right here the malice screamed and stank and shattered, here sacrifice tangled with sacrifice, here I miscarried, here I hurt, here I started bleeding . . .* "I have to get out of here," Fawn said aloud. She could not see clearly. She was shaking so badly she could scarcely breathe. *There is no simple to be had, here.*

"Hey, are you all right?" Whit called as she stumbled out into the air again. There wasn't enough light in the wide green world to make that cave anything but a pit of darkness, to make her anything but *stupid,*

stupid, stupid . . . She became aware she was weeping, not sobs, but weird dry gulps.

Whit, trotting after her, said, "Is the blight making you sick? Here, maybe I . . . I better take you back to Dag, all right?"

She nodded, trying and failing to steady her breathing, which seemed to stagger and stick. She tried to swallow between gulps of air, but her throat was too tight. Whit put a tentative, anxious arm around her waist and half-supported, half-hustled her back down and across the creek. She slipped and put one foot ankle-deep in the stream, gasping at the chill wet, which at least got some more air into her. By the time they reached the ravine's top and Whit boosted her back up into her saddle, she was only wheezing. Her cheeks were wet, her nose beslimed; she dragged an arm fiercely across her face, and coughed.

When they reached the place where they'd sent Dag back, she looked up through the silver blur to see Copperhead cantering up the trail toward them. Dag pulled up with a jerk that made the gelding shake his head and snort. A black scowl, a brutal voice the like of which she'd never heard before from Dag's mouth, demanded of Whit, *"What did you do to her?"*

"Nothing!" said Whit, alarmed. "I didn't do nothing! She was nattering on about, about this and that, and then all of a sudden she took a fit o' the vapors! I thought it might be the blight, though I didn't feel anything like. Here, you take her!"

Dag discarded his menace as he turned a keen look on Fawn; searching her body and her ground both, she thought. He dropped his reins on Copperhead's neck and leaned over to pull her from her saddle into his lap. She clutched him hard around the chest, burying her face in his shirt, inhaling the scents of linen and warm Dag-sweat to drive the deathly cellar-smell away. Arm and strong spread hand, his beautiful hand, clutched her in return.

"I'm sorry," she mumbled into his shirt. "I didn't think it would all pile back into my head like that. It was the smell of the cave. All of a sudden I couldn't breathe. Stupid . . ."

"Shh, no," he said into her hair. His understanding seemed to wrap her more warmly than his arms. He raised his chin, jerked it at Whit. "Bring her horse. We need to get away from this bad ground. Maybe get everyone something to eat."

Copperhead turned obediently at the pressure of Dag's leg, or perhaps ground; in any case, the gelding seemed to grasp that this was no time for tricks. They all rode a good two miles back down the trail before Dag turned off. He led down over a bank and up to a little clearing with a spring seeping out of a rock overhang. A pretty picnic spot. Patroller groundsense at work? In any case, Dag said merely, "This'll do." He murmured in her ear, "Can you get down all right?"

"Yes. I'm better now." Not *all better,* no, but at least she'd stopped sniveling.

He let her slide off Copperhead's shoulder, and he and Whit bustled about pulling food packets from the saddlebags, finding the tin cups, loosening girths, and permitting the horses to browse. Dag kept a close eye on Fawn till she'd settled on a rock, drunk spring water, and taken a few bites of the rather dry cheese wrapped in bread left from yesterday's supply. He finally sat down cross-legged beside her. Whit perched on a nearby fallen log that was not too damp with moss and rot.

"Sorry," Fawn repeated, swallowing and straightening up. "Stupid."

"Shh," Dag repeated, gripping her calf in a reproving, heartening little shake. "None o' that."

Whit cleared his throat. "I guess that malice was pretty scary."

"Yeah," said Fawn. The spring water was welcomingly cool; why did her throat feel so hot? She scrubbed at her scars.

Whit added magnanimously, "Well, you're just a girl, after all."

Fawn merely grimaced. In his own way, she supposed Whit was trying. *Very trying.*

Dag's brows drew in, as if he were struggling to parse what Whit meant; he clearly didn't see the connection between the two statements. And then he did, and got a pretty odd look. He said, "I've seen the first encounter with a malice devastate fully trained patrollers. I was on sick leave for weeks after my first, though the thing never touched me."

Whit cleared his throat, made a wise decision not to try to retrieve his remark, and asked instead, "How many have you seen? Altogether?"

"I've lost count," said Dag. "That I've slain by my hand with a knife of my own, twenty-six."

"Twenty-seven," Fawn corrected.

He smiled at her. "Twenty-six and a half, then. My knife, your hand."

Fawn watched Whit's lips move, counting up kills. No—knives. Lakewalker lives, and deaths. His brow wrinkled.

Fawn put in hastily, "I told Whit about sharing knives. Tried to, anyhow. I'm not sure if he has it all straight." Her anxious eyes quizzed Dag: *Is that all right?*

He ducked his head, answering her look as well as her words. "Oh. Good. Thank you."

Whit scraped his boot toe across the moss. "Is that a lot of those knives to have had?"

"Yes, actually."

"Did you . . . er . . . have a big family?"

Fawn resisted the urge to knock her head—or maybe Whit's—into a tree. He *was* trying.

Dag was trying, too. He replied straightforwardly, "No. Folks—friends, kin of friends, other patrollers—gave them to me, because I seemed to have a knack for getting them used. A patroller can carry a primed knife for a long time and never encounter a malice, which makes the sacrifice seem—well, not vain. But folks like knowing when it all comes to something."

"That makes sense, I guess," Whit allowed. He remembered to take a bite of bread and cheese. "You don't have—do you have—one of those, um. Suicide knives?"

"Unprimed knife, bonded to me?" Dag hazarded.

Whit said, "Well, it would have to be unprimed, wouldn't it? Stands to reason. Because if it was primed you'd be, um."

"I did have. Carried it with me for twenty years, in case. A lot of patrollers do."

"Can I see—no, um. Did, right. What happened to it?"

Dag glanced at Fawn; she gave a small headshake, *No, we didn't get to that part.* "It met with an accident."

"Oh." Whit blinked—daunted, Fawn prayed. But not quite enough, for he added curiously, "Whose bone was it?"

"Kauneo's. She willed one bone to me and the other to one of her surviving brothers. My tent-brother up in Luthlia."

Whit gave Dag a look partway between earnestly inquiring and leery. "Um?" He was already starting to learn caution about these sorts of questions, Fawn thought. And their answers.

Dag took a drink of spring water and managed to reply with tolerable composure, "My first wife."

Fawn gave him a worried look, *Are you all right with this?* He returned her a fractional nod. Yes, he could talk about Kauneo now; they had come so far. Dag cleared his throat and added kindly, for even Whit's feckless curiosity was faltering in the face of all this, "She was a patroller, too. She died in a malice war in Luthlia. She left me her own heart's knife as well as a bone to make one for me. We think she rolled over on her knife in the field after she fell. Her brother said"—he drew air in through his nostrils—"she must have moved quick. Because she could not have been conscious for very long after . . . after she received her wounds."

"Is that where you——" Whit's gaze moved to Dag's left arm.

Another short nod. "Same fight. I went down before she did, so I only have guesses. She was . . . just a girl, then. Five years younger than me."

Just a girl, thought Fawn, and *Dag didn't repeat those words by accident.*

"Oh," said Whit. And, tentatively, "I'm, um, sorry."

Dag gave him another reassuring nod, and repeated his stock phrase, "It was a long time ago."

In your head, it sometimes turns into just yesterday, doesn't it? thought Fawn curiously. *Like me and the malice, back in the cave just now. Yes. Now I see how you knew.* She bent over and took another bite of bread to quell the renewed flutter in her belly.

Whit's brows knit. "Were you really going to stick that bone knife in your own heart?"

"Yes, if it chanced so."

It took Whit a little while to remember to chew and swallow after that one. He finally scratched his ear, and said, "Can't you get another?"

"Whit!" said Fawn indignantly.

Dag made a little gesture with his fingers, *It's all right.* "It's not quite up to me. I'd need someone to give me a bone. Or an unprimed knife that didn't get used that could be rededicated. I want one. I'd be bitterly ashamed to waste my death just for lack of a knife."

Fawn realized she hadn't quite known that, for all she knew of Dag. Whit was reduced to blinking. Silently, praise be.

Whit inhaled. "Folks don't know this. They say Lakewalkers are cannibals. That you rob graves. Eat your dead to make magic."

Dag said gently, "But now you know better."

"Um. Yeah." Whit brightened. "So, that's one farmer boy who's learned something, huh?"

"One down." Dag sighed. "Thousands to go. It's a start."

"Sure enough," said Whit valiantly. Actually, he looked as if he were afraid Dag was about to put his head down and cry.

Fawn was a little afraid of that as well, but Dag just smiled crookedly and creaked to his feet. "Let's go see Glassforge, ducklings."

4

Even in the late afternoon, the straight road approaching Glass-forge was busy with traffic. Fawn watched Whit's head turn as he took in the sight of strings of pack mules, goods-wagons gaily painted with the names of their businesses and their owners, and a big brick dray, returning empty from somewhere. The team of eight huge dun horses thundered past at a lumbering trot, hopeful for home, the bells on their harness shaking out bright sounds like salt along their path. The teamster and his brakeman, too, were impressive in fringed leather jackets decorated with tiny mirrors that flashed in the westering sun, red scarves knotted around their necks. Fawn thought the couple of burly loaders who rode with their legs dangling over the wagon's tail might have been inclined to whoop at her, had she been a girl riding alone, but the presence of her escort turned their lewd stares into self-conscious nods, cheerily returned by Whit. Copperhead pretended to shy at this noisy vision, checked by a growl from his tired rider, and even gentle Warp and Weft swiveled their ears and looked faintly astonished.

Whit patted his mount's neck. "There, there, Warp. Don't let those big bruisers discourage you. Nobody's going to make you pull a ton of bricks." His face rose to stare after the receding wagon. "That'd be a life, though, wouldn't it, Fawn? I bet some of those wagons go as far as Tripoint or Silver Shoals or, or who knows where? Think of it! You'd get to see everywhere, talk to the whole world, and get *paid* for it. Sleep in a different place every night, I bet."

"The novelty of that wears off," Dag advised, sounding amused.

Scorning this with a look that said *Old-people talk!*, Whit went on, "I never thought of it, but I bet a town like Glassforge needs lots of horses, too. And drivers. I know how to drive a team. I wonder if I could get me one of those fancy jackets in town? I wonder if . . ." He trailed off, but Fawn had a clear sense of the mill wheels continuing to turn in his head, even if he'd temporarily disconnected them from his mouth.

I bet you're never going back to West Blue, Fawn thought. *Any more 'n I am.* She grinned in anticipation of showing off Glassforge to Whit, as pleased as if she'd invented the place herself, and wondered if this was anything like the pleasure Dag took in her. Dag never seemed to tire of showing her new things . . . no. It was a little more complicated than that. In her open delight, she made the world new to him again, and so drove his weariness away. It seemed a fair trade.

Whit was gratifyingly amazed by the hotel in Glassforge, three stories high, built of local brick softened by trails of ivy, "bigger," as he cried, "than Uncle Hawk's new barn!" The corners of Dag's mouth tucked up as Fawn earnestly explained to Whit how it was that patrols and couriers were always allowed to stay there for free, on account of some old malice the Lakewalkers had put down in these parts in the time of the present owner's papa, which Whit thought a very good deal.

Fawn was secretly uncertain if the deal would extend to an ex-patroller of dodgy status traveling privately with a tail of farmer relatives, but when they dismounted in the hotel's stable yard, she found she was still remembered from the past summer as the farmer heroine who'd slain the malice. She was welcomed by name by the excited horse boys and made much of by the owner's wife when they went inside. Even more agreeable than having the best available rooms instantly offered up to them was the way Whit's eyes grew wide as he took in her local fame. He didn't even crack a joke about it.

They hauled their bags upstairs to their chambers. By request, Fawn and Dag's room was the same they had slept in before, full of happy memories. Better, it had a nice thick plank door between it and Whit's room, with an oak bar that promised a night free of brothers, mosquitoes, or any other interruptions. Fawn was left with an hour before supper to run around and say hello to all the friends she'd made here in the summer: seamstresses, chambermaids, the cook and scullions. Whit trailed amiably. Fawn wasn't quite sure who she was showing off to which, as several of the younger girls perked up no end at Whit, alarming him enough to make him very polite. The charm he unleashed upon Sal the cook was pure stomach-interest, though, as she was both married and motherly.

"Sal let me do sitting-down chores while I was getting better and waiting for Dag to finish some patroller duties," Fawn explained, inhaling deeply of the mouthwatering aromas of the hotel's kitchen. Pots bubbled, a roast turned on a spit, pies cooled; a scullion ran a hopeful horse boy back outside to wait for scraps till after the patrons were fed. "I must have shelled ten thousand peas, but it kept me from going stir-crazy."

"You were so pale, at first!" agreed Sal. "I think my cookin' helped put those roses back in your cheeks." She patted one, leaving a smudge of flour.

"I think it did, too," said Fawn, brushing at the flour and smiling. "That 'n Dag."

Sal's smile thinned a bit, and she glanced appraisingly at Whit. "So that patroller fellow with the missin' hand must have got you home all right, after all."

Fawn nodded.

"We weren't too sure on him," Sal admitted. "Some of us was afraid he'd gone and beguiled you, like they say Lakewalkers can. Though it's true the ones we get here are usually pretty well-behaved. How they carry on with each other being not our business."

Fawn raised her chin. "If there was any beguiling going on, I'd say it was mutual. We married each other."

"He never!" said Sal in astonishment.

Fawn gestured at her brother. "Whit stood witness."

"Yep," said Whit. "They said their promises in the parlor in West Blue in front of the whole family, and signed the family book, and everything."

"Oh, honey . . ." Sal hesitated, looking troubled. "He was a right disturbin' fellow, the way all patrollers are, though it was plain he'd took a shine to you, but . . . I thought better o' him than that. Don't you two know that Lakewalkers don't recognize marriages to us folks? I'm afraid he was pulling the wool over your eyes, and your family's, too."

"No, he didn't," said Fawn. "We were married Lakewalker-style at the same time—we wove and swapped our binding strings as sound as any Lakewalker couple ever did. See?" She held out her left wrist, wrapped in the dark braid, and wriggled it to let the gold beads on the cord-ends bounce and glimmer, showing it off for the third or fourth time in this evening's rounds.

"Is that what those are?" said Sal doubtfully. "I've seen them hair bracelets on some of the patrollers here, time and time."

"Wedding cords, yes."

Whit said, "It's like they got married twice over. I don't think Dag was taking any chances by that time. I will say, when he ties a knot, it stays tied."

Sal's eyes grew as round as her mouth. "And his people accepted it?"

Fawn tossed her head. "I won't claim his kin were all happy, but they didn't say we weren't married."

"Well, I never!"

The serving boys bounced in, the scullions called, and Sal had to set aside her fascinated pursuit of this gossip in favor of getting supper ready. She shooed her guests out of her kitchen with visible regret.

In the corridor to the dining room, Whit paused in puzzlement. "Fawn . . ."

"Hm?"

"Dag's kin did accept those cords of yours, right? They didn't claim you were just, um . . . running around together, right?"

Fawn lowered her voice. "In truth, there were four or five opinions on that. Some took 'em for true, some accused us of trickery, and some didn't care nohow about the cords, they wanted to deny us any-road. They weren't just arguing with Dag, mind; they were arguing with each other as well. We kind of set the cat amongst the pigeons with those cords. When we left, I expect it took the urgency out of the debate." Truly, Dag hadn't wanted to force a decision, lest it become a quick and simplifying *no*.

"These rules of theirs—do they make them camp by camp, or everywhere at once?"

"Camp by camp, but the camps stay in touch with one another. Couriers carry patrol reports, plus letters between the camp councils. And folks' personal letters. And lots of gossip, Dag says. Young patrollers exchange between camps to train up, and parties travel with trade goods. And folks go on visits to kin, sometimes. So news has ways of getting around. Lakewalkers don't let themselves get cut off from each other." She frowned. "I do wonder how Dag will go on, away from his people. That's not natural, for a Lakewalker. They made us both plenty mad, but . . . I do wonder."

"Huh," said Whit.

Whit must have made a good impression on Sal, because the portions soon set before the three of them at the dinner table were generous. After they had all pretty much foundered on the glut, Whit went off to the kitchen to compliment her. He came back full of a scheme to go reconnoiter Glassforge after dark, which Dag—Fawn was grateful to see—had the sense to discourage.

"It's been a long day," Fawn seconded. "Dag's still recovering, you know." Dag smiled at her from lidded eyes that looked anything but sleepy, dark and a bit glittery, and she dimpled back at him.

"Oh, yeah," said Whit vaguely. "And you weren't doing too well yourself, earlier. Tomorrow, then." He contented himself with going off to visit the horses and maybe chat with the hotel stable's horse boys.

Fawn and Dag went straight to bed, but not to sleep. Where Fawn made the astonishing and delightful discovery that Dag's ghost hand was starting to come back, at least enough to do a few blissful, blushful things with. Fawn's opinion of the medicine maker who had predicted such a recovery went up several notches. They did hear Whit come in, mainly because he knocked on the wall and bade them good night. Fawn smothered a giggle as Dag raised his head and drawled back similar good wishes—very blandly, considering his position just then.

The next morning after breakfast the three of them strolled to the town center, where a street off the market square led down to the little river that flowed past Glassforge toward the Grace. Tributary creeks behind dams fed several mill wheels, though at the moment the dry weather, a boon to harvesters and road travelers all over Oleana, had left the water so low in the main stream that only lightly loaded skiffs and narrow boats could take away the handiwork of the town's artisans. The autumn air was acrid from the wood smoke and coal smoke rising from a forge, a couple of iron furnaces, a wagon-wright's, a big smithy, a pottery yard, and, of course, the town's celebrated glass-makers.

At one of these, as Fawn had hoped, they found Sassa Clay, one of her best friends from the summer's misadventures with the malice. Red-haired Sassa seemed equally delighted to see them, and pleased to meet Whit. He had a refreshing masculine disinterest in marriage customs of any kind, but was very keen on glass and local trade, proudly leading a tour of his glassworks for the new audience. Sassa was not much older than Whit, and the two young men hit it off so well Fawn had no guilt about leaving them to each other's company after lunch and retiring with Dag back to the hotel for—he said—a nap. It wasn't a lie; she was sure a nap would ensue eventually.

She became concerned when Whit did not show up at the hotel for dinner, but Dag sensibly pointed out that Sassa knew perfectly well how to find them here if there were any emergencies to report, and Fawn relaxed. She wondered if she might parlay their two planned nights of rest here into three, but Dag was of the opinion that the dry spell couldn't last much longer, and truly, the night's chill breathed of the coming change.

Whit returned so late, they were actually sleeping. Fawn woke muzzily in the dark to hear him clumping around on attempted tiptoe, and the creak of his bed as he climbed into it. She cuddled back into the warmth of Dag's grip, reassured.

∾

She was less reassured when she went out to the stable in the frosty dawn to tell the horse boys to have Warp and Weft ready after break-fast—Dag would saddle Copperhead himself—only to find the team gone. And so, she discovered when she checked his room, was Whit.

She muffled her panic when she spotted his saddlebags still in a heap by his bed. Descending the staircase wondering whether to drag out Dag and his groundsense for a search, she met Whit breezing back in through the hotel's stable-yard door.

"Where have you been?" demanded Fawn in some exasperation. "Where are the horses?"

"Sold 'em," said Whit smugly.

"What? We still have two days of riding ahead of us!"

"*I* know that. I've made arrangements." At her look of disbelief, he added in a stung tone, "I sold Warp and Weft to Sassa's boss. He gave me a fair price."

"I thought you said you were going to try that coal hauler. On your way back," she added pointedly.

"Yeah, well . . . I liked the glassworks' stable better. Smelled cleaner, y'know? Plus, you have to figure—a glass wagon isn't going to race their horses, or overload them. They're pretty much bound to travel slow and careful." He nodded in satisfaction, apparently picturing his team in this gentle labor.

This appeal could not fail to reach Fawn, but she raked her fingers through her hair nonetheless. "Yes, but—how are we supposed to get to the river? Load all the bags on Copperhead and lead him?"

"No! Don't be stupid. I made a deal. Sassa's boss is sending two wagonloads of glass goods down to the river crossing for the Silver Shoals trade. I get to help drive, and load and unload, and you get to ride for free. Dag can tag alongside on Copperhead."

Fawn hesitated in new confusion. "So . . . are you going to come back and work as a teamster for the glassworks, or what?"

Whit shrugged. "They have fellows for that. I don't know. But anyway, you and Dag have to hurry up. The wagons are all loaded and about ready to leave. They want to catch the light, with the days short-ening."

And so Fawn found herself hustled through what she'd planned as a leisurely breakfast, and forced to make hasty farewells to all the folks at the hotel. Dag, old patroller that he was, adjusted to the surprise de-parture without effort, though he did refuse to be hurried shaving. The extra bags were only piled across Copperhead's saddle long enough to lead him down into town. The well-sprung freight wagon, with Fawn clinging atop a pile of straw-stuffed slat boxes, headed south out of Glassforge before the morning sun had melted last night's frost from the weeds lining the ditches.

They passed the sand-pit where men were digging the fine white sand that was the basis of the town's famous industry. From the loads being hauled away, Fawn guessed Warp and Weft might have some heavier work to do than delivering finished glass, though for the moment they were hitched on as wheelers to this very wagon—on trial, she suspected. Was Whit on trial for future employment, too? The lead wagon of their little train was being driven by a grizzled fellow named Mape, setting as decorous a pace as Whit had envisioned, but which made her wonder just how long it was going to take them to reach the ferry. He had a skinny youth up beside him, Hod, who seemed to be there to help with the horses and load and unload, like Whit. Their own team of four was handled by a comfortably middle-aged man named Tanner, who, Fawn soon learned, was a something-cousin of the owners of the glassworks, and who had a wife and children back in Glassforge.

Whit's questions about the glass business got them over any mutual shyness pretty quick. Fawn edged forward to listen; Dag rode nearby, so quiet and self-contained you might not notice he was listening, too. When Whit paused, Tanner, with a glance over his shoulder at her, took a little breath and asked her about the malice she and Dag had slain this summer. Fawn blinked, first at the realization that his question had been hovering on his tongue for a while, and had taken him some effort to spit out, and then at the oddity of anyone having to work up courage to talk to her. But she answered him steadily, giving him the simplified version, including, after a brief look to Dag, an equally simplified version of how sharing knives worked. This parted Tanner's lips and sent his brows halfway to his hairline; he glanced aside at Dag but shied from speaking to him directly. Whit chimed in with a vivid description of the blight and a recommendation amounting to a sales pitch to visit it.

"I guess I should," said Tanner, shaking his head in wonder. "I didn't have family directly involved with that mess, the way poor Sassa was caught up, but I'd heard a lot about it—except the very center. It all makes more sense, now. Hope you don't mind. I didn't like to ask you about it in front of Mape up there"—he nodded toward the back of the grizzled teamster, safely out of earshot through both distance and the wagons' rumbling—"on account of he lost his wife's nephew in the ruckus, and has feelin's."

"I'm sorry," said Fawn.

"Was he ground-ripped, like?" inquired Whit, morbidly curious.

Tanner looked grim. "I think that would have been easier, all told. He was one of the ones took up by the bandits and pressed into their gang. It was a bad time, after, sorting out who was really a bandit and who was tranced by the blight bogle. In the end it was locals got pardoned and strangers got hanged, mostly, which I don't think was always right. But Mape's nephew was killed outright by the Lakewalker patrollers, in the fight when they caught up with the bandits. Which maybe saved the family a hangin', but I'm not sure Mape's wife sees it that way."

"Oh," said Whit.

Fawn swallowed. "Was he a sort of dun-blond boy?"

"No, dark-haired."

Fawn let out her breath in secret relief. *Not* the one Dag had shot in front of her, then, saving him from a hanging for sure. Dag, riding alongside, had gone quiet—quieter—and expressionless, and it occurred to her that maybe her assailant wasn't the only one whose evil career Dag had personally ended on that patrol. He had been in on the attack on the bandit camp the night before, she knew, which was how he'd happened to be trailing her kidnappers in the first place. He'd run low on arrows. Some must have found targets . . .

"Thanks for the warning," she said to Tanner. "I shouldn't like to step on anyone's feelings." He nodded cordially enough. Glancing at the skinny youth beside Mape, riding along with his back rounded and his hands dangling between his knees, she added, "So what about Hod? Was he caught up in it all?"

"No, he was way too much of a homebody." After a long pause, Tanner added, "Hod's a bit of a sad sack, if you want my opinion. He was an orphan, living with his older sister, till her husband threw him out not long back for laziness and—he said—thievin'. Sassa Clay took a pity on him and let him put up in the glassworks' stable to look after the hosses. Which he does do middlin'-well, I admit, despite us finding him sleeping in the straw half the time."

"Will he work up to driver?" asked Fawn, wondering if this was Whit's competition for the coveted job.

"Hard to say. He's not real bright. Mape wouldn't let him touch the reins of *his* team, for sure." Tanner lowered his voice. "I'm not sayin' the boy's vicious, mind, but it's true about the thievin'. I've seen him sneaking. Only food, so far. Missus Clay slips him extra scraps, now and then, but it doesn't seem to have stopped him. I'm afraid he's gonna work up to something bigger someday soon and get into real trouble. So, um . . . watch your bags."

Did Tanner mean for their sakes, or for Hod's? It was hard to tell.

Truly, when they all stopped for lunch and to water and bait the horses, it seemed to Fawn that the lanky youth had little going for him. Hod's dishwater hair was dull and limp and in need of a cut, his skin was bad, his teeth doubtful, and he moved in a habitual slouch. He was inarticulate to the point of muteness; her couple of attempts to say a friendly word to him threw him into complete confusion. He seemed outright afraid of Dag, and went wide around him. Fawn wasn't even sure if Hod was his real name.

Whit was taken aback when he made the discovery that grub was not provided for the drivers and loaders, but that they were expected to bring their own, a little detail of planning that had evidently escaped his notice—and Fawn's too, in the morning's hustle. Dag let them both flounder and recriminate for a bit before blandly fetching the provisions from his saddlebags that he'd had Sal pack up while he was shaving. He wasn't *too* dry about it, but he did wait and make Whit ask, humbly, for a share before portioning it out. Just enough of a dig, Fawn thought, to make certain that neither of them were like to make a similar mistake again.

Dag enjoyed watching Fawn and Whit take in the scenes south of Glassforge, on a road new to them both, if old to Dag. He hadn't ridden this particular stretch for several years, though. Whit kept asking if the craggy little hills cloaked in color that now rose on both sides of them were mountains yet, and Dag had to keep disillusioning him. Although Dag's personal definition of a mountain was anything high enough to kill you if you fell off it, and thus covered any precipice from ten to a thousand feet high, so he supposed these rucked-up slopes aspired to the name. The land grew less settled as it pinched more sharply, and the hamlets clinging to the straight road fell farther apart.

Darkness overtook them several miles short of the village that was the teamsters' usual stopping point on this route, a mishap that the one called Mape blamed, grumblingly, on their late start, but which the more tolerant Tanner chalked up to the shortening of the daylight. Everyone pulled out their dinner packets and drank from the roadside spring that had prompted the halt while the two men debated whether to rest the horses and continue on slowly—more slowly—by lantern light, or stop here and sleep under the wagons. No rain threatened, but the chill creeping from the hollows pushed consensus toward the lantern scheme; Whit blithely volunteered Dag to ride ahead with a lantern suspended from his hook, a suggestion that made Fawn grimace. The prospect of combining a burning and maybe drippy oil lantern with a cranky Copperhead, tired and bored from the day's plod, made Dag say merely, "I'll think about it."

Dag walked around the spring, stretched his back, and sat down against a buckeye tree, extending both his legs and his groundsense. He'd kept closed all day in the presence of strangers and their chaotic farmer grounds. His reach was out to two hundred paces tonight, maybe? He still felt half-blinded. After pulling off Copper's bridle and loosening the girth, Dag had turned him loose to browse under light ground contact. In the deepening shadows, Dag could better hear the ripping and munching than see with his eyes, but in his groundsense the gelding was an old familiar brightness, almost brighter than the boy Hod. Hod had gone to relieve himself up in the bushes and was now circling back. Keeping to the shadows, easing up toward Copperhead . . .

Dag came alert, though he did not open his eyes. Was the dimwitted boy contemplating a little attempted filching? Dag considered his responsibilities. Hod was no young patroller of Dag's; still, if the boy was to learn a sharp lesson not to go riffling in a Lakewalker's saddlebags, it might be better all around to be sooner than later, with Dag and not with another. It would doubtless be an embarrassing scene, but it might save Hod much worse later on. Dag withdrew his ground contact from Copperhead and settled back to let nature take its course.

Dag was expecting Copperhead's angry squeal, head-snake, and cow-kick. He wasn't expecting the ugly *thunk* or a scream of pain so loud, sharp, and prolonged. *Blight* it, what——? He yanked his ground-sense wide, then recoiled as the hot flush of injury swamped back in on him. Drawing breath, he wallowed to his feet.

The two teamsters pelted past him, with Whit on their heels crying warning for them to swing wide around the horse, who was snorting and backing. Fawn followed, having had the sense to pause and grab a lantern. Trying not to limp on his *right* leg, Dag stumbled after.

Hod was lying on the ground on his back, writhing from side to side, clutching and clawing at his leg and openly bawling. His face was screwed up in pain, mottled red and pale and popping out cold sweat. And no wonder. By whatever evil chance, Copperhead's shod hoof had scored a direct hit on the boy's right kneecap, shattering the bone and pulping the flesh behind it. *Blight it, blight it, blight it . . . !*

Tanner gasped. "What happened?"

Dag said, "Horse kicked him when he went to poke in my bags for grub." Which won him a sharp look upwards from Fawn——*You knew?* They would deal with that aspect *later.* Dag surged forward.

To find himself blocked by the gray-haired and very solid Mape. "Don't you touch him, Lakewalker!"

Whit and Tanner knelt by Hod, trying unsuccessfully to soothe and still him as he beat his fists on the ground and howled.

Dag unclenched his jaw and said to Mape, "I have some skills in field aid."

"Let him through," cried Fawn, at the same moment as Whit called, "Dag, help!" Reluctantly, Mape gave way.

"Fawn, get a fire going, for heat and light," Dag instructed tersely. "We'll need both."

She skittered off wordlessly. Dag knelt by Hod's right knee, and let both hands, real and sputtering-ghostly, hover over it. *Absent gods, I shouldn't be attempting this.* A quick ground match, to slow the internal bleeding—the joint was already swollen tight against the fabric of Hod's trousers—to dull the blazing nerves . . . Dag's right knee screamed in sympathy. He gritted his teeth and ignored the ground-echo. Hod stopped howling and just gasped, staring up wild-eyed at Dag.

In a few minutes that seemed much longer, the men had Hod laid out on a blanket and his trousers off, an operation he tried to resist and that made him cry some more, though whether from pain or shame Dag was not sure. He apparently owned no underdrawers; Tanner dropped a blanket over his nether parts. All four wagon-lanterns and the new fire, bless Fawn, laid golden light on the unpleasant sight of the ruined joint, bulging, mottled, and already dark with blood beneath the shiny skin. Shards of bone pressed against the skin from the inside, and each of Hod's shudders threatened to push one through.

"Can you do anything, Lakewalker?" asked Tanner.

"'Course he can!" asserted Whit valiantly. "I've seen him mend broken glass!"

"This is bad," said Dag. "The kneecap's floating in about six pieces, and one tendon is nearly torn through. This needs a lot more than splint-ing and rest." *I shouldn't even be thinking about this without another medicine maker to guard me from groundlock, or worse. There's good reasons they work in pairs.* Forty miles to the closest other Lakewalkers tonight, down the road to the ferry camp at Pearl Riffle. Eighty miles round-trip. Not even Copperhead could do it, even if a real medicine maker would come out for an injured farmer, an event so unlikely that it would make some kind of history.

"Is he gonna cut off my leg?" sobbed Hod. "Don' let him go cuttin' on me! Can't work, nobody'll give me money, can't go back, Hopper'll beat me again if I go back . . ."

Hopper? Oh, Hod's tent-brother—brother-in-law, Dag corrected himself. *Some tent-brother.*

"Hurts," wept Hod. No one doubted him.

"Dag . . . ?" said Fawn in a small, uncertain voice. "Can you . . . do anything?" She made a little gesture toward his left arm. "Any ground-work?"

A simple ground reinforcement was not going to be enough here, and Dag had, absent gods knew, no prior affinity with this boy the way he did with Fawn to give him subtle routes into his body and ground. He looked into Fawn's huge, dark, scared, trusting eyes. Swallowed. And said, "I can try."

He settled down cross-legged by Hod's right knee, stretched his back, which popped, and bent again. Tanner and Mape, kneeling on either side of the boy, looked at him fearfully. "How hard should we hold him down?" asked Tanner, and "Should he have a leather strap to bite?" asked Mape.

This isn't some farmer bonesetter's bloody amputation, blight it! Dag shook his head. "It doesn't work like that." If it was going to work at all, that is. He brought his right hand and left . . . the sight of his useless hook suddenly irritated him immensely, and he undid the straps of its harness and cast it aside. Try again. Right hand hovering over left . . . stump. *Come on, come on you blighted ghost thing, come out, get in there.* Hod was whimpering, staring up at him in overwhelming horror. His terror beat on Dag in hot waves. *I have to open to this ungodly mess of a child.* One breath, two, three—Hod's breath slowed and Dag's sped, until their chests rose and fell in synchrony. Right hand over left, stroking, coaxing . . . and then it was there, invisible ground projection, sinking down slowly past Hod's skin into the broken flesh and its swirling, agitated ground.

Dag grasped the *ground* of the shattered bone fragments. His fleshly hand darted to the uninjured knee, to test and trace the song of its wholeness. Like that. Just like that. *Sing it so.* Dag began a low humming under his breath, far from musical, but he could feel the power in it. Fragments shifted, moved beneath the tight skin . . .

This was nothing like so simple as welding a glass bowl back together, amorphous and uniform; these structures hid more structures inside them, going down and down and in and in. But this little edge might hook again to that, that to the other, this torn blood vessel find its mated end, and gently, so delicately, kiss and make up. Minute after minute, fragment after fragment. His groundsense was wholly concentrated on the puzzle before him; the world outside both their skins could have cracked open wide with the roar of a thousand thunders and Dag would not have noticed. This vessel and that splinter and that one and that one . . . This was why medicine makers worked with partners for deep healing. Somebody anchored outside had to be able to break into the fascination. Lest you keep spiraling down and in and down and in and not ever come up and out again.

I can't do it all. I have to stop before I spend myself broke. Patch and tie, and let it heal the rest of the way itself—even real medicine makers do it that way. Get out, old patroller, while you still can. He'd thought nothing could be harder than matching his ground with Hod's, until he came to unmatch it again. He sensed Hod's chest rise, and deliberately broke the rhythm of his breath with the boy's. *Let go, old patroller. Get out of here before you hurt your fool self. Let go.*

He blinked his eyes open on firelight and lantern light, and knew himself sinfully lucky not to be groundlocked. *I overdid it, oh, I sure did.* Dag drew a long, long breath, and awareness of his own body returned to him at last.

Unfortunately.

Except that Fawn had three blankets wrapped around his shoulders before the second shuddering shiver shook him, and a basin thrust in his lap before his stomach heaved, and a cup of hot water held steadily to lips like cold clay. He took several grateful gulps, only spilling a little in his ague-like shakes. The hot liquid met his ascending dinner and forced it back down, and his stomach didn't try again. "Guh," said Dag.

"Don't try to talk," said Fawn, and explained over her shoulder to someone, "This happened the last time. He goes all cold and sick for a while, but then he comes out of it." Her worried eyes added to him, *I hope.*

Dag found his voice at last, and mumbled, "Fawn, Whit, find two strong slats and some ties of some kind, cloth strips or whatever. Make Hod splints down each side of his leg like a bonesetter's. Tie above and below the knee, firm but not tight. Keep it straight and still. It's still going to be swollen up, and it has a lot of mending yet to do on its own. Blankets, something, get him warm, keep him warm. He can't walk on it yet."

"He's going to walk?" said someone, in a voice caught between awe and disbelief.

"Not tonight, he's not. And he'd better be carried to the wagon in the morning. He can use my stick later on, I guess." But not tomorrow, because Dag was going to need it himself . . . He leaned toward the blurred, flickering orange light, and added plaintively, "More heat?"

Logs dropped onto the flames, which spewed sparks and danced higher, so some delinquent god had heard his prayer, apparently. It was about ten minutes before he stopped shivering.

"Should you lie down?" asked Fawn anxiously, kneeling beside him. "Eat a bite more?"

Dag shook his head. "Not yet. Not done. There's something else wrong. I felt it, when I was in there."

Her brows drew in, but she said nothing as Dag leaned forward and pulled the blanket a little down from Hod's belly. The boy's eyes widened, and he made a slight whimpering noise, but kept his hands clenched to his sides. Dag let his stump circle above the taut skin, just . . . there.

"Did Copper kick him in the belly, too?" asked Fawn. "I don't see any mark . . ."

Dag gave another brief headshake. "No. Older trouble. The boy's carrying a nasty monster of a tapeworm, inside him there."

Fawn recoiled, making an appalled face. "Eew!"

Dag had dealt with mosquitoes, bedbugs, and lice, but the closest thing to an internal parasite he'd routed routinely was chiggers. All could be repelled with mere persuasion, or an even simpler bounce. They were nothing like this. "It's got quite a grip in there." He eyed Hod. "You, boy, have you been having crampy bellyaches?"

Hod nodded fearfully, then looked around as if afraid to have admitted anything. Tanner and Mape had wandered near and stood watching and listening.

"Yeah?" said Dag. "And bleeding? You bleed when you crap, sometimes?"

Another reluctant nod.

"Ever tell anyone?"

Hod shook his head more vigorously.

"Why not?"

A long silence. "Dunno."

"Scared?" Dag asked more gently.

Reluctant pause. Nod. And a whisper, "Who'd I tell, anyways?"

Dag's brows twitched up. "Hungry all the time even with plenty of food to eat, weak and tired, bleeding . . . y'know, it doesn't take a Lakewalker medicine maker to diagnose a tapeworm. It just takes someone noticin'."

"Not shiftless," said Fawn. "Starving."

Tanner looked a bit sick, and Mape, curiously, looked even sicker.

Dag's arm circled again. "From the signs, I'd guess he's been feeding this pet for a year or more. How long have you been feeling poorly, Hod?"

Hod shrugged. "I always feel poorly, but usually it's my nose. Belly's been aching off and on since this time last year, I guess."

"Uh-huh," said Dag.

"Can you get rid of it?" asked Fawn. "Oh, please! It's so horrid!"

"Maybe. Give me a minute to think."

Ground-ripping the vile thing was right out. It was much larger than any mosquito, and besides just the *idea* of taking in tapeworm-ground was revolting, even if his own ground would convert it eventually. Dag essayed a trifle of persuasion, to no effect; the worm was not normally mobile. Besides, you wouldn't just want it out; you'd want it safely dead, to keep it from spreading.

So if smoothing and reinforcing disrupted ground caused flesh to heal, disrupting ground might . . . ? The blighted thing was large compared to its constricted intestinal world, but in absolute terms, small. Just a tiny ground disruption. Squeeze it, roll it, twist it—turn it inside out—*there*. He felt the head of the creature pop, and a spurt of blood from its anchorage as it tore away. He pinched off the little vessels in Hod's gut, aiding the wound to clot. Then recaptured the thin worm-body and went right down the line to destroy each segment. In a weird way, it felt a bit like spinning thread. With his ground-hand, inside someone else's body . . . *I don't think I want to think about what I'm doing, here.* But the worm was dying, and he managed to keep its roiling, writhing ground from sticking to his own.

Hod made a wary noise, and his hands twitched; Fawn caught one, to keep it at his side, and gave him a big happy reassuring smile. Whit bit his lip, possibly on a bark of laughter, but Hod offered a confused half-smile to Fawn in return, as who could help doing so? And made no further move to fight off Dag.

"Done," Dag whispered at last, and sat up, folding his left arm inside his right. His exhausted ground projection petered out, as if his ghost hand were evaporating into mist, into nothing. *Absent gods, I feel sick.* His groundsense range seemed down to ten paces, or maybe ten inches. But at least he hadn't groundlocked himself to the blighted worm. *Count your blessings. One . . .*

Next time, he would hold out for a medicine shop and some simple dose of vermifuge, a course of treatment he suspected even a Lakewalker medicine maker would prefer. Dag had a vague notion that senior makers saved their costly groundsetting skills for serious dangers, like tumors. More than ever, he regretted turning down Hoharie's offer of real maker's training; then he'd know what to do, instead of having to blunder around by guess. But Hoharie'd had no use for his farmer bride. *Blood over the dam.*

Tanner and Whit settled Hod for the night. Dag dragged his bedroll around to the other side of the fire, away from the sight of his unappetizing patient. Victim. Whatever. He would've liked to retreat farther than that, but hated to give up the heat. Hod, exhausted by the shock and limp from the passing of his pain, dropped to sleep fairly soon. Dag, equally exhausted, did not.

While Fawn, Tanner, and Whit went off to see to the horses, Mape came and squatted on his haunches beside Dag's bedroll. After a while, he said, "I never guessed he was sick. Just thought he was lazy."

"I didn't catch on either, at first." Dag had been led down a false trail by Tanner's talk, yes, but he'd only to open his groundsense to learn better.

"I beat him, couple o' times, when I caught him sleeping on the job," Mape added. His voice was low, flat, expressionless. Suited for things confided in the dark, where no one could see. "I'm just sayin'. Thankee, Lakewalker."

"The knee should be good with a couple of weeks of rest. The other, you'll start to see a difference in a couple of days, I'm guessing." Dag could leave it at that. It was tempting. *Oh, blight it.* "I was cleaning up my own mess. I saw him sneak out to my bags. Thought I'd just let Copperhead teach him a lesson. Instead, I got taught. Can't say as I enjoyed it."

"No," agreed Mape. "Me neither." He nodded, rose. Not friendly, exactly, but . . . acknowledging. That at least. He trod away into the dark.

When Fawn finally came to lie down, Dag tucked her into the curl of his body like one of the cloth-wrapped hot stones she sometimes used for pain. He held her hard. It helped.

In the morning, Hod was laid in his bedroll in the back of Mape's wagon, and Whit took Hod's place as brakeman. Fawn sat up beside Tanner. Dag, too, moved his bedroll, saddle, and bags to the back of the second wagon and continued his lie-down. Copperhead, unnaturally subdued, clopped loose behind, but Fawn supposed Dag had the gelding back under his mysterious groundsense-tie. Dag appeared to doze in the sun, but he was not asleep. It reminded Fawn uncomfortably of that deep, drained fatigue that had overcome him after Greenspring. The

Glassforge teamsters seemed to think little of it, but Whit, familiar with Dag's usual restless energy, cast more than a few concerned looks over his shoulder as they rumbled down the road.

Whit took over helping with Hod during their stops, at least. Hod still didn't say much, but his gaze followed Dag around in something between worry and fascination. Tanner and Mape were kinder to him, which served only to confuse him, as though kindness were a baited trap into which he feared to fall.

Dag was quiet all day. They put up for the night in a barn let by a roadside farm to travelers and their beasts—no hotel, but warmer and more sheltered than last night's uncomfortable sleep on the ground. The next morning, Fawn was relieved when Dag seemed enough himself to climb back up on Copperhead for the last leg of the journey.

Noon found the teams plodding up a long slope along a wooded ridge. Dag edged Copperhead alongside the wagon, and said to Fawn, "Climb on." He had that elusive smile he wore when he looked forward to surprising her, so she stood up, balanced herself, and swung her leg over behind Dag. When she'd adjusted to a secure perch, he let Copperhead roll out in his long patrol walk, and they pulled ahead as though the wagons had parked. At the top of the ridge, he let her slide down, and swung after her. Walking backward, he took her by the hand and brought her to the lip of the road.

The valley of the Grace spread out below them in the gold-blue autumn light. The river seemed to have put on her party dress, her banks and bending hillsides a swirl of color: scarlet and purple-red, glowing yellow, bright brown. The water reflected the azure of the sky, save where it broke into a sparkling shoal, necklace to the dress. Brooches of boats slid upon the water—a distant keel, a broad, blunt ferry—with a girdle of flatboats pulled up along the farther shore. Fawn was dimly aware of Whit, trotting up panting to see whatever there was to see.

She was more aware of Dag, watching her face. She wasn't sure if he was seeing just the river valley reflected there, or something more, but his mouth softened in an ease that handed her joy back to her, to be passed back to him again, redoubled.

"Oh," said Whit, in a voice the like of which she'd never heard come out of him before. She glanced up, startled, to watch his lips part, his mouth grow round. *Wonder,* she thought, though you could well mistake it for a man punched in the stomach.

"Lookit those boats. Lookit . . ." he went on, though she was fairly sure he'd forgotten there was anyone listening. "That's one big river. Even half dry, it's bigger than any river I ever seen. It's like a road. A great grand road, running from mystery above"—he turned with the river's curve, like a man dancing, twirling with his lady—"into mystery below. It's like, it's like . . . it's like the best road *ever.*" He blinked rapidly. His eyes were shining.

No, not shining. Wet.

5

 ack aboard Copperhead, Dag rode close to the second wagon
as they made the turn at the top of the ridge and started down the
road into the valley. Fawn, beside Tanner, sat bolt upright and earnestly
alert, ready to work the wheel-brake at the teamster's word. In the front
wagon, Whit had his head cranked sideways, goggling at the river. Dag's
eye followed his gaze.

Half a mile upstream on this side, Pearl Riffle Camp was just visible
amongst the thinning leaves, a scattering of tent-roofs—Fawn would
have called them cabins, Dag supposed—along the wooded hillside.
Opposite the Lakewalker camp, below the mouth of a creek, lay Possum
Landing, the level stretch of shore where the ferry put in and where
cargoes were traditionally transferred from the old straight road to the
river, or vice versa. There were more farmer houses clustered upslope
from the landing than the last time Dag had ridden through here, and
more sheds for storing goods.

Eight flatboats and a keel were presently tied to the trees along the
muddy bank on that side, waiting for a rise in the water level to dare the
shoals below; a good selection, though if the water rose suddenly from
some big storm upriver, they could all be underway in an hour. But the
water was still falling, judging from both the width of the mud margin
and the fact that a couple of the flatboats, tied imprudently too close to

the bank, now had their bows stuck in the drying mire. Even the wharf boat was half-grounded.

Dag turned in his saddle to look over his shoulder. Half a mile below the glittering shoals on this side, where the river again curved out of sight, was the farmer hamlet of Pearl Bend, which also boasted a wharf boat serving the crossing, as it made sense to offload heavy cargo before hauling a boat up over the Riffle, or wait to load on till after successfully negotiating the hazard coming down. The Glassforge men would take the bulk of their goods there. Pearl Bend, too, boasted more roofs than Dag remembered; practically a village, now.

Dag turned back to find the cautious glass-men pulling their wagons to a halt at a wide space in the road, huddling toward the hillside. A troop of riders was coming up the slope, double file—a Lakewalker patrol, outbound from Pearl Riffle Camp, likely. A dozen and some men, maybe half that many women, a normal complement. Dag drew Copperhead in behind Tanner's wagon and squinted down the track. He fought an impulse to open his crippled groundsense wide, closing it down instead. He could look with his eyes well enough.

Outbound for certain, Dag decided, as first patrollers drew level with the wagons and fell into single file to pass. They appeared far too rested and tidy to be anything else. He suppressed a company captain's inventory of the condition of every horse, rider, and weapon approaching. Not his job, anymore.

The patrol leader, who had barely glanced at the wagons, looked up as he spotted Dag and urged his mount forward. Dag opened his groundsense just enough to keep Copperhead polite as the strange horse loomed near.

"Courier?" demanded the patrol leader, a spare, middle-aged fellow with a shrewd eye.

Because why else would a Lakewalker be riding alone, and if the news Dag bore was bad, perhaps this patrol was about to acquire a more urgent task than their routine search patterns. His mind would not connect Dag, in Lakewalker gear on what was obviously a patrol horse, with the party of farmers that his patrol was rounding.

Dag touched his hand to his temple in a courteous salute, but said, "No, sir. Just travelin' through."

The patrol leader's shoulders eased in relief. "Any news from the north?"

He meant patrol news, Lakewalker news. "All was quiet when I passed through Glassforge, three days back."

The leader nodded. He looked as if he'd like to pause for fuller gossip, but the last rider cleared the obstructing wagons and kicked her horse into a trot to take up her place in the re-forming double file. He contented himself with a return salute and a "Travel safely, then."

"You, too. Good hunting."

An acknowledging grimace, and he trotted after the others.

Dag took back his place as Fawn's outrider as the two wagons creaked into motion again. Fawn twisted around in her seat to watch the departing patrol, turned back, and glanced across at Dag. Concern shone in her big brown eyes, though for what cause Dag was uncertain.

Tanner, too, cast a curious look over his shoulder. "So, all those Lakewalkers are going off to hunt for blight bogles, are they? With their, their ground-senses?"

"Yes," said Dag. "Pearl Riffle Camp doesn't cover as big a territory as Hickory Lake—that's my, was my, home camp. Hickory has eight, nine thousand folks, the biggest camp in Oleana. Doubt Pearl Riffle has eight or nine hundred. They can field maybe two or three patrols, barely a company. But their more important task is right here, keeping the ferry crossing open in case of need. If the Glassforge malice had gotten out of hand— more out of hand—we might have called on Lakewalker camps from south of the Grace to help out. Or the other way around, if they ran into trouble down there."

"The way Hickory Lake sent Dag's company west to fight the malice that came up in Raintree, couple of months back," put in Fawn, for Tanner's sake. And, at Tanner's next question, went on to give him an accurate summary of the summer's campaign, if sketched in broad strokes, and all in terms a farmer might readily grasp, because, after all, Fawn was one. Which drew braver questions from the teamster in turn. Dag listened in grateful silence, backing her with an occasional nod. This fruitful exchange lasted till the wagons reached the bottom of the long slope and turned across the narrow floodplain toward the river.

When they reached the crossroads, Dag said, "Fawn, do you think you'd be all right staying with Whit for a little? I'd like to pay a visit." He jerked his head upstream.

"Sure. This is the camp where Saun and Reela stayed, right?"

The two were fellow patrollers injured in the Glassforge fight, sent down here as the closest place to convalesce. Saun had been Dag's own partner; Fawn had made friends of a sort with Reela, laid up in the hotel afterwards with a broken leg. "Yes," Dag answered.

"Do you have friends here? Or k——" She cut short the last word: *kin.*

"Well, I'm not sure," he said, passing over her little stammer. "It's been a while since I was down this way. Thought I'd go check." Which was not exactly the reason for his detour, but he was reluctant to discuss the real one in front of Tanner. Especially as Dag himself was doubtful of the result. "I'll find you two after my errand. Might be a while. Stay by Whit, right?"

"Dag, I don't need my brother to guard me every minute."

"Who said it was *you* I thought needs a keeper?"

She dimpled, taking this in; he cast her a return wink, possibly more cheerful-looking than he felt. The wagons turned right onto the down-stream road toward Pearl Bend. Dag wheeled Copperhead around and trotted in the opposite direction.

Across a shallow run and over a rise, he came to the camp's perimeter and let his groundsense ease open just a hair, to present himself to the gate guard, if any. He felt an inquiring double-flick in return, and raised his eyes to spot not one but a pair of Lakewalkers lingering on a couple of stumps flanking the road. An older man was whittling pegs; a morning's worth lay piled haphazardly at his feet, and Dag's nostrils flared with the pleasant tang of new shavings. A young woman worked on weaving willow-withy baskets, but a bow and quiver leaned against a rock within easy reach. Patrollers both, on light camp duty.

Dag drew up Copperhead and nodded. "How de'."

The man stood. "Good day to you"—a slight hesitation, as he looked Dag up and down—"patroller." An anxious look crossed his face. "Courier, are you?"

"No, sir, just stopping by. I was hoping you could tell me where to find your camp captain, and who's holding that post these days."

The young woman frowned at his hook, wrapped with Copperhead's reins, and he lowered it a trifle. The man directed Dag to look for Amma Osprey in the third tent to the left past the split oak tree, and Dag, not lingering to get tangled in talk, pressed Copperhead on. A last curious ground-flick touched him. *Pass, friend.*

Both ease and anxiety knotted in him as he rode by the familiar domestic sights of a Lakewalker camp. Tents peeked through trees, the traditional log structures with hide awnings rolled up on their fourth, open sides, mostly looking southwest to the river. Stands of fruit trees, beehives, homely washing on lines. Smoke rising from chimneys, the smells of cooking and preserving. From a distance, a less pleasant whiff of tanning hides. Half a dozen black-and-white speckled chickens squawked and fluttered across Copperhead's path, and the horse tossed his head and snorted.

Downslope near the shore, a couple of men were building a good-sized narrow boat on a rack, hammering in pegs. Twenty-five feet long, double-prowed, broad in the middle, clearly meant for the river trade— its boards looked mill-sawn. A few of the newer tent-cabins, too, were built of such planks; the farmers at Pearl Bend or Possum Landing must have put in a sawmill on one of the feeder creeks.

Dag spotted patrol headquarters by the array of hitching posts in front, and the lack of washing and cook-smoke. The four-sided cabin had Glassforge glass windows, presently hooked open on what had to be one of the last warm days of the season. Dag dismounted, tied Copperhead, and let his groundsense dart out once more. Two folks inside right now, both ground-closed; a woman's voice, sharp, drifted out the open windows.

"If we upped and moved the camp and the ferry a mile upriver— better, five miles—we wouldn't have these blighted clashes."

"And lose the rest of the business from the straight road to the Bend's new ferry? We're hurting already," returned another woman, with a rougher, warmer voice. Not young.

"Let it go. We don't need a wagon road for our patrols and pack trains."

"Amma, three-fourths of the camp's coin comes from farmers using our ferry. And flows right back to them. Everything from flour to horse-shoe nails comes from the Bend goods-sheds these days."

"As it should not. Proves my point, I'd say."

A glum silence fell. When it remained unbroken, Dag stepped up onto the wooden porch and knocked, furling his groundsense more tightly around him.

"Is that you, Verel?" the first voice called. "Come on in. When are you going to let those two—ah." A tough, tall, strongly built older woman, one haunch half-up on a plank table, wheeled as Dag ducked through the door and touched his hand to his temple in polite greeting. He had no trouble identifying her as the camp's patrol captain, given her riding trousers, worn leather vest, long steel knife at her belt, and harassed look. The cabin held the usual headquarters clutter of strewn gear, with maps and record books stuffed on overflowing shelves. The other woman, of like age but rather plumper and wearing skirts, might be some clan head; she seemed to bear herself with scarcely less authority.

"*Now* what?" said the camp captain, in a voice of accumulated exasperation. Her lips began to shape the next query.

"Not a courier, ma'am!" Dag hastened to reassure her, and she let the word fall unvoiced, with a relieved nod. "I'm just passing through. M' name's Dag Bluefield."

This won blank looks from both women. Bluefield was not a Lakewalker name, nor had Dag claimed a camp of origin. Before they could pry into this oddity, he hurried on. "I came about a sharing knife. But I could come back later."

A look of inexplicable enlightenment crossed the camp captain's face. "Oh, no, if you witnessed anything, I definitely want it now. Take a seat, we'll be starting soon." She waved to a bench along the back wall. "Sorry, I thought you were our medicine maker out there."

They were at some cross-purpose, it seemed. But before Dag could open his mouth to uncross them, the other woman peered out the window and said, "Ah, here they come. Absent gods, what a sick and sorry pair they look."

"They're going to be a lot sicker and sorrier when I'm done with 'em." Amma Osprey ran a stray strand of gray hair, escaped from the braid at her nape, back over her ear, then folded her arms and her lips equally tightly as the door opened.

Two young men limped through. One was shorter, tawny-haired, and sturdy with muscle. But his right hand was bandaged, and his arm rested in a sling. His fair, square face was bruised. His shirt was clean and didn't quite fit him—borrowed?—but his trousers were spattered with dried blood. He walked decidedly bent over.

The one who followed was taller, brown-haired, maybe a bit older than his companion, though still very young to Dag's eyes. His face was even more bruised, one eye swollen shut, lower lip twice its proper size. Beneath his torn shirt his ribs were wrapped in cloth strips. Chicken tracks of black stitches marched up two long cuts on his left arm. His knuckles were swollen and scabbed, though he gingerly helped himself along with a stick in his right hand.

Two patrollers who'd lost a fight last night, obviously. To each other? They collected equally cold and silent glowers from the two women as they shuffled into line. The tawny youth made one attempt at a winning smile, wilting swiftly as the scowls deepened. Dag squinted in curiosity. He really ought to excuse himself and go. Instead, he sank back on his bench like a hunter lying up in tall grass, silent and unnoticeable.

Amma Osprey began curtly, "Not the least of your offenses is that I had to pull two of your comrades off their camp leaves this morning to take your places in patrol. You can remember to apologize to them, too, when they get back."

Dag had done that in his time, cut his camp rest short in order to fill in for a sick or injured or bereaved patroller.

The dark one looked, if possible, more hangdog, but the tawny one raised his bruised face and began, "But we didn't start it! We were just—"

The camp captain held up a quelling hand. "You'll have your say in a moment, Barr. I promise you." It sounded more threat than promise; in any case, the tawny youth subsided.

Steps sounded on the wooden porch, and the door swung open once more. A broad-shouldered woman stepped through, nodded to the other two, and scowled at the youths. By the yellow leather gloves stuck in her belt and the thick-soled boots on her feet, Dag identified her as a ferrywoman; by her age and stride, likely the boat boss. She pulled a lumpy cloth from her belt, and said, "I found this piece up in the woods back of Possum Landing this morning."

"Oh, good," said the camp captain. "Remo, do you have the rest?"

The dark youth hitched around and pulled another lumpy cloth from his shirt, reluctantly handing it over to his captain. She slid off the table and laid open both scraps. Dag was disturbed to see the pieces of a broken sharing knife, carved from pale bone. Such a knife was supposed to break when it released its burden of mortality into the ground of a malice, but Dag already had an uncomfortable suspicion that there had been no malice involved, or these two patrollers would be in much better odor this afternoon. Amma Osprey swiftly aligned the shards. "That's got it all, Issi," she reported. The ferrywoman nodded satisfaction; the dark youth, Remo, let out a faint breath.

"Now we have a council quorum," said the skirted woman. The three exchanged nods and settled, two in chairs, Amma hitched up on the edge of the table again. The two young patrollers were not invited to sit.

"All right," said the camp captain grimly to the pair, "start explaining. How did this get started?"

The two exchanged unhappy looks; Remo of the swollen mouth waved a purpling hand at his companion, and said, "Oo 'ell 'm, Arr."

Barr gulped and began, "It was a good deed, blight it! It really got started when that last coal flat tried to take the Riffle when the water'd got too low, ten days back, and tore out its bottom and dumped its load for half a mile down the shoals. Remo and I took out a narrow boat to pick off some of the crew that had got themselves hung up in the white water and the cottonwood wrack. Probably saved three flatties from drowning. Anyway, *they* seemed to think so. We hauled 'em into the tavern at Pearl Bend looking sorry as wet rats. Got them all dried out, on the outside anyway. At least they bought us drinks. Seeing as everyone was saved, they were all in a mood to celebrate, except maybe the boat boss who'd lost his cargo. So some of the keelers who'd helped out and the flatties started some games."

"You *know* you are not to play games of chance with farmers," said Amma Osprey in a dangerous voice. Because Lakewalkers were inevitably accused of sorcerous cheating in such situations. Although only if they had the ill luck or poor judgment to actually win.

"'Ee *'idn't,*" protested Remo.

"It was *arm wrestling,*" said Barr. "With a couple of the keelers. And despite what they claimed, we didn't cheat—though I could have, blight it!" The peculiar indignation of the accused not-quite-guilty livened his voice, and Dag, still quiet on his bench by the wall, suppressed an upward mouth twitch.

"It made me so mad," Barr went on. "So I told them it was true, but they could protect themselves from evil Lakewalker influences with metal helmets, like what you see the soldiers of the old Lake League wearing in the broken statues, which was what those helmets had been for, see. And they bought it. By the next afternoon, we had half the flatties up at Possum Landing walking around with their cook pots and wash bowls stuck on their heads. It was, it was"—he struggled for a moment, eyes brightening in defiant memory—"it was *glorious.*" His jaw set, then slacked instantly as he winced and rubbed its bruises.

"So *that's* where that fool nonsense came from!" cried the ferry boss,

Issi, in a voice that shook in a good imitation of anger. She turned away from the truants and rubbed her face till the betraying laugh lines were smoothed back out. Dag, who could just picture a herd of naive Lakewalker-fearing flatboat crews wandering about the Landing in their clanking makeshift helmets, laid his palm hard over his jaw and kept listening. *Oh, to have been here last week!*

"I was just balancing the scales a bit," Barr continued. "You know what we do for those stupid farmers, and how little thanks we get in return. And it wasn't hurting anyone, till your crew told them it was all a fiddle."

The ferry boss sighed. "It took my girls near three days to talk them out of it. Even then, some of them refused to give up their headgear." She added reflectively, "The rest were plenty mad, though. The Possum folks and the older flatties gave 'em a ripe ribbing for it all."

Captain Osprey pinched the bridge of her nose. "Despite all that, I suppose it would have all passed downstream harmlessly at the next rise, if you two unaccountable fools hadn't *gone over there* last night and stirred them up again. *Why?*"

"I was baited," Barr admitted in a surly voice.

"Tol' yuh," his partner muttered, rolling his good eye.

"How?" demanded the patrol captain.

An even more surly silence.

The ferry boss put in, "I've already heard one version of it over at the Landing this morning, Barr. We'd better have yours."

Barr hunched.

Remo mumbled, "Tell t' truth, blighdit. Can't be worse f'r you th'n f'r me."

Barr hunched lower. With a voice that seemed to come from somewhere around his knees, he said, "A flatboat girl invited me. To meet her in the woods back of the Landing."

Amma Osprey broke the chill silence that followed this with "When and where did this invitation take place?"

"Down at the Bend wharf boat. Yesterday afternoon." He looked up indignantly into the thick disapproval that now blanketed the room. "She seemed all excited. I didn't think she was lying. Well, you know how those farmer girls throw themselves at patrollers, sometimes!"

"You're supposed to throw them back," said the skirted woman in a grim voice.

"Tol' yuh it was a setup," said Remo, with a black stare at his partner. "*He* said, no, it was too obvi'us."

Barr turned redder around his livid bruises. "I didn't ask you to come."

"Y'r muh partner. I'm supposed t' watch y'r back!"

Barr took a long breath, then let half of it out with his protest unvoiced. "Six of the flatties jumped me in the dark. I wasn't carrying any weapon. Neither was Remo. The flatties just had fists and sticks, at first. Then when Remo piled in to help me, and things started to turn back our way, one of the flatties pulled a knife on us. Remo *had* to use his knife to defend himself, it was the only thing we had, except for our bare arms!"

"You drew a primed sharing knife in a common brawl." Amma Osprey's voice was flatter than winter ice. And colder. And harder.

"Wisht 'd just used muh arms," mumbled Remo. And lower, more despairing, "Or muh neck . . ."

It was all becoming clear to Dag, and he almost wished it weren't. He eyed the pale bone shards laid accusingly on the plank table. His heart ached for these two young fools. He curled his right arm around himself and waited for the rest.

"And now we come to it," said Amma. "Why were you wearing your sharing knife at all last night, when you knew you weren't to go out on patrol till today?"

Remo's face set in an agony that had nothing to do with its bruises. "I . . . it was new. I'd jus' been given it. I was trying t' get used to it!"

The picture was plain. Dag knew exactly how excited and proud a young patroller entrusted with a first primed knife would be. A pride sobered, frequently, with personal grief and the heart-deep determination to be worthy of such mortal trust. *Ow. Ow.* Behind their stern facades, he thought the three women shared his pang.

"And then those blighted flatties, those blighted *farmers,* broke it to pieces," Barr went on, remembered rage flaring in his voice. "And then we both, well, we both went after them full-out. I don't even remember getting this." He touched his smashed hand. "And they broke and ran off. Some of them are still running, for all I know."

Dag could picture that, too, rage and outrage and appalling guilt boiling up to a loss of control as terrifying, perhaps, for its sufferers as their victims. *A patroller should never lose control. Especially not around farmers.* It was ingrained, if sometimes not deeply enough. Because when such control failed, everyone was subject to the frightened farmer backlash.

"Your great-grandmother Grayjay didn't share early for *this* fate," said the skirted woman. "She might have had months yet, except that she feared passing in her sleep."

Remo's face went from red to white, beneath his bruises. "I know." His ground-veiling was held so tight, his body was shaking as if with physical effort.

"I was going to take the pieces to your parents, but I think you should."

Remo's eyes closed. "Yes, ma'am," he whispered, dead-voiced. Barr was very quiet.

Amma Osprey gestured at Dag. "You, sir. I gather you were at Possum Landing. You have any information to add to all this?"

Issi stared at the newcomer; she must know he hadn't crossed north over the river by the ferry since last night. Squinting at his arm harness, she asked, "Do I know you, patroller?"

Dag cleared his throat uncomfortably, and rose. "My apologies, Captain Osprey. I actually just rode down from Glassforge. I came to ask you about another matter. I think this isn't a good time for it, though."

An irate look from the camp captain confirmed this belief, but Issi snapped her fingers and pointed. "I have seen you! You used to ride with Mari Redwing of Hickory Lake. You're her nephew, aren't you?"

Yes, Issi and Dag's aunt Mari could well be near-contemporaries. Acquaintances. Maybe even passing friends, who knew? "Yes, ma'am."

The skirted woman said, "But he said his name was Dag Bluefield."

"I'm lately married, ma'am."

"What kind of name is—" the skirted woman began.

The two young patrollers looked wildly at each other. Barr burst out, "Sir! Are you Dag Redwing Hickory, Saun's partner? Who slew the Glassforge malice, single—all by himself?"

Dag sighed. "Not by myself, no." Oh, yes—these two were just the age and sort to have become Saun's boon companions in his convalescence here last spring. Dag winced at the thought of what kind of Dag-stories Saun might have been inspired to tell, to alleviate his boredom and entertain his new friends. Dag could see his hope of anonymity evaporate like morning dew in the heat of those suddenly interested eyes.

Captain Osprey blinked, rocking back. "Then are you also the same Dag Redwing who led the Hickory Lake company to Raintree a couple of months ago, and took down that horrendous malice they had running wild over there?"

Dag set his teeth, briefly. "I was Dag Bluefield by then, ma'am."

"Fairbolt Crow's report on Raintree in the latest patrol circular named a Captain Dag Redwing."

Oh, so that was how the word had got around. Yes, there had been time for such official patrol news to have slipped ahead of Dag while he was lingering in West Blue. Fairbolt kept up. "Then Fairbolt named me wrong." At Amma's rising brows, he offered, "Habit, maybe. I patrolled under him for eighteen years as Dag Redwing. I was in his company even before he became Hickory Lake's camp captain."

"Eh. So what is this other matter?"

Dag hesitated.

Amma made an impatient gesture. "Spit it out and get it over with. It can't be worse than the rest of my morning."

Dag nodded, trying to get over the jolt of having his recent reputation run before him, even if some of it was no doubt due to Saun's exaggerations. But perhaps it would do him some good. "I left Hickory Lake on business of my own, after——as a result of——the Raintree campaign. I expect to travel a lot of territory in the next few months. I used my last primed knife on the Glassforge malice, and haven't yet found another. You don't have to be on patrol to run across a malice——when I was riding courier alone up in Seagate, I once took out a new sessile that might have grown a lot more dangerous before anyone had got back to it with a patrol. I made it a rule after that never to walk bare. I know sometimes folks leave their primed knives to the patrol generally, to outfit patrollers who have none. I was wondering if you happened to have any such"——his eye fell uncomfortably on the broken bone knife on the table, and avoided Remo's face——"spares. Just now."

The camp captain crossed her arms. "Why didn't you get one before you left Hickory Lake, then?" The skirted woman's expression seconded the question.

Because he'd still been reeling, sick and heartsick, exhausted. Not thinking. "I hadn't yet settled my plans."

"What plans?" asked Amma.

"I figure to take the rivers down to Graymouth. Ride back in the spring. After that, I'm not sure. I might be able to return the loan then, if I don't cross a malice." And if he did, and used the knife, no one would ask for a better fate for it. His voice softened. "I promised my wife I'd show her the sea."

The skirted woman touched her lips. "Wait up. Are you also that same Dag Redwing who was just banished from Hickory Lake Camp for consorting with some farmer girl?"

Dag's head shot up. "I was not banished! Where did you hear such a lie?"

"Well"—she waved a hand—"not banished, precisely. But the camp council circular didn't make it sound like a happy outcome."

Buying a moment to gather his wits and his temper, Dag touched his temple, and said stiffly, "You have the advantage of me, ma'am."

The skirted woman gestured at herself. "Nicie Sandwillow. Pearl Riffle Camp council leader, this season."

Therefore a senior tent head, that being the pool from which council members were selected by various sorts of rotations, depending on the camp. With the patrol's camp captain always a permanent member. Dag wondered if the ferry boss was also a permanent member, here. It seemed likely. Making this morning's inquiry doubly efficient, serving the patrol and the council at once. But it meant that one of Nicie Sandwillow's tasks was to receive and pass along critical council news from around the hinterland of Oleana, just as Captain Osprey received patrol news. Dag said carefully, "The Hickory Lake council was deeply divided on my case—"

"So there *was* a charge."

Dag overrode this. "Pakona Pike, our—Hickory Lake's council leader this past summer—was not on the side favorable to my arguments. But I can't believe she'd twist the facts that much."

"No, not if the facts are that you came in alone, late from a leave, dragging some farmer girl with the pair of you wearing Lakewalker wedding braids that you'd somehow cooked up together, claiming she was your wife and not just your whore. The letter warns all camp councils to watch out for similar trickery."

Grimly, Dag rolled up his left sleeve. "I say they're valid cords, and so did a lot of others. Including Fairbolt Crow. See for yourself. Fawn made this one."

A flicker of grounds touched him, felt the spark of Fawn's live ground in her cord, drew back. The women looked nonplussed, the two sagging young patrollers confused. It was like the hearing at Hickory Lake all over again, and Dag was bitterly reminded of why he'd left.

"And Fawn isn't just *some farmer girl*," Dag went on, growing more heated. "It was *her* hand slew the Glassforge malice, with my knife. Or I wouldn't be alive now to tell it. It was a scramble, I admit, but I can't believe the tale you had was this distorted, because Saun knew the truth of it, and so did Reela."

"Hm." Amma Osprey rubbed her chin. "I believe the scramble part."

Dag bit out, "This is beside the point. Do you have a spare knife to lend, or not?"

"Good question, Dag Redwing-Bluefield-whoever," said Amma. "Are you still a patroller, or not?"

Dag hesitated. He could claim to be on the sick list, or pretend to be on long leave. Or disciplinary leave, they'd believe that! But in the midst of all these aggravating half-truths, he refused to lie. "No. I resigned. Although Fairbolt made it clear that if I ever wanted to un-resign, he'd find a place for me."

"And your farmer, ah, woman?" asked Nicie Sandwillow.

"That was the sticking point. One of them."

Amma eyed the gaping, hurting young patrollers, now leaning on each other and looking ready to cave on their feet. Dag was sorrier than ever for their witness of this, because Amma would certainly trim her judgment with an eye to making an impression on them. At least, Dag would never have missed such an opportunity, when he'd been a patrol leader. She said, "Such knives are bequeathed in trust for the patrol, specifically the Pearl Riffle patrol. I can't very well ask the dead if they want to make an exception. As their guardian, it's my duty to conserve them—especially as they seem to be needed here."

Remo flinched.

Them, implying she was not down to her last primed knife. She might lend one and still not strip her patrol's reserve bare. *But not to me. Not today.* Dag had the frustrating sense, watching her face set, that if he'd arrived with the same request yesterday, before this trouble with the boatmen had broken out over at Possum Landing, the balance of her decision might well have tipped the other way. He let his gaze cross the two miserable miscreants with new disfavor.

There were other sources, other Lakewalker camps downriver. He would simply have to try again elsewhere. "I see. Then I'll not take more of your time, captain." Dag touched his hand to his temple and withdrew.

6

Fifty paces up the slope from the Pearl Bend wharf boat, Fawn craned her neck as the wagons halted in front of a plank shed. It seemed to be trying to grow into a warehouse by budding, add-ons extending in all directions. Whit jumped down from the lead wagon to help Hod hobble over to a bench against the front wall, displacing a couple of idlers that Mape, after a prudent sobriety check, promptly hired to help unload his fragile cargo. To Fawn's surprise, they only shifted the top layer of slat boxes from her wagon; after that, Whit climbed up with them and Tanner took the reins to turn the rig toward the river.

"Where are we going?" she asked.

Tanner nodded toward the ferryboat tied next to the wharf boat. It looked like a barn floor laid out on a barge, except for a pole sticking up on one side like a short, stubby mast. "Across the river, and up past the Riffle. This load goes upstream from Possum Landing."

Well, Dag could doubtless find her even over there. Fawn went to Weft's head to coax her up the broad gangplank, which rather resembled a barn door tossed on its side, while Whit did the same for Warp. The horses were dubious, but at last seemed convinced that it was only some sort of strange bridge, and did not disgrace themselves or their former owner by trying to bolt. The boredom of the lead pair also helped.

The stubby mast turned out to be a capstan; a thick hemp rope was wound about it a few times, high up, one end leading to a stout tree up the bank, the other, supported by a few floats, to a similar tree on the other side. Fawn was a little disappointed not to ride on the famous Lakewalker ferry, but watched with interest as the two Bend ferrymen stuck oak bars into holes on the capstan and started turning it. Whit, equally fascinated, volunteered to help and went to work pushing the squeaking post around, winding and unwinding the rope and slowly pulling the ferry across the river. The water seemed clear and calm to Fawn's eye, but she jumped when a log floating just under the surface thumped into the side, and she was reminded that this was no quiet lake. Working the ferry might not seem so pleasant when the water was high or rough, or in rain or cold. From out here in the middle, the river looked bigger.

"How do the other boats get past the rope?" she asked Tanner, watching the big log catch, roll under the obstruction, right itself, and sluggishly proceed.

"The ferrymen have to take it down," he said. "They haul it back and forth across the river with a skiff, usually, but with the river this low nothing's going over the Riffle anyways, so they just leave it up."

When the ferry nosed up to the far bank, the ferrymen ran out the gangplank on that end. She and Whit repeated their reassurances to the horses, and the rig rumbled safely, if noisily, onto dry land once more. They both clambered up next to Tanner as he turned the team onto a rutted track leading upstream.

Fawn sat up in anticipation as they topped a rise and the line of flatboats tied to the trees beyond Possum Landing came into view. They were as unlike the Lakewalkers' graceful, sharp-prowed narrow boats as they could be, looking like shacks stuck on box crates, really. Ungainly. Some even had small fireplaces with stone chimneys, out of which smoke trickled. It was as if someone's village had suddenly decided to run off to sea, and Fawn grinned at the vision of an escaped house waddling away from its astonished owners. People ran away from home all the time; why shouldn't the reverse be true? On one of these, she and Dag would float all the way to Graymouth. All running away together, maybe. Her grin faded.

But even such odd thoughts could not quench her excitement, and when Tanner brought the wagon to a halt in front of another rambling shed-warehouse, she hopped down and told her brother, "I'm going to go look at the boats."

He frowned after her in frustration but stuck with his task as Tanner directed him to unlatch the tailboard and start lugging. "You be careful, now," Whit called. More in envy than concern, she suspected.

"I won't even be out of sight!" She just barely kept herself from skipping down to the bank. She was a sober married woman now, after all. And besides, it would be a tad cruel to Whit. Deciding which, she let herself skip just a little.

Reaching the bank, she caught her breath and stared around eagerly. There were fewer folks in view than she'd expected. She'd seen some fellows hanging around up at the storage shed, others down on the wharf boat, which Tanner had said doubled as a general store for the riverfolk. One or more of the houses in the hamlet, still obscured by the half-denuded trees, probably served as taverns. Maybe some boatmen had gone hunting in the hills to replenish their larders during this enforced delay. But a few men were quietly fishing off the backs of their flat-boats—one, strangely, wore an iron kettle over his head like a helmet, although Fawn could not imagine why. Perhaps he'd lost a bet? A group of several men atop one level boat roof had their heads down over some game of chance; dice, Fawn thought, although she couldn't see for sure at this angle. One looked around to watch her pass and drew breath for what was likely going to be a rude catcall, but some turn of the game sent up hoots and a murmur of comment, and he turned back. A woman came out of the shack on one boat and emptied a pan over the side, a reassuring domestic sight.

Fawn strolled along the row, looking for likely candidates for *their* boat. Some had long top-sheds that clearly left no room for a horse. Others were carrying livestock already—one had four oxen stalled on the bow end, quietly chewing their cud, so the boats *could* carry big animals, but that one was plainly full-up. Several had chicken coops, on top or tucked into a corner, and some had dogs, though none roused enough from their naps in the sun to bark at her. She stopped and studied a likely prospect. A fellow sitting on a barrel in the open bow tipped back his floppy hat and grinned in return with what teeth he had.

"Do you take passengers?" she called to him.

"I'd take you, little lady!" he replied enthusiastically.

Fawn frowned. "It would be me, my *husband,* and his horse."

He swept off the hat with a flourish, revealing greasy hair. "Oh, leave the husband and his horse. I bet I can give you a better ride. If you— *ow!*" He clapped his hand to the side of his head as a small wooden block from seeming nowhere bounced off it with an audible *clonk.* Looking up to his left, he complained, "Now, what'd you go and do that for? I was just bein' friendly!"

Atop the flat roof of the next boat over, a figure in homespun skirts sat in a rocking chair, whittling. As Fawn squinted, she saw it was a surprisingly young woman, almost lanky in build, with straight blond hair escaping from a horse-tail tied at her nape. She had light blue eyes and a wide mouth, both pinched with annoyance.

"To remind you to behave your fool self, Jos," she replied tartly. "Now apologize."

"Sorry, Boss Berry."

This won another wooden missile, which Jos did not dodge quite fast enough. "Ow!" he repeated.

"To *her,* you nitwit!" snapped the blond woman.

Jos put his hat back on, for the purpose of tugging its brim, evidently. "Sorry, miss—missus," he mumbled to Fawn. He shuffled into his boat's shack, out of range.

"Dolt," observed the woman dispassionately.

Fawn strolled on a few paces, noting with interest that while Jos's boat had its hull stuck in the mire, Berry's, moored farther out, still floated. And it had an empty animal pen in one corner of the bow. Some chickens were penned on the opposite side, pecking up a scattering of corn, and their coop didn't stink in the sun, unlike a few she'd passed; someone here cleaned it regularly. She put her hands on her hips and stared up at the woman, who didn't look to be much older than Fawn herself.

"What are you carvin' on?" Fawn called up.

The woman held out a rounded block. "Floats. Cottonwood makes good floats, for ropes and whatnot. A lot of softwoods do."

Fawn nodded, encouraged by the sociable explanation and an almost-smile that erased the earlier tightness from the woman's face. She might have just said *floats,* or *none of your business.* "So . . . does this boat take passengers?"

The blond woman—girl—rocked forward to eye Fawn more closely. "I hadn't thought to. I'm doing a bit of trading down the river, plan a lot of stops. It'd be a slow ride."

"That's all right. We're not in a hurry. How far down the river are you going?"

"I'm not sure yet."

"Can I see inside your boat? I've never been on a flatboat." Fawn smiled up hopefully. Not a request she'd have dared make of the lewd—well, would-be-lewd—Jos; she was in luck to find this woman.

The woman tilted her head, then nodded. She stuck her whittling knife in a sheath at her belt and dismounted from the roof of the cabin by simply jumping down the five feet, ignoring the crude ladder of nailed slats, landing with a thump and a spring of her knees. She grabbed a long board and ran it out to the bank. Fawn eyed the narrowness and flex of it dubiously, but held her breath and picked her way aboard without falling into the mud.

She hopped down onto the deck and straightened in exhilaration. "Hi, I'm Fawn Bluefield."

The woman bobbed her head. She had wide cheekbones, but a pointed chin, lending an effect like a friendly ferret. She was taller than Fawn— as who was not?—and even a bit taller than Whit, likely. Her fine, fair skin was sunburned. "Berry Clearcreek. I'm boss of this boat."

A boat boss was captain or owner or sometimes both; Fawn guessed both, and was impressed and heartened. Berry stuck out a welcoming hand, slim but even more work-roughened than Fawn's. Fawn clasped and released it, smiling. "What lives in the pen?" she asked, nodding toward it, then spotted the droppings in the straw. "Oh, a goat."

"Our nanny Daisy. My little brother took her ashore to graze."

"So you have fresh milk. And eggs." Already this boat seemed homey.

Berry nodded. "Some."

"I grew up on a farm. Up by West Blue." And at Berry's puzzled look, added, "North of Lumpton Market."

Berry still looked geographically uncertain, so Fawn added, "Lumpton's way up the same river that comes out to the Grace near Silver Shoals."

Berry's face cleared. "Oh, the Stony Fork. Big sand bar, there. You know how to milk a goat, do you?"

"Sure."

"Hm." Berry hesitated. "You can cook, too, I guess. Good cook?"

"My husband says so."

The boat boss regarded Fawn's shortness, which, Fawn knew, made her look even younger than she was. "How long've you two been married?"

Fawn blushed. "About four months." It seemed longer, with all that had happened.

Berry smiled a little. "Not sure whether to trust his judgment or not, then. Well, come see my boat!"

A small doorway or hatch in the front of the shack led down by a few crude plank steps into a dark interior. Even Fawn had to duck through; Dag would likely have to bend double, and be very careful when he straightened up. The front of the shelter was full of cargo: coils of hemp rope, rolls of woolen and linen cloth, stacks of hides, barrels and kegs. Fawn could smell apples, butter, lard, and what might be bear grease. One barrel was set up on sawhorses and had a spigot in the end. It hissed a little ominously as the apple cider within hardened, fermenting in the unseasonable warmth. There were sacks of nuts, and smoked meats hanging from the rafters. Tucked everywhere were bundles of barrel staves. All the local produce from up some tributary river or creek of the Grace. At one side was an array of what were obviously Tripoint steel and iron tools and metalwork, from shovel and axe heads, coulters, and kegs of nails, to needles and pins.

"Did you come all the way from Tripoint?" asked Fawn in awe, fingering a shiny new plow blade.

"No, only from about halfway. We pick up things in one place, sell them downstream in another, as chance offers."

The back end of the shack was living quarters, lit by two little glazed windows and another door up to the back deck. Two narrow bunk beds with pallets stacked three-high along the walls had more cargo jammed underneath; one bunk had a curtain. This was one of the boats with a real stone hearth. A few coals glowed under a black iron water-kettle. A cleverly hinged tabletop could be raised up and hooked flat to a wall, its legs folded in tight, to cover and contain a shelf full of metal dishes and cups and cooking supplies.

"How did you come to own this nice boat?"

Berry's smile faded to a grimace. "My papa builds—built—builds one every year, to float down to Graymouth. He and my big brother do the timberwork, and I do the caulking and fitting. He's been taking us kids along ever since my mama died when I was ten." Her expression softened. "He'd come back upriver working as a hand on a keelboat, he and my big brother, with me and my little brother as cargo, till I learned me how to play the fiddle for the keelers. Then I got paid more than him! He used to complain mightily about that, in a proud sort of way."

Fawn nodded understanding. "Papas," she offered. Berry sighed agreement.

Fawn considered the worrisome hesitation in Berry's description of her papa, and how to tactfully phrase her next question. "Does he, um . . . not build boats anymore?"

Berry crossed her arms under her breasts and regarded Fawn with a hard-to-figure stare. She drew breath and seemed to come to some decision. "I don't know. He and my big brother took a boat down last fall and never came back in the spring. Never heard anything about them, though I asked all the keelers I knew to watch out for signs and pass the word back. This here boat, he'd left half-finished. I finished it up and loaded it, and I'm taking it down myself. So's his work won't be wasted." Her voice fell. "If it's his last work, it's about all he left to me. I mean to stop a lot along the way and ask after them. See if I can find out anything."

"I see," said Fawn. "I think that's right clever of you."

There were numerous reasons a man might not come back from a down-river trip, and most of them were dire. A family man, anyway. A young fellow you might picture running off on some new adventure found along the way, selfishly sending no word back to his anxious kin, but not a papa. "How was it you didn't go along, his last trip?"

A brief silence. Berry said abruptly, "Come see the rest of my boat." And led the way out the back, twin to the hatch in front.

Fawn stepped, blinking in the light glimmering off the water, onto what she decided was the boat's back porch. A long, heavy oar mounted on sturdy wooden hinges extended at an angle from the roof above to the water below, and Fawn realized it must be the rudder. Berry or someone had dropped a few fishing lines out over the stern, tied to a cord with a little bell dangling off it.

"Catch much?" said Fawn, nodding to it.

"Now and then. Not much right here—there's too much competition." She glanced down the long row of flatboats, most of which also had similar lines sagging out into the water.

"Dag—my husband—is pretty clever at catching fish."

"Is he?" Berry hesitated. "Does he know boats?"

"A lot more than I do, but that's not saying much. I'm not sure if he's ever been on a flatboat, but he can paddle a narrow boat, and sail. And swim. And do most anything he sets his mind to, really."

"Huh," said Berry, and rubbed her nose.

Fawn gathered her resolve. "How much would it cost to go on your boat? For two people and a horse?"

"Well, there's this," said Berry, and fell silent. Fawn waited anxiously.

Berry looked out over the bright river, absently rolling a fishing line between her fingertips, and went on, "We might find some extra room. But . . . two of my crew, the strong-arm boys who man my sweeps— those are the big oars on the sides—got themselves in some stupid fight up behind the Landing last night and haven't come back." She glanced over to the shore. "It's beginning to look like they've run off permanent. Leaving just me, my brother, and old Bo to run this boat. Me, I can man—woman—the rudder, but I can't do that all day and be lookout and cook the meals as well, which is what I had been doing. You say you can cook. Now, if this husband of yours is a good strapping farm lad with two strong arms who isn't afraid of the water, Uncle Bo 'n I could likely teach him to man a sweep pretty quick. And we could make a deal for you to work your passage. If you've a mind for it," she added a shade uncertainly.

"I could cook, sure," said Fawn valiantly, stirred by the thought of the savings on their purse. Which, to her mind, was none too fat for a trip of this length, though she'd shied from confiding her money doubts to Dag. "I used to help cook for eight every night, back home. Dag, well . . ." Dag did not exactly fit Berry's description of the sort of crewman she was looking for, though Fawn had no doubt he could man any sweep made. "Dag'll have to speak for himself, when he comes."

Berry ducked her head. "Fair enough."

An awkward silence followed this, which Berry broke by saying lightly, "Fancy a mug of cider? We've got lots. It's all going hard in the warm. I've been selling some to the boatmen here, who like it better fizzy, so I've not lost my whole trouble, but even they won't drink it after it goes vinegar."

"Sure," said Fawn, happy for the chance to maybe sit and talk more with this intriguing riverwoman. Fawn had been stuck on one farm her whole life, till this past spring. She tried to imagine instead traveling the length of the Grace and the Gray not once, but eight or ten—no, sixteen or twenty—times. Berry seemed very tall and enviably competent as she led Fawn back inside, picked up a couple of battered tankards in passing, and turned the barrel's spigot. The cider was indeed fizzy and fuzzy, but it hadn't lost quite all its sweetness yet, and Fawn, who had been growing hungry, smiled gratefully over the rim of her mug. Berry led her back to the folding table, and they both pulled up stools.

"I wish it would hurry up and rain," said Berry. "I was done asking around here the first day, but I've been stuck for ten days more. I need at least eighteen inches of rise to get the *Fetch* over the Riffle, and that'd be scraping bottom." She took a pull and wiped her mouth on her sleeve, and said more diffidently, "You haven't been long on the river, I take it?"

Fawn shook her head, and answered the real question. "No, we wouldn't have heard anything of your people." She added conscientiously, "Well, Whit and I wouldn't. Can't speak for Dag."

"Whit?"

"My brother. He's just along for the ride as far as the Grace. He'll go home with the glass-men tomorrow." Fawn explained about Warp and Weft, and Whit's financial schemes. With half her cider gone, Fawn felt bold enough to ask, "So how come you stayed home this past fall?" Fawn knew exactly how agonizing it was not to know what disaster had befallen one's beloved, but she couldn't help thinking Berry might have been lucky not to have shared it, whatever it had been.

"You really got married this summer?" said Berry, in a wistful tone.

Fawn nodded. Beneath the table, she touched Dag's wedding cord wrapping her left wrist. The sense of his direction that he had laid in it, or in her, before Raintree had almost faded away. Maybe, with his ghost hand coming back, he could renew the spell? *Groundwork,* she diligently corrected her thought.

"I thought I would be wed by then, too," sighed Berry. "I stayed behind to fix up what was going to be my——our——new house, see, and so papa left my little brother with me, because I was going to be a grown-up woman. Alder, my betrothed, he went with papa too, because he'd never been down the river, and papa thought he ought to learn the boatman's trade. We were to be married in the spring when they all came back with the profits. Papa said this was going to be his best run ever. 'Course, he says that every fall, whether it's true or not." She drank more cider. "Spring came back to Clear Creek, but they never did, not any of the three *or* their hired hands. I had everything ready, *everything*—" She broke off.

Fawn nodded, not needing a list to picture it: linens and cooking gear all assembled, bride bed built and feather ticks stuffed and maybe all of it garnished with embroidered coverlets, curtains hung, food laid in, the house cleaned and repaired and all sprigged out. Wedding dress sewn. And then the waiting: first with impatience, then with anger, then with helpless fear, then with fading hope. Fawn shivered.

"Strawberry season came and went, and I left off fussing with the house and started fussing with this boat instead. The only kinsman who'd give me a hand was my uncle Bo, who's my mama's older half-brother that never married. The rest of my cousins have got no time for him 'cause they say he drinks too much and is unreliable, which is true enough, but half-help's better than none, I say. And none was what I got from the rest of 'em. They said I'd got no business going on the river by myself, as if I didn't know ten times as much about it as any of them!"

"Think you'll find 'em? All your lost menfolk?" asked Fawn shyly. "They'd have to be stuck somewhere pretty tight, you'd figure." She didn't name the more likely possibilities: a boat broken on rocks or snags and all drowned, or eaten by bears or those appalling southern swamp lizards Dag had described, or bitten by rattlesnakes, or, even more likely and grimly, all dying of some sudden gut-wrenching illness, on a cold riverbank with no one left to bury the last in even an unmarked grave.

"That's why I named my boat the *Fetch* and not just the *Finder,* which was the first name I'd thought of. I'm no fool," said Berry, in a lower tone. "I know what all might have been. But I scorned to go on living with the not-knowing-for-sure for one more week, when I had a boat to hand to go look for myself. Well, partly to hand." She tilted up her tankard to drain the cider. Swallowing, she continued, "Which is why I want a crew to hand, as well. If the rise comes up sudden, I don't want to be stuck waiting for those two scared-off fools to show themselves."

"If they turned up anyhow, would there still be room for us?"

"Oh, yeah." Berry grinned suddenly, making her wide mouth wider; not pretty, but, well, *fetching* was just the word, Fawn thought. "I don't like cookin'."

"If you——" Fawn began, but was interrupted by a plaintive voice from outside.

"Fawn? Hey, Fawn, where'd you go?"

Fawn grimaced and drained her own tankard. "There's Whit. He must be done unloading. I'd better go reassure him. Dag told me to watch after him." She rose to make her way through the gloom out to the bow of the boat, calling, "Over here, Whit!"

"There you are!" He strode down the bank, a trifle red in the face. "You gave me a turn, disappearing like that. Dag'd have my hide if I let anything happen to you."

"I'm fine, Whit. I was just having some cider with Berry."

"You shouldn't be going on boats with strangers," he scolded. "If you hadn't——" His mouth stopped moving and hung half-open. Fawn glanced around.

Berry, smiling, came up by her shoulder, leaned on the rail, and gave Whit a friendly-ferret wave. "That your husband?"

"No, brother."

"Oh, yeah, he looks it."

Whit was still standing there at the end of the board gangplank. Why should he be so shocked that his sister was chatting with a boatwoman?

But he wasn't looking at Fawn at all. The gut-punched look on his face seemed strangely familiar, and Fawn realized she'd seen it there before. Recently.

Ah. Ha. I've never seen a fellow fall in love at first sight twice in one day before.

7

The afternoon was waning when Dag at last caught up with Tanner's wagon at the Possum Landing goods-shed. His roundabout chase had taken him first to Pearl Bend, where Mape had redirected him across the river. A long wait for the Lakewalker ferry, a short ride up the bank, a turn left to the Landing—Dag tensed as his sputtering groundsense, reaching out, found no spark of Fawn. But Whit was out front, waving eagerly at him.

"Dag!" he cried, as Dag drew Copperhead to a halt and leaned on his saddlebow. "I was wondering when you was going to show up. I was just trying to figure how to find you. We've got the boat ride all fixed!"

Tanner climbed up onto his driver's box, gathered up his reins, and regarded Whit with some bemusement. "No messages then, after all?"

"No, not now he's here. Thanks! Oh, no—wait." Whit went to the wheelers and gave Weft a pat and a hug around the neck, then ran around the wagon and repeated the gestures with Warp. "Good-bye, you two. You be good for Tanner now, you hear?" The horses flicked their ears at him; Warp gave him a soulful return nudge—unless he was just trying to use the boy as a scratching post—which made Whit blink rather rapidly.

"They're real good, for such young 'uns," Tanner assured him. "You take care, too." He donned his hat and tugged the brim at Dag. "Lake-walker." And, a little to Dag's surprise, slapped his reins on the team's rumps and drove off minus Whit. A quick look around located both Fawn's and Whit's saddlebags leaning against the porch steps of the goods-shed. A couple of idlers on the shaded bench, one whittling, the other just sitting with his hands slack between his knees, frowned curiously at Dag.

"Aren't you going along to help him?" Dag asked Whit, nodding toward the wagon rumbling away.

"I just helped him load on about a ton of goods from Tripoint and upriver that he's taking back to Glassforge. Mape was going to get up a load from downriver at the Bend—cotton and tea, he said, and indigo if they had any, if the price was right."

"He did. I just saw him."

"Oh, good."

"Mape told me they mean to start home tomorrow morning, after they rest the horses," said Dag. "You, ah, mean to catch up?"

"Not exactly."

"So, what? Exactly?" Gods, he was sounding just like Sorrel. But Whit didn't seem to notice.

"Oh, you have to come see, you have to come *see*. Come on, get our bags up on Copper and I'll show you."

Dag had no heart to dampen such enthusiasm, despite his own lingering foul mood. Dutifully, he dismounted and helped sling the bags across his saddle, wrapped the reins around his hook, and strolled after Whit, who strained ahead like a puppy on a leash. The idlers' eyes followed them, narrowing in suspicion at Dag. Edgy, far from friendly, but not quite the hostility that might have been expected had any of Barr's and Remo's victims died during the night. *Absent gods be thanked.* Walking first forward, then backward, Whit waved and called good-bye to them as well, by which Dag reckoned they'd been briefly hired by

Tanner as fellow-loaders, a typical way for such rivertown wharf rats to pick up a little extra coin.

"So if you're not going back to Glassforge with Tanner and Mape and Hod, what are you going to do?" Dag probed.

"I'm gonna try me some river-trading. I spent some of my horse money on window glass, to sell off the *Fetch*. That's Berry's boat. Boss Berry," Whit corrected himself with a lopsided grin.

"What about that promise to your parents about going straight home?"

"That wasn't a promise, exactly. More like a plan. Plans change. Anyhow, if I get all my glass sold by the time we reach Silver Shoals, I could take the river road home and not get lost, and get back hardly late at all."

There seemed a certain disquieting vagueness to this new plan. Well, Dag would find out what Fawn thought of it shortly. He returned his attention warily to his surroundings.

They passed along the scattered row of flatboats tied to the trees along the bank. A man sitting on a crate in one bow hunched and scowled as Dag went by. A woman frowned, clutched up a wide-eyed toddler, its thumb stuck in its mouth, and skittered inside her boat's top-shed. A collection of flatties idling and laughing on a boat roof fell abruptly silent, stood, and stared across at Dag.

"Why are they starin'?" Whit asked, craning his head in return. "They starin' at you, Dag? I been by here twice and they never stared at *me* . . ."

"Just keep walking, Whit," said Dag wearily. "Don't turn your head. Turn around, blight it!"

Whit was walking backward again, but he obediently wheeled. "Huh?"

"I'm a Lakewalker, seemingly alone, in farmer country. Corpse-eater, grave-robber, sorcerer, remember? They wonder what I'm up to." *They wonder if I'm an easy target. They wonder if they could take me.* He supposed they might also be wondering if he was some sort of consequence of last night, looking for retribution.

"But you aren't up to anything." Whit squinted over his shoulder. "You sure it isn't just the hook?"

Dag set his teeth. "Quite sure. Don't you remember what you thought, first time Fawn brought me into your kitchen at West Blue?"

Whit blinked in an effort of recollection. "Well, I suppose I thought you were a pretty strange fellow for my sister to drag in. And tall, I do remember that."

"Were you afraid?"

"No, not particularly." Whit hesitated. "Reed and Rush were, I think."

"Indeed."

Whit's eyes shifted; the mob of flatties on the boat roof was gradually settling back down. "This feels creepy, y'know?"

"Yes."

"Huh." Whit's dark brows drew in. Thinking? Dag could hope.

"What did you hear up at the goods-shed about the fight last night?" Dag asked.

"Oh, yeah, that was lucky for us!"

"What?" said Dag, astonished. His steps slowed.

Whit waved a hand. "It seems two fellows from the *Fetch* got roped into it by some of their friends, jumping some local Lakewalker they were mad at. When the ferrywomen and a bunch of other Lakewalkers came to break it up, they run off scared, along with some girl and her beau. The other three was in no shape for runnin' and are back on their boats now. But it means Boss Berry needs two stout fellows to pull the broad-oars." Whit pointed to Dag and himself, grinned, and held up two fingers. "And Fawn to cook," he added cheerily.

"Let me get this straight," said Dag. "You've volunteered me—and Fawn—as flatboat crew?"

"Yeah! Isn't it great?" said Whit. Dag was just about to blister him with an explanation of how not-great it was, when he added, "It was Fawn's idea, really," and Dag let his breath huff out unformed.

On his next breath, Dag managed, "Do you have any idea how to man a flatboat sweep?"

"No, but I reckoned you would, and Berry and Bo said they'd teach me."

It wasn't exactly Dag's vision of the marriage trip he'd promised Fawn—or himself, for that matter. It wasn't just the work, which Whit plainly underestimated. Dag was still dragging from his encounter with Hod, though it wasn't his bodily strength that had suffered. But he remembered the recuperative effects of the harvest, and was given pause. He said more cautiously, "Did you tell this boat boss I'm a Lake-walker?"

"Uh . . . I don't remember as it came up," Whit admitted uneasily.

Dag sighed. "Was he wearing a pot on his head?"

"Her head, and no. What kind of pot? Why?"

Dag's terse summary of Barr and Remo's jape surprised a shout of laughter from Whit. "Oh, that's ripe! No, the loaders at the goods-shed didn't tell me that part! I wonder if they was some of the pot-pated ones?"

"Not so ripe in the result," said Dag. "One of the patrollers was wear-ing his sharing knife last night, which he should not have been, and it was broken in the fight. The Pearl Riffle Lakewalkers are pretty upset about it today."

Whit squinted. "Is that bad?"

Dag groped for a comparison. "Suppose . . . suppose you and Sunny Sawman and his friends got into a drunken brawl in the village square of West Blue, and in the tumble one of you knocked over your aunt Nattie and killed her. Gone in a moment. That's just about how bad."

"Oh," said Whit, daunted.

"I expect those patrollers feel as bad as you would, the morning after." Dag frowned. "I wouldn't imagine the friends of those flatties who are laid up feel too kindly toward stray Lakewalkers just now, either." He sighed. Well, one way or another, they needed a boat out of Pearl Riffle, come the rise. Which couldn't come too soon.

And here, evidently, was the boat in question.

Fawn—at last!—stood in the bow talking with a tall, blond girl in a practical homespun shirt, skirt, and leather vest, her sleeves rolled up on slim but strappy-muscled arms. She had a nice wide smile, tinged, as she looked down at Fawn, with a touch of that same excited-to-be-making-new-friends air as Whit. Fawn looked equally pleased. Dag tried not to feel old. In a pen to one side of the bow, a boy knelt milking a goat. He had the same straw-straight hair as the tall girl, cut raggedly around his ears, and the same wide cheekbones flushed with sunburn. Too big to be her child, so likely a younger brother. A much older man, unshaven and a trifle seedy, leaned against the cabin wall looking on blearily but benignly.

Dag nodded to the blond girl. "That your Boss Berry?"

"Yep," said Whit proudly.

Dag eyed him. *So that's the way his wind blows, does it?*

"She ought to be Boss Clearcreek, but she says that's her papa, so she goes by Boss Berry. Wouldn't it be good for Fawn to have another woman aboard? You can see Berry likes that idea, too. They hit it off straightaway."

Dag was getting a certain sense of inevitability about this boat. He let his groundsense flick out. At least the water all seemed to be on the outside of the hull. There was a coherence about its ground that said *boat* not *boards*. "It's a good making, this boat," he conceded.

Fawn saw him, and came dancing over the plank above the mud to hug him as if he'd been gone for days and not hours. He let Copperhead loose to nibble the grass clumps, reins trailing, and folded her in, permitting himself a brief, heartening ground-touch of her. After Pearl Riffle Camp, it felt like bathing a wound in some sweet medicine. He released her again as the boat boss began picking her way across to shore, her wide smile flattening out.

"Dag, I found the best boat!" Fawn un-hugged him just enough to lift her face to his. *Like a morning-glory blossom.* "Berry says we can have passage in exchange for being her crew, if you think that'd work out—"

"I already told him that part," said Whit.

"Don't get ahead of yourself—" began Dag.

The blond girl arrived and folded her arms tightly across her chest, frowning. She said to Fawn, "*This* your Dag?"

Fawn turned out of Dag's one-armed embrace, but didn't relinquish his hand. "Yes," she said proudly.

The frown became tinged with dismay. "But he's a Lakewalker!"

Though it seems there's some question about that, today. Dag nodded politely at the boat boss. "Ma'am."

The frown deepened to a scowl. "Fawn, I know Lakewalkers. A Lakewalker wouldn't no more marry a farmer girl than—than he'd marry my Daisy-goat over there. I don't know if you're trickin' me or if he's trickin' you, but I do know I don't want no trickster-man on my boat!"

Fawn and Whit, in chorus, went into the usual explanation about the wedding braids and West Blue that was beginning to exhaust Dag. It wasn't just Boss Berry, or the suspicious stares from the stirred-up flatties. It was all that atop the scene in the Pearl Riffle patrol headquarters. Dag felt suddenly like a swimmer caught in an eddy between two shores, unable to land on either. He braced himself: *Nobody said this was going to be easy.* But he hoped he wasn't about to lose Fawn their boat-passage. Or her new friend.

Berry touched Fawn's wedding cord, held out in demonstration; her face grew, if not wholly convinced, less tense. Her gaze flicked over the hook. "They say you know boats," she said to Dag at last, the first words she'd spoken to him directly.

He repeated the polite nod. "I've never worked a flatboat or a keel. I've taken narrow boats, big and small, down both the Grace and the Gray, though never the whole length in one trip."

"I've never had no Lakewalker as boat crew, before. Never even seen one doing that, on any farmer boat." But her voice was growing more doubtful than hostile.

"I started out this trip to do a lot of things no one had done before." Dag glanced at Fawn's anxious, upturned face and bestirred himself. "I've been on high water and low, and I know a snag from a sawyer. And I could spot you the channel through the sand bars and shoals in water thick enough to plow, day or dark."

"Oh, your groundsense can do that?" said Fawn in delight. "Yes, of course it would!"

"It's true," said Berry, "you don't hardly ever see a narrow boat hung up. You Lakewalkers use your magic to pilot, do you?"

"In a way." If Berry decided to let Dag and his party aboard, he would have days ahead to explain the subtleties of groundsense. Dag tilted his head at the grazing Copperhead. "Do you have room for my horse?"

"Your wife"—Berry's mouth hesitated over the phrase, then went on—"Fawn mentioned the horse. Can he share the pen with Daisy?"

"He could be persuaded, yes."

"Well, then." The boat boss's pale eyes were still flat with caution; Dag thought they would gleam more blue if she smiled. "I guess you'll do."

Whit whooped in triumph; Fawn grinned. Dag was infected by their enthusiasm to the extent of a crooked smile. Even Berry's lips twisted a bit as she made her way back across the narrow board and down onto her deck.

The bleary man had been listening unmoved to the debate, his head canted; the boy had stopped milking the goat and hung over the bow, wide-eyed. "So, Bo," said Berry to the bleary man, with a jerk of her head toward the three on the shore. "Looks like we got us a Lakewalker oarsman."

One bushy gray eyebrow cocked up; he spat over the side, but only drawled, "Well, *that's* different." He followed her as she ducked indoors.

"How do we get Copper onto the boat?" asked Fawn suddenly, as if she'd only just noticed the problem. "He's a lot bigger than Daisy-goat."

"More planks," said Dag succinctly.

"Oh."

"Fawn, I got my glass goods!" Whit began excitedly, staring after Berry. Dag could only think, *Pull in your tongue, boy, before you step on it.*

Fawn's brow wrinkled in worry; Dag guessed she was thinking much the same thing. She took Whit by the wrist and lowered her voice. "Come over here like we're getting Copper." Dag strolled after, till they were all out of earshot of the boat.

Fawn pretended to be fussing with her saddlebags. "Whit, you went chasing off before I had a chance to tell you something. Berry isn't just taking the *Fetch* downstream for a trading boat. Her papa took a boat down last fall, and never came back. No word. She means to go look for him."

"Oh, we can help—" Whit began.

Fawn overrode this: "Her papa, her big brother, and her betrothed. All gone missing."

Whit's face was suddenly wiped clean of expression. After a moment he said, "She's betrothed?"

"Yes, or maybe bereaved. Even she don't know which right now. So try for a little, a little . . . I don't know. Just try not to be a blighted fool, all right?"

Whit blinked. "Um. Yeah. Well . . ." He gulped valiantly. "Well, we still need a boat. And she still needs a crew, right?"

"Right," said Fawn, watching him carefully.

"Girl like that, in a fix like that, she deserves all the help she can get. A good pair of hands. Three pairs. Well, two and a half." His grin was awkward, unfelt.

"And if you make one more of your stupid hook-jokes," Fawn added levelly, "I swear I'll clout you on the ear."

"Um. Right."

Dag started unloading saddlebags, thinking, *We need some rain. Soon.*

They all settled in quicker than Fawn would have guessed. Berry's uncle Bo accepted Dag's presence without comment, though her little brother Hawthorn, who was rising twelve but not yet come to his growth spurt, gaped round-eyed and mute, and tended to skitter away when Dag loomed too close. But Fawn and Berry joined forces on cooking dinner, Berry mainly showing Fawn where and how things aboard were cleverly kept, and after eating it Bo and Hawthorn both smiled at Fawn a lot.

Thinking she had better start as she meant to go on, Fawn made sure the washing-up fell mainly to Whit and Hawthorn. As the night chilled and the river mist rose, everyone gathered around the remains of the cook fire in the little hearth, augmented by the light of a rock-oil lantern, and were encouraged to drink up as much of the foaming cider as they could hold.

Whit wandered to peer out the back hatch, then came and settled himself again on his stool with a sigh. "Think it'll rain soon?" he asked. Of the air generally, as near as Fawn could tell, and with no expectation of a reply.

Bo held out one battered boot and wriggled it. "My weather toe says no rain tonight."

Whit looked skeptical. "You have a toe that can tell the weather?"

"Yep. Ever since it got busted, that time."

Berry grinned over the rim of her tankard. "Hey, don't you go questioning Uncle Bo's bad toe. It's as good as a coin toss any day."

"The weather in the Grace Valley can change sudden, this time o' year," Bo advised Whit amiably. "Rain, snow, wind—fog. Why, one time when I was workin' a keel up from Silver Shoals, the fog came down so solid you couldn't hardly see your hand in front of your face. It was so thick it held the boat back, it did, and finally the boss said to put down our poles, 'cause he was anchoring for the night. Next morning, we woke up to all this mooing, and found we'd run right up over that fog for a good half-mile onto shore, and the keel was stuck in some farmer's cow-pasture."

Whit sat up, snorting cider out his nose. He rubbed it on his sleeve, and said, "Go on, you did not!"

Hawthorn, looking equally skeptical, said, "So how'd they get the keelboat back in the river?"

"Rollers," said Bo blandly.

Hawthorn's lips twisted in doubt at this logical-sounding reply.

Bo's head went back in mock-offense, those hairy gray eyebrows seeming to jig. "No, it's as true as I speak! Twisters, now, those are good for a tale or two as well."

"Twisters?" said Fawn uneasily. "You get twisters on the river?"

"Now and then," said Berry.

"You ever been in one?" asked Whit.

Berry shook her head, but then Dag's deep voice sounded for nearly the first time that evening. "I was, once, on the upper Gray."

Everyone looked around as surprised as if one of the chairs had suddenly spoken. In the gloom almost beyond the fire circle, legs stretched out, Dag raised his tankard in return and drank. Only Fawn saw his indrawn breath, sensed that he was about to make an effort that did not come easily to him.

"There were six of us, paddling a big narrow boat full of furs down from Luthlia for the river trade. The storm came up sudden, and the sky turned dark green. We pulled in hard to the western bank and tied everything to the trees, which was not so reassuring when the trees started to rip out of the ground and tumble away like weeds. Strangest sight I ever saw, then—the wind had picked up a horse, this white horse, out of a pasture somewhere to the west, and it passed us by straight overhead, its legs churning away like it was galloping. Galloping across the sky."

A little silence followed this; Bo's gray eyebrows climbed. Then Hawthorn said, "So, what happened to the horse? Did you see it come down?"

"We were all too busy gripping the ground and being terrified, right about then," said Dag. "The poor thing was killed, likely."

Hawthorn's face scrunched up in dismay; Dag glanced from it to Fawn, and swiftly offered, "Or it might have spun down and landed in a pond. Swum out, shook its dizzy head, and started eating grass."

Hawthorn brightened slightly. So did Whit, Fawn noticed, and bit her lip.

"That was a tall tale, right?" said Whit, in a tone of some misgiving. Dag let his eyes widen innocently. "Was it supposed to be?"

"Yes, that's how the contest goes, in farmer," Whit explained earnestly. "You're supposed to top the tall tale with another tall tale."

"Oh, sorry," said Dag, ducking his head. "You're not allowed to tell true tales, then? I can see I'm going to be at a disadvantage."

"I . . ." Whit paused and looked confused. "Uh . . ."

Berry scrubbed her lips. Bo's face was unreadable, but he did raise his tankard at Dag in a delicately conceding gesture.

Berry, after a glance comparing the length of Dag to the length of her bunks, offered a place for Fawn and Dag's dual bedroll amongst the forward cargo. It was dank and dark and smelled of the stack of hides that cushioned their blankets, but Berry also donated a length of coarse cloth, which she and Fawn tacked up to the low beams and around for privacy. During this wordless concession to Fawn's recently married state, Berry looked a trifle pensive, but she bade the pair good-night without comment.

So, it seemed the Dag-deprivation that Fawn had feared on this crowded leg of the journey was not to be. A stack of hides had no betraying rope nets to creak in time with any movement in the bodies so supported. Dag had only to muffle her giggles with a lot of kisses, which he seemed quite willing to do, as they undertook the pleasant task of finding each other in the pitchy shadows. She was reminded that his groundsense worked just the same in the dark as in the day. She missed the sight of him, bliss to her eyes, but a careless candle was like to set the curtains on fire anyhow, defeating the aim of all this smothered discretion.

After, lying up under his arm in her favorite position with her ear to his heart, she whispered, "Was that story about the flying horse really true?"

"Yep." He added, "I'll amend it next time. I can see I need to add in that pond." His chest rumbled in an unvoiced laugh.

"Depends on your audience, I expect. Some boys'd likely want to hear all about how the critter burst when it hit the ground."

"It probably did," he said ruefully.

"I like Hawthorn," Fawn decided upon reflection. "He seems kind-hearted, for a boy. But not shy or scared with it." Which said good things about Berry, who'd had the raising of him. "Children and animals, you can usually tell how they've been treated. I mean . . . think of poor Hod."

"I'd rather not," sighed Dag.

They curled tightly into each other, and even the unrhythmic blend of snores from the bunks aft, so few paces away, could not keep her awake in this cozy harbor.

Dag woke in a vastly better mood. He occupied the morning letting Hawthorn and Daisy show him and Copperhead to the patch of meadow just up Possum Run, where the boatmen grazed their animals. They had the place nearly to themselves. Dag spent a peaceful couple of hours stretched out under a tree dozing while Copperhead munched grass, which also allowed him to avoid Whit and his energetic scheme for the day of transferring his cargo, crate by crate, from the goods-shed to the *Fetch*. After failing to recruit Dag, Whit had tried to rope in Fawn, but she cannily claimed to be too busy with stocking the flatboat's larder in support of her more lavish style of cooking, a task no one would let him impede.

After a lunch that testified to the truth of Fawn's excuses, Dag retired to the rear deck. He settled down on a crate with his back to the cabin wall, out of sight of the neighbors. As he'd passed over the plank to and from shore earlier, he'd collected the usual quota of curious stares from the boat folks on the two flats moored to either side of them, cushioned, he thought, by his grudging acceptance by the boss and little crew of the *Fetch.* Berry, it seemed, was held in some respect by this floating community. He eyed her empty trot lines, hanging limply over the stern, and wondered if he ought to undertake to catch some fish by his own methods for everyone's dinner, to show the value of an ex-patroller boatman. Cleaning fish was clearly a two-handed chore, however; it would have to fall to Whit. Dag grinned.

Now, if only this hazy blue autumn day would turn cloudy and rain . . .

Voices from the bow indicated Whit was back with his borrowed barrow and another crate, but then his swift footsteps pounded through the cabin. Whit stuck his head through the rear hatch and said uneasily, "Dag? I think you'd better come out here."

Now what? Reluctantly, Dag sat up. "Where? Why?"

"Up to the bow. It's . . . sort of hard to explain."

Whit ducked back in. Dag stretched himself up and strode across the roof instead, the better to spare his head from the low beams inside. He came to the edge to find Boss Berry sitting with her legs dangling, bemusedly regarding the scene below.

Clutching Dag's stick, Hod perched on a barrel in the bow next to the goat's pen, his long face worried and white around the mouth. Fawn fussed around him. Whit popped out the front hatch and gestured anxiously up at Dag.

"I ran into him up at the goods-shed," Whit explained. "He said he was hunting for you."

Looking at Hod in some bewilderment, Dag eased over the roof edge and thumped to the deck. He was not best pleased to realize they'd acquired an audience. Two flatties from the boat moored closest to them leaned on their own side-rail and gawked with all the interest of men being entertained by a storyteller.

"Lakewalker!" said Hod, glancing up at him with a fleeting smile that faded to uncertainty.

"Hello, Hod." Dag gave him a nod. "What brings you here?" Surely Tanner and Mape had planned to leave at dawn on their two-day rattle back to Glassforge. "Is anything the matter?"

Hod, his throat bobbing, said abruptly, "I brought your stick back!" He held out Dag's hickory staff as if in evidence.

"Well . . ." Dag scratched his head in confusion. "That's right thoughtful of you, Hod, but it wasn't necessary. I can cut another in the woods. It's certainly not something you should have walked all this way on your bad leg to bring me!"

Hod ducked his head and gulped some more. "No, well, yes. My knee. It still hurts."

"I'm not surprised. What is it, a mile down to the Bend?" Dag sucked his lip. To say *That wasn't too bright* to Hod seemed a pretty pointless remark.

"I want—I wondered—if you'd do that thing you do again. What you called it. The Lakewalker magic."

"A ground reinforcement?" Dag hazarded.

Hod nodded vigorously. "Yeah, that thing. The thing that makes me not hurt."

"What would make your knee not hurt would be to stay off it the way you were told," said Dag sternly.

"Please . . ." said Hod, rocking on the barrel. His hand went out toward Dag, dropped back to his knee. His face scrunched up; his eyes, Dag was startled to note, were damp with held-back tears. "Please. No one didn't ever make it stop hurting like that before. Please?"

Fawn patted him somewhat helplessly on the shoulder and looked at Dag in consternation. Dag sighed and knelt down before the feckless boy, laying his right hand over the knee. "Well, let's see what's happening in there."

Gingerly, he extended his groundsense. His ground-glue was holding, certainly, the flesh healing well, but the joint was indeed newly inflamed from the imprudent exercise. He frowned.

"Now, Hod," said Fawn, watching Dag in worry, "you know Dag can't just do those medicine maker tricks anytime. They're very tiring for him. He has to have time to recover, between."

Hod swallowed. "I'll wait." Gazing earnestly at Dag, he sat up straight on his barrel as if prepared to take a post there for the rest of the day, or maybe the week.

Dag rocked back on his heels and eyed the boy. "You can't wait that long. Didn't Mape and Tanner want to leave early?" If they'd been delayed by this foolish side trip of Hod's, they were going to be irate, Dag thought.

"They did."

"What?" said Whit, startled. "They didn't just ditch you here, did they?"

"No, they paid me off."

"But that's not fair. Just because you're off your feet for a week or two, they shouldn't ought to sack you!" Whit scowled in outrage at this injustice.

"Didn't. I asked to be let off."

"Why?"

"I wanted to stay. Here. No, not here." A vague wave around took in Pearl Riffle. "With *him*." Hod pointed to Dag. "He could hire me."

"To do what?" asked Fawn in bafflement.

"I dunno." Hod shrugged. "Just . . . things. Anything." He glanced up warily at Dag. "Well, sitting-down things at first, I guess." He added after a minute, "He wouldn't have to pay me or anything."

"Do you know much about boats?" Fawn asked thoughtfully. She glanced up at Berry, still sitting on the roof edge and watching it all with some perplexity.

Hod gave an uncertain headshake.

Whit's lips screwed up; he strolled over to Berry's dangling feet and whispered up to her, "Hod's not too quick in the wits, I'm afraid."

"Neither was my last two oarsmen. Took me days to get my cook-pots back."

Whit muffled a grin, and went on, "But he's willing. I mean, he could be, once he gets over having his knee kicked in by Dag's evil nag. That's what happened, see, how he got hurt in the first place. Dag fixed him up again Lakewalker-style."

"Mm. The *Fetch* is still a bit shorthanded, it's true."

"He's sort of an orphan, I gather."

Berry's brows rose. "Huh. Funny. So am I, sort of." Her stare down at Hod grew more appraising.

Dag wondered if he'd get anywhere offering to throw Hod up behind him on Copperhead and gallop after Mape and Tanner, delivering their henchman back to them to be firmly returned to Glassforge. Hod plainly wouldn't want to go, and Dag was beginning to have a very ugly misgiving about why. And it wasn't just on account of Hod's unhappy former life.

Could he test his suspicion? Hod was bent over with both hands on his right knee again, helplessly patting at it. It was clear his pain was very real.

Dag swallowed and cleared his throat. "All right, Hod. I can give you just a little more ground reinforcement. But then you have to behave and follow orders about letting that knee heal, all right?"

Hod's face lit with joy; he nodded vigorously. His lips parted as he watched Dag bend down and lay his hand on the joint again.

The wrench of the reinforcement came readily; Dag felt it like a wave of heat passing from his palm into the throbbing joint below. For a moment, all the tension seemed to go out of Hod's body. He gave vent to an *aah* of blissful relief. "That's good," he whispered to Dag. "That's so good."

Fawn patted Hod's shoulder again in encouragement. "There, see? You'll be all right soon."

Berry, watching, scrubbed the back of her hand across her mouth. "That's real interesting, Lakewalker. You some kind of bonesetter, too, are you?"

"Sometimes," Dag admitted, climbing to his feet. His heart was pounding, and it wasn't from the exertion. "Just in emergencies. I'm not trained as a real medicine maker."

Fawn started to explain proudly to Berry how Dag had once mended a glass bowl by groundwork, but broke off as Dag grasped her by the arm and dragged her into the cabin. He didn't stop till they were out of earshot back by the kitchen hearth.

"Is something wrong?" she asked, alarmed. "Isn't Hod healing all right?"

"Oh, his knee's healing fine. So's his gut."

"Well, that's a relief. You know, I'm thinking maybe a trip on the river would be good for Hod, too, now he's not going to be so sick all the time. I bet we all could watch after him better 'n those glass-men did."

"Fawn, stop. It's not that. It's something else."

She blinked at his tone, then looked at him more carefully.

"Hod"—Dag took a deep breath—"is beguiled to the eyebrows. And I don't know how to get him un-beguiled."

8

$\mathcal{D}$ag had the most unsettled look on his face, downright dismayed. Fawn felt pretty dismayed herself. "How did it happen?" she asked.

"Not sure. Well, it must have happened when I healed his knee, yes, but—I didn't mean to. I always thought beguilement was something you had to do on *purpose.*"

"It's something real, then?" She had thought it rumor, tall tale. Slander.

"I'd never seen a case. Only heard about it. Gossip, stories. I've never known a farmer who—well, till I met you, I hadn't really known any farmers at all. Passed through, passed by, dealt with farmers, yes. Never got so close, for so long."

"What's this beguilement like?"

"You saw near as much as I did. Hod wants more. More healing. More ground reinforcement, more pieces of . . . me, I guess."

Her face screwed up in new confusion. "But Lakewalkers have healed me. You, Mari, old Cattagus once a little, when I scorched my hand. And I'm not beguiled." *Am I?* The thought went well beyond dismay. She remembered her own rage when Dag's brother Dar had implied just such a thing, mocking her marriage.

"I . . ." Dag shook his head. It would have reassured Fawn more to think it was in denial and not just Dag trying to clear his brain. "Those were minor healings. What I did on Hod was as deep as any medicine making I know of. I nearly groundlocked myself."

Her hand went to her lips. "Dag, you never said!"

He waved away her alarm. "And you—I'm not sure how to put this. Your ground isn't hungry like Hod's. You're abundant. I don't think you know how much you give to me, every day." His brows drew down, as if he pursued some insight that eluded him. "I'd half-talked myself into thinking the risk of beguiling farmers during healing was exaggerated. That others might have problems, but that I'd be an exception. Looks like I need to think again."

Both their heads swiveled at the sound of footsteps. Boss Berry, frowning, ambled into the cramped living quarters at the back of the cabin. "What do you want to do about that boy, Lakewalker? You takin' responsibility for him or not? He's only about half-useful as he stands. Or sits."

Fawn said, her voice tinged with doubt, "He could be a scullion, I suppose. How long till he could man a sweep, Dag?"

"If he could be taught, you mean? Couple of weeks. If he doesn't do anything to reinjure the knee." He looked at Fawn, his brows pinching harder. "In two weeks, we'll be far down the river."

"If it ever rains again," sighed Berry.

"If he's to be left behind, better here than in some strange place," said Dag. "I can't . . . see my way."

Of how to un-beguile Hod, did he mean? And if Hod were left at Possum Landing, would he still try to follow Dag? How far? "Well . . . if we take him along, you may or may not figure it out. If you leave him here, you never will."

He scratched his chin ruefully. "There's a point, Spark."

Fawn glanced at Berry, who was waiting with her brows up. No, the boat boss's own situation was far too unsettled to ask her for undertakings or promises on behalf of Hod. It was up to them. Fawn said, "I'm willing to try with him if you are, Dag."

Dag took a breath. "Then we'll haul him along."

Boss Berry gave a short nod. "The *Fetch* has itself a scullion, then." She added, in mild regret, "I won't charge nothing for his passage."

～

In the warmest part of the afternoon, Bo led an expedition downstream to the Riffle, where the locals had gathered to salvage coal from a recently wrecked flatboat before the water rose again. Hod stayed on the *Fetch* with his leg up, supposedly keeping watch but probably, Fawn thought, napping. Whit's interest was aroused when he learned that the wrecked boat's boss was buying back coal retrieved from the river bottom by the bushel, albeit at a meager price. Some gatherers preferred to carry off the coal itself, and then, after some jawing, the meager price was paid the other way; Berry explained to Fawn that the going rate had been worked out a few days earlier, when the gatherers had dumped their baskets back in the worst part of the rapids before the boat boss saw reason. Whit stripped to his drawers and sloshed in after Bo and Hawthorn to duck and dive for the scattered cargo—or, contorting, grub it up with his toes. Fawn found herself drawn in along with Berry, skirts tucked up and feet bare as they waded out to receive dripping sacks and pile up the coal on the bank to dry. The water was growing chilly as the autumn waned.

Dag claimed blandly that his one-handed state barred him from the task, which made Fawn raise her brows and snort. He withdrew to sit with his back comfortably propped against a stump and watch. Fawn wondered if giving the ground reinforcement to Hod had set him back, again. He ignored the stares he drew from the handful of families working farther on down the riverside. There were no youths from the Lakewalker camp cashing in on the windfall, Fawn noticed, though clusters of village boys had turned out for the chance.

About an hour into this task, a gang of half a dozen brawny keelers from the boat trapped above the Riffle traipsed past. Some wore striped trousers, others had colored scarves around their waists or sometimes their heads, or feathers in their hatbands if they owned hats. They started to call something rude to Fawn and Berry, but then some recognized the boat boss and hushed the others. Berry waved back amiably enough. Dag opened one eye to observe, but when nothing untoward developed, closed it again.

"Where are they going?" Fawn asked Berry.

"Down to Pearl Bend. To drink, mostly, I expect."

"Isn't there a tavern at Possum Landing?" It was the first place Berry went to look for Bo whenever he vanished off the *Fetch,* Fawn understood.

Berry grinned, lowered her voice, and said, "Yeah, but there's a bed boat tied up down at the lower end of the Bend, just now. Three sisters and a couple o' cousins keep it. There isn't one at the Landing. The ferrywomen won't have it."

Fawn hesitated, reluctant to reveal her ignorance. She had her suspicions. She was the married woman here, after all. "Bed boat?" she finally asked.

"Some of the girls who sleep with the boatmen for money follow the trade up and down the river in their own boats. They can slip away easier if the town mothers object, see, and they don't have to split their pay with the tavern-keepers."

Fawn wondered if Mama had known about this exotic river-hazard. "You ever meet one?"

"Time to time. Playing fiddle for the keelers pulling upriver, I met most every sort sooner or later. Well, not the worst; Papa didn't work on those boats. Most of the girls are all right. Some take it up because they're way down on their luck, but others seem to like it. Some are thieves who give the rest a bad name, same as some boatmen." She grimaced.

By unspoken agreement, the topic was tabled as Whit waved and they waded out within earshot of the males again. Fawn wondered if Whit had heard yet about the bed boat. She couldn't help thinking he'd be even more curious than she was. And he had money in his pocket, just now. She resolved not to mention it in front of him. Then she wondered if Lakewalker men from the camp ever snuck down there. Dag might know. And if she asked him straight out, he would likely tell her straight out, though she bet he wouldn't bring up the subject.

She emptied Whit's sack onto their coal pile as Berry emptied Bo's and Hawthorn's; Berry waded back out in the water to toss them again to the fellows. Whit grinned thanks through purple-blue lips. The shade was already creeping over this patch of bank as the sun sank, and Fawn rubbed her chilly legs together, wondering how long Berry and Bo meant to go on. Dag straightened up and turned his head; he bent one knee and lurched up to a seat on the stump. Fawn followed his gaze.

Coming down the track along the bank were three older Lakewalkers: two women and a man. One woman was dressed like a patroller, the other wore a woolen skirt and buckskin slippers decorated with dyed porcupine quills, and the man was tidy in a simple shirt and trousers, with hair in a very neat queue tied down his back, undecorated. His braid wasn't shot with gray like the others', but his face was not young. His left hand was bandaged. They all wore matching frowns.

They came to a halt in front of Dag. The patroller-looking woman said, "Dag Red-Blue whatever you are, we need a word with you."

Dag opened his hand to indicate welcome to his patch of grass and tree roots.

As Berry came to Fawn's side to stare, the patroller woman glanced at them both and jerked her head over her shoulder. "In private."

Dag's eyelids lowered, opened. "Very well." He heaved to his feet. "I'll be back in a bit, Spark, or I'll find you at the *Fetch*."

All the Lakewalker looks dismissed Berry and focused on Fawn, especially her left wrist. She wrapped her right hand around her wedding cord and lifted her chin. She expected Dag to introduce her, but he didn't, merely giving her a touch to his temple in farewell, and a nod something between grave and grim. Did he know what this was all about? If he did, he sure hadn't told her. He'd said nothing about his visit to the camp when he'd caught up with her yesterday, and in the flurry of news about the boat, Fawn hadn't asked. She'd assumed he simply hadn't found the friends he'd been looking for. Plainly, there was more to it. Fawn watched in concern as Dag trod up the river path after the frowning Lakewalkers.

With his groundsense locked down, Dag could not read the moods of the three Pearl Riffle Lakewalkers directly, but he hardly needed to. Amma Osprey and Nicie Sandwillow were plainly not happy, even more not-happy than when he'd left them yesterday. The man seemed shaken, his right hand protecting the bandaged left held to his chest. He bore no tool bag, but his cleanliness and bearing bespoke his craft.

Captain Osprey turned aside and climbed the bank through the trees till they were out of sight and earshot of anyone happening along the path. The three took seats on a fallen cottonwood trunk, and Amma waved Dag to a place on a recently cut oak stump opposite. As he sank down, her wave continued to the new man, whom she introduced laconically: "Verel Owlet. Pearl Riffle's medicine maker."

Tension leaked from the trio, infecting Dag. He couldn't decide between a belligerent *What's this all about?* or a cool *So, what can I do for you?* He tilted his head instead. "Dag Bluefield."

Their return stares remained dubious.

Amma Osprey drew breath. "First off, I want to get down to the bottom of those rumors flying around Pearl Bend. Is it true you healed some Glassforge wagon-man's broken leg, couple of days back?"

Dag hesitated, then said, "Yes. I was obliged. It was my horse kicked him."

The medicine maker put in anxiously, "Was it really groundwork, or just a bonesetting?"

For answer, Dag held up his hook. But not his ghost hand, tightly furled with the rest of his ground. "I don't do many two-handed chores."

"Ah. I suppose not," said the medicine maker. "Sorry. Did the wagon-men realize what you were doing?"

"Yes. I didn't make a secret of it." He'd just about made it a show, in fact.

Amma hissed through her teeth and muttered, *"Blight* it."

Various premature defenses sprang to Dag's mind, fighting with a desire to demand of the medicine maker everything he knew about beguilement. He settled more cautiously on, "Why do you ask?"

Verel Owlet straightened, laying his injured hand on his left knee. "The first I heard about your stunt was when some farmer fellow from Pearl Bend—I think he's a carpenter by trade—turned up at my tent this morning insisting I come see his sick wife. When I told him Lakewalkers could only heal other Lakewalkers, he started babbling about the wagon-men's story, which was evidently being passed around the tavern down there last night. First he begged, then he offered money, then he drew a knife on me and tried to force me to walk to the Bend. Some of the off-duty patrollers were able to jump us and take the knife away from him, and escort him to the crossroads. He went back down the road crying and swearing."

Verel wasn't just shaken by the knife attack, Dag guessed, but also by his distraught attacker. Medicine makers tended to be sensitive, given their need to be open to their patients. How sick had that carpenter's wife been? A picture of a deathly ill Fawn rose unbidden in Dag's head, and he thought, *I'd have done a lot worse than pull a knife on you.* "But it's not true."

"What's not true?" said Nicie.

"It's not true that Lakewalkers can't do groundwork on farmers."

"It's what we tell 'em around here," said Amma impatiently. "Absent gods, man, use your head. All we have is one good medicine maker and two apprentices, barely enough for our own."

"Not even enough," muttered Verel.

"We'll sell the farmers what remedies we make and can spare, yes," Amma continued. "But they would drain poor Verel dry, if they knew. And then they would keep coming, and scenes like this morning would be the least of our troubles."

"They'd never understand groundwork," said Verel. "What it costs us, what it lays us open to."

"Not if they're never taught, no," said Dag dryly. "Funny, that."

Amma eyed him sharply. "It's all fine for you; you'll be moving on at the next rise. We have to stay here and deal every day with these people."

Verel was frowning at Dag with fresh speculation. "Your partner Saun said you were unusually strong in groundwork. For a patroller, I mean."

Ye gods, yes, the medicine maker here would certainly have treated and talked with the convalescent Saun last spring, and Reela as well. "I did what I could with what I had. Patrol healing can get pretty rough-

and-ready." Granted, since Dag's ghost hand had emerged, he'd seemed to have . . . more. Whether it was new-grown strength, or just new access to strength long crippled, even Hickory Lake's medicine maker, the remarkable Hoharie, had been unable to say.

Verel hadn't mentioned inadvertent beguilement as a reason not to do groundwork on farmers. Did he even know about it, if he'd never healed anyone but Lakewalkers? Was Dag's effect on Hod something unique? Dag suddenly wondered if Amma knew that Hod hadn't gone home with the other wagon-men. It seemed not, since she didn't ask after him.

Nicie Sandwillow rubbed her lined face in a weary gesture. "Just what all have you been telling these farmers and flatties, Dag?"

"Nothing. Or the truth, but mostly nothing." He added darkly, "Leastways I haven't been telling them convenient lies."

"Absent gods," said Amma. "Are you just banished, or are you aiming to go renegade?"

"Neither!" Dag stiffened, indignant. *Renegade* was an even uglier word than *refugee*. Seldom did a Lakewalker of any skill go rogue; not in Dag's life experience, but there were lurid tales from the past. Patrols, who were good at hunting evil things, would surely hunt down such a madman just like a malice. "Fairbolt Crow as much as sent me off with his blessing. If I find the answer, he wants to hear it. He sees the question plain as I do."

"And what question would that be?" asked Amma skeptically.

"I saw it this past summer in Raintree," Dag began, trying to marshal his wits. This was no good lead-in for his pitch, but it was the one he'd been handed. "The Raintree malice almost got away from us because it came up nearly under a farmer town, and had already stolen power from half a thousand people before it even started to sweep south. Because no one had taught them enough about malices. I asked Fairbolt, what if it hadn't been just a little squatter village? What if it had been a big town like Tripoint or Silver Shoals? Instant capital for a malice-king. And the more farmers filter north, the more territory they settle, the bigger their towns will grow—Pearl Bend is twice the size it was last time I was through here—and the more such an ill chance becomes a certainty, and then what will we do?"

"Push the farmers back south," said Amma instantly. "They don't belong here."

"You know they won't go. They've been settled north of the Grace for generations already, on land they've made their own by their labor. And if we're this stretched just patrolling for malices, we for sure can't stop and fight a war with the farmers, which wouldn't be won by either side, but only by the next malice to come along. Farmers are here, so it's here that we have to find another way."

A place for farmers and Lakewalkers both would be a place his and Fawn's children could live, Dag couldn't help thinking. This new and personal urgency to the problem was no more suspect than were the years he'd ignored it when it hadn't seemed so personal. *This crisis has been building all my life. It shouldn't come as a surprise.*

Dag's voice slowed in new thought. "Hickory Lake Camp doesn't deal with farmers, only our patrols do, because Hickory's off in the woods still north of farmer expansion. Here at Pearl Riffle ferry, you've been dealing with the problems for decades. You must have learned something about how to rub along."

"Not really," growled Amma. "Think about those stupid pots, and what it says about how afraid and suspicious these folks are of us. And you think we should hand them proof of what we could really do to them? If the farmers can't be shifted, we should move. Five miles upstream at least. That's my answer." She glowered at Nicie, who glowered back.

Dag shook his head. "Farmers will fill this valley, in time. If it's hard to keep separate now, it will be impossible later, when there's nowhere left to move to. We may as well figure it out now."

"Who is *we,* Dag Bluefield No-camp?" said Amma. "Your happy idea of dealing with farmers nearly got our medicine maker murdered this morning."

Verel raised a hand in faint protest, though apparently only of the notion that he'd come so close to being slain.

Amma went on belligerently, "I'd have told them at the Bend that only Lakewakers with gold eyes could heal farmers, which they might have bought, except I worried for the next fellow to come down the road with your eye color. I should have told 'em it was only folks from Hickory Lake, and let your people cope with the knife-wavers."

Nicie said slowly, "Really, healing farmers is the same problem as fighting farmers. The burden would put us behind, drag us down."

At least she'd been listening. Well, she was a councilor, maybe she was used to hearing folks argue. Dag tried, "But we could keep the balance if the farmers, in turn, took over some of our tasks. Not a gift but a trade." He glanced at Nicie, and dared to add, "Or even a cash business." Dag's own secret notion for making a living in farmer country, before this beguilement problem had taken him so aback.

Nicie raised her brows. "So, only rich farmers would get healed?"

Dag's mouth opened, and closed. Maybe he hadn't quite thought it through . . . well, he knew he hadn't. Yet.

Verel was giving Dag an indecipherable look. "Not many can do deep groundsetting."

"Not everyone would need to. Lots of folks can do minor ground-work. We do it for each other on patrol all the time."

"Just what did you do for that wagon-man?" Verel asked. "Patroller."

Dag shrugged. Gulped. Described, in as few words as he could manage, the trance-deep groundwork that had pulled Hod's bone frag-ments, vessels, and nerves back into alignment and held them there so that they might begin healing. He was careful to call his ghost hand a *ground projection,* since that was the term Hoharie had so plainly pre-ferred. He hoped the medicine maker would approve his techniques, if not his patient. He didn't continue into the unexpected later conse-quences, although he did allow a plaintive note to leak into his voice when he described his wish for an anchoring partner.

"The Hickory Lake medicine maker knew you could do this sort of thing, and *let you get away?*" asked Verel.

Hoharie had seen Dag do much stranger magery than that, in Rain-tree. "Hoharie tried to recruit me. If she'd been willing to accept Fawn as my wife, and maybe as my spare hands, she might have succeeded. But she wasn't. So we left." Verel was regarding him covetously as well as charily, Dag realized at last. Would he take the hint? Between them, Dag and Fawn might add up to a medicine maker and a half, a valuable addition to a straitened camp.

Maybe, for Verel's ground flicked out to touch Dag's wedding cord, concealed from ordinary eyes by his rolled-down sleeve. "It seems just like a real cord," he said doubtfully.

"It is."

Verel was plainly itching to get Dag alone and ask how they'd woven it. Dag longed even more to take the medicine maker aside and squeeze out everything he knew about healing, groundlock, beguilement, and a hundred other complexities. But that wasn't the reason the irate camp captain had tracked him here.

Amma Osprey said grimly, "The old ways have worked for better 'n a thousand years. Nothing lasts that long without good reason. Let farmers keep to farmers, and Lakewalkers to Lakewalkers, and we'll all survive. Mixing things up is dangerous. Which is fine if it falls on your own fool head, but not so fine when it falls on someone else's." She gestured, inarguably, toward Verel's bandaged hand.

"Is that all you want?" Dag challenged. "For the problem to go somewhere else?"

She snorted. "If I tried to shoulder the troubles of the whole world, I'd go mad. *And* Pearl Riffle would be lost. I run Pearl Riffle patrol. My neighbor camps run their territories, and their neighbors do the same, all the way to the edge of the hinterland and on to the hinterlands beyond, and so we all get through. One by one and all together. I have to trust them; they have to trust me. Trust me not to go haring off after swamp gas, for one thing. So I'll thank you, Dag No-camp, to keep yourself to yourself and not stir up these people worse in *my* territory."

"I'll be gone on the rise," said Dag. He pointed to the windless sky, chilling gold-and-blue as the sun slanted. "Though I can't control the rain."

"That works for me," said Amma Osprey. She stood abruptly, signaling an end to the talk. The other two rose as well, though their brows seemed wrinkled as much in troubled thought as in irritation.

Clearly, this was not a good moment to bring up the matter of a spare sharing knife again. Dag sighed and lifted his hand to his throbbing temple in polite farewell.

9

Fawn kept an eye out, but Dag did not return to the scavenging site before the coal boat boss came by with a barrow and bought back their pile. Berry scrupulously divided the scanty handful of coins five ways. On the walk back upstream to the *Fetch,* Bo silently split off and disappeared up the hill in the lengthening shadows toward Possum Landing village.

Berry just shook her head. At Fawn's noise of inquiry, she explained, "Bo and I have a pact. He don't drink the boat's money. He's kept to it pretty good, so far." She sighed. "Don't suppose we'll see him again till morning."

Still huffing with the chill despite dry clothes, Whit and Hawthorn built up the fire in the *Fetch*'s hearth while Fawn and Berry dodged around each other whipping together a hot meal. Dag, looking troubled, strolled in as Fawn was dishing out beans and bacon. He met her questioning look with a headshake.

"Maybe a walk after supper?" she murmured to him as he sat at the table.

"That'd be good," he agreed.

A walk and a talk. There was something pressing on Dag's mind, sure enough. Fawn was distracted keeping her good food coming, happy just to have a real, if cramped, kitchen to cook in after a summer of smoking herself as well as her meals over an open fire. She encouraged the hesitant Hod to eat up, and then he lurched to the opposite extreme and gobbled as if someone were going to snatch his food away. Whit chided him, and Fawn bent her head and grinned to watch Hod earnestly taking Whit for an authority—on table manners, of all things. Hawthorn chattered on about all the different ways he might spend his coal-salvaging coins. Berry encouraged him to save them; Whit advised him to invest them in something he might resell for a higher price downstream.

"Something nonbreakable would be smart," Fawn suggested, winning an irate look from Whit. Dag smiled a little in his silence, and Fawn's heart was eased. A nippy night was falling beyond the cabin's square glass windows—frost might lace them by morning—but inside it seemed cozy and bright in the light of the oil lantern. Comfortable. It felt like friends in here, and Fawn decided she liked the feeling very well.

Dag's head turned toward the bow; he laid down his fork. In a moment, heavy feet sounded crossing the gangplank, and then a thump as someone jumped to the deck. The boat rocked a trifle. A fist pounded on the front door—hatch, Fawn corrected her thought—and a male voice bellowed, "Boss Berry, send out that long Lakewalker you got hiding in there!"

"What?" said Whit, as Dag grimaced. "Someone for you, Dag?"

"Quite a few someones, seems like," sighed Dag.

"*Bother* Bo for not being here," muttered Berry, and stood up from her bench. Whit and Fawn followed her through the cabin; she motioned Hawthorn back. Hod hunched fearfully, and Dag did not rise, though he ran his hand through his hair and then leaned his chin on it.

"Berry!" shouted the voice again. "Out with him, we say!"

"Hush, Wain, you'll wake all the catfishes' children with your bawling," Berry shouted back irritably. "I can hear you fine, I ain't deaf." She pushed open the hatch and strode through. "What's this ruckus, then?" Whit followed at her elbow, and Fawn at Whit's.

One of the big keelers loomed on the front deck between the goat pen and the chicken coop. Dag had left Copperhead tethered for the night to a tree up on shore, well away from the path, with an armload of hay to keep him occupied, but Daisy-goat bleated nervously at the noisy visitor. The man—Wain?—held a torch aloft. The orange light flickered over his broad face, flushed not with exertion or cold but beer, judging by the rich smell wafting from him.

On the shore, a mob of perhaps twenty people had gathered. Fawn stared in alarm. She recognized some of the keelers who had passed them going down to Pearl Bend earlier—you couldn't forget those red-and-blue striped trousers, more's the pity. The others might be towns-men, with one or two women. Some held oil lanterns, and a couple more had torches. Against the shadowy bank, the crowd seemed to glow like a bonfire.

The keelers routinely wore knives at their belts, some of a size to rival Dag's war knife, but not a few were also gripping stout sticks. Six of the keelers were holding up a door on their shoulders, hinges and all, and on it lay a shape bundled in blankets, whimpering. Their frowns ranged from tense to grim, their grins from wolfish to foolish. Fawn thought they seemed more excited than angry, but their numbers were disturbing. Stirred up by the noise, several men came out from the neighboring boats to lean on their side-rails and watch.

"Mark the boat carpenter says those high-and-mighty Lakewalker sorcerers refused to heal his wife. She's in a fearsome bad way." Boss Wain jerked a thick thumb over his shoulder at the huddled shape on the door. "So we 'uns from the *Snapping Turtle* took a show of hands and offered to *make* this one do it!"

A murmur of agreement and a surge forward rippled through the crowd, followed by a sharp cry as the door was jostled. The broad-shouldered keelers holding it up looked awkwardly at each other and steadied it with more care.

Fawn wondered if she should claim Dag wasn't here, and if a violent search of the *Fetch* would follow, but before she could open her mouth, Dag ducked through the front hatch and straightened up to his full height—a good hand taller than the keeler boss, Fawn was happy to see.

"How de'," he said, in his deep, calm, carrying voice. "What seems to be your trouble?"

The keeler's head sunk between his shoulders, like a bull about to charge. "We got us a real sick woman, here."

Dag's glance flicked toward the shore. "I see that."

With his groundsense, he doubtless saw a lot more than that, and had done so even before he'd stepped out into the torchlight. Fawn clutched that thought to herself. Did Dag know what he was doing? Maybe not. But he'd know a lot more about what everyone else was doing than they could guess.

"You healed that wagon-boy's busted knee," Wain went on. "He showed it around at the Bend tavern last night. A lot of us saw. We know you can help."

Dag drew a long breath. "You know, I'm not a real medicine maker. I'm just a patroller."

"Don't you try and lie your way out of this!"

Dag's head came up; the keeler stepped back half a pace at his glinting glare. "I don't lie." And added under his breath, "I *won't*." He rubbed the back of his neck, looked up, and sighed softly to Fawn, who had crept close under his left shoulder, "You see any horse-tails up there in the moonlight?"

The long, wispy clouds that heralded a change of weather. She followed his glance. A few faint bands like skim milk veiled the autumn stars to the west. "Yes . . . well, maybe."

He smiled down at her in would-be reassurance. "Guess we'll take our chances." He turned his head, raised his voice, and called to the shore, "Bring her here onto the bow and set her down. No, there's not room for the all of you! Just her husband and, um, she got any female relatives? Sister, oh good. You come up, ma'am." The crowd rearranged itself as the keelers threw down a couple more boards to make a better gangplank, carried the door across, and grunted onto the deck.

"Whit, stay by me," Dag whispered under the cover of this noise. "Fawn, you stick real tight." She nodded. "That the husband?" Dag muttered on, as a pale young man with dark circles under his eyes came forward. "Crap, he's hardly older than Whit."

Despite the risk of dropping the woman into the mud, the move onto the boat served to thin the crowd considerably. It also shifted the visitors onto Berry's territory, for whatever authority she might have in what was shaping up to be a dicey situation. Once they'd set the door down, Berry was able to shoo most of the keelers back to the bank for the plain reason that there was no room for them aboard. Boss Wain remained, his jaw jutting in resolve. Fawn supposed this expedition had been organized in the Pearl Bend tavern. A good deed combined with a chance to beat someone up seemed an ideal combination to appeal to a bunch of half-drunk keelers. Twenty to one—did they think they could take Dag? He was staring down expressionlessly at the woman. *Maybe not.*

The boat carpenter's wife reminded Fawn a bit of Clover—before this dire sickness had fallen on her, she might have been plump and cheerful. Now her round face was pallid and sheened with cold sweat. The brown hair at her temples curled damply from the tears of pain that leaked from the corners of her eyes. Breathing shallowly, she clawed at her belly, skirts bunching in her sweaty hands. Fawn was aware of Hod creeping out of the cabin door to stare, and Hawthorn as well.

Her husband knelt down and caught up one of her frantic hands; they clutched each other. He looked up at Dag in heartbreaking appeal. "What's wrong with her, Lakewalker? She didn't cry like this even when our baby was born!"

Dag rubbed his lips, then knelt down by the woman's other side, pulling Fawn with him. "Happens I've seen this trouble before. In a medicine tent up in Luthlia, a long time ago." Fawn glanced up at him, knowing just when he'd spent a season in such a tent. "They brought this fellow in, taken sudden with gut pain. Did this come on her sudden?"

The carpenter nodded anxiously. "Two days back."

"Uh-huh." Dag rubbed his hand on his knee. "I don't know if you've ever seen a person's insides"—not the best choice of words, Fawn thought, with maybe half the people here suspecting Lakewalkers of cannibalism—"but down at the corner of most folks' entrails there's this slippy blind pocket 'bout the size of a child's little finger. The medicine makers never could tell me what it does. But this fellow, his had got twisted around or swollen up or something, and took a roaring hot infection that blew it up like a bladder. By the time he came to the medicine maker, it had busted clean open. No, not clean. Dirty. It spilled his guts into his belly just like a knife wound would."

The keeler boss, at least, looked as though he knew what this entailed, and his lips went round in an unvoiced whistle.

"The infection spread too fast for even the maker's best ground reinforcements to stop it, and he died about three days on. Funny thing was, when his gut busted, his pain actually eased for a while, since the pressure went down. I guess it fooled him into thinking he was getting better, till it was too late."

The carpenter's voice went hushed. "Is Cress's belly going to bust inside like that, then?"

"It hasn't yet," said Dag. "This is a right dangerous sickness. But the groundwork to fix it isn't really that deep. There's a host of belly-ills no medicine maker born can cure, especially in women, but this . . ." He let out his breath. "I can try, leastways." He nudged Fawn. "Spark, would you take off my arm harness, please?"

Dag could manage that himself, but having Fawn do it directed their spectators' eyes to her, the patroller's farmer bride. Purposely? She unbuckled the straps and drew off the wooden cuff and the fine cotton sock beneath that she'd lately knitted for Dag to stop the cuff rubbing up blisters, and set them aside. The presence or absence of the arm harness made no difference to Dag's ghost hand as far as she knew, but she supposed Dag thought it would alarm the carpenter less not to have that wicked hook waving over his wife's belly.

"What I can do—what I can try to do . . ." Dag looked up and around, and Fawn suspected only she realized how much uncertainty and fear his stern face was masking. "First I want to wrap a ground reinforcement around the swelling. Most of you don't know what ground is, but anyway, you won't see anything. Then I want to try and pry that swollen end open so's the pocket will drain back into the gut the way it's supposed to. That part I think may hurt, but then it ought to ease. There's a danger. Two dangers. Look at me, you husband, sister." His voice softened, "Cress." He smiled down at her; her pain-pinched eyes widened a trifle. When he was sure he had their attention, he continued, "That little pocket's stretched really tight right now. There's a chance it'll bust while I'm trying to drain it. But I think it's like to bust anyway pretty soon. Do you still want me to try this?"

They looked at each other; the sick woman squeezed her husband's hand, and he wet his lips and nodded.

"There's another hitch. For later. Subtler." Dag swallowed hard. "Sometimes, when Lakewalkers do deep groundwork on farmers, the farmers end up beguiled. It's not on purpose, but it's part of why the Lakewalkers here won't treat you. Now, I'll be gone on the rise. There's a good chance that a touch of beguilement would do no worse to Cress than leave her sad for something she can never have, which can happen to a person whether they're beguiled or not. So, I don't know if you're a stupid-jealous sort of fellow, Mark-carpenter, or more sensible. But if that mood should come on her, later, it'd be your husband-job to help her ease it, not to harry her about it. Do you understand?"

The carpenter shook his head no, then yes, then puffed out his breath in confusion. "Are you saying my Cress would run off? Leave me, leave her baby?" He stared wildly across at Fawn. "Is that what you did?"

Fawn shook her head vigorously, making her black curls bounce. "Dag and I killed a blight bogle together. That's how we met." She thought of adding, *I'm not beguiled, just in love,* then wondered how you could demonstrate the difference. Cress's breath was coming in shallow pants; Fawn caught up her other hand and squeezed it. "She wouldn't run off lessn' you drove her."

The carpenter gulped. "Do it, Lakewalker. Whatever you're going to do. Help her, make the hurting stop!"

Dag nodded, leaned forward, and placed his spread right hand over the apparent gap of his left atop the woman's lower belly. His face got that no-look-at-all Fawn had witnessed while he'd been healing Hod, as if he had no attention to spare for animating it. *Absent* in a very real sense. He paused; his merely expressionless expression returned.

"Oh," breathed Cress. "That eases me . . ."

Fawn wondered if anyone else was thinking of the man who'd been fooled, uncertain if this was the ground reinforcement working or a sudden disaster. Could Dag hope to be gone on the rise before a soaring fever made the difference apparent?

"That was the ground reinforcement," said Dag. His brief grimace was meant to be a reassuring smile, Fawn guessed. "It needs a few minutes to set in."

"Magic?" whispered the carpenter hopefully.

"It's not magic. It's groundwork. It's . . ." Dag looked up for the first time at the ring of faces looking down at him: the two boat bosses, another curious keeler who might be Wain's right-hand man, a worried Pearl Bend couple who could be relatives or relatives-in-law; behind them, Whit and Hod and Hawthorn. "Huh." He set his hand on the deck and levered himself to his feet. Fawn scrambled up with him. He turned slowly, looking at the restive crowd still milling on the shore, craning their necks and muttering. Bending, he murmured to Fawn, "You know, Spark, it's just dawned on me that I got a captive audience, here."

She whispered back, "I figured they were just fixing to beat you to a pulp and then set the pulp on fire."

His grin flitted past. "Then I'll have their full attention while they're waiting their chance, won't I? Better 'n six cats at one mouse hole."

He stepped to the bow in front of the chicken coop. A wide wave of his left arm invited the folks on the foredeck to attend to him, and ended catching Fawn around the waist and hoisting her up to stand on a step-rail beside him, a head higher than usual. He left his stump hidden behind her back, but raised his hand in a temple-touch, half-greeting, half-salute, and began loudly, "Did you all out there hear what I just told Mark-carpenter and Cress? No? I explained that I just set a ground reinforcement around the infection in Cress's gut. Now, I reckon most of you don't know what a ground reinforcement is, nor ground neither, so I'm going to tell you . . ."

And then, to Fawn's astonishment, he went off into much the same

explanation of ground and groundwork that he had practiced so halt-
ingly around the dinner table in West Blue. Only this time, it wasn't
nearly so halting: smoother, more logically connected, with all the
details and comparisons that had seemed to work best for his dubious
Bluefield in-laws. His talk was in what Fawn thought of as his patroller-
captain voice, pitched to carry.

Whit came up behind her shoulder, wide-eyed, and whispered in her
ear, "Are they following all this?"

She whispered back, "I'm guessing one in three are smart or sober
enough. That makes a good half-dozen, by my reckoning." But the crowd
of keelers and townsmen had all stopped muttering and rustling amongst
themselves, and the folks leaning on the nearby boat rails looked as entertained as if Dag were a stump speaker.

To Fawn's greater astonishment, when Dag finished with groundwork and malice blight, he glanced over his shoulder and went right
on with sharing knives. And then the silence grew as rapt as if folks
were listening to a ghost story. "Which was why," Dag finished, "when
that fool patroller boy broke his bone knife in the fight up behind the
landing the other night, all those Pearl Riffle Lakewalkers acted like
someone had murdered his grandmother. Because that's pretty near just
what happened. That's why they've all been so blighted touchy with you
lately, see . . ."

And, Fawn thought, at least some of the men listening did seem to
see. Or at least, they nodded wisely and murmured canny comments, or
parted their lips in wonder, round-mouthed and silent.

"Some of you may be wondering why no Lakewalker has told you
these things before. The answer is standing beside you, or maybe it's in
your own hand. You say you're afraid of us, our sorcery and our secrets.
Well, we're mortal afraid of you, too. Of your numbers, and of your

misunderstandings. Ask poor Verel, the camp medicine maker, if he'd dare to go near a farmer again soon. The reasons Lakewalkers don't explain things to you as we should aren't our fault alone."

A number of the men clutching cudgels looked at one another and lowered them discreetly to their sides, or even behind their backs. One shamefaced townsman dropped his altogether, glanced to either side, and folded his arms somewhat defiantly.

Dag drew a long breath, letting his gaze pass over the crowd; each fellow whose eyes he met rose a bit on his toes, so that a ripple passed along them in response, as though Dag had run his hand through the still water of a horse trough. "Now, Mark-carpenter here asked if ground-work was magic, and I told him no. Ground is part of the world, and groundwork works best running with the grain of the world and not against it. Like the difference between splitting a log or cutting it cross-ways. And it isn't miracle either, at least no more than planting corn is a miracle, which it kind of is, really. Farmer puts four kernels in the ground, and hopes one will sprout, or two will let him break even, or three will let him get ahead, and if it ever came up all four, he'd likely call it a miracle. Groundwork doesn't make miracles any oftener than planting, but some days, we do break even."

Dag glanced again over his shoulder. "Now, if you folks will excuse me, I have some groundwork to try. And if you all are the hoping sort, you can hope with me that tonight I can break even."

He finished with his old self-deprecating head-duck and salute, and turned back to his waiting—patient, Fawn decided. *He's sure not fooling now.*

"Absent gods," he breathed to Fawn's ear alone. "If there's any rules left to bust, I can't think of 'em."

"Flyin', patroller?" she breathed back. That had been Aunt Nattie's shrewd description of Dag the night he'd mended that glass bowl so gloriously, surprising himself even more than he'd surprised the Bluefields.

His lips tweaked up in shared memory, but then his gaze grew grave again. He went back to Cress's side and lowered himself, folding his long legs awkwardly. Hitching his shoulders, he leaned forward and went absent again.

Just as quick as that: here, then gone . . . there, wherever there was. Fawn made mental inventory as she settled again in her place beside him. There was a pot of hot water still on the hearth, blankets just inside the cabin.

A whimper from Cress became a stuttering groan. Fawn grabbed her hand and held it hard as it tried to jerk defensively toward her belly. Fawn was afraid to touch Dag lest she spoil his concentration, but the color draining from his skin made her think he was chilling down awfully fast. The night air was growing raw despite the torches and lanterns held up by their spellbound audience.

The minutes crept by, but in not nearly so many as it had taken for Hod's knee, Dag sat up and blew out his breath. He stretched his shoulders, rubbed his face. Cress had stopped crying and was staring up at him with her lips parted in awe.

"I've done what I can for now. The pocket drained well and the swelling's eased." Dag's brow wrinkled. "I think . . . maybe Cress and her sister and Mark had best stay the night here on the boat. That infection's still pretty warm, could do with another ground reinforcement in the morning. A Lakewalker who'd had gut work, they'd give him boiled water with a little sugar and salt in it to drink, and then maybe tea, but nothing else for a couple of days. Rests up your sore innards while they heal, see. Wrap her up warm by the fire tonight, too."

"But I didn't see you do nothing," said Boss Wain, in a tentative voice that contrasted remarkably to his earlier bellowing.

"You can take my word or leave it, for all of me," Dag told him. He glanced down at Cress, and the ghost of a smile tugged his lips. "If you'd been a Lakewalker, you'd have seen plenty."

He was shivering. Fawn said firmly, "It's time to get you inside and warmed up, too, maker mine. I think you might do with some of that hot tea inside you."

He bent his head to smile at her, then held her tight with his left arm and swooped in for a long, hard kiss. His lips were cold as clay, but his eyes were bright as fire. *Clay and fire makes a kiln,* Fawn thought woozily. *What new thing are we shaping here?*

Despite all the excitement, their exhaustion assured that the boat's visitors were asleep on hides and furs in front of the hearth almost as soon as they'd been tucked in. Dag fell into the bedroll in their curtained retreat as if bludgeoned, and was soon snoring into Fawn's fluttering curls. In the morning, after tea, Dag laid one more ground reinforcement in Cress, then sent the couple and their supporters on their way. Bleary, hungover keelers in the gray mist of dawn were much less threatening than drunken, wound-up keelers by torchlight, though to their credit, they repeated their good deed with the door in the opposite direction without audible complaint.

As soon as the much-reduced parade was out of sight, Dag told Fawn, "Pack up a picnic lunch, Spark. We're going for a ride."

"But it looks to be a nasty, chilly day," Fawn pointed out, bewildered at this sudden scheme.

"Then bring lots of blankets." Dag lowered his voice. "The Pearl Riffle Lakewalkers made it real clear yesterday that they didn't favor me rocking their boat. I think I just turned it turtle. I expect Captain Osprey will hear all about it by breakfast at the latest. I don't know if you ever saw Massape Crow in a real bad mood, but Amma puts me horribly in mind of her. By the time she makes it across on the ferry, I aim to be elsewhere."

And at Fawn's protest, added only, "I'll explain as we ride." He went off to saddle Copperhead.

With Fawn perched on the saddlebags and her arms tight around his waist, Dag sent Copperhead cantering south for a good two miles down the straight road, which was exhilarating but blocked conversation. Despite the double burden, the horse seemed more than willing to stretch his legs after his days of idleness. It wasn't till Dag turned left and began a winding climb up into the wooded hills designed to thwart trackers that he explained about his fruitless first visit to the Lakewalker camp, and how the tavern gossip and its dangerous aftermath with the medicine maker had drawn yesterday's hard-eyed delegations down on him. Fawn grew hotly indignant on his behalf, but he only shook his head.

The gray fog did not burn off as the sun climbed, but rather, thickened. Fawn's stomach was growling when Dag spotted a huge old tulip tree fallen with its roots in the air, sheltering a scooped-out depression blown full of dry leaves. With their blankets atop and below, they soon arranged a hidey-hole as cozy as a fox's den, and settled down to share a late, cold breakfast—Dag declined to light a fire, lest the smoke betray their refuge. His burst of energy departed him as abruptly as it had seemed to come on, and he fell into a drained doze. Happily, he woke sufficiently refreshed after a few hours to while away the leaden afternoon in the best slow lovemaking they'd had for weeks. The mist outside turned to drizzle, but did not penetrate their nest. After, they curled up around each other, Fawn thought, like hibernating squirrels.

Dag woke from another doze with a laugh on his lips. It was the most joyful sound she'd heard from him in a long time. She rolled up on one elbow and poked him. "What?"

He pulled her to him and kissed her smile. "I really saved that woman's life!"

"What, hadn't you noticed?" She kissed his smile back. "Like this medicine making, do you? I think it suits you." She added after a moment, "I'm right proud of you, you know."

His smile faded into seriousness. "My people are full of warnings about this sort of thing. It's not that they think it can't be done, and it's not the beguilement problem—they hardly mentioned that. It's that farmers think it's magic, and that magic should always work perfectly. I won Hod, and I won Cress, but only because I was lucky that she had something I was pretty sure I could get around. I can think of half a dozen illnesses I couldn't have touched."

She curled his chest hair around one finger and set her lips to the hollow at the base of his throat. "What would you have done then?"

"Not started, I suppose. Been a good boy just as Captain Osprey wanted. Watched that poor woman die." His brows knotted in thought. "Some young medicine makers get very troubled when they first lose patients, but I'm surely past that. Absent gods help me, I used to kill people on purpose. But the greatest danger Lakewalkers fear is that if they try to help and fail, the farmers will turn on them. Because they have, you know. I'm not the first to be tempted down this road. And I don't know how to handle it. Heal and run? Amma's complaint wasn't made-up."

"Or maybe," Fawn said slowly, "if you stayed in one place for a long time, folks would get to know and trust you. And then it would be safe to fail, sometimes."

"Safe to fail." He tasted the phrase. "There's a strange idea, to a patroller." He added after a long moment, "It's never safe to fail hunting malices. Someone has to succeed, every time. And not even *at any cost,* because you have to have enough left afterward to succeed tomorrow, too."

"It's a good system," agreed Fawn, "for malices. Not so sure about it as a system for people."

"Hm." He rolled over and stared at the tiny pricks of light coming through the holes in their blanket-tent, held up by the ragged roots. "You do have a way of stirring up the silt in my brain, Spark."

"You saying I cloud your thinking?"

"Or that you get to the bottom of things that haven't been disturbed in far too long."

Fawn grinned. "Now, who's going to be the first one to say something rude and silly about the bottom of things?"

"I was always a volunteerin' sort of fellow," Dag murmured, and kissed his way down her bare body. And then there was some very nice rudeness indeed, and giggling, and tickling, and another hour went away.

❧

They arrived back at the *Fetch* well after dark in a cold drizzle that the boat folk plainly thought a great disappointment, inadequate to the purpose of putting anything bigger than a barrel over the Riffle. Whit reported four visits from tight-lipped Lakewalkers looking for Dag, two from the camp captain, one from the ferry boss, and one from the furtive medicine maker, which Dag said he regretted missing. Dag plainly was keeping his groundsense pricked, Fawn thought from his jumpy mood, but as no one else came by and the night drew on, he relaxed again.

After their long picnic day, neither of them wanted to do anything in their bedroll but cuddle down and sleep, which Fawn thought Dag still needed. She had slept, she thought, about an hour, when she was wakened by Dag sitting up on one elbow.

"What?" she murmured drowsily.

"I think we have a visitor."

Fawn heard no footsteps on the front deck, nor bleats from Daisy-goat or complaints from the chickens. "Berry pulled the gangplank in, didn't she?"

"Not coming down the path. Coming from the river side. Absent gods, I think he's swimming."

"In that cold water? Who?"

"If I'm not mistaken, it's young Remo. Why?" Dag groped for his trousers, pulled them on, and swung off their pile of hides, fighting his way out past their makeshift curtain.

"What should I do?" Fawn whispered.

"Stay here, till I find out what this is all about."

He padded softly back past the piles of cargo and the bunks, careful to wake no snoring sleepers. Fawn barely heard the creak of the back hatch open and close.

10

The oil lantern burning low on the kitchen table was clever Tripoint handiwork, a glass vase protected by a wire cage mounted on a metal reservoir, with a metal hat and wire handle above. As he slipped past, Dag plucked it up. He eased out the back hatch and closed the door before hanging the lantern on the bent nail and turning the valve key to brighten the flame. He peered out over the water. Any moon or stars were veiled by the overcast sky, and the lamplight reflected off the inky surface of the river in snaky orange ripples.

In a few moments, the ripples fluttered and the lines of light broke up as a dark shape emerged from the darker shadows. Dag made out Remo's wet hair, then his paler face as he turned again and stroked toward the rear of the *Fetch*. His left arm, still scored with stitches, was up out of the water towing a makeshift raft, some driftwood hastily lashed together with vines and willow withies. Atop the raft sat folded saddlebags, and atop them a cloth bundle. Remo swam up under the *Fetch*'s rudder oar, and gasped, "Please . . . please will you take these?"

If the boy had swum from the opposite shore in this weather, he had to be chilled to the bone and close to exhaustion, youth or no youth. Dag raised his brows, but bent over the back rail, grasped the cloth bundle, and heaved it onto the deck. Ah, Remo's clothes and boots, of course. Then the saddlebags, containing, from the weight of them, the rest of his life's treasures. Dag grunted, but set them by the first bundle.

He turned to watch Remo trying to lift himself up along the rudder pole on shaking arms, only to slide back. Dag sighed, leaned out, extended his hand, and helped pull the shivering young patroller up over the back rail as well. The abandoned raft ticked against the rudder and drifted away.

Remo nodded gratefully and bent to pick with numb fingers at the knot tying his bundle. He rubbed his naked body down with the wrapping towel and shuddered into his clothes. "Th-thanks."

"Folks are sleeping inside," Dag warned in a low tone. He wondered whether he ought to haul the boy indoors and plunk him in front of the hearth, or throw him back over the rail. Well, he'd doubtless find out shortly.

"Yes, right," whispered Remo. His lip was back to normal size, but the bruises around his eye had darkened to a spectacular deep purple, just starting to go green at the edges. He finished pulling on his shirt and stood with hands clenching and unclenching at his sides, as if his next words were clotting in his throat.

He'd gone to a great deal of trouble for this private talk, Dag thought, only to choke off now. Caution reined in Dag's curiosity just enough to convert his *What can I do for you?* into a more noncommittal general eyebrow lift.

It was enough to break the logjam, anyway. Remo blurted, "Take me with you."

"And, ah—why should I do that?"

The return stare was uncomfortably Hod-like.

"Do you even know where I'm going?" Dag prodded.

"Downriver. Away. Anywhere away from here."

This was the one, Dag reminded himself, who'd had to take his great-grandmother's broken and wasted bone back and present it to his waiting family. It wasn't hard to guess that the scene hadn't gone well, though that still left a wide range of *badly* to choose from. Remo had been the more conscientious of the feckless partners, the one who'd tried to do the right thing. And had it come out all wrong. *Well, you know how that goes, old patroller.* Dag rubbed his head and sat down on the bench against the cabin wall. His arm harness being off for the night, he rested his stump unobtrusively down by his left side and laid his hand on his right knee.

Remo dropped hastily to the deck and sat cross-legged, perhaps feeling dimly that supplication went ill with looming.

"There are ten other boats heading the same way," Dag pointed out. "Why the *Fetch*?"

Remo shot him a look of tight-lipped exasperation. "Because they're all full of *farmers*."

Dag wasn't quite sure how to take that emphasis. He was tempted to haul Remo by the nose in a few more circles till he recanted his tone, but it was late and Dag was tired. One circle, maybe. "So is this one."

Remo's second shaft wobbled closer to the real target. "*You* left."

"I was not—"

"If you weren't banished, they as much as drove you out. Made it impossible for you to stay. I thought you'd understand." His bitter laugh betrayed both his youth and how close to the end of his rope he dangled.

Oh, I do.

"You threw off their old rules. You rebelled. You took your own path, alone. And no one is going to say to *you* it's just because you're a stupid fool kid!"

We see the world not as it is, but as we are. "That's not exactly what I'm about, here. Now, I can say, whatever's going on over there between you and your family, it will pass. Great griefs must, if only because no one has the stamina to keep them up that long." *Not more than twenty years, leastways.*

Remo just shook his head. Too sunk in his own misery to listen? To hear?

Dag thought ruefully of his own family, and revised his sage advice. "And while you're waiting, there's always the patrol."

Remo shook his head harder. "The Pearl Riffle patrol is lousy with my family. Most of my brothers and sisters and half my cousins. Uncles and aunts. And every one of them thinks they should have been left great-grandmama's knife instead, and they're *right*." He gulped and added, "I went to the camp knife maker yesterday to ask for my own bonded knife, and he wouldn't even agree to make it for me!"

In your mood? Dag mentally commended the cautious knife maker. He said patiently, "Whatever your troubles are, you won't defeat them by running away from them. My road's not for you. What I'm saying is, the best thing you can do for yourself and Pearl Riffle Camp is go back over there and pretend this swim didn't happen."

Remo's jaw worked. "I could swim halfway back. That would solve all my troubles."

Dag sighed, but before he could marshal his next argument, the door swung quietly open and Fawn slipped through. She had a blanket wrapped around her nightdress, shawl-fashion, and a lumpy cloth in her hand. She glanced at Dag and tossed her head. "Maybe I can put a word in here. Being the resident expert at running away from home." She opened her cloth. "Here, have a chunk of cornbread. I make it sweet."

Remo accepted it mechanically, but stared at it in some bewilderment. Fawn handed a piece to Dag and took the last one herself. Dag took a grave bite of his own and motioned Remo to proceed. Fawn leaned against the cabin wall and nibbled, then nudged Dag's knee with her bare foot. "This is your Remo, right? Or is it Barr?"

Dag swallowed crumbs and made the demanded introduction. "Remo, yes. Remo, this is my wife, Fawn Bluefield."

Remo, food in hand, made a confused half-effort to stand, then settled back as Fawn waved him down. He returned her nod instead. "You're the farmer bride? I thought you'd be . . . taller."

Dag quelled his curiosity as to what several adjectives Remo had just swallowed along with his cornbread, there. *Older* was undoubtedly one.

"Now," said Fawn cheerily, "the first thing I know for sure about running away from home is, plans made in the middle of the night are not always the best. In the morning—after breakfast—you can generally think of much better ones." She exchanged a meaningful look with Dag, and went on, "It's the middle of the night now, and you're keeping Dag from my bed. But I just laid a big pile o' those furs and blankets we used for last night's visitors in front of the hearth. They're real warm now. Toasty, even."

Remo was shivering, his damp skin clammy in the misty chill. Strands of hair escaping his soaked braid draggled across his furrowed forehead.

"If you got yourself warm, I bet you'd drop off right quick despite your troubles, tired as you look. All that swimming, after all. I expect you're still hurting, too."

In all ways, not just his bruises, thought Dag. He suppressed a smile at the way Remo stared up open-mouthed, blatantly susceptible to what were likely the first kindly words he'd had from anyone for days. A pretty young woman offering him food, a soft bed, and sympathy was not someone he was going to argue too hard with, even if she was a farmer.

"Wise Spark," Dag commended this. "Take her up, Remo; you won't get a better offer tonight." He had the bare wisdom himself not to add aloud, *It beats swimming halfway across the river all hollow.* No good sprinkling salt on wounds, even self-inflicted ones.

Remo glanced as if surprised at his hand, now empty of leftover cornbread, and around at the flatboat and the darkness of the rippling river. Only a few orange lights from Pearl Riffle Camp shone through the half-naked trees on the far hillside.

"This boat's not going anywhere tonight anyhow," Fawn pointed out.

Remo shook his damp head. "No, but a rise is coming on. You can feel it, out in the middle. That's why I swam across now. By morning it'll be too dangerous, and by tomorrow night, these boats will all be gone."

Remo had lived in this ferry camp all his life; Dag expected he knew the river's moods well. Further, swimming the river left no evidence behind of what direction he'd taken. A missing horse would have said north; crossing on the ferry would have left witnesses who could say south. Once he was gone beyond groundsense range, none could guess if he'd gone north, south, east, or west. Or halfway across the river.

A faint breeze raised goose bumps on Remo's lavender-tinged skin, and he yielded abruptly. "All right."

"Be real quiet," whispered Fawn, her hand on the door latch. "They're mostly asleep in there."

"Berry?" Dag murmured.

"I told her you'll explain in the morning. She rolled back over."

"Ah."

With Remo tucked into the bedding before the hearth like an oversized, overtired child, Dag and Fawn at last made it back to their own curtained bed. Their bedroll, unfairly, had chilled down. They rubbed each other half-warm, and laced limbs together for the rest.

"Wondered why you chose just then to come popping out," Dag murmured into Fawn's curls. "You thought he meant it about that half-river, did you?"

"This time o' night, you do. Besides, as ragged as Remo looks, and as big as this river is, the decision might be pulled out of his hands before he made it back to the other shore." She added reflectively, "It's a lot bigger than the river by West Blue, that way. Drowning yourself in that one would have called for a lot more determination. Here, you could do it just by inattention."

He hugged her tight. "No half-rivers."

"Anyhow, I took exception to your advice about not running away from your troubles. You picnicking fraud."

An unvoiced laugh shook his chest. "But I'm not running away. I'm running toward." He sighed. "And just in case I miss any, they follow after and join me. It's going to be a crowded boat, Spark."

In the morning, Fawn found to her excitement that the cracked mud at the bow had disappeared under new water. But Berry said the rise was not yet high enough to get the *Fetch* over the Riffle. Since Fawn suspected the moving boat would not be safe for complicated cooking, she indulged herself instead in what might be the last chance for a while to fix a real West Blue–style farm breakfast.

This resulted in a lot of munching around the crowded foldout kitchen table, and not much talk at first that wasn't requests to pass things, although most everyone shot curious peeks at Remo. Berry was bland about the uninvited guest. Bo was either hungover, or indifferent. Hod seemed intimidated, with lots of looks Dag's way as if for reassurance. Whit was wary—Remo was both older and bigger than he was, as well as being a full-fledged patroller. Hawthorn had a baby raccoon, a prize from one of his coal-salvaging coins, and had no interest in anything else.

Fawn had to admit, the bright-eyed creature was wildly cute. Hawthorn was trying to keep it in his shirt, with limited success; Whit observed that he should have bought a baby possum for that. Bo said raccoons were destructive, and if Hawthorn didn't keep his pet under control, Bo would make it into a hat.

"Now, Bo," said Berry, cutting across Hawthorn's hot protests. "Could be worse. Remember Buckthorn's bear cub?"

Bo wheezed a laugh, and gave over harassing Hawthorn. Hawthorn, Whit, and Hod then fell into a debate about what to name the kit. Dag said little, but Fawn spotted him slipping the curious animal a fragment of bread.

Remo didn't attempt to join the talk. He was medium-tall, broad-shouldered; Dag called him a boy, but he looked like a full-grown man to Fawn. He was not good-looking so much as good-enough-looking, but was probably attractively healthy when he wasn't recovering from a beating. His hair, dry and re-braided, hung halfway down his back. He finished cleaning his plate and looked up at last. "So," he said to Dag. "Did you decide? Can I come with you?"

Dag left off helping to spoil the raccoon kit and returned the look. "I don't know. Can you?"

Remo frowned uncertainly.

Dag went on, "I'm not your patrol leader. More to the point, this isn't my boat. I just work on it. If you want to arrange passage, you have to talk to the boat boss like anyone else." He nodded across at Berry. Remo's head turned to meet her rather ironic gaze, and he blinked.

Dag's response seemed a bit unfeeling to Fawn, but maybe he had a reason. She waited for it to emerge.

Remo finally addressed Berry: "How do I arrange passage, then?"

"Well, you have to either buy it or work it. Everyone else here's decided to work it."

"How much to buy it?"

"How far are you going?"

"I . . . don't know." He glanced at Dag. "Graymouth, I guess."

Berry named a sum of coins that made Remo's face set. No deep purse here, it seemed. Fawn was unsurprised.

"And working?" said Remo.

"I don't know. What can you do? I know you know narrow boats—I heard about the coal-boat boys you fellows pulled out of the Riffle. Can you man a flatboat sweep?"

"I once did it for a day. Barr took me venturing . . ." He broke off.

"Hm." Berry glanced at Dag, who shrugged. "I didn't expect to have one Lakewalker crewman, let alone two. So . . . how's this. I'll take you on trial as far as Silver Shoals. That's my next stop. Papa and Alder were seen there last fall by some keeler friends, so I know they made it at least that far."

Remo made an inquiring noise; Whit explained rather sternly about Berry's quest. Remo looked a bit taken aback to be reminded that people besides himself could have serious troubles, and he squinted as if seeing Berry for the first time. Fawn imagined the view through the haze of his own misery was still a bit blurry.

"Be aware," said Dag, with a hint of challenge in his voice, "that if you choose to work, from the time you set foot on the *Fetch* till the time you step off Boss Berry *will* be your patrol leader."

Remo shrugged. "It's just a flatboat. How hard can it be?"

Whit frowned on Berry's behalf, but before he could wade in, a *clunk* from the back of the boat brought everyone's head around.

"Log," said Bo.

"Current's moving better," said Berry. The *Fetch* shifted, and the ropes from the stern to the shore flexed and groaned a trifle.

Hawthorn ran out to the back deck and returned, reporting, "The river's going browner. Not long now!"

The cleaning up was left to Whit, Hawthorn, and Hod. At home Whit had slacked off abominably on this chore, making game of Fawn, but with Hawthorn and Hod to ride herd on, not to mention Berry watching, he became wonderfully scrupulous all of a sudden. Fawn was considering breaking out her spindle for a little hand-work, when someone on the shore path trotted past the bow and shouted, incomprehensibly, "Hey, Berry! The upstream keelers are on the tow!"

Berry rose, grinning. "Come on, Fawn. You've got to see this."

She picked up an oddly shaped leather bag from under her curtained bunk. Fawn grabbed her jacket and followed; Whit trailed after.

The late morning was overcast and chilly but not foggy. More of the leaves were down from the trees, drifted into sodden yellow piles from yesterday's rain, leaving the bare boles the same gray as the air, receding ghostly up the hill. Berry led down the path past the wharf boat and the ferry landing. The Lakewalkers' ferryboat, Fawn saw in passing, was moored on the other side of the river, and its capstan rope had been taken down. No one would be crossing after Remo just yet.

A little above where they'd gathered coal, Berry hopped up onto some tallish rocks that gave a fine view down over the Riffle. At the bottom of the rapids, which were slowly disappearing under the rising water, two keelboats were moving along opposite shores. On the far shore, the keel was being towed against the current by a team of eight oxen handled by what looked to be a couple of local farmers. On the near shore, the keel was being heaved along by about twenty straining men pulling a long, thick rope. Fawn at last saw why all the trees on the riverside of the shore path had been cut to stumps. Both boats had men running back and forth on their bows with long poles, fending off rocks and clumps of wrack. The two crews were shouting back and forth across the water, rude insults and challenges and a lot of chaff about *We'll be at Tripoint before you!*

"Is it a race?" asked Whit, staring in delight.

"Yep," said Berry, and bent to draw a polished hickory-wood fiddle from the case. She tested the tuning by plucking at the strings and turning the pegs, stood up on the highest rock facing downstream, and drew a long note, starting low and winding high until it seemed to leap off the fiddle altogether. She added, "I've fiddled my keeler boys up over every shoal and riffle on the Gray and the Grace. It makes the work go easier if you have a rhythm. When the boat boss wanted them to go faster, he'd bribe me to play quicker. The boys would bribe me to play slower. It could get pretty lucrative."

Fawn spotted a lot of fellows out on the Pearl Bend wharf boat in the distance, shouting the contestants onward. "I don't suppose you have a bet down on this race, do you, Berry?"

The riverwoman grinned. "Yep." And set her bow to her strings, sending an astonishingly loud ripple of notes echoing down the river valley. The grunting keelers on the near shore looked up and cheered, and bent again to their rope in time to the boatman-music. Fawn guessed it was a familiar tune, likely with familiar words, and likely with a rude version, but the men had no breath to spare to sing along. The oxen on the other side seemed indifferent to the noise.

When the repeats on the first song began to get dull, Berry switched to a second tune, then a third. Some of the other boat bosses from Possum Landing had come out to watch the show, including Wain from the *Snapping Turtle*. Berry moved back from the rocks to the other side of the path as the keelboat drew near and began yet another tune, even livelier, her elbow pumping. Her audience shuffled after her. Strands of her lank blond hair, loose from the horse-tail at her nape, stuck to her face, and she alternated between either blowing them out of her mouth or chewing on them in her concentration. Her fingers stretched, arched, flew so fast they blurred. Everyone else was watching the race; Whit was watching Berry, his eyes alight and his mouth agape.

The sweating keelers, passing, hooted at her, then bent and stamped and strained. She made her fiddle echo their cries almost like a human voice. They were pulling well ahead of the oxen. Berry kept her music chasing them up the shore until they reached the wharf boat, reeled in their keelboat, threw down their rope, and sent up a victory whoop. She made her fiddle whoop back, and finally dropped it from under her chin, panting.

The flatties and locals who had collected along the bank to watch tromped back up the riverside to settle their bets and hoist a drink at the wharf boat, but neither Berry nor the other boat bosses on the lookout point joined them. Instead, they peered upriver, where one of the flatboats had loosed from its mooring and was being slowly sculled out to mid-river. "There goes the *Oleana Lily*," someone muttered. They were all watching, Fawn realized, to see if this scout could clear the shoals without hanging up or tearing out its hull.

"If he makes it, will we go?" Fawn asked Berry.

"Not just yet," said Berry, shading her eyes and squinting at the drifting flatboat, which was picking up speed. "The *Lily* drew a shallower draft than me even before I undertook to load on extra people, a ton o' window glass, and a surly horse. You see that long pole sticking up out of the water below the Landing wharf boat?"

Fawn gazed where she pointed at what looked like a slim, bare tree, stripped of side branches, with a limp red flag nailed to its top some thirty feet in the air. Every half foot along its length, it had a groove circling it daubed with red paint, until a few feet up from the water where it changed to black paint. "That tells you how high the water is, right? Is it safe to take the shoals when it changes from red to black?" There seemed to be several feet left for the water to rise.

"Depends on how low in the water your hull and cargo ride. When it changes to black, any fool can get his boat over."

"The marks go all the way to the top," said Fawn uneasily. "The water doesn't ever go that high, does it?"

"No," said Berry, and Fawn relaxed, until she added, "By the time it's about halfway, the pole usually rips out and washes away."

Fawn finally saw why the river people relied on wharf boats, instead of a fixed dock like those she'd seen around Hickory Lake. The wharf boats would rise and fall with the shifting water, could be pulled ashore for winter, and wouldn't be torn away by floods, drifting trees, or grinding ice. Were less likely to be, she amended that thought.

A few of the boat bosses lined up on the rocks yelled comments or advice to the steersman of the *Oleana Lily,* which were proudly ignored, but most watched in silence. When the steersman leaped to one side and pulled hard, not a few leaned with him, fists clenching, as if to add their strength to his. When the boat sideswiped a rock, scraping along the whole length of its oak hull, the boat bosses groaned in synchrony. They bent like trees in the wind, then all straightened together and sighed at what sign Fawn could not see; but the *Lily* was past the last rock and clump of wrack and still moving serenely.

The group broke up and began to trudge back up the path; a couple of men trotted ahead. Berry detoured only briefly at the crowded wharf boat, collecting a couple of bone-cracking hugs from some keelers and money from several more sheepish boatmen. She refused pressing offers of cider, beer, or the drink of her choice. "I got me a boat to launch, boys. We've been here too long—you've drunk this place dry!"

She paused on the bank to squint again at the ringed pole. "Well, not quite yet. But I think we might load on that horse."

Back at the *Fetch,* they did so, laying extra timber for the gangplank. Dag soothed his dubious mount across the bending boards. Copperhead snorted in dismay, but followed; the boat dipped as he clomped down onto the deck and was penned with Daisy-goat. Whatever groundwork Dag was doing to assure the gelding's cooperation was as invisible to Fawn as ever, but she noticed Remo raising his brows as if secretly impressed.

Berry climbed onto the roof to watch two neighboring boats launch at the same time and tangle their long side oars, with a lot of swearing. Berry scrubbed at the grin on her lips. "I think we'll go next," she said to Fawn at her shoulder. "It's a dice roll, at this point. With a crowd like this, you want to go late enough to get the highest water, but not so late that some hasty fool before you wrecks his boat and blocks the channel again."

Still, the launch seemed leisurely. Hawthorn dodged back and forth untying ropes from the trees and casting off, and Hod limped around to roll them up in neat coils, two at the front corners and two at the back corners. The oarsmen did not sit to their long sweeps, but stood, walking or leaning back, pushing or pulling as needed. Berry took the rear steering oar, with Bo and Whit on one side sweep and Dag and Remo on the other. It made Berry's shouted directions simple: "Farmer side, pull!" "Patroller side, pull!" "Now the other way, patrollers! Turn her!"

A thump shook the boat as the hull glanced off a hidden stump. A crash from the kitchen sent Fawn racing inside to make sure everything was locked down and to check, for the third time, that her cook fire was well-banked and penned behind its iron barrier. When she came out again the boat was in the middle of the river, which still looked bigger than from shore. They swung into alignment with the channel. In contrast to its earlier placid clarity, the water was an opaque bright brown and visibly rolling, carrying along storm wrack from far upstream in an impressive current. She couldn't imagine the bruised Remo swimming it now.

Fawn debated whether to cling to the bench by the front door or climb to the more precarious roof, then decided she was tired of being too short to see things. She climbed up and found herself a spot in the exact middle just beyond the radius of any of the three oars. She sat down firmly, wishing there were side railings, or a handle to grip. Maybe she could talk Bo into adding one. But for now the view was very fine.

They entered the Riffle proper, and the *Fetch* picked up speed. Dag suddenly yelled, "Bear right, boss! There's a big snag about two feet under down there!"

Berry stared where his finger pointed. "You sure? I don't see a boil!"

"Try me!"

"All right," said Berry dubiously, and leaned on her oar to twist the boat past, alarmingly close to some highly visible rocks on the far side. Bo had to lift his sweep to clear them, and shot his boss a questioning look, which she answered with a shrug before leaning on her oar to bring the boat around again. Whit, lending his strength to Bo, looked utterly exhilarated.

"Your boat steers like a drunk pig," Remo said, hauling briefly backward against the current at her next order.

"Yeah, it ain't no narrow boat, is it," Berry returned cheerfully, unoffended. "Live and learn, patroller."

A flatboat crowding close behind them chose to veer wider around the rocks. With a loud *clunk,* it shuddered almost to a stop, then began to swing around its bow. Cries of dismay and a lot more swearing followed as its crew fought to keep it from turning broadside to the current. Berry looked at Dag and raised her brows high. He touched his temple back at her.

"Well, live and learn," Berry repeated, in quite another tone.

Fawn stared back at the receding Lakewalker ferry landing, wondering if they were being watched by irate council eyes. They passed rocks, clogs of dead trees and debris including a bloated sheep, and less visible hazards, then the river widened and the odd swirls like soup boiling disappeared. The surface smoothed.

"Ease up, boys, we're over the Riffle and away at last," said Berry. "It's a straight reach for the next three miles."

Dag and Bo stood down from their sweeps. On the easy stretches, Fawn understood, the oarsmen would take turnabout, and the boat would float along all day without stopping. Dag came over, sat down beside her, stretched out one leg, and gave her a hug around the shoulders. "All right, Spark?"

"It's wonderful!" She stared at Pearl Bend, already falling behind on the far shore, and back to the boat boss, now leaning happily on her oar. "We're going so fast!"

Berry's agreeing grin stretched as wide as the river. "Fast as a horse can trot!"

11

The *Fetch* made thirty river miles before the dank autumn dusk, when they tied to the bank for the night in the middle of, as nearly as Fawn could tell, nowhere. Berry explained regretfully that she didn't want to try running downriver in the dark—Whit's appalling suggestion. In addition to the hazards of rocks, stumps, sand bars, ledges, and wrack, the river divided frequently around shifting islands. A boat choosing the wrong side might find itself stuck in a channel that petered out into impassible thatch, and its crew plagued with the arduous task of towing it up around the head of the island again, difficult enough for a keelboat, designed for such work, worse for a balky flatboat. Boats had been abandoned in such situations, Berry said. Fawn poked Whit to silence when he began to volunteer Dag for a night pilot. Even were Dag's groundsense recovered to its full one-mile range, some of these islands were as much as five miles long. And the river was quite scary enough in daylight.

After that, Fawn was too busy fixing dinner to worry further. With the excitement of the day wearing off, everyone seemed glad to turn in early. In addition, Fawn suspected Dag was still bone-weary from healing the Pearl Bend woman, at some level underneath the mere physical. He seemed to wrap himself around Fawn in their bedroll more for comfort than anything else; from the intensity of his clutch he was feeling low on comfort tonight. She wondered if having Remo aboard bothered him. A curtain gave no privacy from groundsense. Although since farmers couldn't veil their grounds at all, she supposed Remo must have shut himself off, as Dag often did, to spare himself the abrasion. Weary herself, her musings trickled into sleep.

They made a dawn start, and by midday, the clouds had thinned and the sun came through, if still a bit pale and watery, which Fawn thought lifted everyone's moods. At Berry's suggestion she experimented with the clever iron oven that fitted in the *Fetch*'s hearth, and was able to produce pies for lunch without stopping the boat. Or setting it on fire, a fact of which she was more proud than of the pies, which, truly, everyone ate with flattering appetites. In the afternoon, she found Dag taking a break from his oar, lounging on the bench on the front deck keeping pleasantly idle company with Copperhead, Daisy-goat, and the chickens. She leaned over the rail and eyed the smooth, brown water. The *Fetch* seemed to be outracing a sodden log, but that floating leaf was definitely pulling ahead.

"Dag," she said, "do you think you could catch us enough fish for dinner?"

He opened his eyes and sat up. "What kind?"

"I don't even know what kinds there are in this river. Bo was going on about how much he liked a good channel catfish fried up in a cornmeal crust. Do you think you could get enough of them to feed eight?"

His slow smile tucked up the edges of his mouth. "I could try, Spark."

He rose and stretched, only to drape himself over the side of the boat just behind the pen, his left arm trailing down. His hook barely grazed the water. Fawn watched in sudden doubt. When he'd persuaded that big bass to leap so startlingly into their laps at Hickory Lake, they'd been in a much smaller boat, with lower sides. The *Fetch*'s rail seemed awfully high to expect any fish to jump over. Were catfish even the jumping sort? Fawn had a dim idea that they lurked about on the river bottom.

When nothing happened in about ten minutes, Fawn considered wandering back to her domain by the hearth to think about what she could do with bacon for dinner, again, except she was afraid Dag was falling asleep. Granted he would doubtless wake up when he hit the water, and he could swim better than she could, and if she grabbed for his legs he might simply pull her over with him, but still. But then he stiffened, muttering, "Ha." She craned her neck.

And then he was jerked half over the thwart, with a startled scream of *"Blight!"*

Fawn lunged, managing to get her hands around his belt. She snatched one look over the side before she leaned frantically backward, feet skidding on the deck. A huge gray splashing shape seemed to have half-swallowed Dag's hook, and was trying to yank him into the river. In order to eat him, near as Fawn could tell. She supposed turnabout was fair play, but she wasn't willing to give up her best husband to some awful river monster. "Dag, let go of it! It doesn't matter! I don't want a fish dinner that much!"

"I can't! Crap! The blighted thing's stuck on my hook!" Dag clawed futilely at the buckles on his arm harness, then managed to get his knees down far enough to clap them to the inboard side of the hull and give a mighty heave. Fawn added what weight she had.

Several feet of flailing gray wetness rose from the brown water and arced through the air to land on the mid-deck with a thud that shook the whole boat. Dag, still attached to its mouth-end, perforce fell with it, and Fawn with them both. She scrambled back on her hands and knees. The startled Copperhead tromped his hooves in the straw of his pen, jerked his head, and whinnied, and Daisy-goat bleated in fright, whether of the plunging horse or of the river monster Fawn was unsure.

"Whit!" Dag yelled. "Bring a mallet! Quick!"

The uproar brought the entire crew of the *Fetch* rushing to the bow. Whit, Hod, and Hawthorn jammed up in the front hatch. Berry, Remo, and Bo peered down over the edge of the cabin roof. Whit vanished, Hawthorn fell through, and Hod, eyeing Copperhead's antics, hung back. Fawn bounced to her feet for her first clear view of the most enormous fish—if it was a fish—she had ever seen or imagined. It was nearly as long as she was tall. Its head was huge, eyes glaring yellow, mouth wide and ugly, and Dag's left arm was still stuck partway into its gaping gullet. Red gills flexed, and its long barbels snapped like whips as it heaved and flopped. Dag was jerked around with it.

Whit reappeared with a shiny new shovel grabbed from Berry's stock of Tripoint goods, and proceeded to try to beat the fish to death, or at least into submission, urged on by Dag: "Hit it again, Whit! Harder! *Ow!* Aim for its head, blight you!"

The catfish finally stopped moving, mostly, and Dag drew a long breath, sat up, and carefully worked his hook free from inside the thing's mouth. If the monster had succeeded in pulling him overboard, would it have taken him to the bottom and drowned him before he could get loose? Fawn felt faint. Dag shook out his arm, looked around at his riveted audience, and cleared his throat. "There, Spark. Fish dinner for eight."

"Thank you, Dag," Fawn choked. Which won a flash of a smile back, the strain in his face easing. He almost succeeded in looking as if he'd meant to do all this, but she thought he might be picturing that trip to the river bottom, too.

"Fish dinner for forty-eight, more like," said Whit, measuring out the gleaming corpse. "How much does this thing weigh?"

"Looks like about a hundred, hundred-twenty pounds, to me," drawled Bo. An expert opinion, Fawn presumed. Whit whistled.

"Well," said Berry, looking down at Fawn and shaking her head. "You did tell me your husband could catch fish, I'll give you that. Never seen anyone use live Lakewalker for bait, before."

"How do you fit it in a *pan?*" Fawn nearly wailed. She pictured it draped across her skillet with an arm's length hanging over each side. She wouldn't be able to lift it. Could it be cooked on a turnspit, like a roasting pig?

"Whit and Hod will clean it and cut it up for you," said Dag genially. He stretched his back and climbed somewhat gingerly to his feet, wiping his hook on his trousers. "I'm sure Bo will be happy to tell them how."

Whit's look of big-eyed enthusiasm faded a trifle, but he didn't protest. He and Hod hauled the catch to the back deck to butcher under Bo's amused supervision.

Briefly alone with Dag in the kitchen-and-living-quarters while he tidied himself, Fawn reached up and gripped him by the shoulders. "You do know, you don't have to go and do any stupid fool thing just because I ask, don't you? I rely on you to be the sensible grown-up around here!"

He slipped his arm around her back, and protested, "I didn't think a fish dinner was an unreasonable request. Not on a river, leastways. If we were in the middle of a desert, now, that would have been a right cruel demand." He blinked innocently at her.

Demonstrating cruelty, she poked him in his bruised stomach and scowled.

He glinted his eyes at her in a very unfair way, but said, "I admit, it did get a little out of hand."

"If you're saying that thing nearly swallowed your arm, I saw." She gripped him again and shook him, or tried to. "You could have picked out a smaller one. You don't have to prove anything to me!"

His answer was a silent laugh as he dropped a kiss on her curls. She gave up and relaxed into his offered cuddle, even though she wasn't sure whether it was intended as apology for scaring her out of her wits or just as distraction.

She added more pensively, "I don't mind the idea of eating a fish, though on the farm it wasn't a dish we fixed too often. But I'm not sure I like the idea of a fish big enough to eat me."

"Oh, there are channel cats bigger than that one. And there are sea sturgeon that come up the lower Gray that are easily ten times that size."

"Don't tell me!" said Fawn. "First swamp lizards with giant teeth, now fish big enough to swallow the *Fetch*? What parts are you taking us to, anyhow? I'm making a new rule. You don't bring any more fish onto this boat that are bigger 'n me! You hear me, Dag Bluefield?"

All she got back was a smirk and a hug. Which had its own satisfactions, but wasn't precisely an answer.

For dinner, Fawn fried up catfish fillets till everyone aboard was stuffed to the gills and groaning. The white flesh was sweet and succulent, but it went on forever. Breakfast was the same. Mid-river lunch was cold catfish sandwiches. And dinner. And another breakfast. After which Whit led a rebellion and sneaked the remains over the side, where they would feed its cannibal catfish cousins, Fawn supposed. Torn between indignation at the waste and profound relief, she said only, "Huh!"

To which Whit replied, "Yeah, well, be more careful what you ask Dag for, eh? That fellow scares me, some days."

In the late afternoon, Dag asked Berry if they might pull in briefly at another Lakewalker ferry camp, this one on the south side of the Grace. Berry, Fawn knew, was anxious to ride this rise past Silver Shoals, lest the *Fetch* be grounded above that hazard and have to wait again for the next upstream storm. But she eyed Dag and nodded, saying only, "Make it quick, Lakewalker."

The deserted landing was nothing but a bare patch on the bank, the camp up over the bluffs invisible from shore. This ferry served not a wagon road but merely a patrol trail, and so had few farmer customers. Dag hiked off alone, inviting neither Fawn nor Remo, not that Remo would likely have accepted.

The Pearl Riffle patroller had obeyed Berry's boat-boss orders without comment or complaint, but had kept equally silent between work shifts. Whit's most ham-fisted overtures of would-be friendship seemed to slide right over him. Fawn didn't think he even talked to Dag, though she did catch him watching the older man as if he were trying to figure something out and couldn't. Hod was skittish around Remo, but then, Hod was skittish around everyone.

Hawthorn took the goat ashore to graze for an hour. Remo volunteered to do the same for Copperhead, which surprised Fawn, till she noticed it gave him an excuse to settle down well away from the rest of the crew. Whit followed Berry around. Fawn, between chores at last, announced, "I think I'll walk up to meet Dag."

The path up from the shore along the hillside was slick with damp yellow leaves, in need of pruning, and unpeopled. A half-mile up it, she met Dag coming back through the gray-brown woods. From his set face, she guessed his errand had not prospered.

"No luck?" she asked quietly.

He shook his head. "I tried not to repeat my mistakes. I told 'em my name was Dag Otter Hope, and made them think I was a private courier. I might as well have spared my pride. They didn't have any extra knives. Well, it wasn't a big camp, no surprise."

"That's a pity." Fawn turned to stroll beside him. They were not only out of earshot of the *Fetch* right now, they were out of groundsense range. It seemed a good chance to ask. "Your Remo doesn't look too happy. I wondered what you were thinking of doing about him."

"He's not my Remo."

"He's following you, it seems."

"Just because we're on the same boat doesn't mean I've adopted him."

"Is he going to be in a whole lot of trouble back at Pearl Riffle for deserting?"

Dag sighed. "Maybe. I'm not sure he grasps the difference between *banished* and *resigned*."

"He doesn't say much." Fawn considered this. "Or anything."

"He's listening, though." Dag cocked his head. "Think back to when I came to West Blue, before we were wed. It was the first time in a longer life than Remo's that I'd ever slept in a farmer house, ate at the family table. Listened to farmers talk to each other. Remo's never even been an exchange patroller, never been away from his home camp before, any more than Whit. I think it won't hurt to just let his new impressions accumulate for a while."

"Mm," said Fawn. "Yesterday afternoon while he was on break from his oar, he went and stole Hawthorn's raccoon kit. He huddled up in a little dark hidey-hole in amongst the stores, and coaxed it to curl up on his lap. And just sat, hunched up around the one little live thing that wasn't mad at him. Till Hawthorn finally missed it, and found him and made him give it back."

"Nobody on this boat is mad at Remo."

"Nobody on this boat seems real to Remo, 'cept you. And you aren't best pleased with him."

Dag made a noncommittal noise.

Fawn lifted her chin and went on, "I don't think it's good for Lakewalkers to be cut off sudden from everything they know. They get to pining."

"I can't argue with that," Dag sighed.

She cast him a sharp glance. *Yeah.*

"Hod's looking better," Fawn observed after a few more paces, trying for a lighter note. "His skin's a nicer color, and he moves brisker, now he's getting the good of his food. He hardly uses your stick. He watches you. He watches Remo watching you, too." She bit her lip. Maybe not as light as all that. "Jealous isn't quite the right word. Neither is envious. But . . . Hod does make me think of a dog with one bone, somehow."

Dag nodded. "It's the beguilement. Can't say as I've had any fresh ideas about that, yet."

"You trying? Because—ow!" Fawn grimaced and stopped. The branch she'd carelessly shoved out of her face had whipped back, proving to be from a thorny honey locust. After scratching her scalp, it had snagged in her hair.

"Hold up." Dag reached over and gently detangled her, snapped the branch, and bent it down away from the trail. "I do purely hate these evil trees. Find 'em on patrol all over Oleana. They don't bear fruit, their wood's not good for much, and there's just no excuse for those thorns."

"I suppose a hedge of them would be good for stopping unwanted visitors."

"Better for a bonfire." Dag hadn't released the branch; he had an absent look on his face that made Fawn suddenly uneasy. "Nobody would miss this tree. If a malice was to ground-rip a tree like this, it would be a positive good." He paused. "Remember that mosquito I ground-ripped back in Lumpton Market?"

"Yes. It made you very sick."

"I've been wondering ever since what would happen if I tried something else."

"Dag, I'm not sure that's such a great idea." Just what kind of mood was he in right now, after whatever frustrations he'd encountered up at that camp?

"Yes, but see—medicine makers. I've been wondering about medicine makers. The senior ones do have craft secrets. They have such dense grounds—it's pretty much a marker of the gift. Not necessarily long groundsense ranges, mind. Hoharie would never make a patroller, but she can give ground reinforcements day after day. I always thought that was a natural ability, but what if it's something else? I never saw . . ."

"No more mosquitoes," said Fawn firmly. "No more bugs of any kind. Mind what happened to your arm?"

"Yes, but what about this here tree? It never would be missed."

"It's about a hundred million times bigger than a mosquito."

"I grant you, that mosquito did make me itch. Maybe this would make me all thorny and sessile."

"What, are you saying that no one would be able to tell?" And at his bland look, added insincerely, "Sorry." His lips twitched.

Fawn couldn't imagine what taking in the ground of a whole tree would do to a person. Neither could Dag, she suspected. But he was getting an alarmingly intent look on his face, eyeing the thorn-studded branches and bole. The spines were three-pronged and stuck out in jagged packs from every possible part of the repulsive thing.

"Use some sense," she begged. "At least don't start with a whole tree. Start with something smaller." She scrabbled in the pocket of her skirt, found a few tiny lumps still stuck in the seams, and freed one. "Here."

Dag held out his hand to receive the gift. "An oat?"

"I was feeding Daisy and Copperhead earlier."

"One oat?" He stared down at his palm.

"If you ate an oat it wouldn't make you sick, even if you ate a whole bowl of oats. Not like a big bowl of mosquitoes. Or of nasty thorns. Even Copperhead wouldn't eat off that tree!"

"That's . . . an interesting parallel. Huh. We do take in the ground of our food and convert it—everyone does. Lakewalkers, farmers, animals, every living thing. Natural ground reinforcement." He glanced up and down the trail. They were quite alone. He closed his palm, rubbed his hook across the back of his hand, and opened it again. The oat was gone. He wiped a faint gray powder off against the seam of his trouser leg. "Huh," he said again. His face was suddenly very sober.

"What did it do?" Fawn asked anxiously.

He rubbed his left arm. "Well, I can feel that bit of ground stuck in me. Not near as unpleasant as the mosquito's. Got any more oats in your pocket?"

"Remember, your fever and swelling didn't come on right away. Give that one a day. *Then* try another. Maybe."

"Berry's got a whole barrel of oats on the *Fetch*," Dag said thoughtfully. "There's a notion to test. If you can eat it safely, can you groundrip it safely? I think I'd rather just eat my food, but I can see where this might be faster in some emergency."

"I don't know, Dag. I think maybe you need a Lakewalker partner for this sort of experiment." Someone who could tell if he was doing dreadful things to his ground—and warn her, so she could put her foot down. Because, remember that catfish. "Do you think Remo would be any help?"

Dag let his breath trickle out through pursed lips. "I'm not sure I would want to try this in front of young Remo. This is a pretty disturbing sort of groundwork for any Lakewalker who's seen a malice operate."

"Has Remo?"

Dag's brows twitched up. "Maybe not, Spark. There's been no reports of malice finds in the Pearl Riffle patrol area for quite a few years.

If he's never exchanged, then no, he's not had that chance yet."

"So he wouldn't know malice magic if he saw it."

"Maybe not."

Leaving the thorny honey locust unmolested, to her intense relief, Dag started back down the trail. He hugged Fawn close to his side as they dodged hindering branches.

"So," said Fawn, "if dense ground marks a medicine maker, and long groundsense range marks a patroller, what do you call someone who has everything?"

"Knife maker. Sir. Or ma'am."

"There are women knife makers?" She had only met Dar, Dag's hostile knife maker brother. Hostile to farmer brides, anyhow.

"Oh, yes."

"So what do you call someone who hasn't got either density or range?"

"A farmer," Dag replied with a twitch of his lips, then looked down. "Sorry."

Except that he actually was, a little. Fawn tossed her head.

"Only it isn't so," he went on more thoughtfully. "We meet a sprinkling of farmers near the threshold of ground function—at least, we do if we get out of the camps to patrol, and are paying attention. Aunt Nattie. You, in a way."

"Me?" said Fawn, surprised. "I've got no groundsense range. I've got no groundsense to *have* a range."

"None at all," he agreed cheerfully. She almost poked him. "But you have unusual ground . . . not density, though there's that, too, but brightness. Your ground is very beautiful, you know. Why do you think I call you Spark, Spark?"

"I thought it was a pet name. For a pet," she added provokingly.

He gave her a pained look, but said, "No, it's pure description. As natural as it would be to call red-haired Sassa Carrot Top."

"Carrot tops are green. I'm a farmer girl, trust me." Still, she had to smile a little. Was beauty in the groundsense of the beholder? Evidently. Other Lakewalkers had not seemed as entranced by her ground as Dag. Maybe it was a matter of taste, *as the old lady said as she kissed the cow*— Fawn smiled outright in memory at Aunt Nattie's old saw. Yet—elusive thought—what if it was so? What if it was neither flattery nor infatuation, but true report? Dag was a truthful sort of fellow, by preference. What if Dag really did see her as brighter, the way sensitive or sore eyes squinted at the sun? The way thirst saw water . . . ? She asked abruptly, "What do I give you?"

"Breath."

"No, seriously." She stopped; he turned to face her.

"I was serious." He wore his serious smile, anyhow.

"Back when Hod first came on the *Fetch,* you said I didn't know what I gave you, every day. Do you?"

In that moment, she discovered the difference between stopped and stopped cold. "What?" he said.

"What do I give you *in your ground?*"

A slow blink. He wrapped her in a hug, bent his head, and explored her mouth in a long kiss. Not evading the question—testing it. He released her at last, his brows drawn in, and she came down off her toes.

"Balance," he said. "You—untangle me."

"I don't understand."

"Neither do I."

"Dag . . ." she protested. "If you can't figure this out and tell me, who else can?"

He ducked his head in wry accord. "You make my ground disappear. No, that's not right," he continued, as she began to protest again. "Imagine . . . imagine your muscles all full of knots, pulled and sore and stiff, fighting you with every move you try to make. Now imagine your muscles when they're working smooth and warm, effortlessly, without thought. To will is to have is to be, all one. Like a perfect shot."

"Hm?" He wasn't there yet, but he had hold of the tail of something, she could tell. Something elusive.

"When I make a perfect shot with my bow. Which happens from time to time, though never often enough. I don't just mean get the arrow into the target, which I can do pretty consistently. In a perfect shot, everything's there the same as any ordinary shot, yet not. For that fleeting moment, it's like—my worries, my body, my bow, the target, even the arrow disappear. Only the flight is left." His hand closed, opened. "My left-hand groundwork is like the flight of the arrow without the arrow."

He stared down as if his words had fallen into his palm as unexpectedly as a jeweled tooth.

He just said something important. Hang on to that, farmer girl, even if you don't quite get it yet. "So why am I not beguiled, yet Hod is? You've done groundwork on us both. The why and how has to lie somewhere in the space between us three."

His mouth slowly closed; the gold of his eyes turned flat and unreflective. But he said only, "We're keeping Berry," and walked on.

Fawn matched his pace, satisfied that her question had not been dismissed; his sudden abstraction only marked the wheels in his head turning creakily in unaccustomed directions. *So maybe I should keep that axle grease coming, huh?*

12

Despite the delay from Dag's fruitless errand, the *Fetch* made another eight downriver miles before darkness drove them to shore. At supper, Berry opined that they would reach Silver Shoals by tomorrow, if the river didn't fall overnight. Dag smiled into his mug of fizzy cider as he watched Fawn's and Whit's eyes light up at the news. They both quizzed Berry and Bo about the famous rivertown, which filled the time until Hawthorn and Hod carried the dirty dishes to the back deck to wash up. This looked to take a while, as Hawthorn was attempting to teach his raccoon kit to ride on his shoulder at the same time. There was still a long stretch of evening left, and it wasn't raining, windy, or excessively cold.

"Bow lessons?" suggested Dag to Whit. "It's been a few days." Since before the distractions of Glassforge and Pearl Riffle.

Whit looked up eagerly, but said, "Isn't it too dark? The moon won't be up for a while, and even then it's none too full."

"The *Fetch* has plenty of lanterns, if Berry'll lend us a couple."

Berry nodded, looking interested.

"Set up one by the target, the other by us," Dag continued. "Easy."

"Sounds like a waste of good rock oil. And lanterns," said Bo.

"Whit will aim by it, not at it. Or so we hope," said Dag. Whit grinned sheepishly. "You need to learn to shoot in all kinds of light. If you were a Lakewalker, I could teach you to shoot in complete darkness, by groundsense. Those slow-moving trees in broad daylight are getting too easy for you. We'll have to shift you on to peppier targets soon. But tonight we can borrow Copperhead's and Daisy-goat's spare straw bale and set it up above the bank a ways."

Fawn said, "Wait, who has to go grope for the misses in the dark? We'll be losing my good arrows!" Arrow retrieval had been her job in Whit's prior camp-side lessons, mostly due to an understandable protectiveness of her craftwork.

"Not a one," Dag promised. "You collect the hits, and I'll undertake to find the misses." He cast a mock-stern eye on Whit. "That means you'd better tighten your aim, boy."

With Fawn carrying the lanterns, Whit thumped off to lug the straw bale onto shore. Berry followed after. Bo got up to poke the fire, then settled back with his feet to the hearth. Dag finished his tankard of cider in a more leisurely way.

Remo had listened to all this with a frown. Now he said, "You're really teaching that mouthy farmer boy Lakewalker bow-work? Why?"

"That would be my tent-brother, yes, and because he asked."

Remo hesitated. "I suppose it's been a long time since you had a chance to handle a bow yourself," he said more quietly. "Were you good, once?"

Remo hadn't heard all the Dag stories from Saun, it seemed. Maybe it was the livelier Barr that Saun had struck up his acquaintance with. From his tone, Dag guessed Remo was attempting to apologize. *Pity he isn't better at it.* Dag let a couple of tart replies go, including *I was a fairly dab hand last week,* in favor of "Come on along and make yourself useful, if you like. There are some things I just can't show Whit about his left-hand grip, for one."

Remo looked taken aback at the notion.

Dag added evenly, "You know, if you're going to be living with farmers, it's time you started learning how to talk to 'em."

"I'm not going to be living with farmers!"

"Well, it doesn't appear you mean to be living with Lakewalkers, either. What, do you figure to perch up a tree with the squirrels and eat acorns all winter? It's got to be one or the other."

Remo's lips compressed. Dag just shook his head and rose to stroll after Fawn and Whit. He called over his shoulder, "If you change your mind, come on out."

Whit had set up his bale on some deadfall a reasonable distance upstream, that being the direction with fewer trees and more level footing, and was arguing with Fawn over where to place the lantern. They compromised on a nearby broken cottonwood stump. Fawn pinned the increasingly tattered cloth target with the two concentric circles painted on it to the bale. The white fabric showed up well in the modest yellow glow. They returned to the boat, and Whit ran inside to get his bow and arrows. When he came back out, Remo followed slowly, though only as far as the boat's front rail, on which he leaned.

The night was quiet—the songs of frogs and insects stilled by the recent frosts, the current barely lapping the dark shore. Dag settled comfortably on a fallen log by the second lantern, offering corrections to Whit's stance and grip as he sped his dozen arrows. After that, Dag had to grunt up and go with Fawn to find six of them. But the next round, he only had to collect two. Pleased, he made Whit back up ten paces for the following round.

Then Hawthorn arrived, agog to be let try. At least his hands were clean from the dishwashing and wouldn't leave grubby prints on the bow. Dag promptly set up Whit as Hawthorn's instructor, a good old-patroller trick to force a novice to focus on his problems from the outside for a change. Dag grinned to hear some of his own phrases falling glibly from Whit's lips. Remo, Dag was bemused to note, kept creeping closer, first to the end of the gangplank, then to the end of Dag's log. Every once in a while his hands twitched. If Remo owned a bow, he had not brought it with him on his cross-river swim. Well, if he wanted to play with this one, he would have to ask Whit, just like Hawthorn.

When Dag returned from seeking the next set of misses, and had suggested Whit move Hawthorn rather closer to the target, Remo said suddenly, "Collecting spent arrows was always work for the beginners. Not for a captain."

Not for a captain with twenty-seven malice kills to his name, did he mean? On whose behalf was Remo offended? "You fetch back your share when you were a tad, did you?"

"Yes!"

"Good for you."

Fawn wandered back to watch over Dag's head, finding a task for her restless hands by kneading Dag's shoulders, which disinclined him to get up and run down the shore again. She said, "What about you, Dag? You haven't practiced in a while either."

"Now, Spark, I've been pulling a sweep half the day. I'm tired. If I can't hit that target it'll make me look nohow in front of all these youngsters."

"Ha," she said unsympathetically, abandoned her lovely task—he tried not to whimper out loud—and dodged back up the gangplank. In a couple of minutes, she came back toting Dag's adapted bow and his well-stocked quiver.

Remo sat upright, eyes widening. "What's that?"

"That's my bow." Dag unscrewed his hook from his wooden wrist cuff, dropping it into the leather pouch on his belt. He stood, put his weight into bending the short, heavy bow, and strung it. Setting into his cuff slot the carved bolt that stuck out where the grip would be, he rotated the bow once to seat it, making sure the string ended up to the inside, and snapped the lock down.

"A farmer artificer that Fairbolt Crow knew up in Tripoint made it for me, some years ago," Dag went on. "And my arm harness and all my gear that goes with it. It took us four tries to get a design that would work. Interesting fellow. He started out making wooden arms and legs for miners and foundry men, see, as the folks in those hills do a deal of that dangerous work. He'd been a friend of Fairbolt's back when Fairbolt was a young patroller up that way. Seems you never know when you'll need an old friend."

Remo's ground was as shuttered as his expression; hard to tell how he took this pointed moral. He said only, "It looks like it has a heavy draw."

"Aye, it's a right bear. It was all compromises by that point. We needed a short length, to keep it out of my way if I had to move in a hurry, because putting it down takes a minute and dropping it isn't an option. At the same time, I needed penetrating power. When I had two hands, I used a much longer bow, matching my height and arm length. Took me months of practice to finally change all my long-bow habits." His remaining fingers had bled.

"You're pretty matter-of-fact about it all."

Dag had no idea what Remo was going to hear out of this, but he chose the truth anyway. "I wasn't at first. I took a long time getting over it." A little jerk of his left arm made his meaning clear. "I won't say no one can be a blighted fool forever, because I've seen some try for it. But I finally decided I didn't care to be in that company."

Remo grew rather quiet.

The appearance of this fascinating new device brought Hawthorn back, bouncing in curiosity. Whit, trailing amiably, said, "Oh, yeah, give us a show, Dag!"

"This rig's no good for teaching you, mind. It takes a different stance and style than your bow, and besides, I'm full of old bad habits you likely shouldn't be allowed to watch."

Whit grinned. "Do as I say, not as I do?"

"There is that," Dag agreed.

Hawthorn pulled one of Dag's heavy, steel-tipped arrows from the quiver. "Hey, these are lots fancier than the ones we were using! I bet these'd work better!"

"Nothing wrong with the ones you were using. They all had the same maker." Dag winked at Fawn. "Here, give yours to me—put that one back, now . . ."

Hawthorn said *Ow*, and Fawn pried the arrow out of his bloodstained grip, saying, "Give that over before you poke your eye out. Those are Dag's good arrows. He doesn't waste them on target practice."

"Well, what does he use 'em for?"

Dag prudently let that one go by unanswered, and swapped for Whit's quiver. He strolled up to a distance from the target about equal to Whit's longest range, hitched his shoulders, and spent a leisurely few minutes putting the dozen flint-tipped arrows into the general vicinity of the two circles. It felt good enough. "Nope, Hawthorn, they all work just fine. See? You can go collect those." Hawthorn scampered off.

"My style isn't pretty enough for contest bow-work," Dag remarked to Whit. "I argue with the purists about that. I claim a patroller is going to have to shoot from all sorts of strange positions, and that it doesn't pay to get too fussy. They claim—well, maybe I won't repeat what they claim."

His muscles felt reasonably warm and loose, now. Fawn was watching him. Humming unmusically under his breath, Dag took up his quiver, clamped it awkwardly under his left arm, and removed about half its contents to give to her for safekeeping, leaving twelve of the heavy arrows more loosely packed. He shrugged the quiver up over his shoulder and walked back to the shooting spot. Made an estimate of the range to the straw bale, turned, and added another dozen paces to it. Stretched, emptied his mind, turned back.

The first arrow went its way with a notably louder twang; Whit's head snapped around from the gangplank where he'd been talking to Berry. The second followed before the first hit the target, then the third. One after another, Dag reached, set, pulled, released. The extra range hadn't been just swagger; he needed all that distance to get that lovely streaming effect of two and three arrows in the air at a time.

Twelve shots in less than a minute. *It's been a while since you did* that, *old patroller!*

He lowered his stubby bow and studied the results. Well, they had all ended up somewhere within the outer circle. Not a tidy heart-shot, but that straw bale sure wasn't getting away. He rather regretted not being able to spell out *D + F* in quivering feather shafts. He could imagine them spelling a trailing sort of *argh!* maybe, if he squinted a lot, which was almost as good.

Fawn came up beside him, peering in fascination. "Was that the pure flight? My stars, it did look like something!"

"Almost," Dag said in satisfaction. "Right workmanlike, leastways. You can go fetch those, Whit."

Whit trotted off. Dag sensibly decided to quit while he was ahead. He did off his equipment and turned the makeshift range back over to Whit. Hawthorn was ruthlessly set aside when Berry, watching from a seat on the gangplank, barely hinted that she might like to try her hand. Dag gave himself over to an indolent seat on the log and a cozy cuddle with his wife. It was getting chilly; he'd favor going in soon.

Fawn nudged him and pointed, grinning. Remo was now standing up talking to Whit, earnestly demonstrating some fine point of gripping a bow. Dag replied with a finger laid to the side of his nose and a lift of his eyebrows. His lips twitched up. When next it came time to collect Berry's misses, Remo waved Dag back and went with Whit.

A loud thump from the boat turned both Berry's and Dag's heads around. "What was that?" said Berry. But as no more noises followed, she turned back to watch Whit and Remo.

Dag stayed twisted, brows knotted. *Hod. What's the fool boy gone and done now?*

In another few moments Bo stuck his head through the front hatch, and called, "Lakewalker, you want to come in here for a minute?"

No, I don't, Dag could not answer. He rose, waving the concerned Berry back to the game with Whit and Remo. Fawn gave him a sharp look and tagged along.

In the kitchen and bunk space, he found Hod sitting on the floor in front of the hearth with his right trouser leg rolled up, rocking and whimpering.

"What happened?" Dag asked.

"I fell down out on the back deck," sniveled Hod. "Hurt my knee. Fix, can't you fix it again, please?"

Fawn drew breath in ready sympathy. Dag sighed, knelt, and let his palm hover above the joint, opening himself briefly. The damage was not deep, but Hod had definitely re-cracked one of the healing fissures in his kneecap, blight it.

Fawn said sternly, "Hod, were you trying to carry too much at a time again? Remember what I told you about a lazy man's load?"

"No, I just fell down," Hod protested. He seemed to think a moment. "I was trying not to step on the raccoon."

A quick groundsense check found the kit snoozing peacefully in Dag and Fawn's bedroll. Dag looked up and frowned.

Bo caught his gaze and lifted his hairy brows. After a long, considering pause, he said slowly, "Actually, that kit was nowhere around. Didn't sound like Hod tripped on the deck, either. I think he slammed into the back wall."

Hod blurted in a flustered voice, "You didn't see me!" Then added belatedly, "Yeah, that's right. I tripped and fell against the wall."

Dag sat back on his heels, taking in the ugly implications. "Hod, tell me the truth. Did you just go and knock your own knee into the wall *on purpose?*"

Hod would not meet his gaze. "Fell," he muttered belligerently.

Dag drew a long breath. Hod's was a real injury, but not a real emergency. There was no need for hasty stopgaps. Dag could take time, slow down, think. That didn't feel like his best skill, right now, but maybe, like bow-work, it took practice. *I wonder if my brain will bleed?*

Hod seemed stupid and surly, but maybe those were just other words for inarticulate and terrified. Dag had won this trouble by making assumptions about Hod. When his own habits of concealment met Hod's mute bewilderment, it wasn't any wonder that enlightenment didn't generally follow.

"Hod, you were standing right there on the front deck when I did the groundwork on Cress's belly-hurt. Did you hear what I said to her and Mark about beguilement? Did you understand it?"

Hod managed somehow to shake his head yes and no at the same time. Dag couldn't tell if that meant he hadn't heard, hadn't understood, or was just uncertain if it was safe to admit to either.

"Do you even know what beguilement is?" Did Dag? It seemed he was finding out.

Hod shook his head again, but then offered, "Lakewalker magic? They make people give them bargains. Or make the girls"—he shot a glance at Fawn and turned red—"want to go out to the woodpile with 'em."

The latter, Dag guessed, being a Hod-ism, or perhaps Glassforge slang, for seduction. "It's not either of those things," he asserted, possibly untruthfully. At least it wasn't either of those in this case, and he didn't want those slanderous—or cautionary, pick one—notions cluttering up Hod's thinking. Or his own. "You and I are both finding out just what beguilement really is, because I beguiled you by accident when I healed your smashed knee. It seems to happen when a farmer—that's you—experiences Lakewalker groundwork and wants it to happen again. Wants it so bad he or she will do crazy things to get it." He let his finger tap the swollen skin over the knee; Hod whimpered.

"Hurts," said Hod. Complaint, or placation?

"No doubt. What I want to know is why you want a ground reinforcement again so bad you'd go and hurt yourself to coax one out of me?"

Hod looked as panicked as a possum in a leg-hold trap. He gulped, but kept his lips clamped.

"It's not a trick question, blight it!" Hod jumped; Dag gentled his tone. "Lakewalkers give each other ground reinforcements all the time—well, often—and they don't work like that on us. I have to know. Because I've a notion, a dream, leastways, that I'd really like to settle down with Fawn someplace and be a medicine maker who heals farmers, but I sure can't do that if I'll make all my patients crazy. I'm really hoping you can help me figure it out."

"Oh," said Hod. In a voice, absent gods, of Hoddish enlightenment. "Me, help you? Me?" He looked up at Dag and blinked. "Why didn't you say?"

Why hadn't he said? Maybe *he* should go out to that back deck and hit, say, his head against the wall . . . He glanced up to find Fawn looking at him with her arms crossed and her brows up as if she quite seconded Hod's question.

Evading answering, Dag went on, "First off, this has to stop. You can't go on hurting yourself just to get a ground reinforcement."

Hod looked up in hope. "Would you give me one without me hurting?"

"I don't think I'd better give you any more at all. I'm not sure if beguilement wears off over time or not, but I'm pretty sure repeating makes it worse."

"Oh." Hod gingerly petted his knee and blinked tears. "You gonna make me . . . wait?"

"If only I had two hurt Hods, I could make one wait and one not, and compare, and then I'd know."

"Which one would I get to be?"

Dag couldn't quite figure out an answer to this. He ran his hand through his hair.

Fawn put in, "In a way, you do have another Hod to do the waiting. Cress. If we ever get back to Pearl Bend, say, next spring, you could check up on her."

"Good point, Spark."

Hod, too, brightened. He looked at Fawn almost favorably.

"I guess that frees me up to try something else." Dag squinted into the fire. He hated to interrupt the first voluntary interchange Remo had enjoyed with his boat-mates since the start of this trip, but needs must. "Fawn, would you go ask Remo to come inside for a moment, please?"

Her brows twitched up, but she nodded and went off. In a few minutes, Remo shouldered through the shadowed supplies into the firelight and lantern glow of the kitchen area, Fawn trailing. He frowned at Hod and looked his question at Dag, *What's this?*

"Ah, Remo," said Dag. "Glad you're here. Have you been taught how to give minor ground reinforcements, out on patrol?"

"Verel taught all of us who had the knack," said Remo cautiously. "I've never had a chance to try it out for real."

"Good, then it's time you had some practice. I would like you to put a reinforcement into Hod's hurt knee, here."

Remo stared, shocked. "But he's a farmer!"

"I thought you wanted to break the rules?"

"Not that one!"

You're choosy all of a sudden. Dag rubbed his lips, reminded that Remo hadn't been there to witness Cress. Or Hod's original injury, either. Dag steeled himself and gave a brisk description of both incidents, finishing, "With Hod beguiled by me already, the last thing I want to do is make it worse. What I don't know is what would happen if a beguilement was divided amongst two Lakewalkers. I'm hoping—wondering, leastways—if the division might halve the problem."

Remo's lip jutted in suspicion. "Are you trying to foist this off on me?"

"No," said Dag patiently, "I'm trying to solve a groundwork problem. For myself, yes, but if I can solve it for myself, there might be a chance I'd solve it for a lot of other medicine makers as well. It seems worth a shot."

"I thought you were a patroller."

"Old habits die hard. Did you think I quit only because I ran mad over a pretty little farmer girl a third my age?" Fawn raised her brows ironically at him; he tipped her a wink. "I'm also becoming—trying to become—a maker." *I'm just not sure of what.* "Take a good look at Hod's knee, down to the ground, and tell me if I'm wrong about that ambition."

Reluctantly, Remo knelt down next to Dag beside Hod, who gave him a worried smile. He glanced aside at Dag and opened his ground for the first time in days. Dag saw Remo's wince as the unveiled farmer grounds pressed upon him: the dark old knots of the watching Bo, the mess of Hod, Fawn's brightness. It took him a moment to draw his focus in upon the injury. When he did, his brows climbed. "You did all that? *Verel* doesn't pull breaks together that tight!"

"I could have wished for Verel. Or someone, to guide and guard me. I almost groundlocked myself."

Remo's ground, open to Dag at last, was in about the uproar he expected. Upset patroller—he knew the flavor well. Sometimes he regretted that reading grounds did not give access to thoughts, although most of the time he had better sense. *We already know too much about each other.* Who knew what Remo would perceive of him? "What's on your mind?" he asked gently.

Remo licked his lip, still a little sore. "I don't know what you want from me!" he blurted. "You didn't have any use for me before."

Dag almost said, *I just told you what I wanted*, but hesitated. "How do you figure?"

Remo hung his head, and muttered, "Never mind. It's stupid." He made to lumber up, but Dag held out his spread hand, *stop.* Remo drew breath. "When you got in trouble the other day with that fish. You called for Whit. The farmer. Not for me. Remo the botch-up. Well," he added fiercely, "why would you?"

Remo, who hadn't been able to save his partner from trouble before? Leaving aside the flash of jealousy about Whit, Remo was wounded, it seemed, in his oversensitive conscientiousness. Dag couldn't hand him back his self-esteem gift-wrapped. He wondered if it was time for the full tale of Wolf Ridge again. He was reminded of Mari's trick of hauling him and his maiming along when she wanted to shame local farmers into pitching in with pay or supplies after a malice kill in their area, and grimaced in distaste. No. Parading his old griefs to shame Remo was not the right road; Remo had shame enough for two already. *You're making this too hard, old patroller. Keep it simple.*

"You were on your oar. Whit was off duty. That's all." *Not everything is about you, youngster, though I know you can't see that right now.* He was also reminded of Fawn's farmer joke about the parents' curse: *May you have six children all just like you.* Was there an equivalent patrol captain's curse? That would explain a lot . . .

Remo swallowed. "Oh." A flush bloomed and faded in his face, but some of the tension went out of him.

Dag refrained from pointing out that he'd have yelled for Remo before Hawthorn or Hod, lest the touchy Pearl Riffle boy just think himself called the second-best of a bad lot. *Tact, old patroller.* They were getting somewhere, here.

Remo's hand went out toward Hod's knee, then drew back. "Is he going to end up following me around like he does you?"

Dag rejected both *If I knew, I wouldn't have to test it* and *He can't follow both of us, leastways* as answers. He glanced down at Hod, who was staring up anxiously. "Why don't you ask?" *Otherwise you're about to do intimate ground-work upon a person you haven't spoken to directly since you came into the room.*

Remo reluctantly looked Hod in the face. "Are you going to get stuck on me?" he demanded.

Hod did that yes/no headshake again, as confusing to Remo as to everyone else. "Dunno?" He offered after a moment, "Don't want to. But my knee hurts all throbby, and I want to help Dag. Don't you want to help Dag?"

Remo scratched his head, glanced sideways. "I guess I do."

Dag had talked young patrollers through their first fuzzy ground-giftings before; Remo gave him no surprises on that score. The actual transfer was the work of an instant. Hod gasped as the palpable warmth eased his joint. Dag gave Hod some stern warnings about taking better care of himself hereafter, and no more tricks. Hod shook his head hard and unambiguously at that one.

Whit, Berry, and Hawthorn came in then, cheeks pink from the night chill, to put away their assorted equipment. Dag, feeling as drained as if it had been him rather than Remo to give the ground reinforcement, sagged wearily into a chair by the hearth and let Fawn explain to the boat boss just what all had been going on in here, which she did with an accuracy almost as embarrassing to Remo as to Hod. Since she managed to do this while simultaneously feeding everyone warm apple pie, however, they all got over it pretty smoothly.

Dag was then treated to an entirely unexpected half-hour of listening to a lot of farmers sitting around over plates of crumbs seriously discussing problems of Lakewalker-farmer beguilement not as dark magical threat but as something more like navigating a channel that had just had all its snags and sand bars shifted by a flood. Save for Fawn and Whit, their ideas were confused and their suggestions mostly useless; it was their tones of voice that subtly heartened him. Remo, hearing mainly the confusion, at first folded his arms and looked plagued, but then was drawn despite himself into what Dag suspected were his first halting efforts to explain Lakewalker disciplines to outsiders.

The party broke up for bed with the woes of the world unsolved, but Dag felt strangely satisfied nonetheless.

Fawn, passing Hod, caught him on the shoulder, and said, "You know, you could have come out and asked for a turn on Whit's bow, too, same as Hawthorn. Try it next time."

Hod looked startled; his lips peeled back in a grin over his crooked teeth, and he bobbed his head in a gratified nod. Had he just needed an invitation? What brooding over a purely imagined exile had led him to the wall? What distress was so painful that such a brutal self-harm seemed a better choice? Dag, wondering, managed to add a, "Good night, Hod. Sleep hard," to Fawn's shrewd words, which won another gratified head-bob and a flush of pleasure. Following Fawn forward, Dag blew out his breath in contemplation.

After calling Hawthorn to come collect his raccoon, who after its nap now wanted to romp, they curled around each other in their warming nest. Fawn murmured, "How's your oat doing?"

Surprised, Dag rubbed his left arm. "I'd almost forgotten it. Huh. It seems to be converted already. Hardly anything left there but a little warm spot. Maybe tomorrow I'll try ten oats."

"I was thinking, two."

"Five?" He hesitated. "I think I'm glad you talked me out of that tree."

"Uh-huh," she said dryly. He could feel her sleepy smile against his shoulder. She added after a moment, "You really got Remo going tonight. If only we could get him to quit confusing farmers with their livestock, I think he'd be a decent sort."

"Is he that bad? He doesn't mean ill."

"I didn't think he did. He's just . . . full of Lakewalkerish habits."

"Or he was, before he got tipped out of his cradle. I 'spect our river trip isn't quite the rebellion he thought he was signing up for."

She snickered, her breath warm in the hollow of his skin.

Dag said more slowly, "He was just an ordinary patroller, before his knife got broken. But if ordinary folks can't fix the world, it's not going to get fixed. There are no lords here. The gods are absent."

"You know, it sounds real attractive at first, but I'm not sure I'd want lords and gods fixing the world. Because I think they'd fix it for them. Not necessarily for me."

"There's a point, Spark," he whispered.

She nodded, and her eyes drifted shut. His stayed open for rather a long while.

13

To the excitement of everyone aboard—although Fawn thought that Dag and Bo concealed it best—the *Fetch* approached Silver Shoals around noon. It was another gray, chilly day, promising but not delivering rain. Climbing to her mid-roof perch again, Fawn was glad for her jacket.

On the north bank of the river lay a village and ferry landing, which Remo at his sweep eyed uncertainly. "Is that Silver Shoals? It's four times the size of Pearl Bend!"

"Oh, that's not the town," said Berry, leaning on her steering oar to keep the flatboat mid-channel. "That's just a road crossing. Wait'll we get around this bluff and the next curve." She did shade her eyes and frown at the water-gauge pole sticking up near the landing. "River's falling again. I think we'll take the Shoals while we still can, and tie up below. I don't want to get caught above for another week."

Remo grew very quiet as the shore shifted and the town covering the southern hillsides eased at last into view; Dag, joining him at his oar, seemed to study his stare. Many of the houses were painted white, or even colors, spots of brightness amongst the now nearly leafless trees. Some newer, taller buildings were brick, and Fawn wondered if one might be the famous mint. Wood and coal smoke smudged the damp air, and the shoreline was crowded with smelly but lively businesses needing access to water—tanners, dyers, a soap-maker, a reeking mussel fishery, a boatyard. Mills, Fawn supposed, lined the feeder creeks—she could see at least one from here, partway up the hill, a sawmill at a guess. Wagons drawn by straining teams rattled up and down the muddy streets, and pedestrians strode on boardwalks. The town was bigger than Lumpton Market and Glassforge put together, and easily forty times the size of Pearl Bend.

At Berry's sharp reminder, all the gawkers turned their attention to navigating the growling shoals, which were much like Pearl Riffle only more so. A few skeletal boats hung up in the wrack gave warning of the fate of the unwary or unlucky. Dag passed back laconic remarks about hidden hazards to Berry, which by now she took in with no more comment than nods, and they cleared the shelves, boulders, and bars without once scraping the hull, which made her grin. There followed some heavy pulling by all the oarsmen to bring the *Fetch* in to shore.

A couple dozen boats, both flatboats and keels, were tied along a more level stretch amongst not one but several wharf boats, each with its own collection of goods-sheds upslope from it. The road between was dotted with wagons drawn up either by the sheds or the boats, and toiling teams of wharf rats loading or unloading goods. "You could get *lost* up in that town," Remo muttered in dismay, which made a smile flit over Dag's mouth. Whit frankly gaped. Hod, a Glassforge boy, was less impressed, instead earnestly intent on carrying out with Hawthorn his task of throwing and tying ropes as they nudged into the bank.

Once the *Fetch* was safely wedged between another flat and a keel, Berry made inquiries of the neighboring loiterers for downriver news, but both boats were from upstream, like themselves. Bo ran out the gangplank, and Berry led the way on a climb up to the nearest goods-shed, Fawn following her by invitation, Whit just following.

In the front rooms of the goods-sheds they found counters with clerks or clerk-owners. With the latter, Berry bartered for her cargo—hides and barrel staves, bear grease and the dying cider; with all, she asked after news of her papa's boat which might have passed through here last fall. This mostly drew headshakes, but also remarks about *some Tripoint feller* who'd been by lately asking similar questions about missing boats, and *he'd likely want to talk to you.* Which would have been more useful if they'd remembered his name or direction.

But in the third goods-shed, the merchant not only pulled out his record book from eleven months ago and found an entry of a purchase of hides from the *Clearcreek Briar Rose the Fourth,* recognizably initialed by Boss Clearcreek, but identified the curious Tripoint man. He told Berry to look for a trader by the name of Capstone Cutter, likely to be found this time of day at a mussel tavern up the street behind the goods-sheds. From this clerk-owner Berry made her only purchase, some boxes of pearl and mother-of-pearl buttons that were one of the rivertown's more famous products.

Berry told Whit to hang on to his window glass, just as she was hanging on to her Tripoint tool stocks, because he'd get a much better price downstream. Which made plain what Fawn had suspected for some time: Whit wasn't heading back home from Silver Shoals after all. Fawn supposed she ought to at least make him write a letter to Mama and Papa. Or write one herself. She wondered how to get her missive to West Blue without a Lakewalker courier to tap; likely that last merchant, the smart one, had ways of getting news to and from Lumpton Market at least. She would ask him later.

Meanwhile, she hurried up the boardwalk after Berry, Whit following cumbered with the button boxes, then across the mucky street to a building with a swinging sign announcing it as *The Silver Mussel,* painted with a picture of a shell with little feet, buggy eyes, and unlikely smiling teeth. If those creatures at all resembled their portrait, Fawn didn't think she wanted one anywhere near her mouth, cooked or not. But the smell, as they entered the door, was nothing at all like the stench from the mussel fishery down on the riverbank, being mainly a heady steam of garlic and onion intertwined with the sweet tang of fresh beer. Whit inhaled and smiled.

Inside was a big room with sawdust on the floor and a long counter along one side. Scullions and serving boys were clearing tables in a leisurely fashion that suggested the lunch rush was over. Fawn's eye followed Berry's as it swept the room and caught up on a man who could well be their quarry, sitting alone at a table at the far end. *A big fellow about my age,* the fortyish merchant had said, *running to fat, curly brown hair, very nice-trimmed beard. Dresses like a riverman, right enough, but all his gear was the best.* Berry nodded, as if in confirmation, and wove amongst the tables toward him.

He looked up from the mussel shell he was exploring and smiled vaguely at the two young women, but swallowed what he was chewing in quick surprise when Berry stopped by his side and said, "Mister Cutter? From Tripoint?"

"Cap Cutter, and aye," he replied. "What can I do for you, miss . . . and miss?" An afterthought of a nod also acknowledged Whit.

Berry stuck out her work-roughened hand. "I'm Boss Berry Clearcreek, of the *Fetch*. This here's my sweep-man, Whit Bluefield, and my friend and cook Missus Fawn Bluefield."

Cutter's eyebrows rose a little at her claim, but lowered again as he shook her hand and she returned his boatman's grip. He nodded to Fawn and Whit. "Married?" And corrected himself even before the Bluefield grimaces with, "Oh, brother and sister, aye."

"I hear you been asking about missing boats," said Berry.

His general friendliness gave way to something more urgent. "Did you all come from downriver?"

"No—the *Fetch* is a flat—but we're heading that way. See, last fall my papa and brother took a flat down from Clearcreek and never came back. No word. It was like they just vanished. So I'm on the lookout for them, or news of them."

"The boats we're missing disappeared in this spring's rise, much later, but here, sit . . ." He half-rose, gesturing at the other three chairs around the square plank table. An uncleared plate opposite him, piled high with empty shells, indicated that a companion had left—perhaps another informant? Cutter sank back, frowning a little, as they settled themselves.

"Boats?" asked Fawn curiously. "More than one?"

He nodded. "I started out as a keeler out of Tripoint, till I married and the tads started coming along, and my missus wanted me more settled. So I took up a goods-shed there and started sending cargoes instead of hauling them. First cargoes, then a boat, then two boats, then four. My luck was fair in general, and I've mostly found steady men for my bosses. They were good boats, too, solid work out of Beaver Creek. Not like those homemade tubs the hills boys cobble together, with green or rotten timbers and bad caulking—I lost a cargo on one of those flats, once, learned my lesson. It went down on a sunny day in nineteen feet of clear water, stove in, I swear, when it struck nothing harder than the head of a yellow-bellied catfish."

Having seen a channel cat, Fawn was not so sure this represented defects in the boat, but she held her peace.

"Sound boats, sound crews," Cutter went on, "but two out of four didn't come back this summer. And when I got to asking around, turned out they weren't the only ones. There's nine boats or flattie crews out of the Tripoint area didn't come back when they should of. You might expect to lose one or two a season, but nine? And even sunk boats come up again, or are seen, or salvaged. Bodies come up, too, and folks who have the snagging and burying of 'em generally pass the word along.

When we all got together and figured it, it was right plain someone needed to go take a closer look, and I was it. Losing those two boats was a blow to me, I don't mind telling you."

A scullion interrupted then, clearing the odd plate and asking if they'd like anything. Fawn shook her head warily, and Berry, intent on Cutter, waved the offer away, but Whit ordered a plate of mussels and a beer to go with.

"My papa was twenty years and more on the river," Berry said after the scullion departed. "A good boat-builder, and his crew was all local fellows who'd gone down and back with him before. I usually went along myself, 'cept this last time."

Cutter's eyes opened. "Say, do you play the fiddle?"

Berry nodded. "I got good pay, playing the keeler boys upstream."

His smile turned a shade more respectful, not that he'd been at all rude before. Some kind of river fellowship at work, Fawn guessed. "I've heard tell of you! Yellow-headed gal who travels with her daddy and scrapes real lively, has to be." He sucked out the contents of another mussel shell, and went on, "My keel tied up down the bank is the *Tri-point Steel,* and I picked my crew special. Big fellows all, and we've come pretty well-armed, this time. Some of them were missing friends or kin, too, and volunteered when they heard what I was up to. Whatever this trouble is, we're hoping to find it."

Berry rubbed her nose. "Steel won't help if it was sickness or ship-wreck, but I admit it sounds right heartening. Are you thinking it was some kind o' boat bandits? Boatmen's been robbed before, it's true, but usually word gets out pretty quick."

Cutter scratched his short beard in doubt. "There would be the hitch in it. So many gone, so quiet-like . . . Some of us think there's some-thing uncanny about it." His mouth tightened. "Like maybe sorcery. Or worse. Thing is, not only are the boats and bodies not showing up between the outlet of the Grace and Graymouth, neither are the goods, seemingly. Which makes a fellow wonder—what if they were diverted north to Luthlia instead, up the Gray into that wild Lakewalker country?"

Fawn sat up in indignation. "Lakewalkers wouldn't rob farmer boats!"

Cutter shook his head. "They were valuable cargoes. Fine Tripoint steel and iron goods, plus I'd sent a deal of silver coin along with my keel bosses to buy tea and spices with, down south. Anyone could be tempted, but for some, it might be . . . easier."

"It makes no sense," Fawn insisted. "Leaving aside that Lakewalkers just don't *do* things like that, Luthlia's one of the few Lakewalker hinterlands that makes iron and steel on its own, and it's good work, too. I've seen some. Dag says Luthlian mines and forges supply blades to the camps north of the Dead Lake nearly to Seagate! They can make steel that doesn't even rust! Why would they rob yours?"

Cutter's voice lowered. "Yeah, but there's also the missing bodies to be accounted for. I can think of another reason they might not turn up downstream, and it ain't a pretty one." He ran a thumbnail between his teeth in a significant gesture, then glanced guiltily at the paling Berry. "Sorry, miss. But a man can't help thinking."

Fawn wanted to jump up and stalk out in a huff, but Whit's mussels and beer arrived just then, and by the time the scullion took himself off again she had re-mastered her wits. "I can think of a reason a lot more likely than Lakewalkers—who *do not either* eat people—for folks to go missing, and that's malices. Blight bogles. I was mixed up in that malice kill near Glassforge last spring—as close a witness as I could be. Bogles take farmer slaves, if they can. If one's set up on the river, it'd be just as happy to take boatmen slaves, I'd imagine. And it wouldn't necessarily know about selling stolen goods downstream." Although its new minions might. Could a malice dispatch them to such a distance without risking losing control of them? Maybe not.

And yet . . . the whole Grace Valley was well-patrolled, not only by Lakewalkers from the several ferry camps strung along the river, but also by any Lakewalkers passing up or down in their narrow boats. It wasn't a neglected backwoods region, by any means. Could a malice as strong as the Glassforge one pass undetected for a year or more? *The Glassforge one did,* she reminded herself. *I need to tell Dag about this.*

Cutter looked as if the idea of a river bogle didn't sit well with him, but he didn't reject it out of hand. If it was a malice snatching boats, all Cutter's big men with big knives would be no use to him. *But a lot of use to the malice.* Fawn shivered.

Whit, watching her mulish expression anxiously, said, "Hey, Fawn, try one of these!" and pushed his plate of gaping mussel shells toward her. She picked one up and eyed it; Berry leaned over and showed her how to detach the morsel from its housing. Fawn chewed dubiously, without as much effect as she would have thought, gulped, and stole some of Whit's beer for a chaser. Berry absently helped herself to a few more.

"If you find a pearl," Cutter put in, watching Fawn with some amusement, "you get to keep it. They take back the shells, though."

All those buttons, after all. Still, the notion of a pearl was enough to make her try one more, till Whit pulled back his plate in defense.

Cutter turned more seriously to Berry. "Your missing folks aren't necessarily connected to ours. Or else the problem goes back farther than I thought. But my keel will be downriver before your flat, I expect, and I can ask after your folks, too, while I'm asking. What are the names again?"

Cutter listened carefully to Berry's descriptions of her papa, brother Buckthorn, Alder, and their crewmen. She didn't mention her betrothal, and from the pause in his chewing Fawn thought Whit noticed this. Re-marking that two sets of ears were better than one, Cutter returned the names and some descriptions of the Tripoint boats and bosses—bewildering to Fawn, especially as some boats were named after men, but Berry seemed to follow it all. Berry even remarked of one boat, or boss, "Oh, I know that keel; Papa and us worked it upriver from Graymouth 'bout three years back," which made Cutter nod.

Cutter leaned back, looking over the two young women and Whit, and asked, "So what do you have for muscle on your *Fetch,* 'sides this sawed-off boy here?" Which made Whit sit up and put his shoulders back, frowning.

"Two tall fellers and my uncle Bo, who's canny when he's sober. Couple of boat boys."

Not mentioning, Fawn noticed, that the two tall fellows were shifty Lakewalkers. Was Berry actually growing protective of her unusual sweep-men?

Cutter's mouth tightened in concern. "If I were you girls I'd find another flat or two to float with, so's you can watch out for each other going down. If it's river bandits, they're more like to cut out a stray than tackle a crowd. There's safety in numbers."

Berry nodded acknowledgment of the point without precisely agreeing to the plan, and they took their leave of the Tripoint man.

❧

Fawn, still fuming over Cutter's slander of Lakewalkers, hadn't been going to repeat that part to Dag when they all got back to the *Fetch,* but, alas, the excited Whit promptly did. Dag responded only with his peculiar expressionless expression, lowering and raising his eyelids, which Fawn recognized as his *I am not arguing* look that could conceal anything from bored weariness to silent rage. Dismissing the slur, however, Dag was a lot more interested in the news about the other lost boats. He agreed with Fawn's hopeful suggestion that a river malice seemed unlikely due to the heavy patrolling in the region, but his hand, she noticed, absently rubbed his neck where a cord for a sharing knife sheath no longer hung.

❧

Just before supper, finding herself briefly alone on the back deck with Whit, Fawn said, "You know, Berry's still betrothed to her Alder, as far as she knows. What are you going to do if we find him downstream somewhere?"

Whit scratched his head. "Well, there's this. I figure if we find out he's died, she'll need a shoulder to cry on. And if we find out that he's run off with some other girl and don't love her anymore—she'll still need a shoulder to cry on. I got two shoulders, so I guess I'm ready for anything."

"What if we find him and rescue him from, from I don't know what, and they still want each other?"

Whit twitched his brows. "Rescue from what? It's been too long. If he loved her proper, he'd have come back to her if he had to crawl up that riverbank on his hands and knees all the way from Graymouth. Which he's had plenty of time to do, I'd say. No, I ain't afraid of Alder."

"Even if Alder's out of the picture, one way or another, doesn't mean you're in."

Whit eyed her appraisingly. "Berry likes you well enough. It wouldn't hurt you to put in a good word for me, now and then." He added after a moment, "Or at least stop ragging me."

Fawn reddened, but replied, "The way you always stopped ragging me, when I begged or burst out cryin'?"

Whit reddened, too. "We was *younger*."

"Huh."

They stared moodily at each other.

After another moment, Whit blurted, "I'm sorry."

"Years of tormentin' to be fixed with one *I'm sorry*—when you finally want something from me?" Fawn's lips tightened. She hated to be so weakly forgiving, but under the circumstances . . . "I'll think about it. I like Berry, too." But couldn't help adding, "Which puts me in a puzzle whether to promote your cause or not, mind you."

"Well"—Whit sighed—"maybe we'll find her Alder, and you and me'll both look nohow." Turning away, he muttered dolefully under his breath, "I wonder if he's tall?"

❧

Dag sat on the edge of the *Fetch*'s roof in the dark, legs dangling over, gingerly testing his groundsense. The familiar warmth of Copperhead, Daisy-goat, and the chickens, the known shapes of the people near him: Whit and Hawthorn out back cleaning up after supper and amiably arguing, Spark's bright flame collaborating with Berry on rebuilding a bed-nest after their stack of supporting hides had been sold out from under them today, Remo sitting in a corner with his ground wrapped up tight, a nearly transparent smudge. Bo had gone off, he said, to ask around the taverns after further news of the *Clearcreek Briar Rose,* a plan that had made Berry grimace; Hod had gone along.

Dag widened his reach to the other boats nearby, holding dozens of people more. Up to the line of goods-sheds, more comfortably deserted except for a night watchman or two, and a loiterer who might or might not be looking for an unlocked door. The river behind, lively with moving water, plants, a certain amount of floating scum suspiciously rich in life-ground, a few fish with their bright fishy auras, crayfish creeping and mussels clinging in the rocks and mud. Still wider, across

the street to the buildings thumping with lives boiling in his perceptions—awake, asleep, arguing, scheming, making love, making hate,
the warm ground-glow of a mama nursing a child.

That's three hundred paces. Try for more. On the far shore of the river,
ducks slept concealed in the scrub, heads tucked under their wings.
In a barn up the bank, tired oxen dozed after a day of hauling boats
up over the shoals along the well-beaten tow-path. A dozen houses
were clustered around the towing station and ferry landing, and more
goods-sheds; Dag could have counted their inhabitants. *That's over half
a mile, yes!*

He studied the ground in his own left arm. The five oats that he'd
surreptitiously ground-ripped this morning, stolen from a handful fed to
Copperhead, were all turned to Daggish warm spots. The ten he'd
snitched at lunch were well on their way to conversion. His ground
seemed healthy and dense, the old blighted patches fading away like
paling bruises. He quietly extended his ghost hand, drew it back in.
And again. Once so erratic and frightening, the ground projection was
coming under his control, even fine control. *Why did I fear this?* Perhaps
he'd try ground-ripping something even bigger tomorrow. Not a tree—
impressed with Spark's shrewd guess, he'd stick to food, for now.

The shadow of Remo's closed ground, like a ripple in clear water,
moved beneath him; the young patroller ducked out the front hatch
and straightened by Dag's knee, looking up at him. A brief flicker as he
opened a little and found Dag open wide. Remo turned his head and
stared back up the hill toward the many lights of Silver Shoals, scattered
up the slope and over the slopes beyond. Even at this hour, there were a
few wagons and people wandering the streets. Beyond the line of goods-
sheds, light and laughter burst from the door of the mussel tavern as it
swung open and closed, loud enough to carry down to the waterside.

"How can you stand the noise?" Remo asked, pressing his hands to his head in a gesture of pained dismay. He didn't, of course, mean the sounds of the actually quite peaceful autumn night that came to their ears. Silver Shoals had to be the largest collection of unveiled humanity he'd encountered in all his short life.

Dag considered him, then gestured friendly-like to the space on the roof edge beside him. Remo clambered up easily. He'd pretty much fully healed from his beating, due to a combination of Verel's earlier ground treatments, plenty of good food, and simple outdoor exercise, although mostly, Dag suspected glumly, due to youth.

"Farmer ground's a bit noisy," Dag said, "but you can get used to it. It's good ground, just a lot of it. It's blighted ground that hurts. *Malice* ground, now *that* hurts like nothing else in the wide green world."

Remo looked appropriately daunted by this reminiscence; Dag went on, "Still, it's a lot to take in. Even for townsfolk. If you study them, you'll notice that they pass by each other in the street with a lot less looking or talking than village or hamlet farmers do. They have to learn not to look, because there's no way they can stop and deal with everyone when there's thousands. It's not ground-veiling, but it's something like, in their heads, I think. In a way, it makes big towns saf—more comfortable for Lakewalkers alone than tiny ones. Townsmen are more used to ignoring odd folks."

"But there's more of them to gang up on you if there's trouble," said Remo doubtfully.

"Also true," Dag conceded. "Try opening up to the limit of your groundsense range, just once, to see what happens. I promise it won't kill you."

"Not instantly, maybe," muttered Remo, but he obeyed. Brows rather clenched, he opened himself, wider and wider; the water-shadow of his ground gradually thickened and became perceptible to Dag in all its dense complexity.

The boy's got a groundsense range of a good half-mile, Dag thought in satisfaction. Remo was clearly well-placed as a patroller, maybe a future patrol leader, if he could be lured away from wrecking himself on the rocks of his own mistakes.

With a muttered *Oof!*, Remo let his groundsense recoil. But not, Dag noted, all the way; it was still open to perhaps the dimensions of the *Fetch* and its residents. And to Dag. Remo rubbed his forehead. "That's . . . something."

"Town like this has a tremendous ground-roil," Dag agreed. "It's life, though—the opposite of blight, as much as any woods or swamp. More. If our long war is meant to hold back the blight and sustain the world's ground, if you look at it rightways, a place like this"—he nodded at the slopes, the lamplights spread across them like fireflies out of season—"is our greatest success."

Remo blinked as this odd thought nudged into his brain. Dag hoped it would stir things up a bit in there.

Dag drew breath, leaned forward. "The fact that this town is also a vast ground-banquet for any malice that chances to emerge too close troubles me hugely. What all had you heard down at Pearl Riffle Camp about the losses in our summer's campaign over in Raintree?"

Remo replied seriously, "It was bad, I heard. A place called Bone-marsh Camp was wholly blighted, and they lost seventy or a hundred folks in the retreat."

"Did the name of Greenspring even come up?"

"Wasn't that some farmer village the malice first came up near?"

"Praise Fairbolt, at least that much got in. Yes. Had you heard their losses?"

"I didn't read the circular myself, just heard talk about it. Lots, I'd guess."

"You'd guess right. They lost nearly half their people, about five hundred folk in all, including almost all their children, because you know a malice goes for youngsters first. Absent gods, you should have seen that malice when we slew it, after that fair feast. I never knew one could grow so ghastly beautiful. Sessiles, early molts, they're crude and ugly creatures, and you get to thinking ugliness is what malices are all about, but it's not. It's not." Dag fell silent, but then shook off the haunting memory and forged on while he still had Remo's ground and mind open. "I took my patrol through Greenspring on the way home, and we came upon some townsmen who'd come back to bury their dead. It was high summer, but most of the victims had been ground-ripped, so they were slow to rot. I counted down the row, so pale they were, like ice children in that gray heat . . . How long a trench do you think you'd have to dig, Remo, to bury all the youngsters in Silver Shoals?"

Remo's lips parted; he shook his head.

"It'd be about a mile long, I figure," said Dag evenly. "At the least estimate. I'd have dragged every Lakewalker I know down that row if I could have, but I couldn't, so now I have to do it with words." And maybe his clumsy words were working better here, with Silver Shoals spread in front of Remo's eyes, than they would have in the comfortable isolation of Pearl Riffle Camp.

"I can see the problem," said Remo slowly.

Absent gods be praised!

"But I don't see what more we can do about it. I mean, we're already patrolling as hard as we can."

"It's not our patrolling that needs to change. It's . . . see, the thing is, if the Greenspring folks had known more about malices, about Lake-walkers, about all we do, someone might have got out with word ear-lier. More lives—not all, I know, but more—might have been saved at Greenspring, and Bonemarsh need not have been blighted any, if we could have been warned and taken the malice quick before it started to move south. And the only way I know to get farmers to know more is to start teaching 'em."

Remo's eyes widened as he gauged the lights of the town. "How could we possibly teach them all?"

Already Remo was past the usual response, *How could we teach any of 'em? Farmers can't . . .* followed by whatever Lakerwalkerish conceit first occurred. Dag nearly smiled. "Well, now, if we had to lift and carry each and every farmer all at once, we'd break our backs, sure. But if we could start by teaching *some* farmers, *some*place—maybe after that they could teach each other. Save each other. If they can only grab the right tools. These folks are good at tools, I find." He raised his left arm; his hook and the buckles of his harness gleamed briefly in the faint yellow lantern lights.

Remo fell silent, staring up the shore.

After a while, Dag said, "Fawn and Whit are mad to see the town mint tomorrow morning, before we go on down the river. Want to come along?"

Remo's ground closed altogether. "Is it safe for Lakewalkers alone up there?" Remo had barely ventured off the *Fetch*; if he hadn't been pressed into helping with the unloading earlier, Dag wasn't sure he would have set foot on land at all.

"Yes," said Dag recklessly. He suspected that Remo would follow him from sheer habit if he displayed a patrol leader's confidence, and no need to enlighten the youth as to how hollow a confidence that so often was. "Besides, we won't be alone."

"I'll think about it," said Remo cautiously. He added after a little silence, "Whit sure likes his money. Yet it's nothing, in its ground. Just metal chips."

"If money has a ground, it exists inside folks' heads," Dag agreed. "But it's mighty convenient for trade. It's like a memory of trade you can hold in your hand, and take anywhere." Anywhere it was recognized. Four great farmer towns—all along this river system, curiously enough—coined their own money these days, in addition to odd lots of coin left from the ancient days that turned up from time to time. The clerks in the goods-sheds were gaining a lot of practice in figuring, Dag guessed, making the coins all dance fairly with one another—or sometimes, he'd heard, not so fairly. In which case, people got a lot of practice at arguing. Even Lakewalkers used farmer coin, and not only while out patrolling.

"Lakewalker camp credit is better," said Remo. "Bandits can't knock you on the head and take it away from you. It's not a temptation to the weak-willed or cruel."

"It can't be stolen with a cudgel," Dag agreed, his mood darkening in memory. "But it can be stolen with words. Trust me on that."

Remo looked over at him in some wonder. But before he could inquire further, Bo and Hod turned up at the foot of the gangplank. Hod had one of Bo's arms drawn over his shoulder and was getting him aimed down the middle of the boards.

Dag was surprised to see them. One of the reasons Berry had been amenable to the proposed trip to the mint in the morning, despite the delay to their departure, was that she hadn't expected her uncle back tonight. She'd figured she and Hawthorn, who had been taken to the mint once by their papa on a previous trip, would use the time looking for Bo while Fawn and Whit went off touring.

Bo was saying querulously to Hod, "I still don't see the point of making me drink all that water. It just took up space for better bev'rages. And I have to piss just as bad."

"Your head'll feel better in the morning," Hod assured him. "It's a good trick I know about, really."

"Yeah, well, we'll see," muttered Bo, but let Hod steer him over the gangplank. His knees buckled on the jump down, but Hod kept him upright. Despite several hours of following Bo around Silver Shoals riverside taverns, Hod was pretty sober, Dag noted. Hod looked up at Dag and Remo, watching from the roof, and cast them a shy smile. He maneuvered the old man inside, to be greeted with even greater surprise by Berry.

"Well, that's interestin'," murmured Dag.

"How so?" said Remo.

"Seems Hod's got a talent for managing difficult drunks. I wasn't expecting anything like that. You wonder where and how he learned it, so young."

Remo's brows drew down. He was quiet for a long time. "Kind of disturbing, in a way. In light of how he flinches at most everything."

"Uh-huh," said Dag, pleased at Remo for following through that far. The boy might make a patrol leader someday after all, if he survived. Remo was open enough again to sense the ripple of approval in Dag's ground, and his spine straightened a bit, unwittingly.

Dag smiled and slid down off the roof to go find out what Fawn had arranged for their bedding.

14

To Fawn's bemusement, Remo tagged along on the trip to the mint, which made her wonder what Dag had been saying to him last night. She'd thought Remo had been too terrified of the town to set foot in it. He started the tour with a set look on his face that could more easily be mistaken for disapproval. Which made her wonder in turn what emotions some of Dag's grimmer looks masked—a Lakewalker bride would not have to guess, she reflected with a sigh. At the last moment, Dag thought to ask Hod if he wanted to come along, which made the boy turn red with pleasure and nod mutely and vigorously.

Disappointingly, the mint was not in operation that day, but in return for a few copper crays a man took visitors around, answered their questions, and, Fawn suspected, kept an eye on them. He certainly eyed the pair of Lakewalkers askance. Even idle, the coin-stamping presses were fascinating, almost as complex as Aunt Nattie's loom, and much heavier. "Sessile," Dag muttered, staring at them over her shoulder with profound Lakewalker suspicion of sitting targets. Remo nodded agreement.

On the walk back through town, she and Whit were diverted by a shop selling tools and hardware—not a blacksmithery, as nothing but small repairs were done on the premises, but more like a goods-shed. Most of the items for sale seemed to come from upriver, including a fascinating Tripoint stove cast entirely of black iron, with an iron pipe acting as a chimney to take the smoke away. It was like an iron hearth-oven box turned inside out, made to stand out into a room with the fire on the inside.

"Look!" Fawn told Dag in excitement. "It has to be so much better for heating, because a fireplace only shows one face to a room, and this thing shows, what, six. Six times better. And you wouldn't have to bend and crouch to cook on it, and it wouldn't blow smoke in your face, either, and you're less like to catch your clothes or hair on fire, too!" *Oh, I want one!*

He stared at it and her in mild alarm. "You'd need a wagon and team to shift it, Spark!"

"Naturally you wouldn't cart it around with you, any more than you would a fireplace. Fire pit," she revised, thinking of Lakewalkers camps. "It would have to be planted someplace permanent."

"Hm," he said, looking at her with one of his odder smiles. "Farmer tool."

"Well, of course." She tossed her head, imagining someplace permanent where you could plant such a stove, and a garden. And children. Not a Lakewalker camp, they'd proved that. Not a farmer village, or at least not West Blue. A town like this one? Maybe not, as such a big concentration of folks plainly made Lakewalkers deeply uncomfortable. *Where, then?* Regretfully, she allowed Dag and Remo to drag them away from the fascinating emporium.

Back on the *Fetch,* they found a crisis brewing as Berry and Bo were ready to cast off, but Hawthorn's raccoon kit had disappeared. Bo was all for leaving without the pesky creature, assuring the distraught Hawthorn that his pet would swim down the river and find a new home in the woods just fine. Hawthorn envisioned more dire fates, loudly. Then the listening Remo made himself hero of the hour—or at least of Hawthorn—by walking along the bank and retrieving the kit from a boat down the row where, caught raiding the pantry, it was about to meet its end at either the hands of the boat's irate cook or the jaws of the excited boat-dog. Remo had a dangerously attractive face-lightening smile like Dag's, Fawn discovered as he handed the little masked miscreant back to its ecstatic owner. Berry noticed it too, and smiled in pure contagion; Whit first smiled at her smile, then frowned at Remo.

As the boat made midstream and peace fell, Fawn pulled out her wool and drop spindle and took a seat on the bow to spin, watch the riverbank pass by, and think. Remo had to have opened and used his groundsense for that swift rescue, despite his aversion to farmer grounds. For Lake-walkers, hunting must be a very different activity than for farmers, if they could just stroll into a woods and find prey as easily as a woman picking jars off her pantry shelf. Although she supposed convincing, say, a bear to submit to having its skin peeled was just as dangerous to a Lakewalker hunter as to any farmer. Or was it? Were there other practical uses for persuasion than just on farmer merchants and maidens? *And horses and mosquitoes and fireflies.* She would have to ask Dag.

Twisting her yarn plump for warmth—it would knit up faster that way, too—she made quite a bit of progress before it was time to break off and go start lunch. An iron stove, she thought longingly, could be installed on a boat like this one and not be so sessile after all. But it would be a short love affair—you'd have to sell it downstream just as the boats were sold off at journey's end, sometimes as houseboats for the poorer riverfolk but more usually broken up for their lumber. Most of Graymouth was built of former flatboats, she'd heard. She hated to think of the *Fetch* so dismembered, and hoped someone would buy it for a cozy floating home.

As she made her way into the kitchen, she found Dag sitting at the drop-table, his head bent strangely. He was staring down at a distressing lumpy gray blob on a pie plate, his face drained and almost greenish.

"What in the world is that thing?" Fawn asked, nodding at the plate. "You're not going to eat it, are you?" The man certainly needed to get more food inboard, but preferably something wholesome. This looked like something dead too long that had been fished from the bottom of the river.

"Last piece of apple pie from last night," he said.

"*That's* not my—" She looked more closely. "Dag, *what did you do?*"

"Ground-ripped it. Tried to. I think I just found my upper limit."

"Dag! Two oats, I said!"

"I tried two oats. They were good. So were five and ten. Time to try something else. This was food, too!"

"Was, yeah!" As she stared in a mix of exasperation and horror, Dag abruptly clawed off his arm harness and dropped it, bending over with his left arm held tight to his body. He swallowed ominously. Fawn darted for a washbasin and shoved it under his nose barely in time. He grabbed it and turned away from her, trying to retch quietly, but he didn't bring up much. Wordlessly, she handed him a cup of water with which to rinse and spit.

"Thanks," he whispered.

"Done?"

"Not sure." He set the basin on the bench beside him, ready to hand. "This feels bizarre. It's like my ground is trying to get rid of it, but it can't, so my body tries instead."

"But there wasn't anything in your stomach."

"I'm right grateful about that, just now."

"Is this the same way you get sick after your healing groundwork?"

"No," he said slowly. "That's more light-headed, like blood loss except it passes quickly. This . . . is heavy like indigestion. It just sits there. Except in both cases the disruption of my ground is affecting my body."

"So is your ground like a horse, or like a dog?"

He blinked at her in dizzy confusion. "Say what?"

"We had some farm dogs that would wolf down any garbage you left around, and then heave it back up if it disagreed with 'em, which it generally did. Usually someplace where you were going to step, seemed like." She scowled in memory. "Then there was that dog of Reed's whose joy was to roll in smelly things—manure, dead possums—and then rush up to share his bliss with you. But that's dogs for you."

Dag pressed the back of his hand to his lips. "Indeed . . . Are you ragging me, Spark?"

She shook her head, though her fierce glance said, *You deserve to be ragged.* "Then there's horses. Now, horses can't vomit like dogs do. Once they've eaten something wrong, they're in big trouble and no mistake. Papa lost a good pony to colic, once, that had got into the corn, which is why Fletcher is so careful about fixing fencerows and keeping the feed bins latched tight. It'd been his pony, see. So if you ground-rip something bad, can you get rid of it or not?"

"Evidently not." Dag's brow wrinkled. "I couldn't get rid of those toxic spatters after I ground-ripped the malice back in Raintree, either, come to think. They were blighting me, poisoning my ground. They were drawn out and destroyed with the rest of the residue when we broke the malice's groundlock, but that trick wouldn't work for this."

"Will this kill you?" she asked in sudden terror. "Just a piece of pie— *my* pie?"

He shook his head. "Don't think so. It's not poison. And I didn't— couldn't—rip it all the way. But I sure wish I hadn't done that." He hunched tighter, grimacing.

"Then will you get better slow like after the mosquito?"

"I guess we'll find out," he sighed.

"Ground-colic," said Fawn. "Eew."

She took away the plate and basin and emptied them over the back rail, then returned to put Dag firmly to bed. It was a measure of his malaise that he went without argument.

She made his excuses to the others, come lunch——*he thinks it's something he ate*——which were accepted without question but with lots of speculation as to what it might have been, since everyone else had eaten Fawn's boat-food as well. In desperation——and in defense of her reputation as a cook——she finally suggested it might have been something he'd got hold of up in town that morning, which was allowed with wise nods. Remo seemed the most disturbed by the development, stopping by their bed-nook to ask Dag if he was all right and if there was anything he could do. Dag's response was muffled and repelling. Fawn thought that Dag should take the only other Lakewalker available into his confidence about these alarming ground-ripping experiments, but wasn't certain enough to force it. She was out of her depth, here. The notion that Dag might be too was not reassuring.

Dag's loss was Hod's gain, as he was suddenly promoted to sweepman that afternoon in Dag's place. Hod was clumsy and timid and mixed up his right and his left, but responded slowly both to Berry's patience and Bo's familiar hungover bluntness. His panicked mistakes became fewer as his confidence grew, though he seemed so surprised to be told he was doing well that he almost dropped his broad-oar overboard.

To Fawn's immense relief, Dag revived enough in the evening to eat real food, although she noticed he left his arm harness off. He was still very quiet, answering most queries with a headshake and then pressing his forehead as if in regret of the sudden motion. But the next day Dag went back to taking turns on the oars, although only after a promise to the eager Hod that he would now be added to the regular rotation.

They pulled in that noon at a village that was seemingly a traditional stop for the Clearcreeks, where Berry found a fellow who both knew her and remembered the *Briar Rose* stopping last fall. So her papa had made it at least this far. The goods-shed man couldn't recall Boss Clearcreek saying anything unusual about the trip, was very sorry to learn of his disappearance, and shook his head over the news about the lost Tripoint boats. Whit sold his first batch of window glass, and they took to the river once more. The cool autumn sun that made the water sparkle and the riverbanks glow delighted Fawn, but was not welcomed by Berry, eyeing the falling water.

Late that afternoon Berry's glumness was unfortunately vindicated. The boat boss was sitting with Fawn, Dag, and Hod at the kitchen table, nibbling leftovers and asking about life in West Blue, when a grinding noise from the hull made her look up and set her teeth. She stared at the ceiling, thumping with sudden bootsteps, and muttered, "Bo, you're too close to the bank, bring her over hard now——" but broke off with an aggravated snarl as the *Fetch* quite perceptibly ground to a halt.

"What is it?" asked Fawn sharply; Hod looked equally alarmed.

"Sand bar," Berry called over her shoulder as she swung out the back hatch. They all followed her out and clambered up onto the roof, where she was peering over the side with her hands planted on her hips and saying to Bo, "What did you want to go and do that for? We're scrunched in good now!"

Bo was apologetic, in a guilty-surly sort of way, blaming the island they were stuck beside for growing that bar out in an uncalled-for way. Whit was rather red-faced, and Remo, catching Dag's eye, looked hangdog. Berry sighed in exasperation, which reassured Fawn that this was a normal sort of emergency, and Berry and Bo took up a practiced routine for efforts to push them off again.

The first step was to swing the oars down and use them as stilts to walk the boat off the bar. Dag and Remo actually broke their big oar with their grunting effort, but the *Fetch* did not budge, and Berry abandoned that method before they either broke another—she was not over-supplied with spares—or ripped out the massive oak oarlock as well. The next step was to send all the men ashore, lightening the load, to try tugging with ropes. Copperhead, whom Berry kept calling *Dag's land-skiff,* was sent too, with a rope tied to his saddle. The men stripped to their drawers and boots and waded into the chill water, grimly or with yelps, which was pretty riveting—Fawn caught Berry staring too, and her wide grin flashed back—but still didn't shift the boat.

The third method was to settle back and wait for a rise to float the *Fetch* off the bar, a choice the shivering crew had scorned a couple of hours back but now applauded. As they were yelling this debate across the little stretch of water between the boat and the churned-up bank, a long, low hoot, rising to three sharp toots, sounded from upriver. "That's the *Snapping Turtle*'s horn," Berry said, her head swiveling.

The keelboat appeared around the bend, riding easily down the center of the channel. A man in—dry—red-and-blue striped trousers cheerfully waved a tin horn as long as his arm at the mud-splashed crew of the *Fetch* strung along the shore. "That there's a boat, not a plow, Boss Berry!" he called. "You tryin' to dredge a new channel over there?" Berry snorted indignation, but her lips twitched.

As Boss Wain strode to the bow and stood with his thumbs in his green leather braces, grinning at them, Berry cupped her hands and shouted, "Hey, Wain! You've got muscle over there! How's about a tow?"

He cupped his hands and yelled back, "I dunno, Berry—how's about a kiss?"

Over on the bank, Whit, despite being mostly blue, flushed red.

"Daisy-goat'll pucker up for you!" Berry shouted back. "You'll think you're back with the home girls!"

Wain shook his head. "Not good enough! What's your cargo?"

"Mainly salt butter, Tripoint tools, and window glass!"

Wain's grin stretched as the *Snapping Turtle* slid past. "Then I guess we'll sell our tools and glass downstream before you!" He patted his lips in a broad gesture. "Unless you want to change your mind about that kiss?"

"Muscle-headed turkey-wit," Berry muttered under her breath. "He never changes." She raised her voice and shouted after him, "What, are all your fellers too weak and worn out with flipping those dice to pull a bitty flatboat anymore? All little girly-arms on the *Turtle,* so sad!" She flapped hers limply in mockery.

Wain raised his arm and slapped his massive biceps. "Nice try, Berry!"

Fawn considered volunteering a kiss in Berry's place, in support of the *Fetch,* but looking over the rowdy keelboat men decided better of the impulse.

"I'll play you over the bar!" Berry raised her arms back and mimicked fiddling.

This actually started a hot debate amongst the dozen or so men of the *Snapping Turtle*'s crew; before it could quite turn to mutiny, Wain shouted, "A concert and a kiss!"

Berry gritted her teeth. "I'll wait for the rain!"

Moans of disappointment drifted back from the keelboat, but the river bore it inexorably on, and in a few more minutes it had floated out of hearing and then sight. Berry heaved a frustrated sigh. It had all been fairly good-humored, Fawn thought, but—they were still stuck on the sand bar.

Copperhead was turned loose to graze on the island, since, although he had jumped into the water readily enough under Dag's practiced persuasion, getting him back aboard would be nigh impossible until they could again tie the *Fetch* to the bank bow-first and run out the gangplank. The men washed in the river and came back aboard, crowding the hearth where Fawn was trying to start an early supper, there seeming to be little else to do for the long evening. They stamped and shivered and rubbed their hands, all but Dag who tucked his under his left arm, but eventually settled down enough out of her way that she could make pies and stew. Dag asked if Fawn wanted him to catch her some fish, but for some reason this amiable suggestion was voted down.

In the night Fawn awoke to find their bedroll empty of Dag. At first she thought he'd gone to piss, but when he didn't reappear after a reasonable time, she wrapped a blanket around herself and crept out to look for him. A light was seeping in from around the bow hatch, too amber to be the moon. She slipped out the door and closed it behind her. The night air was cold, damp, and smelled of fallen leaves and the river, with a whiff of warm goat and sleepy chicken, but overhead the stars burned bright.

The bench was pulled out from the wall, and Dag was sitting astride it, with a lantern glowing at the other end. He seemed dressed by guess, hair sticking up, and was without his arm harness. He was frowning down at two little piles of mixed oats and corn kernels on the board between his knees, although when she came to his shoulder he looked up and cast her a quick smile.

"What are you doing?" she whispered.

He ran his hand through his hair, to no good effect. "I've gone back to oats. Figured you'd approve."

She nodded provisionally. "Are you planning to ground-rip some?" She didn't see any little piles of gray dust, so perhaps she'd caught him in time. Which begged the question *In time for what?*——although it was possible her mere presence would inhibit him from dodgier trials.

He made an odd face. "I got to thinking. Even a malice doesn't normally ground-rip its victims down to deep physical structure—that gray slumping's more an effect of prolonged draining blight. It only snatches the life-ground. The cream off the top, if you will."

She frowned in concentration. "I remember when Dar told me about how sharing knives are primed. The knife just draws in a person's dying ground. The whole person doesn't dissolve. So it's not just malices."

His lips parted, closed. "That's . . . a better thought. Though I don't think of sharing knives as ground-ripping so much as accepting the greatest possible ground-gift. I . . . hm." His brows drew in. After a moment he shook off the distracting notion, whatever it was, and went on. "Live ground is more complex than the ground of inert or dead things—lighter, brighter, more fleeting . . . and it seems"—he reached out with a fingertip beneath his hovering stump and shifted one more oat from the pile on his right to the pile on his left—"more digestible. Speaking of ground-colic."

She estimated the number of grains in each pile. It was a lot more than ten. "Dag," she said uneasily, "how many of those are you planning to try?"

He chewed on his lip. "Well, you remember back in Raintree when every patroller in camp who knew how gave me a ground reinforcement, trying to get me better quick so's we could all ride home?"

"Yes?"

"After a while I started seeing these wavering purple halos around things, and Hoharie made them stop. She said I needed more absorption time."

"You didn't tell me about any purple halos!"

He shrugged. "They went away in a day. Anyway, the experience gave me a notion to try. I figure I'll have hit my daily limit in live-ground theft when things start looking sort of lavender around the edges."

She pursed her lips in doubt. But how could she demand he not explore his abilities when she was so full of questions herself? There was no expert here for him to beg explanations of. He could only question his own body and ground with these trials, and listen carefully to the answers. Truly, somebody had once had to try *everything* for the first time, or there would be no experts.

"Are you still thinking that if you could get more ground-food to restore yourself, you could do more healing, faster?"

He nodded. "Maybe. Of Lakewalkers, leastways. But I want to heal farmers, and if I can't figure out this beguilement problem . . ." He moved another oat. Then a corn kernel. Then he sat up, blinked, twisted around, and stared at her face.

"Do I have a purple halo now?" she asked a little grimly.

He reached back, moved another oat, and blinked again. "Now you do," he said in a voice of tentative satisfaction.

"Then stop!"

"Yes," he sighed. He rubbed his night-stubbled chin and stared down at the two little heaps. "Huh."

"Hm?"

"This pile"—he pointed to the one on his right—"is live seeds. If you put them in the ground and watered 'em, you'd get new plants."

"Maybe," said Fawn, from a lifetime's experience on a farm. "Anyhow, if you planted enough of them, you'd likely get something. Plus the weeds."

"*This* pile," he said, ignoring the commentary, "is dead seeds. Plant them and they would just sit there and rot. Eventually."

A bleak look crossed his face, and Fawn wondered if his mind's eye was seeing a long row of uncorrupted little corpses. Blight it, oats weren't children. Well, she supposed they were the oat plant's children, in a way, but down that line of thought lay madness for anyone who meant to go on living in the world. She put in quickly, "Seeds won't sprout once you cook them, either. How is this different from cooking our food, really?"

His squint, after a moment, grew grateful. "There's a point, Spark."

She peered more closely. The heap on the left did seem a bit duller to her eye than the bright yellow grains on the right. She pointed to the dull heap. "Could you still eat those, like cooked food?"

He looked a bit taken aback. "I don't know. You'd think they'd have lost something."

"Would they poison you?"

"I have no idea." He stared down at the little pile for a long time. "I'd try feeding that handful to Copperhead, but he's over on the island, and, well, a horse. We've no dog." His eye fell speculatively on Daisy-goat.

"We drink milk from that goat," Fawn said hastily. And, as his face swiveled toward the chicken pen, "And we eat the eggs!"

He frowned, then got a faraway look for a moment. A scratching sound made Fawn glance down to find that Hawthorn's raccoon kit had appeared at Dag's ankle and was pawing at his trouser leg. Dag reached down and gathered up the creature, tucking it in the crook of his left arm. Its little leathery paws gripped his sleeve, and its bright black eyes twinkled from its furry mask.

"Dag," Fawn gasped, "you can't!"

"The horse, goats, chickens, and you are out," he said patiently. "What's left on this boat that'll eat grain? Well, Hod, but no. I don't think it will poison the little critter, really."

"It's just not right. I mean, at the very least you should ask Hawthorn's permission, and I can't see you explaining all this to Hawthorn!"

"I can't even explain it all to myself," Dag sighed. "Very well." He scooped up the pile of grain and raised his palm to his own lips.

"No!" Fawn clapped her hand to her mouth to muffle her shriek.

Dag raised his brows at her. "You can't say I don't have the right."

Fawn bounced up and down in dismay, lips pressed tight. And finally blurted, "Try it on the raccoon, then."

He tilted his head ironically at her and offered the grain to the kit. The kit seemed only mildly interested—spoiled, Fawn thought, by the tastier fodder that everyone aboard slipped to it—but at Dag's urging and, she suspected, sorcerous persuasion, it did nibble down a spoonful or so of the grains, whiskers twitching. When Dag let it go, it toddled off, apparently unaffected, or at least it didn't drop over dead on the spot. Dag tossed the remaining handful of dead seeds over the side, wiped his palm on his shirt, and picked off a few raccoon hairs. His eye fell on the chicken coop. "Food, huh," he said in a distant tone. "I wonder what would happen if I tried to ground-rip a chicken? Next time you mean to serve up a chicken dinner, Spark, let me know."

Fawn mentally took chicken off her menu plans for the indefinite future. "I don't know, Dag. The idea of you ripping seed grains doesn't bother me a bit. But if you could rip a chicken, could you—" she broke off.

He eyed her, not failing to follow. "Ground-rip a person? In full malice mode? I don't know. A person's bigger. I begin to suspect I could rip *up* a person's ground, at least. And yes, the idea does trouble me, thank you very much."

Fawn scrubbed her mouth with the back of her hand. "You can rip up a person's body *and* ground with your war knife, and you have. Would this truly be different?"

"I don't know yet," sighed Dag. "Spark, I really do not know." He folded her in to him then, leaning his forehead against hers. "I've been wondering for some time if I've stumbled across some craft secrets of senior medicine makers. Now you have me wondering if it's secrets of the senior knife makers, instead. They're even more close-mouthed about their work, and it may be with good reason. Because . . ."

"Because?" she prompted, when he didn't go on.

"Because I can't be the only person with these abilities. Unless I truly have been malice-corrupted, somehow. I wish I had someone to . . ."

"Someone to ask?" Alas, not Remo; a nice young patroller, but no maker.

Dag shook his head. "Someone *safe* to ask."

"Urgh." She didn't fail to follow, either.

"Hoharie might be, but she's back at Hickory Lake. She saw me—I don't think I told you about this . . ."

Fawn rolled her eyes. "More purple halos? Yes?"

"Sorry. At the time, I didn't know what to make of it, so I didn't talk about it. But when her apprentice Othan was trying to give a ground reinforcement to my broken arm, he couldn't get in. I ended up sort of . . . ripping it from him as he was trying to give it. Hoharie was right there, watching."

"And?"

"And her only reaction was to try to recruit me for a medicine maker. On the spot. Till I pointed out my little problem with fine hand-work." He waved his stump. "Later, she came up with the idea of partnering me with Othan's brother, for my spare hands. If she'd offered to partner me with you, I might have taken her up on it, and we'd still be there instead of here. But she shied off from that suggestion."

Fawn couldn't decide if that would have been good or not, so only tilted her head, *I hear you.* But she pounced quickly on the important point. "That was well before you ground-ripped the malice in Raintree, right?"

"Yes . . . ?"

"So these new abilities"—she leaned back and gripped his left arm— "can't be some sort of malice-contagion you picked up then, because you developed them before. I don't think you're turning into a malice." *Or you would be more scary, instead of just more aggravating.* "If that's what's worrying you."

From the play of expression on his face—first dismay, then relief— she realized she'd just spoken his most secret fear. And that, once dragged out into open air, it shrank hearteningly. "It . . . was a passing thought, I admit." He ducked his head, then smiled crookedly and held her closer. "So if I turned into a malice, would you still love me?"

"If you really turned into a malice, you'd just eat me, and the question wouldn't arise," she said a bit tartly.

"That's how we'd know, I suppose," he allowed.

"You'd know, anyhow." She thought about it. "Or maybe you wouldn't. You'd be too stuck inside your own torment to even see mine."

"Ah. Yes. You did look one straight in the eye, that time." His fingers brushed the scars on her neck, not to say *I forgot* so much as *I should have realized.* His eyes darkened with his own memories. "From what I've seen of the inside of a malice, you're right. You have an uncomfortably acute way of looking at things sometimes, Spark."

Fawn just shook her head. This conversation was spiraling into the dark, or at least into the creepy, in a way that suggested it was time for bed, because no further good could come of it tonight. She picked up the lantern and led the way.

15

D ag was reassured early the next morning of the health of the raccoon kit, as it woke him by nosing curiously in his ear. It also conveniently left a scat on the end of their blankets, not for the first time, as the creature seemed to have a partiality for their bed-nook. Dag took the pellet outside to the goat pen in the gray light to squash open with a stick. He would not have been surprised to find that the ripped grains had passed through whole, or even some odder effect, but they appeared to have been digested normally, with no sign of blood or blight to the kit's gut. So it seemed he could leave a trail of sterile seeds in his wake and do the world no harm. Though he was still deeply suspicious of their reuse as feed; perhaps he would buy his own chicken at the next stop to test them upon in a more methodical way. And put Fawn in charge of it, as he was by no means sure of his ability to keep a chicken alive in the first place, and he wouldn't want to make a mistake, here.

He leaned on the boat rail and watched the sky lighten from steel to silver to gold in a pure autumn sunrise, color seeping into the low hills lining the mist-shrouded river. It looked to be another brisk blue day like yesterday, which did not bode well for getting the *Fetch* off the sand bar. But a day of rest would be welcome. Perhaps he and Fawn could take a two-person picnic to the other end of the island. He extended his groundsense to check the chances of privacy, assuming they could successfully lose Whit, Hod, Remo, Hawthorn, and the raccoon. The island was a good two miles long, rich in natural ground, free of blight-sign, and, he found, unpeopled.

His breath drew in sharply, and he tested that range again, turning slowly. To both ends of the island, yes; he could clearly sense the head and tail where the stolidity of land met the melting motion of water. He cast his inner senses up along the farther hills, taking in the trees set-tling down root-deep for their winter sleep; drying, dying plants with bright seed-sparks armored in burrs; a multitude of small creatures burrowing, nesting, nosing through the brush, flitting from branch to branch; the slower lumbering of a family of black bears in the shadow of a ravine. *It's back. It's all back, my full range!* If only he were still at Hickory Lake, he could go out on patrol again.

He could hear the rattle of Fawn starting breakfast, and her voice scolding the kit out from underfoot and Hawthorn out of his bunk to take charge of it. His mouth quirked in the sure realization that if he were given, right this minute, the unfettered choice of whether to go back or go on—he'd go on. Smiling, he ducked inside and made his way to the back deck to wash up.

The morning meal was leisurely, abundant, and prolonged; the sun was high over the hills before Fawn stopped thinking of amusing new treats to try cooking up out of the *Fetch*'s stores. The younger male eaters, originally ravenous, showed signs of going sessile, losing inter-est in the idea of hunting on the island in favor of lazing on the boat, at least till Berry starting reeling off a long list of maintenance chores that a fellow with time on his hands could turn to.

On impulse, Dag interrupted this: "Actually, I'd like to borrow Remo and Hod this morning. And Fawn. I want to try some things."

Berry looked up shrewdly. "Is this about Hod's beguilement thing?"

"Yep," said Dag, and marveled at how far they'd come, that he could say such a thing openly—and be understood, at least well enough to go on with.

Boss Berry nodded. "Fine by me." She added wistfully, "Say, I don't suppose you two Lakewalkers can magic up some rain for us while you're at it?"

"I don't know of any groundwork that manages weather, sorry," said Dag seriously. "Though who knows what the old lake lords could do, back before the world broke?"

Berry eyed him. "That was a joke, Dag."

"Oh."

Fawn patted his hand. "That's all right. I don't always get patroller humor, either. Though if something's appalling, patrollers likely think it's hilarious."

Remo looked as though he wanted to object to this, but his mouth was too full.

Dag originally thought to retreat to the boat roof for the trials he had in mind, but then decided it would be best to get more out of groundsense range from the others. They rowed to shore dry-shod in the *Fetch*'s little skiff, though they might almost have waded, and hiked up the bank, waving good-bye to Berry and Whit, who were setting up a makeshift water-gauge in hopes of spotting some slight rise that might be just enough to lift the flatboat out of its sandy trap. At a high-ish spot near the towhead, with a view up the river valley framed by sand bar willows, Fawn laid out a blanket, and they all settled cross-legged in a circle and looked to Dag. Hod gulped nervously. Remo frowned in misgiving. Fawn just waited, watching him.

Dag cleared his throat, wishing he were more sure of, well, anything. "Fawn said the answer to this puzzle ought to lie between us all, if only we could see it. I mean to try harder to see it. Why is Hod beguiled, but Fawn not? Why don't Lakewalkers beguile each other? What are our grounds really doing, when we feel what we feel? My notion is that Remo and I will each open our grounds as wide as we can, try trading little ground reinforcements all around, and watch each other."

"What would we be looking for?" asked Remo, a trifle plaintively. "I mean—it's not like we haven't done this before."

Dag shook his head. "Watch for the things we don't usually notice. Especially watch for the things we think we know that might not really be so. Watch for the differences between Hod and Fawn. Is it the receiver that makes the difference, or is it the way the ground is gifted? I hope it's not all in the receiver, because that would mean I couldn't fix it—I could only heal some sick or hurt farmers but not others, and how would I tell which was which, in advance? How could I say to someone in mortal trouble, no, you go away, I can't—" Dag broke off. Swallowed. Said, "You start, Remo. Give a small reinforcement to Hod."

Remo's lips twisted in doubt. "In his knee again?"

"How about his nose?" Fawn suggested. "I think he's getting the sniffles from being in that cold water yesterday. And it wouldn't be mixed up with the old groundwork there."

Hod, who had in fact been making some ominously juicy snorting noises all morning, turned red, but nodded. Acutely aware that he would be laying himself entirely open to Remo's perceptions, Dag dropped his every guard and closed his eyes. He felt the whorl of ground coming away from Remo's face and floating between the two, the quick blink like water droplets joining as it settled into Hod's ground in turn, a palpable touch of warmth. Remo sneezed, and Dag's eyes shot open again.

Hod rubbed his nose and looked bewildered. "Feels nice," he offered.

Dag squinted, but no, with neither sight nor groundsense could he detect anything out of the ordinary. He ran his hand through his hair. "Well, all right. Do the same for Fawn, then."

"Are you sure, Dag?" asked Remo. "I mean—I wouldn't want to risk accidentally beguiling your wife." His glance at Dag was sidelong and wary.

"Fawn's already received some pretty complex ground reinforcements from me, and minor ones from Mari and Cattagus—is that all, Fawn?"

She nodded. "Old Cattagus fixed that little burn on my hand that time, and Mari—you were there when she helped me out." She made a vague gesture to her belly and the slowly healing malice scars hidden there that still rendered her monthlies so painful.

"She's not been beguiled yet, and this is lighter than even a minor healing reinforcement," said Dag. "Go ahead."

"Where?" said Remo. "I mean, Barr claims if you put a ground reinforcement in a farmer girl's—" He broke off abruptly, his face flushing. His ground shuttered.

"Out with it," said Dag patiently. "Who knows what overlooked thing could be important?"

Remo's ground only eased back by half. He looked up the river valley, meeting no one's eye. He said distantly, "Barr says if you put a ground reinforcement in a farmer girl's t . . . c . . . p . . . private parts"—this last choice barely got past his teeth—"it makes her eager to, um, be with you."

"Huh?" said Hod.

"Go out to the woodpile with him," Dag translated into Hoddish.

"Oh." Hod nodded wisely. "Sure."

From the look on Fawn's face, she did not require a translation. But she sat up straighter, her brow wrinkling. "Dag . . . is that why, when we first met, you said you couldn't heal my womb after the malice ripped me there?"

Remo's head swiveled at this, and his inspection of her malice scars dropped below her neck for the first time. His eyes widened.

Dag answered, "No! It was what I was always taught about field healings. For folks who aren't trained up as medicine makers, ground reinforcements flow best from body part to the same body part—the way Remo did Hod's nose, just now. Without a womb to pull ground from, I'd no such ground to give you." He hesitated. The healings he was trying nowadays through his ghost hand—his *ground projection*—certainly didn't work that way. "I wouldn't put much faith in Barr's hearsay."

"But it wasn't hearsay," Remo blurted. "He said he did it."

Dag, after an unmoving moment, pursed his lips. "You know this for sure?"

Remo nodded in discomfiture. "We'd put up out on patrol in this farmer's barn. He went after one of the sisters. The prettiest, naturally. He dared me to try with another one, but I said I'd tell our patrol leader if he ever pulled a stunt like that again, and he shut up about it." After a moment, he added, "I'm pretty sure he's done it more than once, though."

"He could hardly have pulled ground from his womb," said Dag slowly, still not convinced he believed Barr's brag.

"No, he said it was from his"—Remo gestured crotch-ward—"parallel parts. Because he had plenty to spare. He claimed."

Fawn said, in a coolly thoughtful tone, "That wouldn't have been a *healing* reinforcement then, exactly. Maybe it was just . . . stimulatin'. You know, Dag, what you were taught may just be what they tell the young patroller boys—and girls—so as to save trouble. And in the next generation, if no one tested it, they'd pass it along for fact. So you could both be right, in a way."

Dag rubbed the back of his neck as he considered this proposition. Maybe there ought to be another experiment, later, in private . . . he wrenched his mind back to the present trial. "Elbow. Try a tiny reinforcement in her elbow."

"Yes, sir," said Remo, in a tone that added, *And if anything goes wrong later, sir, remember you told me to do this.* He leaned forward again.

This ground reinforcement, as nearly as Dag could tell, worked identically to Hod's. Fawn rubbed her elbow and squinted at Remo, then sat back with an unperturbed smile.

Well, that had gone nowhere in particular. "All right," Dag sighed. "Now me, I guess. If you're up to it. Or do you need a rest?"

Remo shook his head. "Not for those little bits."

Dag sat up and opened his ground as wide as he ever had, trying for a listening quietude. "Elbow's fine for me, too. Better stay away from my left side, it's still pretty roiled over there."

Remo's head tilted, and his lips parted. He said uneasily, "Dag, yours is the strangest ground I've ever seen. Scarred up one side and knotted down the other, but dense . . . you're as dense as any medicine maker I've met. It's hard to know where to *put* a reinforcement!"

Dag nodded. "That calling has been growing in me for some time, I suspect. Longer than I've known. Try a foot. They're always happy for some help." He cast a glint at Fawn, recalling her very alluring foot rubs; she glinted back.

Remo gathered himself, touched his own right foot, then Dag's. Dag felt the whorl of ground flow past. *There!* An echo of ground—like the fainter second rainbow that sometimes mirrored a first—passed back between them even as the bit of Remo's ground joined to Dag's. The ground in Remo's foot closed again like some thick liquid settling around the warm return gift.

"Did you see that?" Dag said in excitement.

"What?" said Remo cautiously. "It seemed like a usual reinforcement to me."

"That little backsplash from me to you, like an undertow of ground."

"Can't say as I noticed."

Dag's teeth gritted in frustration. He bit back a sharp rejoinder of *Then open wider, blight you!* Remo was only a young patroller. It was more than probable that an improved sensitivity to ground was growing in Dag along with his other maker's talents. Had his younger self ever experienced such simple field reinforcements as anything other than diffuse blobs? Although if Remo truly couldn't sense this, he wasn't going to be much help as a check on Dag's perceptions.

Dag sighed and straightened. "All right. My turn. I need you to watch really closely, Remo. I'll start with Hod's right elbow, as there's no other groundwork there." That had been a good notion of Fawn's, to keep the trials separated for clearer comparisons.

He unfurled his ghost hand, reached out, and spun off a tiny reinforcement into the target. No ground-echo returned, hah! The reinforcement was swallowed up greedily as though gulped. Hod sighed contentedly.

But Remo almost fell over in his scramble backward. Up on one knee and looking ready to bolt, he pointed toward Dag's hook and cried, "Blight! What *was* that?"

Dag had forgotten he'd not introduced Remo to his new talent. "Settle down. It's just my gh—ground projection. Instead of mirroring body parts, it pulls ground generally from all through me. Hoharie— she's Hickory Lake Camp's senior medicine maker—says it's a maker's skill. It doesn't usually take quite this form in other makers, but you can kind of see why it would for me."

"Uh," said Remo. "Yeah." Dag wished he wouldn't look quite so bug-eyed, but he did settle back cross-legged and tried to be attentive.

"I will wait," said Dag patiently, "till you can get your ground open again."

Remo swallowed. It took him a few minutes, but he eventually achieved the relaxed openness Dag needed.

Dag rubbed his jaw, and said, "Think I'll try you next. I need you to watch not my reinforcement, but for a little echo of it coming back from you to me. I'd say underneath, but it's more like the return ground passes right *through* the other, lagging a bit. Ready?"

Remo nodded. Dag leaned forward and extended his ghost hand again. He paused while Remo's ground flickered in alarm, then steadied. He nodded and spun off the reinforcement toward Remo's right forearm. This time, watching for it, the ground return was distinctly discernible. The faint Remo-ground-echo was converted so rapidly it seemed to disperse through Dag's arm like a blown dandelion puff. Dag's brows rose.

"I saw . . ." Remo began excitedly, then slowed. "I'm not just sure what I saw."

"You saw your ground-echo. I felt it slide into me. It converted a lot faster than . . . um . . . a primary ground reinforcement." The one Remo had placed in Dag's foot was still there, comfortable but distinct. Dag's return echo in Remo's foot was almost fully absorbed already. Dag blew out his breath and turned to Fawn. She was watching him closely, clearly struggling to follow all this. He gave her a reassuring nod, but it only made her lift her brows wryly.

Dag centered himself, opened all his heart to her, reached out, and spun a reinforcement into her opposite elbow. The return echo came back to him like a kiss, and his lips softened in a smile.

"I saw that thing again!" said Remo. "I think . . ."

Dag sat back and rubbed his forehead. "I saw. Felt. Yes. The reason

Fawn is not beguiled is that her ground is acting like a Lakewalker's—at least—it did when *I* gave her the reinforcement. But it didn't when you did. That's . . . odd."

"Is it because you're married?" said Remo.

"I'm not sure." Marriage—Lakewalker marriage—was certainly a ground-transforming act, as their binding strings testified. But Dag could hardly marry all his potential patients. A stumper, this.

They'd gone all the way around with each of them. The answer had to be here, hidden in the crisscross of ground flow—or its absence. Dag fell onto his back and glowered up at the nearly leafless willow branches, at the cool, blue sky brightening toward noon. Dag and Remo had exchanged ground with each other; Dag only had exchanged with Fawn. Neither had exchanged with poor Hod.

Or was that, neither had *accepted* an exchange with poor Hod . . . ?

Oh ye gods. Can I do this? I don't want bits of Hod in me!

So do you really want to be the farmers' own medicine maker—old patroller? Because a real maker can't pick and choose his patients. He has to take whoever and whatever comes, equally.

"It's not true," he said to the sky in sudden wonder. "It was *never* true."

"What's not true, Dag?" Fawn asked in that long-suffering voice that suggested she was about to snap. His lips curled up, which made her growl, which made them curl up more.

"It's not true," he said, "that Lakewalkers don't beguile each other. We beguile each other *all the time*."

"What?" said Remo, sounding startled.

Dag sat up, his smile twisting. He raised his left arm toward Hod. Spun off a neat reinforcement into the nearly healed knee. And held himself open: not sternly, not rigidly, but warmly and without reservation.

The backsplash this time was so blatant that Remo cried *Whoa!* There was, after all, a deal of accumulated ground-load for Hod to dump so suddenly.

Hod bent, blinked, and touched his forehead, then gripped his leg. His smile flickered very uncertainly. "Uh," he said. "I felt . . . it went away . . ." And added piteously after a moment, "But . . . can I still be your friend?"

"Yes, Hod, you surely can," said Dag. "You surely can."

"Dag," said Fawn dangerously, "do you want to explain that for the rest of us? Because if you haven't just done something worse 'n that catfish, I'll eat my hat."

"I just un-beguiled Hod!" Dag exulted, choking back a thoroughly undignified chortle. "In a sense."

"The first half of that sounds good," allowed Fawn, and waited with understandable suspicion for him to explain the second.

"I think—I'm guessing—that the hunger a beguiled person has for repeated ground reinforcements isn't only because they feel real good. It's really an urgent attempt by their ground to rebalance itself. To complete the thwarted exchange. Except that it just gets worse with each addition if the Lakewalker doing the reinforcements still blocks—rejects—the return ground-gift."

Dag went on in growing elation, "That also explains why beguilement's so blighted erratic. It depends on how open—or not—the Lakewalker feels about farmers—or about that particular farmer, leastways. I've been open to Fawn since almost the beginning, so no imbalance has ever built up in her. Hod . . . not. Till just now. Ha!" He supposed he'd only frighten Hod and Remo if he jumped up and danced around them all whooping like a madman, but he really wanted to.

Remo looked less enthusiastic. "What do you mean, we beguile each other all the time? We don't!"

"Beguile and un-beguile both. Ground exchange, in balance, not thwarted. I swear it starts with our mother's milk, and goes on—not a Lakewalker child comes of age without having received dozens of little reinforcements from dozens of kinfolk or friends for this or that ailment or injury. Grown up and out on patrol, or in camp with our tent-kin, we're always swapping around. We float in a lake of shared ground. I'd not be surprised to find it's part of why, when a Lakewalker is cut off from others, we feel so odd and unhappy."

Remo looked wholly interested but only half-convinced. "Dag, are you sure of this?"

"Nearly. You'd best believe I'll be watching out for it from now on."

Fawn asked, "Does this mean you really could teach other makers to heal farmers?"

"Spark, if I'm right, any medicine maker who knew this could treat a farmer without beguiling—if only the maker was willing to take in farmer ground." He hesitated. That might be a bigger *if only* than it looked at first. Still, medicine making had never been for the squeamish.

Remo said slowly, "But what would happen to that lake of shared ground if a lot of Lakewalkers started taking in farmer ground? What would happen to the maker?"

Dag fell silent. "I don't know," he said at last. "I came out here this morning determined to wring some answers to my questions—and we did!—but it seems I've just stirred up a pack of bigger questions. I'm not getting ahead, here."

After a longer pause, Fawn clambered to her feet and motioned them all off the blanket so she could roll it up. The walk back to the *Fetch* was very subdued. Although at least Hod had stopped sniffling.

∾

In the warmest part of the afternoon, Dag took Fawn down the island to, as they explained to Hawthorn, scout for squirrels. Hawthorn promptly begged to go along, brandishing a slingshot. Remo, bless him, understood the patrol code, and diverted the boy long enough for them to escape.

Finding a warm nook took a little searching, as the wind was freshening and showing signs of veering northwest, with horse-tail clouds spread in gauzy lines turning the light paler. But a low spot in some deadfall, once it was lined with the good supply of blankets they'd packed along, lent both privacy and comfort.

Over the next few delicious hours, Dag discovered that with his growing control of ground projection he could indeed lay reinforcements in select body parts that did not match his own, but, Fawn reported, it did nothing that his ghost hand didn't already do better. They compared the techniques a couple of times, to be certain, during which Fawn's solemnly helpful expression kept dissolving into giggles. Dag chortled in, he trusted, a more dignified fashion. Well, maybe not so dignified in that position . . . He was unable to test Barr's assertion about making farmer girls suffer desire because he couldn't force himself to stay closed to Fawn, and anyway, it would have been like pouring milk into milk and looking for a color change. But he hoped this new support around her hidden malice scars would help with the pain of her next monthly, coming up soon.

"A ground reinforcement doesn't actually heal a person," he explained as they lay drowsily intertwined, bodies and investigations temporarily exhausted. "It just strengthens a body to heal itself quicker, or to fight infection better. If the damage is too great or the sickness spreads too fast, the maker's work gets overwhelmed, too."

Fawn's lips pursed. She turned her head in the crook of his arm to dot kisses across his skin. "Can the maker get overwhelmed? Give away too much ground to live?"

Dag shook his head. "You'd pass out, first. It's not like bleeding, that can go on without your will or awareness. Although the exhaustion can lay the maker open to sickness, too, same as anyone else." He hesitated. "A reinforcement's not to be confused with a medicine maker's ground-lock, mind you. If a maker's gone down and in too deep, till matching grounds turns into mixing them, and his patient dies on him, the maker can die, too. The dying ground disrupting the other, see."

She blinked. "Huh. I wonder if that's how your ancestors first got the idea for sharing knives?"

Dag rocked back. "Huh! Could be, Spark! Could well be." *Bright farmer girl!*

She nodded, brows drawing down. "One way or another, seems like it would be a good idea to keep your strength up."

"Same as a patrol leader keeping his patrol in good shape, I reckon," he allowed thoughtfully.

"And the other way around."

He bent his head and nuzzled her hair. "That, too, Spark."

The next morning Dag woke to gray skies and extra kisses. Fawn sat up on one elbow, and asked, "Do you know what day this is?"

"I've lost track," he admitted. "Better ask Berry."

"Guess I'd better." She grinned and went off to start breakfast.

The clouds thickened but did not deliver rain; the *Fetch* stayed stuck. After lunch, Whit insisted on dragging Dag off to explore the back side of the island. A wedge of fallen trees and thatch across the channel made a temporary bridge to the mainland, and they picked their way precariously across despite Dag's assurances that there was nothing over there of note for at least a mile in any direction. When they at last returned to the *Fetch*, Remo met them on shore with strict instructions from the cook to go catch some fish for dinner, specifically not catfish. This entailed another trip across to the back channel, from which they returned with heavy strings of walleye and three kinds of bass. Bo and Hod took the catch in charge to clean and gut. Then Whit suggested an archery lesson. Remo and Dag set up a target while Whit took the skiff out to the boat for their bows and arrows. In a while Hod and Hawthorn rowed to shore for a turn as well, and by the time they'd worn out everyone, especially the chief instructor, the leaden skies were darkening with early nightfall.

The air of the *Fetch*'s cabin, when Dag stepped inside, was warm and moist and smelled amazing. He walked into the kitchen area to find it crammed with busy people and festooned with bunches of autumn wildflowers and dried milkweed pods tied with colored yarn. Berry and Fawn were frying up a mountain of fish and potatoes and onions, and Whit and Bo were tapping a new keg of beer set up on a trestle, and where had that come from?

"What are we celebrating?" Dag inquired amiably.

Fawn set aside her pan, walked over, stood on tiptoe, snaked an arm around his neck to pull his face down to her level, and said, "You. Happy birthday, Dag!" And kissed him soundly, to the hoots and clapping of the whole crew congregated. He pulled back, once she released him, with his mouth gaping in astonishment.

"Yes!" Whit whooped. "We *got* him! We got him good!"

"How did you know this was my birthday?" Dag asked Fawn. It had been upwards of twenty years since he'd paid the least attention to it himself, and he certainly hadn't mentioned it recently.

"Dag!" said Fawn in fond exasperation. "You gave it to the town clerk when we were married in West Blue! Of course I remembered!"

And Fawn's was in about six more weeks, as he had learned at the same time and not forgotten—he'd thought they might be in Graymouth by then, and wondered what farmer birthday customs might please her, and been glad that Whit would be there to ask and maybe help keep her from feeling too alone in a strange place. *She'll be nineteen, gods.* Dag wasn't sure whether to feel old, or good, but as Remo pressed him into his seat and Bo thrust a tankard of beer into his hand, he decided on good.

Then came tender fish and melting potatoes and a tide of beer, and jokes and tales and laughter, and yes, friends, and his own real tent-kin. He was glad, too, for Remo at the table—whatever the exact interplay of ground and body, mind and heart, it seemed a wider world to have both farmers and Lakewalkers in it. Celebrating each other.

The beer, Dag learned, had been secretly laid in by Whit for precisely this purpose at that last stop where he'd sold his window glass. Its status as a present had apparently kept it from any premature depredations by Bo, a fact Bo himself pointed out with a certain pride. The Bluefield conspiracy had been going on for some days, it seemed, for when no one was able to force down another bite, Fawn brought out a package wrapped in cloth and tied with another jaunty yarn bow. Dag opened it to discover a new-sewn oiled cloth cape and hood, such as boatmen wore.

"Bo let me use his old one for a pattern," Fawn explained in satisfaction. "I traded making new ones for him and Berry for the cloth to make some for you and Whit, but I haven't got to the others yet." Her second packet was a sweater sleeve, incomplete but promissory. "I expect to make some real good progress on it next week. Remo said Lakewalkers give new clothes and weapons on birthdays, and maybe when you start patrolling, a horse. You have a horse and a whole arsenal already, but at least I made you a few more arrows. Berry gave me the Tripoint steel heads, and Hawthorn had the eagle feathers." She added a bundle of half a dozen new shafts to the stack, and Dag decided he would let his tongue be cut out before explaining that such gifting customs were mainly meant for youngsters.

Outside in the dark, the wind blew a spatter of rain against the walls and windows, and Berry looked up intently. But as the wind and water didn't yet shift the boat, she settled back and sipped at her tankard. Dag would have been quite content to just take a seat near the fire with a warm wife in his lap for the rest of the night, but Fawn extracted herself from his embrace and flitted off again.

"More?" said Dag.

"Remo said Lakewalkers don't make birthday cakes, exactly, but if you're going to be a real Bluefield, you need to have one," Whit explained as Fawn came tottering back with a huge cake on a platter. "With candles. It's the farmer thing to do, or at least it always was at our house."

"I love the candles best. One for every year," Fawn expanded upon this, thumping the platter down in front of Dag. Which explained the size of the cake, bristling with a small forest of thin beeswax sticks. "I made this cake with ginger and pear, and honey-butter frosting. Because I was getting right tired of everything apple, even if we still have barrels of them."

"Where did you find all the candles?" Dag asked, fascinated and a bit taken aback. "Same goods-shed where Whit got the beer?"

Fawn shook her head, dark eyes and curls all sprightly. "Nope, the ones they had were all too big. I made these myself, this afternoon, with some wax Berry gave me from her stores and some string I plaited a while back."

Dag plucked one up and rolled it between his fingers, smelling the faint honey scent. "They're a good making, Spark."

She smiled in pleasure at his praise.

"The deal is," Whit advised, "you're supposed to light them, then make a wish. If you blow them all out in one breath, you get your wish."

Dag could not picture the groundwork that would effect such a thing, so decided it must be a farmer superstition, if a pleasant one. "It sounds right difficult."

"It's easier when you're six than when you're fifty-six," Whit conceded.

"Indeed. Well, all right. I'll try." Certain Lakewalker makers produced groundworked candles that made the task a snap; this would call for a greater effort on his part, Dag suspected. But these wax lights were sound work, and of Fawn's own hands. Just like their marriage cords. He set the candle back in its hole in the frosting, centered himself, aligned his ground, called up his hottest persuasion, and swept his ghost hand back and forth across the bristling top of the cake. To his pure delight, all fifty-six little golden flames sprang up in its wake with a faint *foomp! foomp!* sound.

He looked up in satisfaction to find Fawn and Berry both standing at his sides with lit spills in their hands and their mouths open. A silence stretched around the crowded table. Hod was blinking. Hawthorn's eyes were wide. Bo seemed to have bitten his tongue. "Was that . . . not right?" Dag asked hesitantly.

Whit said, in a rather hollow voice, "And I'd have been impressed if he'd *blown them out* all at once!"

Remo laughed out loud. Actually, Remo *cackled,* Dag decided. Dag might have been more annoyed, particularly as Remo didn't stop for quite a while—choking himself off, eventually, into his sleeve—except that it was the first time ever he'd heard the boy laugh.

"That was just fine, Dag," Fawn assured him valiantly. "You can light all our birthday cakes from now on." She blew out her spill and handed him a knife.

Dag waited a while for Fawn to enjoy the glow—or conflagration—while he enjoyed the play of the warm light on her face, like a summer sunset here on the edge of winter. He didn't cheat much, blowing out the candles again. Fawn extracted the wax stumps for reuse, sharing the task of licking off the frosting with Hawthorn, an eager volunteer. The pocked cake was divided into generous slabs, with half still left for breakfast. After, Dag was made to sit by the fire with Fawn just as he'd pictured, while Whit and the crew took charge of the cleanup. The rain drummed on the roof as Hod and Hawthorn pestered Remo to show them how Lakewalkers cheated in games of chance, Remo protesting that he didn't know how to either play *or* cheat.

And then, with a faint groan and a definite jerk, the *Fetch* lifted from the sand bar. Berry whooped, and everyone dropped all other tasks to turn out and get the boat away from the bar and down the island to a safe landing, to be tied properly for the night. Both of the Lakewalkers, with their ability to move surely in the dark, were pressed into this task, but when they all came trooping wetly back inside Fawn had hot tea waiting and prewarmed towels stacked by the hearth. Sodden clothes were stripped off and hung up—except for Dag's, adequately protected by his new boatman's rain gear— dry clothes were donned, and those with room snagged more cake and beer. The patter of rain gusted into a rattle of hail, but the guide ropes held the boat in its new mooring as they all settled around the hearth once more.

Then Berry pulled out her fiddle and gave them three tunes, two lively, one slow and plaintive. There wasn't enough room to dance, but while Berry shook out her fingers and rested up the Clearcreeks debated teaching boatmen's songs to the Bluefields. Hawthorn claimed he knew all the rude words.

"Yeah, but you don't understand 'em," drawled Bo.

"I do too!"

"Maybe it's time for a lullaby," Berry suggested.

"No, not yet!" Hawthorn protested. Hod looked torn. Whit looked wistful.

Remo was sitting on the floor near the fire, the overfed raccoon kit asleep in his lap; his head came up, turning.

"What?" Dag said quietly.

"There's a Lakewalker out on the river in a narrow boat."

"In this weather?" Bo snorted. "Fool should be on shore with the boat turned upside down and him under it. Tied down at both ends, too, if he'd a lick of sense."

Dag silently agreed, but stretched his groundsense outward. A Lakewalker indeed, and just as miserable as you'd expect. Their grounds bumped, and the narrow boat changed course, fighting through the wind waves.

Remo's eyes widened. He set down the kit and scrambled to his feet. "It's Barr!"

A clunk and a thump were followed by the muffled pounding of a fist on the side of the hull.

"Remo, you fool!" Barr's voice called hoarsely. "Blight you! I know you're in there! Come give me a hand before I freeze in this blighted rain!"

16

Fawn watched in alarm as Remo took up the lantern and made his way with Dag and Whit out into the wind and rain of the back deck. Hod hovered uncertainly till Bo, staying planted in his chair beyond the hearth, told him sharply to go in or out but stop blocking the doorway like a fool cat, and Hod drew back. Hawthorn bounced impatiently behind Hod; the raccoon kit skittered off and hid in the stores. Berry put her fiddle away in its leather bag and slid it back under her curtained bunk.

Voices outside rose in debate, Dag's deep tones overriding: "Just tie it to the rail. We can deal with it in the morning. Shipping more water's not going to make much difference—it's already half-swamped."

More thumps, grunts, and muffled curses. Whit shoved the door open and handed in a bedroll, a pack, an unstrung bow and quiver coming unwrapped from a trailing blanket, and a couple of lumpy cloth bags, all equally sodden. Hod dropped them in a heap. Whit came back in, followed by Dag and a very wet Lakewalker who Fawn didn't know. Remo trailed with the lantern, which he put back on the kitchen table, then leaned his shoulders against the door and crossed his arms, face set.

The fellow stood dripping before the hearth, breathing heavily, strained with exhaustion and cold. His lank hair, plastered to his forehead and hanging in a sorry rattail down his back, might be tawny blond when dry. He shrugged broad shoulders out of a soaked deerskin jacket, then just stood holding it in his hands as if confused where to put it, or just confused altogether. He scowled faintly at the *Fetch*'s crew, who were staring at him with expressions ranging from dumbfounded to dubious, but he eyed the bright fire with understandable longing.

Barr, presumably. Fawn tried not to take an instant dislike to him simply on the basis of Remo's tale about the pretty farmer sister; such a seduction, if it had occurred as described or even at all, could well have been a two-way enterprise. And he'd been brave to help rescue those coal flatties from drowning in the Riffle. Or maybe he just liked excitement, although at the moment he seemed more distraught.

Apparently continuing an exchange started outside, he looked to Remo and said, "I was afraid I wasn't going to catch up with you for another hundred miles!"

"Why are you trying to catch up with me at all?" said Remo, in a voice devoid of encouragement.

"What do you mean, why? I'm your partner!"

"Not anymore. I left."

"Yes, without a word to anyone! Amma and Issi turned me on the grill for a blighted hour about that alone—like I should have known. How? By magic? You owe me for that, as well as for paddling three hundred miles in three days after you."

"If you came from Pearl Riffle, that would be 'bout two hundred miles, unless you took a detour," Berry observed, her hands on her hips. Hers was one of the more dubious looks.

Barr waved this away. "It was too blighted many miles, anyway. But that's done now." He stretched his shoulders, which cracked a bit, shook out the jacket and laid it on the hearthstones, and edged his backside closer to the fire, spreading his hands briefly on his knees. Big, strong hands, Fawn noted, although at the moment cramped from his paddle and chapped with cold. "I admit, I was glad not to find you floating facedown anywhere between there and here. We can start back in the morning."

"Back where?" said Remo, still dour.

"Pearl Riffle, snag-brain. If you come back with me now, Amma says she'll let us both back on patrol." Barr straightened up with a look of, if not triumph, at least accomplishment.

Remo's lips folded as tightly as his arms. "I'm not going back."

"You have to come back! Amma and Issi ripped me up one side and down the other, like it was my fault you ran off!"

"So it was," said Remo uncompromisingly.

"Well, it's water over the Riffle now. The *important* thing is, if I bring you back, all is forgiven. I'm not saying things won't be edgy for a while, but sooner or later someone else will win Amma's ire, and it'll blow over. It always does." He blinked and grinned in a way that might have seemed charming, to some other audience at some other season.

"Not this time."

"Remo, you're making no sense. Where else would you go but back?"

"On," said Remo. He nodded at Berry. "Boss Berry, whose boat you are dripping in, will likely let you sleep the night inside if you ask politely. In the morning, you go upriver, I go down. Simple."

"*Remo*, no. Not simple. If I don't fetch you back alive and in one piece, Amma swears I'll be discharged from patrol permanently! I'm not joking!"

Fawn was beginning to get the picture, here. It wasn't simply worry for a partner; Barr was on a mission to save his own well-scorched tail.

Remo looked furious. "Neither am I."

Barr stared at him with the genuine bewilderment of a fellow who'd slid by on charm all his life whose charm had inexplicably stopped working.

Dag had been watching from the sidelines without comment. Before the go-round could start again, his unmoved voice put in, "Best dry your weapons, patroller. Your bow is starting to warp from the wet."

Barr made a discomfited gesture, as if he'd like to protest this interruption but didn't quite dare. He eyed Dag warily. "And you, Dag Red-Blue whatever. Amma *also* wanted me to tell her if *you* talked Remo into this. Like I knew!"

Remo snorted in disgust.

"I said I didn't think you'd seen each other since that first day in the patrol tent. I'm not sure she believed me." He added bitterly, "I'm not sure she believed anything I said."

With heavy sarcasm, Remo intoned, "Why, Barr—why *ever* would she not?"

Before Barr's return growl could find words, Berry exchanged a glance with Dag and shouldered forward. "It's boatmen's bedtime, patroller, and you're making a tedious ruckus in our bunkroom. If you want, you could have some mighty tasty leftovers and a dry bed in front of the hearth. If you two'd druther keep arguin' instead, take it outside to the riverbank where you can keep it up to your heart's content or dawn, whichever comes first. Your choice, but make it now." A rattle of sleet against the windows lent a sinister weight to her cool remark.

After a long, long moment, Barr swallowed down whatever he'd been going to snap back at Remo and nodded to the boat boss. He said stiffly, "I'd be grateful for a bed, yes, ma'am. And food." He shot Remo a surly look that made it clear he was giving up only temporarily.

The occupants of the *Fetch*'s kitchen-bunkroom shuffled back into almost-normal preparations for sleep. Barr did look after his weapons, with a sidelong glance at Dag. Whit and Hod helped lay out the rest of his things to dry; Hawthorn and Berry settled the guest-furs in front of the fire; and Fawn reheated the fish, potatoes, and onions. Barr wolfed down the meal as though starved, and gaped in wonder at the tankard of beer Bo shoved in front of him. He found the bottom of it quickly. Awkwardly, everyone dodged around one another in the shared sleeping space that had suddenly become a little too shared, but all found their beds at last.

As the lantern light dimmed to the faintest red glow through the curtains of their nook, Fawn interlaced herself with Dag for warmth and whispered, "You didn't happen to wish for Barr on those birthday candles, did you?"

Dag choked down a laugh. "No, Spark." He grew quiet for a moment. "Not exactly, leastways."

"Just so's you know that last surprise was not my doing."

"It seems to have been Amma Osprey's. Wish I could have been listening at the window for *that* talk. I'll bet it was blistering. Sounds like it was past time she put the fire to that boy's feet, though."

"Do you think Remo should go back with him?"

"It's not my decision to make."

"You wanted him to go back, that first night."

"It's good for young patrollers to get out and see the world."

"You said you weren't adopting him."

He drew back his head to look down over his nose at her, squinting in the shadows. "Do you remember everything I say that clearly? That could get downright burdensome on a husband."

She snickered.

He added, "Seems they can both drag back home with their tails between their legs, and Amma'll let them in. I'm not too surprised. Nobody wants to waste patrollers. Still . . . I'll hate to see Remo go, if he goes. I thought I might be starting to get somewhere with him. And he was a huge help with Hod."

Fawn grew more pensive. "There is this. You can't ever run away from one thing without running toward something else." She slid a small hand up his shoulder. "You, for example. I ran away from home, and right into you. And the wide world with you. I'd never be here if I hadn't first left there."

"Do you like it here? This boat?"

"I'd like any boat with you in it." She stretched up and kissed him. "Was it a happy birthday?"

"The best in years." He kissed her back, and added slowly, "The best in all my years. And that's a lot of years, Spark. Huh."

She considered poking him and demanding what that *Huh* was all about, but he yawned fit to crack his jaw, her feet finally warmed up, and she melted into sleep.

At breakfast, Fawn discovered that like most fine young animals, Barr was cuter when he was dry and fluffy. She'd been uncertain of his age in the strain of his last night's exhaustion, but now she was sure he was the junior of the partners. He'd also regained his temper, or at least his arguments shifted to being less about Barr and more about Remo.

"Your tent-folk are all really worried about you," he offered.

"Not when I last saw them," Remo replied. "Notably not."

"Remo, you have to realize, Amma's only giving us a grace period, here. You can't expect forgiveness to be held out on a stick forever."

Remo said nothing.

Barr soldiered on. "If we don't get back timely, she'll have had a chance to get over being worried about you, and revert to being riled. We need to grab the moment."

Fawn couldn't help asking, "Won't she be worried about the both of you?"

Barr glanced at her as if uncertain whether to speak directly to the farmer bride or not; unable to resist a chance to vent, he said, "Since she as much as told me to come back with him or not at all, I don't think so."

"Barr the expendable," murmured Remo.

Barr's jaw set, but he made no rejoinder; Remo looked mildly surprised.

After a little silence broken only by munching and requests to pass the cornbread and butter, Remo said, "Speaking of expendable, what in the world were you doing out in that weather last night?"

"It wasn't my first plan," said Barr. "There's a ferry camp somewhere near here that I was trying to reach by dark, and the worse the rain got, the more it seemed worth holding out for. I sure wasn't going to get any drier camping on shore in that blow. But I came to you before I came to it."

"If you mean Fox Creek Camp," Dag put in, "you passed it about ten miles back."

"I can't have missed it!" Barr said. "I've had my groundsense wide-open almost the whole way—looking for you," he added aside to Remo. "Or your floating body."

"Water this cold, my body might not have come up so soon," said Remo distantly.

Dag's brows twitched, but he said, "Fox Creek Camp mostly lies behind the hills. They dammed the creek to make a little lake back there. Likely there wasn't anyone out on the ferry landing after dark."

"Oh. Crap." Barr looked briefly put out, then cheered up. "This is better anyway. If I'd stopped there, I wouldn't have caught up with you till tonight at the earliest, and that'd be yet another fifty upriver miles to backtrack. At least." He turned again to Remo. "Which is another reason to come back with me now. Every mile you go down is going to be that much more work going up."

"Not my problem," said Remo.

"Well, it's mine!" said Barr, baited into personal outrage again. "With this current running, a narrow boat with only one paddler couldn't even make headway going upriver! It needs at least two, and better four!"

In a practical spirit, and to divert whatever crushing thing Remo was fixing to say next, Fawn suggested, "You could trade your narrow boat for a horse at the next town and ride back to Pearl Riffle overland."

"That's a stupid idea," objected Barr. Failing to notice either her stiffening or Dag's, he plunged on, "I couldn't get one good horse in trade for that old boat, let alone two!"

"You wouldn't need two," said Remo.

Whit, falling back into his old bad habits of pot-stirring, put in cheerfully, "And who says it has to be a *good* horse?"

Barr clenched his teeth and eyed him unfavorably.

Boss Berry's drawl cut across the debate. "There's this, Remo. You hired on as my sweep-man. If you jump my boat now, you'll leave me shorthanded in the middle of nowhere, and that's not right. Now, this ain't my argument, but if you want to quit, at least do it at a village or town where I can hire on your replacement."

"That's only fair," Remo allowed, looking at Barr in a challenging way. Barr didn't have an immediate answer, although by his grimace Fawn thought she could see him mentally adding the upstream miles.

"Sky's lightening," said Bo. "Time to get out on the river."

Berry nodded. "Me, Remo, and Whit for the first watch."

Which ended the squabble for the next two hours at least. Breakfast broke up, and Remo and Barr went out to get the water emptied from Barr's boat, hoist it up, and tie it down across the back deck, where, Fawn thought, it was going to be mightily in the way. Hod and Hawthorn turned to their scullery duties. Dag went ashore to collect Copperhead, who had been standing amongst the dripping leafless trees and whinnying plaintively since predawn, answered by bleats from Daisy-goat. Copperhead actually seemed glad to scramble back onto the boat, and touched noses with Daisy; the two animals had become unlikely friends. The lines were untied, the top-deck crew took to their sweeps, and the *Fetch* pushed off from the muddy bank, turning slowly downstream. The river was dark and fast and scary this morning, the wind funneling up the valley cold and raw, whipping the mist to tatters. Fawn put her mind to sewing up more rain cloaks and retreated inside to find her work basket, glad for an indoor task.

⚬

Fawn had her oilcloth pieces laid out on the table near the window for the light, stitching industriously, when Barr came into the kitchen, shot her a guarded look, and began puttering around setting his dried gear back in order. Patrollers were doubtless taught to travel tidy, she reflected. She returned him a nod, in case he wanted to talk but wasn't sure he was allowed. Although maybe that was more for rigid Remo; Barr apparently had found no trouble talking with farmer girls in the past. Except not farmer brides inexplicably married to other Lakewalkers, it seemed, for when he finally opened his mouth, what came out was hardly smooth.

"You're pretty stuck on Dag, aren't you?" He'd sat down in front of the hearth with his knees up, to oil some leather straps, incidentally blocking the heat. But perhaps he was still core-cold from yesterday.

For answer, Fawn held up her left wrist and the marriage cord wrapped around it. "What does your groundsense tell you?"

His nose wrinkled in wonder, but not denial. "Can't imagine how you two did that."

"We wove them together. As partners, you might say. I made my ground follow my blood into the cord that Dag wears, which Dag's brother Dar said was a knife-making technique. It worked, anyhow."

Barr blinked. "Saun said you two had jumped the cliff at Glassforge, which surprised him right off, as he hadn't thought Dag was the sort—stiffer than Remo, even—but nobody ever . . . Lakewalkers don't usually marry farmers, you know."

He was actually being sort of polite: *don't ever* would have been more accurate. "Dag's an unusual man."

"Do you realize how old he likely is? To farmer eyes I know he looks thirty-five or forty, but I can tell you he has to be a good deal more than that."

What are you on about? "His fifty-sixth birthday was yesterday. We had a real nice party. That was the leftovers you bolted last night."

"Oh." Barr squinted at her in increasing puzzlement. "Do you realize he has to have beguiled you?"

"Do you realize you are amazingly offensive?" she returned in a level tone.

By his discomfited head-duck, that wasn't the response he'd been expecting. She bit off her short strand and tied it, then drew out a new length to thread her needle. "Dag hasn't beguiled me one bit. He and Remo have been doing some studying on that, how beguilement really happens in groundwork, and have found out some pretty terrific things. You should get Dag to teach you." Barr did not seem the most promising learner, but there was certainly worse out there. If Dag's schemes were to work, they had to reach ordinary folks, Lakewalker and farmer alike, and not just a tiny elite.

But Barr had other matters on his mind. He muttered, "Can't be her. *Has* to be the blonde." Raising his voice, he said, "Remo's after that Berry girl, isn't he? That's why he won't turn around . . . taking after your Dag, maybe? Absent gods, he doesn't mean to marry her, does he?"

Fawn stared over her stitches in increasing exasperation. "Berry's betrothed to a farmer boy named Alder, who went missing on a downriver trip last fall along with Berry's papa and brother. She's going to look for 'em all, which is why she named her boat the *Fetch*. She carries on steady, because she's that sort and it's a long haul, but inside she's anxious and grieving. You want to make yourself real unpopular with everyone on this boat in a big hurry, you try botherin' Berry *in any way*." Had she hammered in that hint hard enough to penetrate Barr's self-absorption? Well, if not, she knew someone with a bigger mallet. Dag had been a company captain, twice. She doubted a patroller boy like Barr would present him an insurmountable challenge.

Barr looked down, finished treating the straps, and returned to re-organizing his pack.

Fawn stared at his sandy hair tied in that touchable fluffy queue down his back, shoved her needle through the heavy cloth with her thimble, and said abruptly, "Ha! *I* know who you remind me of! Sunny Sawman."

Barr looked over his shoulder. "Who?"

Fawn smiled blackly. "Farmer boy I once knew. He was blond and broad-shouldered like you."

Straightening up, Barr cast her a probing smile. Gleaming enough, but she wondered why it wasn't as face-transforming as Dag's or Remo's. Not as genuine, maybe? Barr said, "Good-looking fellow, was he?"

"Oh, yes." As Barr brightened further, she went on, "Also completely self-centered, a slanderer, and a liar. It wouldn't quite be fair to call him a coward, because with those muscles he didn't need to be, but he sure was eager to skim out of the consequences of his choices when things went sour." She looked him over, pursing her lips in consideration, and added in a kindly voice, "It's likely your hair color does it, but boy howdy, it's not a recommendation. I'll try not to let it set me against you. Too much."

Barr cleared his throat, opened his mouth, and prudently closed it again. He made his way—or fled—out of the kitchen to pretend to check on his boat on the back deck. Fawn stabbed her cloth once more, satisfied.

❧

At lunch, Remo stopped responding to Barr's continued badgering altogether, which left Barr floundering. Fawn shrewdly followed Remo's example, and Whit followed the crowd. Hod and Hawthorn didn't talk to Barr in the first place, Hod because he was fearful, Hawthorn because he liked Remo and didn't want him to go away, and so took Barr as an unwelcome interloper. Bo was bemused, Berry unamused, and Dag, well, it was hard to tell what he was thinking. Nothing simple, anyhow.

It was late afternoon and forty river miles before they again came upon a village big enough to boast a wharf-boat and goods-shed. The *Fetch* tied on and most everyone trooped up to the goods-shed, if only to stretch their legs and enjoy a change of scene.

The goods-clerk, when he saw the three tall Lakewalkers shoulder into his shed, leaned under his counter and came up wearing an iron helmet fashioned from an old cook-pot with one side newly cut out, before turning on his stool to do business with these fresh customers. He adjusted the loop of handle comfortably under his chin. Remo choked, Barr nearly went cross-eyed, and Dag pinched the bridge of his nose in a weary way.

Berry bit her lip but, not wishful to waste daylight, rattled off her questions without any comment on the unusual headgear. Regrettably, the goods-clerk knew of no local river-rat wanting to hire on for a downriver hitch as sweep-man, nor had he any memory of the *Clearcreek Briar Rose* stopping here last fall, although he did remember a couple of the Tripoint boats from Cutter's list in the spring. Fawn made a few little purchases for the *Fetch's* larder, and Whit sold one crate of window glass.

As they finished settling up and turned to go, Barr abruptly turned back.

"Mister," he said to the clerk, pointing at the iron hat, "where did you get the idea for that?"

The clerk smiled at him triumphantly. "Wouldn't you like to know, eh, Lakewalker?"

"Because it doesn't do a blighted thing. It was a joke got up on some flatties stuck up above Pearl Riffle a few weeks back, and they bought it. We laughed at them."

Some flatties, obviously, who had made it downriver this far ahead of the *Fetch,* Fawn realized. She stuffed her fist in her mouth and watched in fascination.

"Yep, I just bet you'd like to trick me into taking this off, wouldn't you, young fellow?" said the clerk in growing satisfaction. "Laugh away. We'll see who laughs last."

"What, I haven't tried to buy anything off you! Or sell anything, either."

"Yet." The clerk nodded, then reached up to adjust the slipping pot more firmly. "And nor will you."

Barr's hands spread in a frustrated plea. "Look, I *know* it was a joke because I *made it up myself*!"

The clerk sat back, eyes narrowing shrewdly. "You would say that, aye."

"No, really! This is crazy. Groundsense sees right through a bitty thing like that. An iron hat doesn't do anything. It was just a joke! I made it up—"

Berry gave Dag a significant look; Dag reached out and gripped Barr's shoulder. "Come along now, Barr, and stop arguing with this fellow. Boss Berry wants to cast off."

"But it's—but he's—"

Remo helped propel his partner through the door and down the muddy slope. Barr skidded to a halt and tried to turn back. "It was a *joke,* I made it up . . ."

Dag sighed. "If you want to stay here and argue with that fellow, I'm sure we can offload your boat and gear. Me, I predict we're going to be seeing pots on people's heads up and down the Grace and the Gray for the next hundred years, so we might as well get used to it. Or for as long as folks are afraid of Lakewalkers and ignorant about our groundwork." He hesitated, looking down the sodden, dreary valley in a considering way. "Though I suppose if it made people feel safer, it might could be a good thing . . . no, likely not." He shook his head and trudged on.

"It's not my doing," said Barr plaintively, head still cranked over his shoulder even as he stumbled in Dag's wake.

"Yes, it is," said Remo irately, blended in chorus with Fawn's "Whose else would it be?" and Dag's reasonable drawl, "Sure it is. Might not be your intention, but it was certainly your doing. Live and learn, patroller."

Barr's lips thinned, but he finally shut up. Except Fawn heard him mutter, as he stepped aboard the *Fetch* once more, "I *made* it *up* . . ."

❧

The next morning at breakfast, Barr's campaign upon Remo was temporarily silenced when the entire crew of the *Fetch* united in telling him to pipe down or prepare to go swimming. It didn't quite cure the problem, because Barr took to staring instead: imploringly, or angrily, or meaningfully. Remo gritted his teeth and attempted to ignore him. Fawn had no idea what-all the pair were doing with their grounds and groundsenses, but would not have been the least surprised had Remo burst out, just like her brothers when they'd driven their beleaguered parents into threats of a whipping if silence did not ensue, *Boss! Dag! He's lookin' at me! Make him stop lookin' at me!* Barr watched the shoreline slipping past and glowered harder.

Fawn herself took to sewing, spinning, and unambitious cooking, hugging the hearth. Her monthly had begun last night, and she dared to hope that Dag's new treatments were helping her to heal, because today's pain was merely uncomfortable, not crippling. Other hopes rose in her mind as the dull tasks filled the hours. Dag had used a number of Lakewalker tricks to avoid starting a child in her half-healed womb, but it sure would be nice someday not to need those tricks. What was wanted, Fawn decided, was not time, but a place.

She pictured it in lavish detail while she jammed her needle through the tough oilcloth and occasionally her fingers—she preferred cooking to sewing, generally. The new Bluefield place would need to be near a farmer town big enough to give Dag steady medicine work, but not so big or near as to overwhelm him. There ought to be a little lake, or at least a big pond, to grow those Lakewalker water lilies with the edible roots. A kitchen garden, of course, and room for Grace and her foal and surly Copperhead. She spent considerable time working out the garden plan, and what other sorts of animals to have. If they weren't to follow the migrating seasons of a Lakewalker camp, she could have a house with four real walls. And an iron cook stove like the one she'd seen at Silver Shoals.

She mulled over all the names she'd ever admired, and not just for children, because they did grow up and what was pretty for a baby might sound downright silly in a mother or grandmother—*Fawn,* for example. Whatever had Mama and Papa been thinking? She and Dag would have more than one daughter, anyhow, that was for sure . . . Dag would like that. Should they be close to some Lakewalker camp, too? Would any Lakewalkers want to be close to them? What if any of those children with the dignified names turned out to have strong groundsenses . . . ?

She was just considering whether to pick out a name for Grace's foal, too, when a distant hail from the river broke up her daydreams. Bo, who had been dozing in his bunk during his off-watch, rolled over and slitted open one eye, listened a moment, and rolled back. Fawn set aside her sewing and rose to venture out on the cold front deck to see what was happening.

A keelboat was rapidly overhauling them. On this long, straight reach the wind was coming more or less from upriver for a change, and the keel had its sail up to push it along even more briskly than the heavy current drew the *Fetch*. The name *Tripoint Steel* was painted on the prow in fancy letters, with all the *T*s in the shape of drawn swords. As the gap closed between the two boats, Boss Cutter and Boss Berry bellowed the news back and forth across the moving waters.

Berry reported the names of the boats that had been seen by the helmeted goods-clerk from their stop yesterday. Cutter mentioned a man who knew a man who'd seen the *Briar Rose* at a town still forty miles downstream, which made Berry narrow her eyes and wave especial thanks; it would save stopping before then. Berry wished Cutter luck, and Cutter called back, as the gap again widened and the *Tripoint Steel* splashed bravely on, "You girls be careful now!"

"We're not all girls," Fawn heard Whit mutter from the roof. "The *Fetch* can look after its own. Blight it."

Dag came out to cloak Fawn in his arms and listen carefully while this was going on, and Barr leaned on the rail to watch in curiosity. Fawn explained to him about Cutter's quest for the missing boats. "Like a river patrol, sort of. They're looking for trouble, and armed for it."

Barr just shook his head.

❧

That afternoon, Barr jittered around the *Fetch* as restlessly as a bedbug at a family reunion, swearing under his breath at each passing mile. Fawn would have bet that kidnapping schemes now revolved behind his silvery-blue eyes, but how to bring them off in a crowded flatboat in the view—and groundsenses—of all those aboard defeated him at least till bedtime. When she trod across the bunkroom after her last visit to the back deck for the night, his open eyes still gleamed from his nest of blankets in the fading firelight.

The next morning, when she came out to start tea, she found him up and dressed before anyone else. As Fawn cut bacon and calculated how to stretch limited eggs over unlimited potatoes, Berry's bunk curtains stopped moving. She yanked them back and rolled out dressed in her usual shirt, vest, and leather skirt, shoving her sock feet into her waiting boots. When she came in from the back deck after a brief morning wash, Barr was waiting by the door.

He lowered his voice. "Boss Berry, can I speak with you—in private?" He waved vaguely toward the bow.

She put a hand on one hip and regarded him without favor. "Might it get you off my boat?"

"Maybe."

She looked dubious, but led him through the stores, tying her hair in its horse-tail with a scrap of cloth on the way.

Whit sat up on one elbow in his bunk and blinked. "What was that all about?"

"Barr wanted to talk to Berry. Alone. They went up to the front deck."

Whit frowned, rose, and padded over to peer out the window. "No, they went ashore. They're walking upstream. He's kinda got his arm . . . huh." His frown deepened to a scowl, and he went back to the bunk rack and shook Remo awake. Remo sat up looking less than delighted, but after a whispered consultation, both drew on trousers, boots, and jackets and went out as well. Hawthorn and Hod, wakened by the rustling, followed curiously.

Dag wandered into the kitchen from their bed-nook amongst the stores and sat at the table, smiling as Fawn handed him a mug of strong tea. "What's the parade?" he asked, nodding toward the bow. He sipped gratefully and opened his second eye. In the bunk rack, Bo rolled over and groaned, then stumbled out to the back deck.

"It's a little hard to say," said Fawn, standing on tiptoe at the window to look up the shore. Dripping trees, gray mist, muddy bank, and no one in sight. She went back to cracking eggs and cutting onions, cheese, and bread.

She almost sliced her hand when sudden shouts broke out in the distance. Dag sat up, his head turning, brows drawing down. He tensed, but did not rise. The yelling diminished, then rose again, then stopped. Fawn certainly made out Whit's voice, and probably Barr's and Remo's both.

"What's all that ruckus?" Bo asked, coming back in and helping himself to tea.

Fawn stretched up again, squinting out into the mist. "They're all coming back. Uh-oh. Barr's holding one hand to his face, and Remo has the other arm twisted up behind his back. Really hard. Whit's got hold of a big stick, and is waving it and talking. Berry's kind of . . . stomping. Wow, she looks mad. Hod's bringin' up the rear as usual, and Hawthorn's running ahead."

Dag rubbed his forehead and took a long, preparing breath. Fawn took heart that he did not, himself, jump up; but then, it seemed the emergency was coming to him. Hawthorn's thumping feet across the gangplank announced his excitement even before he burst into the kitchen to cry: "Dag! Barr's tried to magic Berry, and Whit and Remo says they're gonna kill him!"

More shuffling footsteps crossed from shore, the boat dipped as many feet thudded onto the deck, and the rest of the party arrived on a wave of raised voices too mingled to make out the words, except for some *You did*s, an *I didn't!*, and rather a lot of *Dag! Dag!* Dag winced and took a long swallow of tea, then turned in his chair as the whole mob piled into the little kitchen-bunkroom.

The left side of Barr's face was deeply reddened; his eye was already swelling shut. Any other damage Fawn could not see, but both Remo and Whit were out of breath, and Hod, of all people, was rubbing his knuckles and looking ready to burst into tears. Barr's voice broke briefly above the babble: "I did *not*! Use some sense! Is this the time of day for that sort of thing? Ow, stop that, blight you!" He rose on his toes as Remo hoisted him higher.

Dag pitched his voice, Fawn noticed, really deep: the rumble somehow cut through the noise. "One at a time, please. Boss Berry?"

The uproar died as Whit and Hod poked each other for attention to Dag, and even Hawthorn swallowed his squeaks. Berry stepped forward, grim and angry.

"That patroller of yours"—she pointed a shaking finger at Barr—"tried to do something to my head. Some sorcery."

"Yeah, and we know what it was, don't we?" said Remo, hoisting again.

"Ow, no, blight it!"

"Dag?" said Fawn uneasily from the place of safety she'd sought behind his shoulder. "Can you tell who's telling the truth?"

Dag looked around, pursed his lips, and dipped his chin. He cleared his throat. "Boss Berry, may I touch your head?"

She hesitated a long moment, then looked up to seek Fawn's eyes: Fawn nodded vigorously. Berry shrugged and stepped forward. Dag leaned back and collected Fawn in the circle of his arm, not for his own reassurance or hers, but for Berry's, Fawn realized. Very carefully, Dag touched the back of his hook to Berry's pale forehead. He had to have done something with his ghost hand, because Barr's mouth dropped open and even Remo's eyes widened.

"I thought he was just a patroller!" Barr whispered to his partner.

"You thought wrong," Remo growled back.

"Well." Dag sighed without pleasure. "There's a new bit of ground reinforcement here. It's trying to be shaped as a persuasion, but it isn't very well made, so I'm not quite sure what it was intended to do if it had been finished."

"Can you get it back out o' there?" said Berry nervously.

"I can release any beguilement, and undo the shape so it's no more directed than any healing reinforcement. Your own ground will convert it in a couple of days. There shouldn't be any other effect than, well, you won't be getting any headaches for a bit. Shall I do this now?" His voice, Fawn realized, had gone very gentle.

"Yes!" said Berry. "I don't want no one puttin' things in my head I can't see."

The little bit of absence in Dag's eyes passed faster than a blink. "There," he said, dropping his left arm. "All undone now."

Berry rubbed her forehead. "I suppose I have to take your word for that."

"I'm afraid so."

"I didn't——" began Barr.

"What?" said Dag.

Just that word, with a faint twist of astonishment, but the look that went with it was like nothing Fawn had ever encountered in Dag's eyes before. She'd never seen his waking face so absolutely wiped clean of any humor whatsoever.

Barr flinched. "I wasn't trying to seduce her," he got out, in a much smaller voice.

"What were you trying, then?" said Dag, still in that dead-level tone.

Barr's teeth clamped.

"I know where Berry keeps the rope, up in the stores," said Whit grimly. "We could hang him. Plenty of trees back in those woods."

"I wouldn't stop you," said Remo. Barr winced.

Berry pressed her temples uncertainly. "It seems I took no harm. Thanks to you boys," she added a little gruffly, with a nod all around at her crew. The young men all stood a bit taller. "Hanging might be too much."

"Too much, or too good?" said Whit.

Hod offered helpfully, "My sister made me drown some extra barn kittens once—tied 'em in a sack with some rocks, see. We got some feed bags up front, and there's plenty of rocks on the bank. We could do that."

Barr's eyes shifted toward Hod in deep uncertainty.

"Dag?" said Whit, and "Dag?" echoed Remo and Hod.

"Wait, how'd I get elected judge, here?" said Dag. "It's Berry's boat. She's boss; any decision's hers."

"You're the expert in Lakewalkers," Berry said. *The only trusted one*, she did not add aloud, but it sort of hung in the air implied, Fawn felt.

"I'm not Barr's patrol leader. I'm not even a member of Pearl Riffle patrol. Dag No-camp, indeed. Closest thing Barr has to a senior officer here would be Remo." Dag tilted his head invitingly at the dark-haired patroller.

What are you thinking, Dag? Fawn wondered. *Besides ahead . . .*

Barr said desperately, "Remo, Amma's holding me responsible for you, and I can't make you do anything! It's not fair!"

"Now you know how I've always felt about you." Remo took a breath, nostrils flaring. "It's Berry's boat. Whatever she decides, I'll abide."

"It *wasn't* what you *think* . . ."

Berry stalked up to Barr, sweeping her blistering gaze from his boots up to his blond hair. "You are about the most worthless sack of skin I ever met. You ain't payin', you ain't workin', and you ain't welcome on my boat. So *git*!"

"No!" cried Barr in ill-considered defiance. "Not without my partner!"

Dag's brows went up. "You heard the boat boss. Hod, Whit, get his boat in the water. Fawn, Hawthorn, fetch his things and bung them in. Remo . . ." Dag stood to his full height as Barr started to struggle. "I'll lend you a hand."

The crew of the *Fetch* scattered into action. Fawn brought the bedroll, conveniently already rolled up, and the bow and quiver, and flung them any which way into the rocking narrow boat right after Hawthorn tossed down the pack and the sacks.

Dag and Remo manhandled the struggling Barr through the door, although he stopped fighting and froze once Dag's hook eased around and pressed into the corner of one eye. "Don't move sudden. That's better. Now, you got two choices," Dag advised. "You can climb down into your boat from the deck, here, or you can climb up into it from the water, over there."

The water was black and utterly opaque this morning, and even here by the shore the current raced, making strange patterns on the surface. And it looked so cold Fawn would not have been surprised to see little skins of ice jostling, but it was likely still too early in the season for that.

"I'll climb down," Barr choked. The two released him, and he scrambled over the rail, bitter fury in every jerky motion. The narrow boat rocked only a little as he sank, balanced, into his seat. Remo bent down and gave it a hard shove out into the swirling current.

Barr looked around him. "Hey!" he said indignantly. "Where's my paddle?" He held up both empty hands in protest as his boat drifted farther from the bank.

"Oh, leave him go, just like that!" cried Whit in delight. "Downriver bass-ackwards!"

Berry, lips clamped, stalked over to retrieve one of the narrow boat's paddles from where they lay by the cabin wall. She strode to the back rail and launched it endwise; it landed a good thirty feet downstream of Barr's narrow boat, and was caught by the current. If she'd thrown it the same distance upstream, it would have drifted right to Barr's reaching hand.

"There's your paddle, patroller boy! Chase it!" she yelled after Barr.

"Nice," said Whit, leaning on the rail with eyes aglow.

Barr, with a lot of choked muttering in which *Blight!* was the most frequent word Fawn could make out, leaned from side to side and began clawing the water with his hands in an effort to overtake his paddle's head start.

"Who gave Barr the shiner?" Fawn asked, leaning beside Whit.

"Remo. And me. And Hod, but he was too scared to hit him very hard."

"Ow," said Fawn.

"He earned it."

"I won't argue with that."

The clinging river mist closed around the narrow boat, although the disembodied cries of *Blight it!* drifted back for a while longer.

Berry squinted out in satisfaction. "Right. That should make the *Fetch* a sight more peaceful." She dusted her hands and led her crew back in to find breakfast.

Fawn hesitated by Dag, who stood with his hand on the rail looking out into the layer of gray damp, but seeing, she suspected, much more than she did. There was scant satisfaction in him, only close attention. "There," he said at last, straightening. "He's got his paddle back."

"Is that the end of him?" Fawn asked hopefully.

Dag smiled down at her. "Well, there's this. He's a Lakewalker boy away from home for the first time, all alone. He's not going upstream by himself, that's for sure. His only choice is to keep going down, like us. So we'll see."

She frowned at him in doubt. "Do you want him to come back?"

"I don't like losing patrollers."

"You kept Remo. That's one."

"I don't like losing two patrollers 'bout twice as much as I don't like losing one."

"Well, I hope you can find more value in Barr with your groundsense than I can with my eyes and ears."

"I hope I can, too, Spark," he sighed.

17

Though the weather stayed cloudy and chilly, the *Fetch* made steady downriver progress all that day. The enclosing hills flattened out, sign, Berry explained to Fawn, that they were passing west out of the hinterland of Oleana into level Raintree. The riverbanks were drained of color, sodden brown with gray tree boles broken only by an occasional glum-looking river village, or sometimes dun farm fields open down to the water. No longer autumn . . . not yet winter.

Berry kept Remo on the sweeps with her—possibly, Fawn figured, to avert another grounding, since she encouraged Remo, in a way Bo had not, to offer warnings. At least Bo did not ignore Dag's laconic remarks. Clearly, river pilot could be another job for Lakewalkers amongst farmers, in addition to medicine maker. When Fawn started sorting through the possibilities with an open mind, it seemed to her that farmers and Lakewalkers offered vast possibilities to each other, for all that Lakewalkers scorned any task that diverted them from hunting malices. Yet someday the last blight bogle ever had to emerge and be destroyed. What would patrollers do when there was no more need for patrols? *Not in my lifetime,* Dag had said. Maybe Lakewalkers were better off not dwelling on an end none of them would live to see.

She glimpsed Barr's narrow boat ahead of them a couple of times that day, and what might have been a campfire on the far shore that night, till the rains came again and doused the distant glow. The following day she saw his boat trailing far behind, an ink-stroke on the gray water, before the *Fetch* rounded another curve and the shifting shoreline hid it.

"Isn't a narrow boat faster than us?" she asked Dag, peering under the edge of her hand when they were both out on the back deck for a moment. "I'd think he should have pulled ahead. Or stopped somewhere and bought that broke-down horse."

"He imagines he's trailing us just out of groundsense range. Which he is—of his and Remo's. Though not of mine."

"How long d'you think he'll follow us?"

"Not much longer. With all his gear we threw into his boat, no one included any food. And I doubt hunting in the rain and dark on shore is likely to offer him much reward, especially without a cook fire."

Fawn hadn't noticed Barr's lack of supplies in the rush. *Dag did.* And had said nothing. What was he up to?

Dag went on, "Rain again tonight, I expect. Perfect."

"Perfect for what?"

"Sober reflection, Spark. Fasting is supposed to be good for meditating on one's sins." His dour smile faded a trifle. "Barr's in trouble and he knows it. He's getting his first taste of banishment. There are reasons in our grounds that Lakewalkers regard banishment as the next thing to a death sentence. If he's let his bow-strings get as wet as I think, I give him till tomorrow night, tops."

"To do what?"

"Well, that'll be somewhat up to him."

"I dunno, Dag. If I wanted some particular thing, I don't think I'd leave it entirely up to Barr."

He gave her a reassuring nod. "I'm not planning to, Spark."

The narrow boat trailed them disconsolately all the following morning. Around noon, it spurted forward as if in sudden decision. Fawn wondered if this had anything to do with the smell of the baking apple pies wafting in their wake, which Dag had asked for especially for to-day's lunch. She and Dag stepped out onto the back deck to lean on the rail and watch as Barr paddled close to the side of the *Fetch* where Remo held a sweep. Berry and Whit were on roof crew with him, this hour. They all stared down coldly as Barr hailed them. He looked pinched and pale, and nothing like as self-righteous as upon his first arrival.

Berry glowered over the side. "What are you doin' back here?"

Barr jerked his chin. "It's a free river."

Berry shrugged; her frown did not change.

"Remo," Barr called plaintively, "what is it you're planning to *do* once you get to the blighted sea, anyway?"

Remo gave his sweep a long pull. "Turn around. Or keep walking, maybe. Depends on how I feel about things by then."

Barr winced. "All right. It's plain you won't come back with me. I, um, accept that."

Remo said nothing.

Barr took a fortifying breath. "Can I come with you?"

Remo's brows flew up. "What?"

"To the sea. Can I come with you?" Barr stared up in something very like pleading.

Remo stared down in unflattering astonishment. "Why would I want you? Why would anyone?"

"*I* sure don't," said Berry.

"Ma'am." Barr ducked his head at her. "I could pay my passage. Part-way, at least."

"I wouldn't have you on my boat for any money," said Berry.

"I could work? Like Remo?"

"You?" She snorted. "I ain't seen you lift a hand yet."

"You wouldn't have to pay me . . . Look, I'm *sorry,* all right?"

Dag's lips twitched; he gave Fawn's shoulder a squeeze and climbed up onto the *Fetch*'s roof. Bending his head, he murmured to Berry. She shot him a startled frown, then a slow, respectful look that started at his boots and traveled to his serious face, and said, "I don't know, patroller. I suppose you can try."

He nodded and dropped back down to the rear deck. "Barr, bring your boat alongside. You and I need to have a private talk about some things."

He motioned Barr closer. When Barr brought his boat clumping up to the hull, Dag climbed down and lowered himself into it, facing Barr, and shoved them away. Barr stroked slowly backward till they were well out of earshot, then set his paddle across his lap. Only then did Dag lean grimly forward and start talking.

Fawn scrambled up onto the roof to stand in the line with Remo, Whit, and Berry, watching.

"What's Dag doing?" asked Whit, craning his neck.

"Well," said Berry, "he said he wanted to talk to the boy, patroller-to-patroller like. And then we'd see what we'd see."

Barr waved his hands; Dag's spine straightened in skepticism. He leaned forward and spoke again, and Barr rocked backward.

"I think that may be more like company captain to patroller," Fawn allowed.

"Was he a—oh, yes, in Raintree," began Remo. "I suppose the famous Fairbolt Crow wouldn't have given Dag that command if he hadn't thought he could handle it."

"Fairbolt didn't just think," said Fawn. "He knew. Dag'd been a company captain before, when he patrolled up in Luthlia."

"Luthlia!" said Remo. "That's tough country. I met a couple of patrollers from there once, came across our ferry. They scared me." He eyed Dag in new speculation.

Barr, perhaps inadvisably, vented some protest. Dag gestured at his hook and spoke more fiercely.

"Uh-oh," said Fawn. "If Dag's bringing up Wolf Ridge, that boy's in bigger trouble than he can guess."

"Wolf Ridge?" said Remo. "*The* Wolf Ridge? Dag was *there?*"

"That's where the hand went," said Whit, waving his left. "Torn off by one of them dire wolves that malice made, he says. He doesn't much talk about it. But he sent the skin to Papa as one of Fawn's bride-gifts. Big as a horse hide. The twins swore it had to be faked, but Papa and I didn't think so."

Remo's breath trickled out through pursed lips. "There were only a handful of survivors—wait, *company captain* at Wolf Ridge?"

"Yeah, which is why he don't care to talk about it," said Fawn, "so don't you let on I told you. It gave him an aversion to captaining. Despite beating that malice."

"Absent gods," said Remo. He watched the pair in the narrow boat. Dag was saying more. Barr was saying much less. By the time Dag's hand clenched in a venomous fist—for some emphasis rather than threat, Fawn judged—Barr had shrunk to half his former size. Crouching in his seat, really, but the effect from this angle of view was pretty startling. And if Barr backed up any more, he risked falling off the stern.

Barr's lips had stopped moving altogether. It was just head bobs, now, or sometimes head shakes. At length, Dag sat back. Barr straightened his slumped shoulders, picked up his paddle, and aimed his narrow boat back toward the *Fetch*. As they pulled alongside again, Dag sat with his hand on his knee, waiting. Barr looked up and cleared his throat.

"Miss Clearcreek—Boss Berry, that is," Barr corrected himself as her frown deepened. "First off, I apologize for what I tried with you the other morning. What I was trying, see, I was trying to put a persuasion in your ground to get you mad at Remo so's you'd fire him and he'd have to come back with me. That was wrong. I also didn't quite have a strong enough—" he caught Dag's rising brows, and finished hastily, "I was just plain wrong, is all."

He drew a long breath and continued, "And I apologize to you, Remo. First for what I tried with Boss Berry, which was as much out of line to you as to her, and also for getting taken in by that flattie girl up in Pearl Bend even though you told me better, and for flirting with her in the first place, and for getting your great-grandmama's knife broke when you came in after me in the fight, and for that stupid joke with the pots that started it all, which I guess I'm still going to be apologizing for when my hair turns gray. Which is going to be next week at this rate, but anyway. I'm really, really sorry." He looked up. He looked, Fawn thought, ready to cry. *Gods, Dag, you don't do things by halves, do you. But I knew that . . .*

Remo's mouth was hanging open. "Oh," he said.

"And I apologize to everyone on board the *Fetch*," Barr concluded valiantly, "for being a walking, talking blight on you for the past few days."

Dag's deep voice broke in. "Here's the offer. I'll stand good for Barr, Boss Berry, if you'll let him back aboard your boat to work his passage. In return, Barr will place himself under my discipline as his patrol leader. Barr, if you agree, you can come back on board. If not, you're on your own."

Barr stared around the wide, flat, empty riverscape, gulped, and murmured, "I agree, sir." He looked up. "I agree, ma'am."

Berry leaned over, skeptically sucking her lip. "You understand, patroller boy, you're here on Dag's word. He's earned my respect, which you have not, and it's his wallet you'll be drawin' on. I don't know how you plan to pay that debt; that's between you and him. But I don't have to put up with you, and if you give me one lick more trouble, I won't. Clear?"

"Yes, ma'am."

She glanced at Dag, who nodded. "All right, then. You can come on my boat."

Dag climbed back over the rail, and Barr once more handed up his gear; he and Remo manhandled the narrow boat across the rear deck and tied it down. At lunch, which came up shortly, Barr ate hesitantly, though he left nothing to wash off his plate. Which was his gain, because his first assignment was scullery duty with Hod, which he fulfilled almost wordlessly. It was equally quiet up on the roof when he did his first stint on the oars with Dag and Bo. At dinner he was slightly less ghostlike, actually exchanging three or four unexceptionable remarks besides requests to pass the salt or cornbread.

Cuddling down with Dag that night, Fawn whispered, "What in the world did you say to Barr out in that boat today? I've seen frogs run over by a cart wheel that weren't squashed that flat."

"Well, I think that'd better be between me and him, Spark. But don't fret too much. Barr's resilient. You have to calibrate, see. A reprimand that would have poor Remo trying to fall on his knife is just about enough to ruffle Barr's hair."

"Did you, um, *persuade* him?"

"Didn't need to. He was ready. Reminds me of how you train a Raintree mule. First you whack him between the ears with a fence post, hard as you can. This gets his attention. Then you can start in."

"That works on patrollers, as well as mules?"

"Or on patrollers who are like mules. You have to give Barr credit for that two hundred—or three hundred—miles he hung on after his partner, despite all. That boy's wrong-headed in a lot of ways, but you can't accuse him of giving up easy."

"How'd you learn to handle mule-headed patrollers, anyhow?"

His lips twitched against her brow in the dark. "Studied my own patrol leaders, as a youngster. Up really close."

"That would be, like, face-to-face close?"

"Uh-huh."

Her dimpled grin brushed his collarbone. "Mule-man. Why am I not surprised? Though I'd have guessed you more for a young Remo."

"Remo and Barr each have their moments that throw me back in memory. Between the pair of 'em, they put me in a real humble frame of mind toward my old patrol teachers, I will say."

During the next day, Barr settled in to be a pretty good crewman, as far as Fawn could judge. Topside, both his muscle and his groundsense proved useful, and adding the extra man to the rotation gave everyone a bit more ease, with the possible exception of the cook. Only Hod resented the reductions of his turns on the sweeps, but he was much consoled when Barr was assigned to dishwashing duty in his place one meal out of three. The good fellowship on the *Fetch* slowly began to recover from the setbacks Barr had brought.

Berry put in at a largish rivertown, too briefly for Bo to wander away and find a tavern, just long enough to learn of another sighting here of her papa's boat last fall. The news left her frowning thoughtfully and counting out the river miles still left till the junction of the Grace and the Gray; the *Fetch* was better than two thirds of the way from Tripoint to the Confluence. Not exactly running out of either river or possibilities, but as the distance shortened, Fawn thought she could feel Berry's tension grow.

Dag begged one short stop at another Lakewalker ferry camp, though Remo stayed aboard and Barr with him. Dag came back soon, shaking his head. "Too small, these camps strung along here. I'd likely do better to wait for Confluence Camp, which is the biggest in these parts. Better chance there."

Fawn had thought the Grace a big river at Pearl Riffle, but she began to see she'd been naive. It was a lot wider now, and not just because of the rains and the rise. It was also starting to be more bendy, turning in large loops that added river miles without getting them westward much and utterly confusing Fawn's sense of direction, especially under the thickly overcast skies. But toward the afternoon of the next day, the scudding clouds broke up and genuine sunlight broke through once more. When the chill wind also died, Fawn climbed up to the roof to sit at Berry's feet and watch the passing scene. The shores turned a sharper gray and a richer brown, glowing soberly, and the water shone a dark, metallic blue.

As the sun's light grew level and the shadows stretched, they rounded a tight bend to find a familiar keelboat drawn up to a high place along the bank. Smoke rose from cook fires, with the boat's crew lazing around them. When they saw the *Fetch,* some rose and waved, and Boss Wain actually ran out to the back of the *Snapping Turtle* to cup his hands and hail them.

"Hey, Boss Berry! How's about a mutton dinner in exchange for a tune or three?"

Berry grinned and bent her head to Fawn. "What do you say? Would the cook like a night off?"

Fawn looked dubiously at the rowdy keelers, now adding whooping welcomes to that of their boss. "I don't know. Is it safe?" Berry had always been with her papa and big brother before, keeping an eye out for her.

"Oh, aye. Wain's a loud lout, but he'll keep the line if you do. Not that he won't push his luck, mind. Doubt he'll bother you, though—I mean, you have Dag."

Dag indeed. And Whit, Remo, Hod, Bo, and she supposed Barr, and Hawthorn for the cheering on. Fawn decided to be brave, like Berry. "All right. Sure."

Berry waved back. "You got yourselves a fiddler, boys!" She leaned on her steering oar to bring the *Fetch* to shore just above where the *Snapping Turtle* was moored. Keelers ran out to help tie their lines to the trees.

"What, *more* Lakewalkers?" Boss Wain cried as they all trooped up to his fires. "What are you doing, Berry, collecting 'em?"

"In a manner of speaking," she replied, swinging her fiddle-bag. "This here's Remo and Barr; Dag you know."

Wain tugged on the brim of his hat in uneasy, respectful acknowledgment of Dag, and promptly begged his attention for a crewman with a hurt foot, if he'd a mind. Dag returned a nod, eyelids lowering and lifting. Nobody brought up the sand bar; maybe Wain was trying to make amends, in which case Berry seemed willing to let him.

"What's this, Wain, stealing sheep again?" asked Bo, with a nod at the nearest cook fire, where two crewmen were turning a browning carcass on a makeshift spit. Dripping fat made the fire lick up in smoky, orange spurts, and sent a rich aroma into the cool air. Fawn's mouth watered, and Whit licked his lips.

Wain stuck his thumbs in his braces and puffed out his considerable chest. "I'll have you know that farmer *gave* us this here mutton." His wave took in not only the roasting carcasses, but three more worried-looking live sheep tied to the trees beyond the camp.

His brawny lieutenant put in, "Yeah, he told us to take them as a present. He begged so pitiful, we finally gave in."

"That I just plain don't believe," said Berry.

"It's true as I stand!" Wain cried in indignation. A sneaky grin stretched his mouth. "See, we passed this sheep pasture up the river a ways, and the boys allowed as how fresh mutton for dinner would go down good, but the farmer likely wouldn't give us a fair price. And I said, no, I wouldn't allow no sheep-stealing, a riverman should be above that, but I bet Saddler here a barrel of beer I could get us them there sheep for free, and he said, No, you can't, which was as good as a red rag to a bull, you know me."

Berry nodded, though her blond brows had a skeptical lift to them, which only seemed to encourage the other boat boss.

"So we tied up the *Turtle,* and me and a couple of the boys snuck up on some of those sheep—that was a job, let me tell you, sliding around that muddy pasture—and chucked a good slug of Graymouth pepper sauce in the mouths of the six slowest."

"Or tamest," Fawn muttered, suddenly not liking where this tale was going. She edged closer under Dag's arm.

"You should've seen those sheep run around then, shaking their heads and drooling all orange at the mouth!"

Wain's lieutenant, Saddler, wheezed with laughter and took up the tale. "Then Boss Wain, see, goes up to the farmer's barn and calls him out, and tells him there's something wrong with his sheep—that they've taken the Graymouth murrain, horrible contagious. The fellow was practically shakin' in his boots by the time Wain got done tellin' him how he seen it wipe out a whole flock in a week, down on the lower Gray. And the farmer asked, what's to be done? and Wain says, There's no cure and nothing for it but to cull the sick ones, quick, and maybe bury the carcasses in lime, miles away from the others. And this fellow was practically crying for his sheep, so when Wain suggested he'd take away the sick ones and dispose of 'em for him, the farmer was most pitifully grateful. Which we did do, and here we are."

"And you owe me the next barrel!" Wain said, slapping him on the back in high good humor.

"That I do," coughed Saddler. "But it was worth it, to see the thankful look on that farmer fellow's face when we carted off his poor sick sheep. And you have to admit, Wain spoke true—they didn't live the day!"

The gathered boatmen laughed, and even Barr and Remo smiled. The tale finished, the group broke up to tend to the dinner preparation, including tapping a new keg set up on a nearby stump. Dag went off to see the fellow with the bad foot. Fawn caught Whit's eye and scowled the grin right off his face.

"What's your trouble?" he whispered at her.

"Those could've been Papa's sheep," she muttered back.

His brow wrinkled. "I don't think Papa would have been taken in by some smoky fiddle about the Graymouth murrain, Fawn. He knows his sheep better than that."

"That's not the point. That farmer may not be as smart as Papa, but I'll bet he works as hard. Tricking's same as stealing, in my eyes. And it was *cruel* on him."

The smoke wafted their way, and Whit inhaled appreciatively. "Well, those sheep are beyond saving now, Fawn. Best anyone can do now is see they didn't die in vain. Waste not, want not, as Mama herself says."

"Well, *I'm* not eating any!" she declared. "And you shouldn't, either."

"Fawn!" he protested. "We can't go complaining and being—being walking, talking blights and spoiling everybody's party. These keeler men work hard; this is a pretty innocent pleasure, here. A picnic and a sing-song!"

"That farmer worked hard, too. Harder than rivermen, or you wouldn't be thinking of switching, now would you?"

"That's not why I—oh, crap anyways. Don't eat that tasty-smellin' mutton if that's what pleases you, but don't be ragging me." He stalked off, to console himself pretty promptly with a tankard of the *Turtle*'s fresh Raintree beer.

Fawn's jaw set, but truly, what right had she to blight the party? Especially if it was, more or less, Wain's apology to the *Fetch* and its boss about that sand bar. But she remained determined to touch no tricked-away mutton. Remo was now helping Dag with the fellow with the hurt foot; she withdrew quietly to the *Fetch* and watched the camp on shore from a perch on the edge of the cabin roof. The sun set, and the firelight blazed brighter and more invitingly.

The noisiness of the boatmen grew more repellent. Bo was staggering already, grinning foolishly, though Hod seemed to be looking out for him. Hawthorn was showing off his raccoon kit's tricks, such as they were, to an appreciative or at least tolerant audience. Barr and Remo were sitting together eating along with the man with the freshly bandaged foot, so even they weren't being standoffish Lakewalkers. Wain, Saddler, and Whit were all grouped tightly around Berry. Fawn began to wonder what the point was of spurning the affair for principle's sake if nobody was going to even take notice.

At least one person noticed. Dag walked across the gangplank and lifted himself up to the roof to dangle his legs over beside hers. "What's the trouble, Spark? You feeling all right? I thought your monthly was past."

"It is." She shrugged. "I just keep thinking about that poor farmer that Wain robbed. Or tricked, whichever. It's just not fair!" She eyed him suspiciously. "Are you going to eat that stolen mutton?"

"Er . . . I'm afraid I already have."

"Well, don't try and kiss me with those greasy lips," she said grumpily.

He cleared his throat. "I actually came aboard to find my tambourine and a couple of buckets for the boys to thump on. Berry's about to tune up her fiddle, and she allowed as how she'd like some help."

"Oh, that'll be good . . ." It had been ages since Dag had played music with anyone around a campfire, and she knew that had been one of his pleasures out on patrol. A tambourine was not much as a solo instrument. *Blight that Boss Wain . . .*

Up the bank in the shadows, a dim, white shape uttered a mournful *m-a-a-a*. It occurred to Fawn that not *all* of that poor farmer's sheep were beyond saving. And a faint thump against the side of the hull reminded her that the *Fetch*'s skiff was presently tied to the stern down in the water, rather than onto the side of the cabin where it often hung in rougher weather. She could never have launched it by herself. Could she row it by herself? Upstream?

She eyed Dag sideways. Could he be roped into helping with her scheme? Maybe not. Sometimes, catfish notwithstanding, he could be a little *too* grown-up and responsible. That left Whit, maybe, but he seemed to have gone over to the other side. In any case, she now had good reason to cheer the party along merrily, with *lots* of food and beer all around. And any boatman or Lakewalker who was lagging—not that this seemed to be a problem—should certainly be encouraged to drink up. "I wouldn't miss your music for all the mutton in the world." She smiled at Dag, who looked heartened by her change of mood; she even let him kiss her brow with muttony lips as he swung her down from the roof.

And as for fickle brothers, well, when you'd watched someone all his life while he hardly noticed you, you ended up knowing a lot more about him than he might credit. A *lot* more. She almost skipped across the gangplank after Dag.

⌘

The moon rode high above the river valley, shedding silvery-blue light on the mist that wisped above the water. The night air was as silent as though some ancient sorcerer had cast a spell of enchantment. Clearly a midnight made for romance, although the chill suggested the kissing might better be conducted beneath a thick quilt. The one she'd left Dag snoring under would have suited Fawn fine. Instead, well . . .

"Fawn, this is crazy," Whit hissed at her.

"Lift your end, Whit."

"Someone will hear us."

"Not if you shut up and lift. They're all sodden-drunk over there, pretty much."

"Wain'll be mad."

"*I'm* mad. Whit, if you don't help me hoist this stupid sheep into this stupid skiff, not only will I tell Berry what you and the Roper boys did with Tansy Mayapple in Millerson's loft, I'll wake her up and tell her *right now.*"

"*M-a-a-a,*" bleated the confused sheep, its hooves slipping and splashing in the mud and stones of the bank.

"You shut up, too," Fawn whispered fiercely. "Now, *lift!*"

A grunt, a swing, and the last sheep was rocked over the thwart to join its two companions. Twelve cloven feet thumped and clattered, echoing on the planks of the boat's bottom. Round yellow eyes rolled in long white faces. Fawn leaped to thrust back the front legs of one trying to struggle out again, soaking her shoes.

"We better get in and start rowing," she said. "You don't think they'll try and jump out when we're out on the water, do you?"

"They might. And probably get their fleece waterlogged and drown, to boot. Sheep are stupider than chickens."

"Whit, nothing's stupider than chickens."

"Well, that's true," he conceded. "Almost as stupid as chickens, then."

Fawn scrambled aboard after Whit, to find that the boat's end was now stuck in the mud from the added weight. She climbed back out and prepared to give it a push off the bank, only to freeze when a puzzled voice behind her spoke: "Why are you taking sheep for a boat ride?"

She spun around to find Barr standing in the moon-striped shadows of the bare branches, scratching his head and peering blearily at them.

"Why aren't you asleep?" she hissed at him.

"I was asleep. I got up to piss," he replied. "Good beer those keeler boys had. What are you doing?"

"None o' your business. Go back to your bedroll."

Barr ran a hand over his jaw and squinted at them. "Does Dag know you two are out here?" The absent look of a groundsense consulted slipped over his face. "No, he's asleep."

"Good. Don't you dare wake him up. He needs his sleep." Fawn stuck one already-wet shoe into the mud and gave them a hard shove off. The skiff slid away from shore.

"If you don't want Dag to know what you're up to, then I'm *definitely* curious," said Barr stubbornly, beginning to follow them up the bank.

"We're un-stealing sheep," said Whit. "Don't look at me like that. It wasn't my idea."

"Won't Boss Wain be mad?"

"No," said Fawn. "He'll think they chewed through their ropes and ran off. I made sure to leave the ends ragged and all over sheep spit."

She rubbed her hands on her skirts and took up her oar. Unfortunately, Whit's pull, once they got coordinated, was about twice as strong as hers, which resulted in the skiff turning toward shore unless he waited for her to stroke again. And in the pause the down-bound current pushed them back. Barr was having no trouble keeping up, even with the need to pick his way across the rocks and fallen logs.

"You two are never going to make it upstream against this current," he observed.

"Well, we're gonna try, so get out of our way." Not that Barr was actually *in* the way, but he was being very annoying off to the side.

Barr continued walking up the bank. Very slowly. A passenger said *M-a-a-a.*

"You're not making much progress," he said again.

"Let's try farther out in the channel, Whit," suggested Fawn.

"That makes no sense," said Whit. "Current's stronger out there."

"Yes, but it'll be more private."

M-a-a-a. M-a-a-a.

"Dag'd flay me if I let you two babies go drown yourselves in the Grace," Barr complained.

"So don't tell him," said Fawn through her teeth. Her hands were beginning to ache.

After a few more minutes, Barr said, "I can't stand this. Give over. Come inshore and I'll take Fawn's oar."

"We don't need your help," said Fawn.

"Yes, we do," said Whit, and rowed harder. Fawn splashed madly, but was unable to keep the skiff from turning in.

"No, the stupid sheep'll try and jump out!"

"Well, go nab 'em. You herd sheep, Barr and I will row."

Fawn gave up. Barr edged past, and he and Whit pushed the boat out into the river once more. Fawn settled irately on the next seat and shoved a sheep face out of her lap. But she slowly grew consoled as their upriver progress became more visible. Whit's muscles were on the whippy side, but a farmer son's life had left them harder than they looked, and he kept up with Barr's broader shoulders well enough.

The sheep dropped dung, trampled it around the bottom of the boat, and bleated. One attempted suicide by leaping into the river, but Fawn lunged and pulled it back with her hands dug into its greasy fleece. Another tried to follow the first's example.

"Can't you settle these sheep down with your groundsense?" Fawn asked Barr. "I bet Dag could."

"I don't do sheep," said Barr distantly.

"No, only boat bosses," said Whit, which resulted in a chilly silence for a time. The moonlit woods slid slowly past, silvered and remarkably featureless.

"I'm getting blisters," Whit complained. "How much farther?"

"Well, we're looking for a sheep pasture that comes right down to the water," said Fawn.

"What if the sheep are in the fold for the night?" said Whit. "There are lots of pastures that come down to the water. We've been passing 'em for days."

Fawn was quiet.

"Do you even know which one we're looking for?" asked Barr.

"Er . . . well . . . not really."

"Fawn!" protested Whit. "It could have been any farm for the last twenty miles—or more! Likely more—stands to reason Wain wouldn't stop too close, in case that farmer figured out he'd been diddled and came after 'em."

"I'm not rowing any twenty miles!" said Barr.

The mutiny was unanimous. The skiff put in at the first likely-looking pasture it came to, and Barr and Whit united to heave the bleating cargo overboard. The sheep cantered off a few paces and clustered to glower ungratefully back at their rescuers. Whit yanked Fawn back into the boat and turned it downstream.

"I sure hope they find a smarter owner," she muttered.

"Yeah, sheep, don't bother thanking us for saving your lives or anything," Whit called sarcastically, turning and waving.

"Whit, they're sheep," said Fawn. "You can't expect gratitude. You just . . . know you did the right thing, is all."

"Just like f—" Barr began, and abruptly shut up. Fawn shot him a suspicious look. After a moment, he said instead, "They sure did stink. Who's cleaning up this boat?"

"Not me," said Whit.

"Somebody'll have to," said Barr. "I mean . . . evidence."

"I will take care of it," said Fawn through her teeth.

Lovely moonlight and less lovely silence fell. They came in sight of the *Fetch* in about a third of the time it had taken them to labor upstream.

"Thank you both," said Fawn gruffly. "Even if I couldn't make it right, it seems less wrong now. I couldn't have done it without your help."

"I'll remember that," said Whit.

"Don't you two un-sheep-stealers go congratulating each other too soon," said Barr, with a nod toward the *Fetch*. Fawn followed his glance and went still to see Dag sitting cross-legged on the roof in the moonlight, gazing upstream.

"Crap," said Whit.

"Though I'm suddenly glad you're here, Whit," muttered Barr. "To prevent misunderstandings and all." He glanced circumspectly at Fawn.

Fawn thought the greater fear might be perfectly correct understandings, actually. As the skiff eased alongside the flatboat, Dag dropped down to the back deck to catch the painter-rope Fawn tossed up to him.

He sniffed, and inquired dryly, "Nice boat ride?"

"Uh-huh," said Fawn, staring up in defiance.

"Whit, Barr . . . you look a mite sheepish, one could say."

"No, we only smell it," muttered Whit.

"It wasn't my doing!" Barr blurted.

Dag's lips twisted up. "This time, Barr, I believe you."

He leaned down to give them each a hand up in turn, and oversee the skiff properly tied.

Whit said uneasily, "Are you going to turn us in?"

"Who to? They weren't my sheep." He added after a moment, "Or yours."

Barr breathed stealthy relief, and Dag shepherded Fawn firmly to bed.

He actually kept his face straight until he had a pillow stuffed over it. The chortles that then leaked through had Fawn poking him. "Stop that!"

It took a while till he quieted down.

❧

The *Fetch* left its mooring soon after dawn, when the *Snapping Turtle*'s bleary crew were just beginning to search the nearby woods for their escaped mutton. The sweep-men draped on their oars maintained just enough motion to give steering way to the rudder, and sometimes not even that. Even Berry seemed content to drift at the river's pace. Despite being as cotton-headed from lack of sleep as everyone else was from other excesses, Fawn kept strong tea coming, and as the morning wore on folks slowly recovered.

The river's pace picked up abruptly around noon, when a great brown flood swept in from the right, and the current grew rolling.

"That's not the Gray already, is it?" Fawn asked Berry, startled, when she looked out her moving kitchen window to find the shore grown alarmingly distant.

"Nope," said Berry, in a tone of satisfaction, and took another swig of tea. "That's the Beargrass River. It swings up through Raintree to Farmer's Flats. We're three-fourths of the way from Tripoint to the Confluence now! They must have had heavy storms in Raintree this past week—I haven't often seen the Beargrass this high."

"Do boats go on it?" Fawn peered some more.

"Sure. All the way to Farmer's Flats, which is the head of navigation, pretty much. Which is why the town is where it is, I 'spect. The Beargrass is almost as busy as the Grace."

Blighted Greenspring had lain on one of the Beargrass's upper tributaries, as Fawn recalled soberly. Bonemarsh Camp, too. Last summer's grim campaign against the malice had all played out north of the big town of Farmer's Flats; the disruption hadn't reached down here. Dag might thank the absent gods, but Fawn thought the thanks were better due to Dag.

With the addition of the Beargrass, the Grace nearly topped its banks, and in some places overflowed them. Some of the lower-lying islands were drowned already, bare trees sticking up from the water as if growing out of a lake, except that the lake was moving sideways at a fair clip. Fawn sometimes saw animals trapped up the island trees; possums and raccoons, of course, a couple of black bears, and once, excitingly, a catamount, quite close. They passed a wild pig swimming strongly in the current, and the men aboard were barely restrained from trying to hunt it from the boat. Floating wrack either lodged on or broke loose dangerously from towheads, those accumulations of trees and logs at the top ends of the islands that from a distance resembled, the boatmen said, the unruly locks of a fair-haired boy, hence the name Beargrass.

Toward evening, Berry put two men on each sweep to fight the unwieldy *Fetch* in to shore. As they were tying up in the lee of a bend, a peculiar arrangement floated past in the dusk: two flatboats lashed together side by side. The crew apparently struggled in vain to steer this lumbering rig, because it was slowly spinning in the current.

Out on the back deck, Bo called across the water for them to break up and tie to shore before dark, but the men on the double-boat either didn't hear or didn't understand; their return cries were unintelligible.

"Why'd they fix their boats together like that?" asked Fawn curiously, coming out to look.

"I expect because they're fool Raintree boys who don't know a thing about the river and have got no business being on it," said Bo, and spat over the side for emphasis.

"For company, maybe, or not to lose each other in the dark. It likely made 'em feel safer, out on this big river," said Whit slowly. "Even the *Fetch* is starting to look pretty small."

"Do you see why it don't make 'em safer?" said Berry.

"Oh, I do!" said Fawn excitedly, staring after the receding Raintree flatties.

Berry grinned. "I bet you do. Now wait for Whit."

Whit squinted into the dusk and said slowly, "They're trying to move twice the weight with half the oars."

Fawn nodded vigorously.

"That's right," said Berry, straightening in satisfaction. "We may make a riverman of you yet."

Whit smiled blindingly at her. "I sure hope so."

She smiled back involuntarily; not her usual wry grin, but something unwitting and almost unwilling. She rubbed her lips and shook her head. "And to top it, they're running at night. Unless they got themselves their very own Lakewalker aboard, not too bright, I'm afraid." She leaned on the back rail and stared down the river, her eyes growing grave and gray in the gathering gloom. Fawn barely heard her mutter: "Papa was no fool country boy. So *what happened?*"

18

During an easy stretch of river in the morning, Berry took Whit topside to give him a lesson on the steering oar. Mildly inspired, Dag assembled the Lakewalkers on the front deck for a drill in ground-veiling. He'd a shrewd suspicion such groundwork had been somewhat neglected by these two partners in favor of more vigorous training in bow, knife, sword, and spear.

Dag took the bench, Barr leaned against the goat pen, and Remo settled cross-legged on the deck. Eyes closed or open, they went around the lopsided circle taking turns at that inward-furling blindness that sacrificed perception for privacy—or invisibility. Unfairly, Barr had the stronger native groundsense of the pair, though unsurprisingly, Remo was more disciplined at handling what he had.

"You can't veil yourself any better than that, and they let you out on patrol?" said Dag to Barr. "Amma Osprey must be harder up for patrollers than I thought."

Barr waved a hand in protest. "Going blind like this feels like being a little kid again," he complained. "Back to before my groundsense even came in."

"There's a deep difference in vulnerability. But leaking like you do, you'd never get close enough to a malice to make a rush with your knife." *If you had a knife.*

"At that range, it could see me, couldn't it? I mean, they do have eyes, right?"

"Usually. But that's not the point. A good ground-veiling also resists ground-ripping, at least by a weak sessile or early molt. Which you'd better hope is what you'll find yourself facing." It occurred to Dag that this could be another use for his own weak ground-ripping ability—training young patrollers to resist it. He was tempted to test the notion, except for the certainty that it would scare the crap out of these two even worse than it scared him, and then there would be all those awkward explanations. But it was a heartening realization that any patroller who could resist a malice could resist Dag, as readily as a brawler could block a blow to his face. *If he saw the blow coming, leastways.*

But not any farmer.

He bit his lip and pushed that troubling thought aside for later examination. "And whether you're the patrol member who places the knife or not, the better your ground-veiling, the better the chance of not spending the week vomiting your guts out from the blight exposure, after."

Remo eyed him. "You ever do that?"

"It was closer to two weeks," Dag admitted. "After that, I took my ground drills a lot more seriously. Let's go around again. My turn to veil. You two close your eyes, but leave your groundsenses open and try to watch me."

Dag furled himself firmly, watching as the two obediently scrunched their eyes closed. Softly, he rose from his seat.

Barr grinned. "Hey, where'd you go?"

"Here," he breathed in Barr's ear.

The boy yelped and jumped sideways. "Blight! Don't do that!"

"It's how you get close to a malice. You need to learn, too."

"I've heard an advanced malice can ground-rip you all the same," said Remo dubiously.

"I've only tangled with two that strong, in my forty years of patrolling. The Wolf Ridge malice I didn't see close-up, just heard about from the survivors of the actual attack on the lair. The Raintree malice I saw eye-to-eye. That malice opened up one of the best ground-veilers in my company as easy as you'd gut a trout."

"How can you even take down a malice that strong?" asked Remo.

"Gang up on it. Go after it all at once with a lot of patrollers with a lot of knives, and hope one gets through. Worked at Wolf Ridge, worked the same at Raintree." He added after moment, "*Well-veiled* patrollers. So let's go around again."

After a couple more circuits, Barr remarked, "So, are you saying if I stayed this lousy at my ground-veiling, I'd never be chosen for one of those suicide-rushes?"

"In Luthlia, we'd set you out for bait," Dag said.

Remo sniggered. Barr grimaced at him.

"Again," said Dag. Interestingly, Barr improved; but then, Barr had more room for improvement. Judging by his increased flickering, Remo was growing fatigued. Time to wind up.

"That's enough for today," said Dag, easing back onto the bench. "I think we'll spend an hour a day in this drill from now on."

Barr stretched and rolled his shoulders, squinting. "So much for the benefits of running away from home."

"Depends on what you run into," Dag drawled. "If we rode slap into a river malice around the next bend, would you be prepared?"

"No," said Remo bitterly. "None of us has a primed knife."

"Then your job would be to survive and run for help to the next camp. Which is where?"

"Blight," said Barr. "I'm not even sure where *we* are."

"Amma made us memorize the locations of all the camps in Oleana," Remo offered.

"Good," said Dag. "Too bad you're in Raintree now." And led the boys through a list of every Lakewalker ferry camp and its location in river miles from Tripoint to the Confluence, and made them each recite it back, individually and in chorus. Granted, the obscene version of the old memory-rhyme sped the process.

The cool morning was failing to warm, the climbing sun absorbed by graying skies. Dag glanced down the river valley to see dense mist advancing up it. Berry popped her head over the roof edge.

"If you can spare one of your patroller boys to pilot duty up here in a few minutes, I'd be much obliged," she said. "Looks like we're in for a real Grace Valley fog, and I don't want to run up over it into some pasture half a mile inland like in Bo's tale. The *Fetch*'d look funny on rollers."

"I'll come up," said Dag. "I could do with a stretch."

He joined Berry and Whit on the roof; Bo and Hod climbed down for a turn at the hearth.

"If I'm right in my reckoning," said Berry, "we're coming up on a big island around this next bend that I don't want to get on the wrong side of."

"Do we want the right- or left-hand channel?"

"Right-hand."

"Will do, Boss." Dag took a sweep and matched Whit's slow sculling—just enough to give Berry's rudder steering-way—which they had learned how to keep up for hours if necessary. The mist thickened about them, beading on Dag's deerskin jacket, which Fawn had lately lined with quilting to help fit his scant summer gear for fall. They followed the main channel as it hurried around the wide bend; Dag extended his groundsense to its full mile range to locate the split in the current before they were swept wrongside-to.

"Hey," he said. "There's somebody on that island."

"Can't be," said Berry, peering into the clinging damp. They could see maybe three boat-lengths ahead, now. "With this rise from the Bear-grass, that island's under three, maybe four feet of water."

"That could explain why they don't seem too happy." Dag reached, opening himself as wide as he could, ignoring the familiar, and much louder, grounds close-by. "Seven men. Blight, I think they may be those same Raintree flatties who passed us by backwards last night." He added after a moment, "And a bear. They've all taken refuge from the flood up in the trees!"

"Must be exciting for the one who's sharing with the bear," said Whit dubiously.

"Bear's got his own private tree." After a moment, Dag added, "No sign of their boats. Not moored within a mile, leastways. I think those fellows are in trouble over there, Boss. At least one ground shows signs of being hurt."

Berry drew breath through her teeth. "Bo!" she bawled. "Hod! You patroller boys, git out here! We need to get the skiff in the water afore we float too far!"

The rest of the crew turned out onto the back deck, and Berry leaned over and explained the situation. After Dag confirmed the head-count of men stranded on the island, they decided to launch both the skiff and the narrow boat, in the hope of rescuing them all in one pass; also, Dag pointed out, so the two boats could partner each other in case of snags literal or figurative. Dag stayed with the *Fetch* to guide it down the channel. Whit and Remo each took an oar in the skiff; Barr paddled his narrow boat.

"You sure about those fellows, Dag?" Remo called up from the water, once they'd all clambered down and were ready to push off.

"Yep. Just over half a mile that way." He pointed.

Barr's head turned. "Oh, yeah, I've got 'em now! Follow me, Remo! It'll be just like old times." His boat shot away as his paddle dipped and surged.

Remo snorted, but trailed dutifully. Whit's voice drifted back through the fog: "Beats shifting sheep, anyhow . . ."

"Sheep?" said Berry.

Dag shook his head.

Long minutes slid past as the *Fetch* slipped downstream. Floating with the current, the banks obscured, it felt as if they'd stopped altogether in a quiet, fog-walled harbor. Running full-tilt into a snag or a big rock at five miles an hour and opening the *Fetch*'s seams would cure that illusion right quick, Dag thought; he kept all his senses alert.

"Them Lakewalker boys'll be able to find their way back to us, won't they?" said Berry uneasily.

"That's why we put one in each boat," Dag assured her. "They've made it to the island; ah, good for the narrow boat! Barr can get it right in between the trees."

"Just so's he don't catch it sidewise to the current and lean too far over. He could fill it in an eyeblink that way."

"These Pearl Riffle patrollers are up to the river's tricks, I expect," said Dag. "Handier than I would be. And those narrow boats are made to float even full of water. Air boxes in the prow and stern, tarred up and sealed."

"So that's how they do that! I always wondered." She added after a moment, "We thought it was magic."

Fawn took Hod and Hawthorn below to help assemble a warming welcome for the expected influx of unhappy boatmen—or boatless men. It was nearly an hour before the narrow boat appeared out of the fog astern. Two cold, wet strangers crouched in a miserable huddle in the center, clutching the thwarts nervously, but a third sat up in the bow, helping Barr paddle. Bo and Hod gave them hands to climb stiffly out—one nearly dumped the boat over in his clumsiness, but Barr kept it upright.

"Whee-oh!" said the paddling man, straightening up and pulling off a shapeless felt hat much the worse for wear. He was a lean, strappy fellow, unshaven and shoeless; his feet were scratched and his toes purple with the cold. "We sure are glad to see you folks. We hit the top of that there island broadside in the dark last night, and it just sucked our boats down under that big towhead like the river was swallowing 'em!"

Bo leaned over the steering oar and nodded sagely. "Yep. It would." Fawn, hovering in the rear hatch, looked on wide-eyed.

They had barely hoisted the narrow boat back aboard when the skiff, too, emerged from the mist, Remo and Whit rowing strongly. The skiff rode low in the water with the weight of the four rescued men. One was not only shoeless but shirtless, the skin of his shoulders and torso scraped bloody, some hanging in ugly strips. He handed up an ash boar spear, of all the things to have hung on to in the wreck. He groaned as he was hauled and pushed up by his anxious companions, but when he found his battered feet and gingerly straightened, clinging to the upright spear, he gazed around with a lively smile. Unbent, he proved a tallish man by farmer measures, with black hair straggling down his neck, and bright, brown eyes.

"This here's our boat boss, Captain Ford Chicory," the paddling man explained.

"I'm Boss Berry, and this is my boat, the *Fetch*," said Berry, raking an escaped hank of hair out of her eyes. "You're right welcome aboard."

The skinned flattie blinked at her in frank appreciation. "Well, ma'am, you folks sure fetched us out of a heap o' trouble! We called all night from those trees as the water was gettin' higher, till we got so hoarse we couldn't yell no more, but you're the first as heard us."

"Thank the Lakewalker, here," said Berry, nodding to Dag. "He's the one that spotted you. We'd have passed you right by in this soup."

"Yeah, and if we had heard you, we'd likely've thought you was ghosts crying to lure us to our doom in the fog," Hawthorn offered helpfully.

The skinned flattie's startled eye was drawn from Dag by this; he looked down at Hawthorn in bemusement and scratched his head. "Yeah, I could see that."

"Too many tall tales," Berry explained, cuffing Hawthorn on the ear. "Go help Fawn." She turned to her crew. "I want at least one of you patroller boys topside with Bo." Both volunteered, and climbed up. "And, Bo," Berry called after them, "this time, if Remo tells you it's a sand bar or snag, you mind him!"

His crew herded their skinned boat boss—or former boat boss— through the back hatch; Dag ducked in after, mentally locating his medicine kit. The crowded kitchen was warm and steamy, and there he found Fawn had prepared gallons of hot tea and a huge heap of potatoes fried with onions and bacon, drenched in salt butter. A basket of apples stood ready. Warmed, if not hot, water waited for washing up. Stacks of every blanket and towel the boat carried were heating in front of the hearth. The exhausted men fell on it all with moans of gratitude. The limited supply of spare dry clothes was shared around as best as might be, with blankets making up the rest.

Hot water, soap, and Dag's kit waited by the hearth as well. It seemed he was expected to take on the injured, which he was willing enough to do. It was mostly cuts and scrapes, which he set Hod to washing with strong soap. Whit helped bandage, with a little instruction. The flattie leader was the worst off, and Dag set him on a stool before the fire and borrowed Fawn's hands to help clean the odd injuries on his torso.

"What in the wide green world happened to you?" Fawn asked him as she started in with rags and soap. "Did that bear claw you?"

The fellow smiled back at her the way most sane fellows did, despite his winces from her scrubbing. "Not this time, missy."

"Why didn't you bring back the bear, too?" demanded Hawthorn of Whit, both pausing to watch this process.

"It wasn't a *cub,* Hawthorn," Whit said impatiently. "It would've sunk the skiff, if it didn't try to eat us."

Boss-or-Captain Chicory told Hawthorn kindly, "Bears can swim fine, if they've a mind. It'll get itself off that island when it gets bored." He whispered to Fawn, "I've got a boy about that size at home, and his little brother to keep him in trouble in case he runs out. Which he never has yet, I admit." He raised his voice, "No, see, how it was—ow!"

"Sorry," said Fawn, folding a cloth to pat new blood leaks from a scrubbed scab.

"Keep on, missy, I can tell you're doing me good. How it was, was, we'd come up shorthanded just before we reached the Grace, because three of our fellows got scared at the size of the river and run off with our skiff. So we lashed the boats together, but now I think that wasn't such a good idea, as the rig was mighty obstinate after that. We pretty much gave up and just went with the river, figuring we'd get a chance to sort out and maybe hire on a real pilot downstream a ways."

"Had any of you been on the river before?" asked Berry, joining the circle.

"No, not down this far. Some of my hands had worked the upper Beargrass a time or two, but boats are a new start for me. My main line is hunting—bear and wild pig mostly, though my missus keeps her garden. I'm no hand at farming. Tried it once. If things are mainly going to die on a man anyway, hunting's a more natural trade for him, I figure." He took a long swallow of tea, warming to his tale.

"I was sitting down by the fire last night in the trailing boat, trying to get my feet thawed and wishing I was back hunting bears on hard land, where a man can at least pick his own direction, when I heard the fellows running and yelling over my head. Then we struck that towhead, *thunk!* I knew right off we were getting sucked under tail-end first, because the upstream side o' the floor tilted down like a rooftop. I bolted for the hatch, which was in the middle of the roof, but the river was already a-pouring in like a regular cataract. The only other opening was this little window in the side, which we'd mainly used for dipping up water before we'd lashed the boats together."

Berry glanced fore and aft to the *Fetch*'s two exits, and its generous pair of windows. "I see. You boys make those boats yourselves?"

"Not exactly. I bought 'em from a widow woman whose man was killed in that ruckus in north Raintree this summer. Seemed a way to help her out. He'd been in my company, was how it was." He took another swig and continued, "I scrambled over to our dipping hatch, but it was plain to see it was too small for me. But with the river pouring in, it was plainer it was go through it or be drowned, and my papa always said I was born to be hanged, so I chucked out my good ash spear, stuck my arms through, and yelled for Bearbait and the fellows to grab me and pull with all their might or I was a goner."

The man with the battered hat—Dag trusted that Bearbait was a nickname—nodded earnestly. "We didn't so much pull, as just hang on tight and let the boat get yanked off around you. I was mainly thinking how much I didn't want to go back to your wife and explain how you was drownded, after all that. She being strongly not in favor of this whole scheme in the first place," he added aside to Fawn, who nodded perfect understanding.

"That little hatch scraped off my shirt and skinned me like a rabbit, but they got me through!" Chicory beamed around at his crew, who grinned back despite their fatigue. "We all scrambled onto the towhead before the second boat went after the first, and spent part of the night clinging to the wrack like wet possums, till it started to break up, too. Then we waded back and found some trees that were right-side-up and not moving. You know, I suppose I should have been glum, having lost my boats and lading and all my trouble, not to mention my clothes and skin, but I felt prime, up in that fine tree. Every once in a while I'd break out chuckling. Couldn't help it. It felt so good to be breathing air and not river." He sighed. "I don't suppose I'll ever see my poor boats again."

"You never know," said Berry. "If they weren't busted to pieces when they went under the towhead, sometimes they come up again all waterlogged and get picked up downstream by folks. What was your cargo?"

"Barrel staves, mostly, and bear and pig hides. Kegs of bear grease and lard. I don't care for the staves, but I regret the other. A passel of bears and pigs, those were, and not easily come by." He glanced at his ash spear, leaning in a corner.

"Your staves would likely be too warped to be anything but fire-wood, later, and the hides, well, it'll depend on how long they soak, and if they can be dried again without going moldy. Some of your kegs might make it, if they're good and tight."

Chicory brightened at this news; his partner Bearbait looked less enthusiastic.

Fawn finished washing and drying the wounds, then traded places with Dag, who bent in for a close inspection with both eye and ground-sense. Dag reported, "You're well gouged and scraped, and your joints are wrenched sore, but nothing's dislocated or broken. Bleed pretty freely last night, did you?"

"He was a sight," confirmed Bearbait. "I was ready to bust him in the jaw for laughing like that while looking like that."

"But the bleeding's mostly stopped on its own, now." Dag gently worked out a few deep splinters with his ghost hand and tweezers. "The rips are too ragged to make stitching you up worthwhile, I think." He fingered a hanging ribbon of skin, considered whether to detach it with knife or scissors, then, on impulse, ripped its ground crossways in a slice as thin as paper. The strip fell away into his hand; he pitched it into the fire. "Did that hurt?"

"What?" said Chicory, trying to crane his sore neck to see over his shoulder.

The tiny bit of the Raintree man's ground in his own felt little different than a normal ground reinforcement; not even as odd as a mosquito or an oat. Dag removed the other two bad strips the same way, trying for as fine a slice as he could. They did not bleed. *Better stop here and think about this one, eh?* "You're going to have scars there."

Chicory snorted indifference. "I've done worse to myself."

Dag didn't doubt it. "Give me your say-so, and I'll put a little Lakewalker-style ground reinforcement in the deepest gouges to fight infection, which is the biggest danger left. Then have Fawn put some ointment on and wrap them up so the scabs don't crack when you move. In a few days, a clean shirt should be enough to protect them while they finish healing."

Chicory's brows arched wryly. "If I had a shirt, I could wash it, sure, if I had a bucket. And soap." He hesitated. "What's that thing you say you want to put in me?"

Fawn translated, "A touch of Lakewalker magic healing."

"Oh." Chicory looked both impressed and alarmed. "That'd be a new start, for sure. All right . . ." He craned suspiciously as Dag laid in lines of ground, but his lips parted as his hurts eased. "How de'! That's a strange thing. Never had a Lakewalker offer me anything like *that* before!"

"I aim to be a medicine maker to farmers, once I learn more of the trade," Dag explained. "It isn't anything anyone's done before."

"Mighty strange place, this big river," sighed Chicory.

Plans were made to deliver the boatwrecked men to a town two days down the river, where Chicory hoped to find an old friend who would help them to shoes, clothes, and enough gear to commence walking home. Meanwhile, Berry undertook to watch for signs of their lost boats. The exhausted men slept in piles and didn't wake again until the *Fetch* tied to the bank for the night and Fawn had to clear the decks of her kitchen to start supper.

Dag wasn't sure if he wanted to wrap a cloak of husbandly protection around Fawn, or clutch her to him like a talisman against such a concentration of strange farmers. Just who was supposed to be protecting whom? But with fifteen people crammed aboard the *Fetch,* privacy—not to mention private conversation—was out of the question.

Dag quickly learned that Chicory's crew were mainly his friends and neighbors from a small town on a feeder creek to the lower Beargrass, southwest of Farmer's Flats and so not in the direct path of last summer's horrors, news both Dag and Fawn took in with relief—his covert, hers warmly expressed. Chicory had acquired his tag of *Captain* by getting up a troop of local volunteers to go help out when the troubles began, when the malice had grown advanced enough to kidnap and mind-slave Raintree farmers, marching them to attack other settlements in turn. By the looks they exchanged, Barr and Remo were inclined to mock this self-appointed rank; Dag, the more he listened, was not.

Ford Chicory proved to be an excellent tale-teller. He was no blowhard like Boss Wain; his place at the center of his tales was as often as the butt of the joke as the hero, but he had a knack for holding his listeners in thrall either way. After dinner, aware of his audience and perhaps in return for the boat's hospitality, he even told a creepy ghost story that had both Hawthorn and Hod bug-eyed and half of the crew pretending not to be.

Tales now being as readily exchanged as coins in a dice game, everyone clustered around the hearth as Chicory and his crew learned in turn about Berry's quest, Dag and Fawn's West Blue marriage, and—inevitably, Dag supposed—Dag's place in the campaign against the Raintree malice. Dag did not willingly volunteer his words, but with Fawn, Whit, the crew of the *Fetch,* and once in a while even Barr and Remo chiming in, he didn't need to do much more than adjust their Dag-tales for overenthusiasm. As the Raintree men's picture of him shifted from itinerant medicine maker to ex–patrol captain, they grew warier—Dag could not decide if this was a relief or an annoyance—but Chicory's attention sharpened.

"I'd seen old blight bogle lairs when I was out hunting, from time to time," Chicory told Dag. Dag wondered how often the man had ventured into forbidden territory above the old cleared line, but now did not seem the time to ask. Chicory went on, "Gray patches, all nasty and dead. It didn't take no high-nosed patrollers to convince me to stay off 'em, no sir!"

Dag let his groundsense flick out. A successful hunter like Chicory might well possess a rudimentary groundsense like Aunt Nattie's, if some passing Lakewalker had climbed his family tree a few generations back. It was impolite to inquire, though, and since Chicory seemed to have led an irregular wandering life far from his birth kin, he might not know himself.

The Raintree man continued, "I've met your patrols, run across your camps—they never invited me in, mind, more like invited me to move along—but I'd never seen Lakewalkers *run* before."

"They went streaming past us like rabbits, when we got up north of the Flats," said a crewman in a faintly scornful tone.

"Now, that was the women and their young shavers, mostly," said Chicory in a fair-minded way.

"Malices snatch the youngsters first, by preference," Dag said. "When a malice goes on the move, Lakewalkers have learned to get the little ones out of the path as fast as they can, with the rest—off-duty patrollers, other adults—for rearguard. Likely you didn't get far enough north to meet the rearguard, or the malice might have taken you, too."

"We met plenty of them mud-men," Bearbait put in, face darkening in memory. "Both before and after they lost their wits. Ugly mugs, they were."

"The malice makes them up out of animals it catches, you know," Fawn said. "By groundwork." She went on to describe the grotesqueries of the mud-man nursery she'd seen at Bonemarsh Camp, with such simple directness that she seemed unaware of how thoroughly she was topping Chicory's ghost story for keeping folks awake in their bedrolls later.

Upon reflection, Dag was not surprised to learn that Chicory's troop had acquitted itself well upon the mud-men—hunting and killing bears and wild pigs would have trained them in both methods and daring. But Chicory's face grew graver when he remarked, "Ugly as they was, they didn't bother me near as much as those bogle-maddened farmers we met up with. Because they *weren't* driven witless. It took you a little to realize they weren't right in the head, because they walked and talked as if what they was doing was sensible, and they looked just like anybody else, too. You couldn't hardly tell who was on what side, till they jumped on you, and then it could be too late. What we did find, though"—he rubbed his chin and frowned at Dag in the lantern glow and firelight—"was that if we rode in and grabbed up a few, and took 'em back south far enough, they'd come to their senses. We first found that out trying to capture one to make him talk. Got him far enough away and he talked, all right—not that you could make much sense of it through the crying. After that, we tried to catch as many as we could, and carry 'em away till they found their lost minds again. Wouldn't any of them join us to go fight, after, though."

Dag's brows rose in increased respect. "I didn't realize farmers could do that, on the edge of a malice war. Huh. That would be . . . good. Draw down the malice's forces."

"You took a chance," said Remo in disapproval. "If you'd got too close to the malice, it might have caught your minds in turn, and then the malice's forces would have been up, not down."

Chicory said stiffly, "Seems to me such a chance would've overtaken a man sitting still, just the same." He eyed Dag sidelong, and added, "I was never too fond of Lakewalkers, and the ones I've met have pretty much returned the favor—but I do admit, after last summer I don't like blight bogles a whole lot more."

The lead-in could not be spurned; Dag set Fawn to describing Greenspring again, as he did not think he could bear to. Fawn and Whit together managed a creditable explanation of groundsense and sharing knives. Barr and Remo listened with troubled faces to these deep Lakewalker secrets being bandied around; the boatmen, with expressions ranging from disturbed to disbelieving. Chicory, though, just grew quiet and intent.

Chicory seemed a village leader of sorts—if a terrible boatman—with initiative and wits enough on dry land to persuade friends and kin to follow him into discernible danger, for a good cause. His words, as well as the slices of his ground, gave Dag much to digest as he retreated with Fawn to their curtained nook. The bits of ground were converting far more readily than those of the mosquito or even the oats, nearly indistinguishable from an ordinary supporting or healing ground reinforcement. As with malices, it seemed people made the best food. *Lakewalker cannibals, indeed.* Neither Chicory's ghost tales nor his war stories had unnerved Dag, but as Fawn cuddled into the curve of his body and drifted into sleep, that last reflection kept him awake for a long time.

✧

The *Fetch* didn't handle any worse for its added passengers, but neither did it handle any better, Dag noted the next morning as he took his turn on the roof. Hod was on the opposite oar and Whit at the rudder, very proud to be permitted to steer all on his own down this straight stretch. Berry would be coming up shortly to take over, as, she said, the next bend would bring them to one of the trickiest passages on the river. Berry had allowed a few of the Raintree flatties to volunteer for oar duty, but only one at a time and under her or Bo's close supervision. The rest seemed willing to help out with the increased scullery chores their presence as inadvertent guests had caused, so except for the unavoidable crowding and the friction on the Lakewalkers' groundsenses, a day more of their company seemed likely to pass pleasantly enough.

Since a chill wind funneled up the valley, with sunshine intermittent between the scudding blue-gray clouds, most everyone stayed inside near the hearth or curled up in nests amongst the stores. As Dag studied the river, two men in a skiff put out from a feeder creek beneath a bluff, rowing in their direction. When they pulled to within shouting distance, the older one rose up on one knee from his bench and hailed them, waving his hat.

"Hallo the boat!"

"How de'!" Whit called cheerfully in return. "What can we do for you fellows?"

"Well, it's more like what we can do for you. That last flood messed up the channels all through Crooked Elbow something fierce! I'll undertake to pilot you through safe."

This was a common way all along the river for local men to earn a bit of coin. Berry, now that she'd come to trust her Lakewalker crew's groundsenses, usually turned down such offers politely, though she did enjoy the exchange of river gossip that went with. Sometimes, the rowboats also brought out fresh food or other goods to sell or trade.

"I'm not the boat boss," Whit called back, "but what do you charge?"

"Just ten copper crays to the Elbow. Twenty to the Wrist."

A nominal sum, well worth it to the average boat given the time— or worse—that could be lost to an accident. Dag opened his ground, furled to block out the uproar of the crowd on the *Fetch*. And paused in his sculling.

"Huh," he said to Hod and Whit. "That's funny. One of those fellows is as beguiled as all get-out."

"By a malice?" said Whit in alarm. Hod gaped curiously.

"No, there's not a touch of blight-sign. He must have had some encounter with a Lakewalker, lately." Dag stared as the men rowed nearer.

The beguiled man was middle-aged, shabby, rough-looking, a typical tough riverman. He hardly seemed the sort to have attracted the attention of some female Lakewalker lover. Perhaps he had less visible attractions, but his ground was certainly no brighter than the rest of him. He hadn't been healed of any obvious injury lately. The other, Dag could imagine drawing a female eye: well built, young, open-faced, with crisp brown hair, and cleanly in his dress and bearing. But no beguilement distorted his ground, for all that it was furrowed by old stress. It was a puzzle.

"You can come up and talk to our boss, I guess," Whit called down as the skiff came alongside. "I don't think we need a pilot, but we have some things to trade, if you're interested. Some real fine Glassforge window glass, to start."

The skiff men waved apparent understanding. Hod shipped his oar and swung down to the bow to help them tie their boat and clamber up past the chicken pen. They both gazed around with interest. The pilot could have been watching his prospective customers approach for the past ten miles from a vantage on that bluff, Dag realized.

"Hey, Boss!" Hod called through the front hatch. "More visitors!"

Dag locked his oar and walked forward to the roof edge. He looked down to see the top of Berry's blond head bob through. She stopped as if stone-struck; the tin cup in her hand fell to the deck with a clank and rolled disregarded, spilling a last mouthful of tea.

The handsome young man looked up at her with recognition in his gray eyes and, Dag would swear, a flash of horror.

"Alder!" Berry shrieked, and flung herself forward to wrap around the startled fellow nearly from top to toe. His arms hesitated in the air, then closed around her to return the hug. "Alder, Alder!" Berry repeated joyously, her face muffled in his shoulder. "You're *alive*!"

19

Berry's radiant joy seemed to light up the air around her; in contrast, Alder's roiling ground darkened in consternation. Dag set his feet apart and stared down, hand on his jaw, fingers spread hard across his lips. *What is this?* Hod grinned uncertainly. Whit abandoned his steering oar and came to Dag's side to peer over, his eyes widening in a suddenly set face.

"Hawthorn, Bo! Fawn, come on out here! I've found Alder!" Berry called.

Alder's hand made a futile gesture and fell to his side; he stretched his mouth in a smile as Hawthorn came bolting out of the hatch with a yell of glee. The boy might have hugged Alder if Berry hadn't already held that space with no sign of giving it up; as it was, he danced around the pair, whooping. Fawn and Bo followed at a less violent pace. A curious Remo dodged the crowd by hoisting himself up from the back deck and strolling forward to watch.

As the cries of greeting swirled around Alder, his skiff mate looked up and spotted Remo. "Alder!" he gasped. "There's a Lakewalker on this here boat! We have to leave off. You know Crane don't want us to mess with no Lakewalkers."

Alder stared up at the row of spectators lining the edge of the cabin roof. He drew a short breath. "No, Skink—there's two. That tall one's haircut fooled me at a distance."

Berry grinned widely at him. "Three, actually. Dag and Remo've been in my crew since Pearl Riffle, and Barr, um, signed on later. They're all real tame, though—you don't have to be scared of 'em."

Alder gulped. "No, not scared, but—I guess you won't be needing a pilot, huh?"

"No," agreed Skink loudly. "These folks don't need us. Come on away, Alder."

Alder swung to his companion. "No, you don't understand. This girl here"—he waved at Berry—"she's my betrothed. Was. Is. From back at Clearcreek. Did you come all the—no, yes, of course you came from Clearcreek. Had to have. We *can't* . . . hire on this boat, Skink."

Skink said uneasily, "Right, that's what I said. What you want t' do, then?"

Hawthorn interrupted urgently, "Alder, where *were* you? Where's Papa and Buckthorn and the *Briar Rose*? Where's the other boat hands that was with you?"

Berry stood a little away from Alder, wrenched unwillingly from her elation by these harder questions. "Oh, Alder, why didn't you come home? Or write, or send word up the river with someone? It's coming on eleven months since you left. We've been worried sick about you all!"

Alder's lips moved wordlessly. He swallowed and found at least a few: "I'm so sorry, Berry. The *Briar Rose* sank in a storm near here last winter. I was the only one as got off. Some fellows from"—he glanced at Skink—"from a hunting camp up in the Elbow picked me up off the shore, nearly dead. I was sick for weeks—lung fever. By the time I got better, there was no sign of the boat but a few boards caught in a tow-head. The river took the rest."

"Are you sure?" asked Berry anxiously. "They might have got downstream of you and thought *you* was lost—no, they would have sent word somehow . . ." Her breath went out of her in a long sigh.

Hawthorn's hopeful face crumpled; Berry folded him in one arm. His back shook. "Shh, Hawthorn," she said, hugging him tight. "We always sort of knew, didn't we? Because Papa and Buckthorn and . . ." she hesitated, ". . . they wouldn't have left us without saying, unless . . . well." She scrubbed her free arm across her damp eyes. "Why no word, Alder? It was so cruel on us!"

Alder drew breath. "It took me months to get stronger, and then I owed the camp fellows for their help, and then I thought—I went down the river to get us a grubstake, and I didn't want to come dragging back to you with my hands full of bad news and nothing. I meant to at least replace the value of the *Rose* for you. But it's took longer than I thought it would."

Remo whispered urgently in Dag's ear, "Dag, he's—"

Dag held up his hand and murmured back, "Wait. Let him finish." He stared down intently at the anguished people on the front deck, groundsense as open as he could bear. Which was not wide, at this point.

Berry cried, "Alder, you're making no sense! You know me better, you must! How can you think I'd put a bag of coin above my kinfolks' lives, or even the knowing of their fates?"

"I'm sorry, Berry," Alder repeated helplessly, hanging his head. "I was wrong, I see that now. I never dreamed you'd come after me."

A variety of expressions had moved across the listening Bo's face, from muted pleasure to muted grief; now he was simply mute, chewing gently on a thumbnail. Fawn had tumbled out onto the deck almost as excited as Hawthorn. Her face had fallen in mirror to her friend Berry's. Now she stood by Bo with her arms folded, listening hard. On the whole, Dag was glad she did not seem to be swallowing all this down as readily as Berry, but then, she had less reason to: Alder had sworn no heart-oaths to Fawn, and any hopes she held for Berry's happiness teetered on a balance against fears for Whit's. *My Spark's shrewd; she feels the twist in this.*

Berry went stiff. "Alder—you're going to have to tell the truth sometime, so it may as well be now. If there's another girl, you'll have to betray one of us or t'other, so you can't win that toss nohow. If she—maybe—nursed you back to health or something, I don't suppose I can even hate her . . ." Berry stared beseechingly at him. They were standing wholly apart now.

"No!" said Alder in surprise. "No other woman, I swear!"

Remo whispered, "Blight. S' the first true thing that fellow's said."

"Aye," replied Dag. And sorry he was for it; it would have been a tidy wrap for the tragedy. He added softly, "Keep an eye on that beguiled fellow. He's getting ready to bolt." Skink was edging toward the skiff. Remo nodded and slipped quietly down past the chicken pen. Skink stopped and edged back, looking furtively around the crowded bow.

Berry searched her betrothed's face and decided—however wishfully, even Dag could not tell—that he spoke true. "Then come with me now! We'll sell the *Fetch* in Graymouth and have all the grubstake we need. The house in Clearcreek is waiting." Her voice skipped a breath. "I had it all ready for us."

Alder ran a harried hand through his hair. "I can't run off with no word to the camp fellows as helped me."

"Of course not!" said Berry. "We can stop around the bend. I'd want to thank them myself for their care of you. Or"—she paused as a new realization apparently overcame her—"if you have debts to them, well, I have some coin as will clear them. It's not much, but it's enough to cover a sick man's keep and nursing." She hesitated again in unwelcome suspicion. "Unless they were gambling debts that got all out of hand on you . . . ?"

"Berry, they're a pretty rough lot. Better I should deal with them, and you take your boat straight on. I'll . . . collect my things and meet you at the Wrist."

Bo's slow voice broke in. "You never found any bodies to bury proper?"

Alder shook his head. The roil in his ground was growing frantic.

"You don't have to soften it for me," said Berry in a low voice. "I know what this river can do."

Was this Dag's business? He glanced at Fawn, who was anxious for Berry but more anxious for the stricken Whit. At Bo, at the bewildered Hawthorn. Dag was not above supporting lies to shield someone from futile pain, but all directions seemed bad, here. *So let's have the truth out, and see where the pain falls fairly.* He looked down gravely and said, "Berry . . . ? Alder is lying to you."

Her face turned up, white and wild. "What about?"

"Everything."

Skink lunged for the rail.

He was caught by Remo and by Chicory, who had come out partway through the uproar to lean against the cabin wall and listen in baffled fascination. Chicory was quick enough to help catch Skink before he went over into the water, a hunter's reflexes, but his face twisted up in doubt once the struggling man was held between them. "What are we doing here, Lakewalker?" he called up to Dag.

"I'm not sure, but that fellow is beguiled to the gills. I don't know who did it, or when, or why." Had it been on purpose?

"Oh, that's no good," said Hod. "Can you fix him, Dag?"

What would happen if he unbeguiled the unsavory Skink? It was gut-wrenching to imagine having to take in that repulsive ground-release, but beguilement was a hurt in its own way. If Dag would not leave a man bleeding or lying with a broken bone, could he turn away from this? "Why are you trying to run off, Skink? I won't hurt you."

Skink glared around madly. "Crane won't like this!" he told Alder.

The fear from both their grounds pulsed like a stench, but Alder at least held his stance as Dag eased down from the roof and approached Skink. *On my head be it.* He lifted his left arm, not that he needed to touch the man at this range, but aligning body and ground helped him concentrate. The act was growing easier with practice; Dag flinched as the backwash of Skink's agitated ground poured into him, but he forced himself to accept it.

Dag wasn't sure what response he'd been expecting, but it certainly wasn't Skink's collapse into utter shock and violent weeping, a sudden shuddering heap on the deck. "No, no, no!" he wailed. "No, no, no . . ."

Chicory bit his lip in appalled fascination, tense with surmise.

Yes, Dag thought. *The troop captain's seen something like this before. And so have I.*

"Skink, pull yourself together!" Alder snapped. He looked around at his gaping audience, now augmented by Barr and Bearbait. "Sorry, folks, sorry. It takes him like that when the drink wears off, sometimes. I better get him back to camp . . ."

Any one of Alder's lies might have been plausible; the accumulation was surely not. *What truth does he fear so desperately?* This was Dag's last chance to avoid finding out. Alas, there wasn't much to choose between regret for a disaster from a mistake, or regret for a disaster from being perfectly correct. *Strike at the weakest point; strike fast.*

He strode forward, yanked up Skink's head by the hair, and bought his attention with, if not a fence post between the ears, his harshest company-captain's voice. *"Look at me."* Skink stared up, his breath catching in mid-snivel. Dag demanded, *"What are you really doing here?"*

"Boat bandits!" babbled Skink. "We're supposed to check the down-bound boats, and if they're any good, bring 'em in to Crane and the boys for the plucking. Oh, gods!"

"What?" cried Berry. "Alder, what?" She wheeled to stare in horror not at Skink, but at her betrothed.

"The man's in a drunken delirium!"

"The man," said Chicory thoughtfully, "reminds me a whole bunch of those fellers we used to pick off the edge of the blight bogle's camp."

Dag just barely kept himself from saying, *It's related.* Not a parallel he wished to draw attention to. He compromised on, "Maybe, but this is human mischief, it seems." He yanked Skink's hair again, refusing to let him retreat into breathless weeping. "How many bandits, where?"

"Thirty. Forty. And Crane, always him."

"Where?"

"Cave, there's this cave up around the Elbow. Thirteen river miles around the loop, but just three across the neck. Gives time to scout out the boats and prepare, see . . ."

He's spouting good, now. Keep up the pressure. "Was there ever a malice in the cave?"

"What?"

"A blight bogle."

Skink shook his head. "Ain't no blight bogles around here. Just Crane, that's bad enough. And them Drum brothers. Before the Drums come, Alder was Crane's right-hand man, but he likes them better now, and even Alder's not crazy enough to be jealous of them two Drums."

Dag shook Skink again, leaning down on his shoulder as if Skink were a leather water-bag and Dag was trying to squeeze out the last drops. "So you lure in the boats with offers of piloting, and then what? Steal their valuables? What do you do to the crews?"

"That wasn't how they got *my* boat. When I first come, the cave was still fixed up as Brewer's Cavern Tavern. Bring us in, get us drunk, set on us while we was in a stupor . . . except the ones Crane saved out for his game . . . oh, the blood and pitifulness of it all!"

Very quietly, Bo and Barr had moved in on either side of Alder, Dag was glad to see. Berry had stepped back, her face drained, cold, distant. Fawn gripped her bloodless hand, in support or restraint or both.

"What happens to the crews nowadays?" Dag kept on.

"Kill 'em in their sleep or from behind, if we can. Can't let any run off to tell. Ride 'em down if they run. Crane can always find 'em. Burn the boats or hide them in the blocked channel back behind the island. Can't let any boats go down to be recognized, either. Brewer used to do that, but Crane is cannier. Brewer invented the game, too, but Crane won it in the end."

"And the bodies?"

"Used to plant 'em in the ravine, till Little Drum showed how you could slit their bellies and load 'em with rock, and sink 'em in the river so's they don't come up. Faster than buryin'. Oh, gods. See, them Drum boys don't always kill 'em first . . ."

Was this enough? *Too much.* Dag knew their urgent danger now, and surely decanting more grotesque details—what was *the game?*—could wait till they were not in front of Fawn, Berry, Hawthorn, and Hod. *One more.* "Who is Crane?"

"The Lakewalker. *Our* Lakewalker."

Barr and Remo both took that in immediately; Dag could tell by the way their grounds snapped shut like mussels. *A renegade? A madman? A malice's pawn?* "Where did he come from?" Dag pressed relentlessly.

"Don't know. He was here already when I come along. Oleana somewheres, I guess."

"Did he start the gang?"

"No! Fellow named Brewer, I said."

"Was Brewer a Lakewalker?" Surely not, with that name.

"No, 'course not! Before me—before Alder—Crane was just a passenger on a down-bound flatboat that Brewer lured in to the Cavern

Tavern. Somehow he talked Brewer out of killing him, and then he was Brewer's right-hand man for a time, and then . . . no more Brewer. Just Crane." Skink hesitated. "Brewer, they say he just wanted to get filthy rich, but nobody can figure out what Crane wants."

"He's alone?"

"No, there's about thirty or forty of us, depending."

"I mean, no other Lakewalkers with him?" Dag clarified.

"Oh. Yeah. Alone like that, I guess."

"Where is he right now, do you know?" Nowhere within a mile, but a mile seemed suddenly much too short a distance between this madness and Spark.

Skink shook his head. "Cave, last I seen." Alder seemed to cringe inward. Dag looked up and eyed him in cold speculation.

Berry swallowed and said to Dag, "Ask him if they took . . . saw the *Tripoint Steel.*"

"Them struttin' keelers?" Skink snorted. "They was through here last week. Crane, he said to lie low and just let them fools float on by. Which they did."

Dag met Berry's eyes and read the message: *No help there.* But it set his mind to spinning. The *Fetch's* complement was outnumbered by at least two to one, but other boats came behind in a steady stream. Clever of the bandits to take only the richest and let most pass unmolested, but even so their crimes could not go unmarked much longer. How much time did the *Fetch* have to prepare? *Prepare what?*

Some of the Raintree flatties had taken over the oars, or the *Fetch* would have drifted into a sand bar. They were much closer now to that feeder creek with the good lookout just above it. Dag motioned to Chicory and Bearbait. "Did you ever have the hunting of bandits up in Raintree?"

"Once," Chicory admitted, scratching his head. "It was only a couple, not thirty or forty. Brought them in alive to be tried before the village clerk, but we didn't have to stay for the hangings. Not my favorite sort of hunting, but it needed doin'."

Dag said, "It seems to need doing again. I've helped take out bandit gangs a couple of times, plus the big one that plagued Glassforge. First trick is, you make sure you outnumber the targets. The *Snapping Turtle* is not too far behind us, and there may be other boats following soon. If we can get enough help by nightfall, are you fellows in?"

Chicory glanced at Bearbait, who nodded. "Might as well be."

"If I could, I'd prefer to leave the farmers to the farmers. And the Lakewalker to the Lakewalkers," said Dag. Barr and Remo both flinched at the word of their new task, but returned his nod. "This Crane is likely to be dangerous in ways you can't fight."

"That would suit me," said Chicory slowly. "As long as they're all brought to the same justice after." His gaze at Dag was hard and questioning.

"If he's guilty of half the horrors Skink suggests, that won't be a problem. Three's been a quorum for field justice before this."

Chicory gave this a very provisional nod. "Well, if you want to make a rabbit stew, first you catch your rabbit."

"Aye," said Dag.

After the *Fetch* tied up at the mouth of the feeder creek, Fawn watched anxiously as Dag and most of the rest of the men took their prisoners ashore for further questioning. They all returned in about three-quarters of an hour, looking even grimmer, although neither Alder nor his shattered partner showed signs of much new roughing-up. Bo closely supervised the chaining of Alder's hands behind him, around one of the sturdy posts holding up the *Fetch*'s roof between the kitchen space and the stores. He advised Dag, "I'd put a gag in his rotten mouth, too."

Dag just shook his head, but he told Berry and Fawn, "Don't let those chains loose for any reason. If he has to piss, turn your backs and have Hod hold a bucket." He held Berry's eyes as he said this; she nodded shortly. Then they all settled down to wait for reinforcements.

Whit signaled from the bluff fairly soon; he and Bo went out in the bandits' skiff to explain matters to a down-bound flatboat, which then rowed in to tie alongside the *Fetch*. Its nine able-bodied flatties were shocked at the news, not to mention at their own narrow escape, and readily volunteered for the attempt to burn out the river robbers.

The *Snapping Turtle* came into sight around noon, and Fawn saw Dag start to breathe a little easier. Its raucous crew pronounced themselves all in for the dirty job. The serious planning began then amongst the cadre of leaders and bosses gathered on the shore: Wain and Saddler, Chicory and Bearbait, the new flattie boss, and Dag. Wain, claiming to be the best brawler on the river bar none, was inclined to assume leadership. He called for a roundabout river attack, although it was plain Dag preferred Chicory to lead a land strike up over the neck. When the blustering threatened to grow loud and prolonged, Dag took Wain aside for a brief word. Fawn, watching from the *Fetch*'s bow, was not at all sure it had been words alone that persuaded Wain to settle down, and she nibbled on her knuckles in worry as Dag looked darker than ever. But the land ploy was finally agreed upon.

The men spent the afternoon assembling or devising weapons. All had knives, and cudgels were readily fashioned, but there were fewer spears and bows amongst them than Dag plainly would have preferred. He set Whit with the bowmen.

"Does Whit have to go?" Fawn murmured to Dag in a rare private moment snatched out on the *Fetch*'s back deck.

"He volunteered. It would be an insult to leave him with the boats.

And I'm short on archers." He pushed a curl of hair back from her brow. "At least bow-shot puts him farther from the rough and tumble."

"There's a point," she conceded.

"And . . . I'd rather not leave him with Alder."

Her gaze flew up. "Dag! No matter how heartbroke he is for Berry, Whit's not an assassin!"

"No, but Alder has as twisted a tongue as I've ever encountered. If he talks Berry into . . . anything, there's as much danger of Whit being persuaded to some foolishness out of misplaced nobility as there is of his going to the other extreme. I'm as happy to remove him from the dilemma altogether." He hesitated. "We're all going to have to turn hangmen come morning, you know, if this goes as it should. Berry'll need all the support you can give her through that."

"Does Alder have to hang? I mean, he was beguiled by this Lakewalker Crane, wasn't he? Is he guilty, if he did what he did under compulsion? Is Skink? Isn't that going to be a real problem to figure out, come . . . come morning?"

Dag was silent for a long time, staring out across the river. "I'm not planning to bring it up if the others don't. Please don't you, either. They're all guilty enough."

"Dag . . ." she said reproachfully.

"I know! I know." He sighed. "No matter what, first we have to capture the bandits. We need to get through that with a single mind. Argue after, when it's safe to."

Her lips twisted in doubt.

He held her, bent his face to her hair, and murmured into it, "I thought when I quit the patrol this sort of work would all be behind me, and I could turn my whole heart and ground to fixing folks instead of killing them." And even lower-voiced: "And once I'd fixed as many as I'd ever killed, I'd be square. And then start to get ahead."

"Does it work like that?"

"I don't know, Spark. I'm just hoping."

She gave him a hug for support and turned her face up. "Can't you at least unbeguile Alder, before you boys go off tonight? It'll be horrible for Berry to watch him fall to pieces like that Skink fellow, but at least he mightn't be so dangerous."

"I can't unbeguile Alder."

"Why not? You did the other. It's not like ground-gifting, is it, where you can only give so much before you collapse yourself? Or is it like that piece of pie, too much at once?"

"No," he said in slow reluctance. "I can't unbeguile Alder because he's not beguiled in the first place."

A silence. "Oh," said Fawn at last. *Oh, gods. Poor Berry* . . . "Just when were you planning to mention this to her?"

"I don't know. I have way too much tumbling through my head right now to trust my judgment on that. Get the bandits, first. And their leader Crane especially. I know that much. It may well be the only thing in the world I know for sure, right this minute."

It seemed old-patroller thinking to her: *Get the malice first. Everything else after.* She didn't think he was wrong. But *after* was starting to loom in a worrisome way. She settled on reaching up to give a heartening shake to his shoulders and say, "You get those bandits good, then."

He gifted her back a grateful smile and a jerky nod.

In the afternoon, another flatboat arrived, but it proved to hold a family. The papa and the eldest son volunteered, along with two boat hands, to the dismay and fright of the mama who was left with four youngsters and a grandpa. No one expected arrivals after nightfall, when most sensible boats tied to the banks, but at the last glimmering of dusk one more keelboat came, almost slipping past in the shadows. Its crew of tough-looking Silver Shoals men, when the awful litany of deceit, murders, and boat-burnings was recited yet again, made no bones about joining up. Then there was nothing to do but feed folks, talk over plans in more detail, and keep the men quiet and sober till midnight.

There was little work to getting Dag's war kit ready, as he planned to be gone for mere hours, not weeks. Fawn had thought they were done with these partings in the dark when he'd quit the patrol; the returning memories unnerved her. But the crowd of river men assembled on the bank was encouraging in its numbers and bristle. Dag had set Barr and Remo and some of the Raintree hunters out ahead as scouts. The rest tramped away over the hill by the light of a few lanterns, doubtless noisier than a company of stealthy Lakewalker patrollers, but with determination enough.

Sleep was out of the question. Fawn and Berry turned to assembling on the kitchen table what bandages and medicines the *Fetch* offered, in readiness for the men's return—at dawn, Dag had guessed. Fawn hoped there would be no need to break out any of Berry's stock of Tripoint shovels for burial duty, at least not of folks on their side. It was likely much too optimistic a hope, but she had to fight the bleak chill of this night somehow. With nearly everyone gone off, the row of boats tied along the bank of the feeder creek seemed much too quiet.

Hawthorn had disappeared up amongst the nearby trees for a while, most likely to cry himself out in privacy. When he returned, he lay down in his bunk with his back to the room. As his hands loosened in deep sleep, the kit escaped his grip and went to hide in the stores. Bo went out to take a walk up and down the row of boats and talk with the few other men, some older like himself, one with a broken arm, left to watch over them. Hod, detailed as Bo's supporter as well as boat guard, tagged along.

Alder's head came up from an uncomfortable doze. He didn't look crisp and handsome anymore, sitting on a stool with his back to his hitching post, just strained and exhausted. Fawn wondered if he'd often been sent out on decoy duty because his clean looks and glib tongue reassured folks. His eyes shifted in the lantern light, a furtive gleam, then focused on Berry.

"I couldn't escape," he said. "You don't know what Crane does to deserters."

Berry stared across at him from her place at the table, but said nothing. Fawn ceased fiddling uselessly with her sewing kit and wondering if she would have to sew up live skin and flesh with it, and turned in her chair to watch them both. "Just what does this Crane do to deserters?" she asked at last, when Berry didn't.

"He's clever, horrible clever. One or two he's killed outright in arguments, but mostly, if a fellow or a couple of fellows demand to leave his gang, he pretends to let them. He lets 'em load up with their pick of goods, their share, the lightest and most valuable, then trails after 'em in secret. You can't get away from his groundsense. Ambushes 'em, kills 'em, hides the goods for himself. Nobody back at camp even knows. You can't get out alive."

It seemed almost inadvertent justice to Fawn. With a few hitches. She glanced up, wondering if Berry spotted them, too. "If it's so secret, how do you know? 'Cause it seems to me Crane wouldn't be doing all this ambushin' and buryin' by himself."

Alder shot her a glance of dislike.

"How come there's any bandits left?" Fawn went on. "Or is that Crane's plan, to be the last one left at the end?"

"Men drift in. Like the Drum brothers. Sometimes he recruits from captives. Like Skink."

And like Alder? Fawn wondered if she wanted to ask how in front of Berry. Maybe not. She suspected Bo already knew, from that earlier interrogation that had left the men all so grim. And there would likely be other witnesses taken alive to tell the tale tomorrow.

"I tried to save you," Alder went on, looking longingly at Berry. "Out there today, I tried everything I could think of to get you to go on. I always tried to save as many as I could, when I was put on catching duty. Boats with families, women or children, I waved them on."

Likely they were also the poorer boats, Fawn suspected. "Bed boats?" she inquired.

Alder flinched. "We never got any of those," he mumbled. Berry's gaze flicked up.

If Crane was as clever and evil as Alder said, more likely he let the women in to ply their trade, loaded them up with presents, and disposed of them on their exit just like his deserters. Or else word of the lucrative Cavern Tavern would have trickled out in at least some channels before this, and Berry had not overlooked the bed boats in her inquiries. But it was undoubtedly true that Alder had tried frantically to convince Berry to go on.

His voice grew lower, more desperately persuasive. "But we could get away now, you and me. When I saw you, it was like I woke up from a yearlong nightmare. I was so afraid for you—I would never have let Crane have you. I never imagined you'd rescue me. But see, I know where some of Crane's caches are. If we slipped away now, tonight, while the others are busy, we could both go back to Clearcreek rich and never have to go on the river no more. I never want to see the river again; it's been the ruination of me. We could wipe all this out like a bad dream and start over."

"Is that what you was plannin' to bring back to me?" said Berry in a scraped voice, staring down at her clenched hands. "Bags of coin soaked in murdered folks' blood?"

Alder shook his head. "Crane owes you death payment for the *Rose* at least, I figure."

"Why, if it sank in a storm?" Fawn inquired, lifting her eyebrows. His return glare was nearly lethal.

Alder recovered himself and went on. "It's all that Lakewalker sorcerer's fault. He messes with folks' minds, puts them in thrall to him. Destroys good men—delights in it. You saw Skink. He was just an ordinary boatman, not a speck different from your papa's hands on the *Rose,* before Crane caught him and turned him. That's why I could never get away. Gods, I hate Crane!"

That last had the ring of truth. Berry looked up at him, and for a moment, Fawn thought she saw her hard-pressed resolution waver, if that wasn't just the water in her reddened eyes.

"If Crane beguiled you," said Fawn, "then you're still beguiled right now, and it isn't safe to let you go, because you'd just run right back to him. You couldn't help it, see, just like you couldn't help the other."

Alder's lips began to move, then stopped in confusion. Did he see the dilemma he'd backed himself into?

Berry spoke at last. "'Course if you ain't beguiled, it's hard to see how it was you couldn't get away before this. Seems to me a man who just wanted to escape, and didn't care about no treasure, could've swum out in the night and set himself on a bit of wrack and floated away most anytime this past summer. Come to the first camp or hamlet past the Wrist in about a day and gone ashore for help, and gave warning what nasty things was hiding up in the Elbow. And this would all have been over long before now. If you wasn't beguiled. So which is it, Alder? Make up your mind."

Alder's mouth opened and shut. He finally settled on, "That Lakewalker. He's sorcelled me all up. I can't hardly think, these days."

"Then I daren't let you loose, huh?" said Berry, and rose to her feet.

"Come on, Fawn. There's ain't no sleeping in here. Let's go set to the roof. The air's cleaner up there, I expect."

"I expect it is," said Fawn, and followed her out the back hatch into the chill dark.

The night sky was clear and starry over the river valley. A half-moon was rising above the eastern shore. They sat cross-legged on the roof, looking around at the black bulk of the bluff, the few dim lights leaking from the boat windows down the row. The creek water gurgled in the stillness, giving itself to the Grace. Fawn heard no shouts or cries of commencing battle, but from three miles away on the other side of a hill, she didn't expect to.

"Alder was a good man all his life, up in Clearcreek," said Berry at last.

Fawn said nothing.

"The river really did ruin him."

Fawn offered, "Maybe he just never met such hard temptations, before." And after a little, "Spare me from ever doing so."

"Aye," breathed Berry. No insect songs enlivened the frosty night; their breath made faint fogs in the starlight. She said at last, "So, is Alder beguiled or not? Did Dag say?"

Fawn swallowed. It wasn't as if there would ever be a better time or place to tell Berry the truth. "He said not."

A long inhalation. "I sort of realized it must be that way, after a while. Or Dag would've released him along with Skink." Cold haze trickled from her lips. "I can't think which way is worse. Ain't neither is better."

"No," agreed Fawn.

"I don't see no good way out of this."

"No," agreed Fawn.

They huddled together in silence for a long time, waiting for light or word, but the cold drove them inside before either came.

20

Dag braced one knee on a fallen log, checked the seating of his bow in his wrist cuff, and locked the clamp. He opened himself for another quick cast around, cursing, not for the first time, his groundsense's inability to penetrate more than a hand's breadth into solid rock. Barr and two of Chicory's bowmen had reached their position on the opposite side of the cave mouth. Remo and another Raintree hunter were creeping up on the opening in the cave roof, through which a trickle of wood smoke, steel-gray in the light from the rising half-moon, made its escape. It would be Remo's job to see that nothing else escaped by that route. Lastly, Dag checked on Whit, clutching his own bow at Dag's side. Whit's face, striped by the shadows from the bare tree branches, was nearly as pale and stony as the moon, entirely drained of all his wearing humor. The effect was not as much of an improvement as Dag would have thought.

He choked back anger, not only at the cruelty of the bandits, but at finding them *here, now,* in the middle of the journey he'd intended as Fawn's belated wedding gift. She'd been terrorized once by the bandits at Glassforge, and he'd sworn that no such horror would touch her again. Granted, she hadn't seemed terrified tonight, just tense and resolute. He would keep the ugliness well away from her this time, if he could. He tried not to think about the fact that her monthly fertile days were starting up, a lovely sparkle in her ground, normally the signal for them to switch to subtler Lakewalker bed customs. Far from bandits of any sort. *Don't dwell on that threat, old patroller, you'll just make yourself crazy. Crazier.* But he was determined that none should escape this cave trap to trouble her, or Berry, or anyone else. He bit his lip in frustration, unable to make a count of targets through the shielding rock walls.

Wonder of wonders, the two trampling gangs of boatmen, one led around the upstream side by Chicory, the other around the downstream side by Boss Wain, nearly joined again by the entrance to the cave before the guard there woke from his drunken stupor and yelled alarm. *Too late,* thought Dag in satisfaction. His groundsense flexed open and shut, wavering between picking up events and blocking the flares of the targets' injuries. All his fooling around with medicine making seemed to have left him much more sensitive to such . . . he cringed, taking in the sizzle of a knife cut, the explosive flash of a thump with a cudgel, still searching for his true target.

Where was this Crane, blight it? They must have caught the Lakewalker leader asleep inside, just as Dag had hoped, or else the boatmen would never have crept this close before being spotted. Because none of the *Fetch*'s Lakewalkers had bumped grounds with him outside, not within a mile.

Cries, crashes, and screams sounded from the cave mouth, borne outward in the orange flickering from torch fire and wildly wavering lantern light. A bandit trying to lift himself out the smoke hole was knocked back in by Remo's partner, like a man hammering down a peg. Remo followed, disappearing from both view and groundsense. Good, Dag had at least one scout inside to help the rivermen deal with the renegade. He ruthlessly stifled worry for Remo's inexperience as a group of five bellowing bandits clumped together and fought their way out the cave mouth past Wain's men, breaking and running toward Dag and Whit.

"See 'em?" said Dag, raising his bow and drawing hard.

"Yep," said Whit through dry lips, and mimicked him. Both steel-tipped arrows flew together; both found targets.

"Great shot!" said Dag. *Beginner's luck, more likely.* Dag's second arrow was on its way before Whit's shaking hands could nock his next. It wasn't a disabling hit, lodging in the bandit's thigh; the man was not felled but only slowed. This bunch must realize how little mercy they could expect from their boatmen prey-turned-hunters. The three still on their feet turned back and began running, or limping, the other way, around the cave mouth and up onto Barr's position. None made it past.

Dag waited a few more minutes, but no more fugitives broke free. Archers' task accomplished, he eased forward and led Whit down the slope, more anxious now to reach the cave than to keep Whit away from it. One of their victims lay dead, an arrow through his eye. The other whimpered and shuddered in the fallen leaves, clutching a shaft that was lodged deep in his gut.

"Should we——?" Whit began uncertainly.

"Leave him for now. He won't be running off," murmured Dag. He would worry about men due to be hanged in the morning only after he had tended to the injured on their own side. If there was time or any of himself left over for the task.

"But I—which one did I hit?" Whit stared back over his shoulder.

"Yours was that brain-shot. Clean, very quick."

"Oh."

Whit's expression teetered between triumph and revulsion, and Dag realized it wasn't just Barr and Remo he ought to meet with when this was all over, to check for damage due to leaks from targets. *And who will check my ground?* Never mind, first things first. Reeling, disarmed bandits were already being passed out through a gauntlet of boatmen and tied to trees. Dag trusted the rivermen knew their knots.

The inside of the cave was arrested chaos. Benches and crates lay knocked over, bedrolls kicked around. Goods of all kinds were strewn across the floor, including an inordinate number of bottles and jugs, broken and whole. The cave seemed to be composed of two chambers, one behind the other, each about twenty feet high and forty across. The fire beneath the smoke hole spouted up around a broken keg, emitting a glaring light. Burning oil from a broken lantern spread and sputtered, but already a boatman was stamping it out. Some men lay groaning on the ground, others were being tied up; there seemed to be at least two boatmen standing for every live bandit left—good. Dag winced, trying to hold his groundsense open long enough to get an accurate head-count. He still couldn't find the Lakewalker leader. Was Crane ground-veiled and hidden amongst the others? No . . . Remo was upright and uninjured, though, better still.

Bearbait sprang up at his elbow and grabbed him by the arm; Dag controlled a reflexive strike at him. "Lakewalker, quick! You have to help!"

He jerked Dag toward the cave wall, a little out of the way of the noisy mob. Two boatmen lay there on hastily tossed-down blankets. A kneeling friend held his hands frantically to the neck of one of them; blood spurted between his tight fingers. The other was Chicory, lying stunned, breathing irregularly, his face the color of cold lard. *Oh, no!* Dag let his groundsense lick out. The Raintree hunter had taken a cudgel blow on the left side of his skull, fracturing it just above the ear. *Bad . . .*

Bearbait wet his lips and said, "He'd took on two with his spear, see, when a third one got him from behind. I wasn't quick enough . . ."

The one with the cut to the neck was now or never. Dag dropped to his knees, unlocked and tossed his bow aside, and let his hands real and ghostly slide over those of the frightened friend, one of the Silver Shoals fellows. "Don't move," he murmured. "Keep holding tight, just like that." The man gulped and obeyed.

The jugular vein was only nicked, not sliced in two; this might not be impossible . . . The uproar of the cave faded from Dag's senses as he descended, down and in. Felt with his ground projection, caught up the cut edges of the big vessel, and mated them one to another once more. A shaped ground reinforcement, not large, but dense and tight . . . would it hold against internal pressure, external jostling? Had the pallid young man already spent too much blood to recover? The soil beneath Dag's knees was soaked in red, sticky and caking. He drew breath and backed out, evading groundlock, staring around in disorientation at the dire scene in the cave, unholy noises, men's shadows leaping in the wavering torchlight.

Dag shook his head and swallowed, chilled and shaking. "You can let up now," he told the bloody-handed friend, removing his own hand and wrist cuff from above. "Get blankets around him, get him warmed up any way you can. But don't bump him, or that big vein will bust open again. That surface cut needs stitches, if you have anyone with a real light hand to do it. Not right away, but in a bit." The jagged, ugly gash across the victim's neck still gaped, but blood only oozed now, instead of flowing like some terrible spring. "Don't try to move him yet." Later, the Shoals lad would need as much drink as they could get into him, but he daren't be made to swallow while still out cold. Choking could kill him.

Dag tried to remember what he'd been doing. Medicine making and captaining didn't mix well, it seemed; each took all of a man's attention. Chicory, yes, oh gods. He didn't want to lose Chicory, and not just for his affable humor. He was exactly the sort of natural leader who could go home and make a difference in his village, and amongst a widespread array of friends, if he could be convinced to see things Dag's way. *If he lives.*

Dag lurched half up and over to Chicory's side, and knelt again.

Watched closely by the fearful Bearbait, he cradled the hunter's head in his spread fingers. The skull was cracked in spider-web-like rings around the blow, pushed inward, but no sharp shards had pierced the brain beneath. But atop that strange thin skin that overlay brains in the smooth goblets of their skulls, a pocket of blood was collecting, actually pushing the skull dent out again. But also pressing into the delicate tissue beneath, like a grinding fist. *I'm pretty sure that's not good.* A real medicine maker or a farmer bonesetter might drill into the skull to let the bad blood out. At any rate, he was sure he'd seen such drills amongst Hoharie's tools. Dag's medicine kit included a fine knife, tweezers, needles and threads of gut and cotton, fluid to clean wounds, bandages, herbs, and powders. No drills. *Do I really need one?*

Dag recentered himself and ground-ripped a pea-sized hole in skin and bone. A spurt of blood trickled out, making a slippery mess of Chicory's black hair, seeping through Dag's fingers. As the pressure in the bulging pocket lessened, he found the bleeding inside starting up again. Not good. *Groundlock, you're risking groundlock . . .* He drew back out, still holding Chicory's head in his spread hand, and looked around woozily.

A few paces away, a man with a knife wound to his gut choked out his last breath and died. Bandit, Dag hoped, although he was blighted if he could tell the difference between bandits and boatmen from this confused vantage.

"Lakewalker . . . ?" said Bearbait.

Dag shook his head. "Skull's busted, but you knew that. It's too soon to say if he has a chance." He surreptitiously dropped another general ground reinforcement into the brain flesh around the blow, and blinked at his own dizziness. A big figure trod past; Dag called, "Wain!"

The boat boss wheeled around. "There you are!" He thrust out a suspicious chin. "What are you doing?"

"Best as I can," said Dag wearily. "I can't leave off here just yet. You find that Crane by now? If he's not here, find out where he's gone, and if there are any more bandits missing with him. Get exact numbers, get names. Don't let them hold out on you." Wain had wanted undisputed leadership of the boatmen—but to his credit, not at such a cost to his rival Chicory. The boat boss chewed his lip briefly but decided not to argue; he cast Dag a curt nod and moved off, bellowing for his lieutenant, Saddler. If Dag wanted questions answered, Wain was the man for the job, he was pretty sure. Most of the captives would be surly and hopeless, tight-lipped, but amongst a group this large, there were bound to be a few babblers. Beguiled or not.

Skink and Alder, blight them, had both claimed Crane was at the cave, and Dag would have sworn neither had been lying by that time. But they had been camped on their lookout for more than a day. Dag had seen good-once-but-too-old-now information devastate plans before this. *Blight.*

The little hole in Chicory's skull was clotting off. With his ground projection, Dag teased the clot out, letting the blood keep trickling. Was this right? When would it stop? He wanted to go back in to find the source of the flow and pinch it off, but didn't dare yet. One more of these deep ground-explorations, and he wasn't sure he'd be able to get up and walk, after. Let alone fight. This fight did not seem finished.

Whit had been drawn off to help the Raintree men secure prisoners. He returned to Dag's side and draped a blanket around his shoulders. Dag smiled up gratefully. Whit stared wide-eyed at the gray-faced Chicory. "Is he going to die?"

"Can't say yet. Can you find me Remo or Barr? Where the blight have those two gone off to?"

"Back of the cave, I think. I'll go check."

"Thanks."

Whit nodded and picked his way through the rubble. Dag thought his young tent-brother was holding up well, thrust into scenes of such lethal brutality for the first time in his life. He wouldn't have sent Whit to assist Wain, though. Dag grimaced at the ugly thumps and yells from the interrogation going on over at the far side of the cave, cutting through the moans and groans.

Whit brought Barr and Remo back in a few minutes. The pair looked black indeed, and not only from their first experience with putting down farmer bandits.

Remo held up a sharing knife. "Look what we found back there."

"Yeah, there's a cache piled to the ceiling," Whit put in, sounding amazed. "All the most valuable stuff, I guess."

Dag squinted. The knife was unprimed. "Could it be Crane's?"

"I found it in amongst what has to be a whole narrow-boatload of furs," Remo said. "Looks like Crane's crew didn't always avoid Lake-walkers."

Dag carefully set Chicory's head between his knees and raised his blood-soaked hand to take the knife. Remo recoiled to see Dag's sleeve wet with darkening red, but he reluctantly released the knife to the gory grip. Dag held it to his lips. Unprimed, yes. And with a peculiar stillness in its embedded involution.

"Whoever this knife was bonded to is dead now." So, probably not Crane's, though Dag supposed he could hope.

Barr, startled, said, "You can tell that?"

"My brother is a knife maker," Dag said vaguely; the two patrollers' brows rose in respect. "Keep this aside." He handed it back.

Remo slipped the bone blade back into its sheath and hung the thong around his neck. As he hid it all inside his shirt, his voice hushed in outrage. "They must've murdered a Lakewalker without even letting him *share*!"

Or her. Dag didn't want to think on that. There would have been women amongst the boat victims from time to time, but there weren't any around now. *Can't let any run off to tell,* Skink had claimed. Should Dag hope that they'd died quickly, and were his hopes worth spit?

Chicory's drainage was clotting off again, blight it, the pressure in the blood pocket growing once more. "Did you find any sign at all of Crane?" Or of those mad Drum brothers who seemed to have become his principal lieutenants; Dag definitely wanted to locate them—dead, alive, or prisoners.

Barr shook his head. "Not within half a mile of here, anyway."

"We have to find him. Take him." And not only for his monstrous crimes. If the Lakewalker leader was not tried with the rest, perfunctory as Dag suspected the trial was going to be, the boatmen would always suspect the patrollers had colluded in his escape. "Blight it, what's taking Wain so long . . . ?"

As if in answer, Saddler crunched across the cave to stare down at Dag, shake his head in worry at Chicory, and report that all the bandits were accounted for but five. Two, it seemed, had left the night before last, cashing out their stakes and quitting the gang permanently, unable to stomach the Drum brothers' grotesque cruelties any longer. Crane and his two lieutenants had left separately early the next morning, some hours before Alder had flagged down the *Fetch*. It had been a chance to the boatmen's benefit, it seemed, because the bandit crew, bereft of their leader's supervision, had broached some kegs Crane had been saving, and had been a lot drunker than usual this night.

So, up to five bandits still loose out there, including the worst of the bunch. *Have we left enough men to guard the boats?* Dag suddenly didn't think so. But he dared not move his two charges yet, and besides, there would be no point jostling them up over the hill in litters when the boats had to come downriver anyway. The convoy could float around the Elbow in the morning and tie up below the cave, carrying them smoothly. *But I can't wait that long.*

Dag wet his lips. "Anyone on our side killed?"

Saddler looked dubiously at Dag's two patients. "Not yet, seems. Nine of the bandits are goners. Twenty-one here left to hang, though there's one that might not live for it."

Dag stared in frustration at Chicory's drained face. He must bring the Raintree man to a point where he could be left for a while, because Dag *had* to start moving after Crane. But in what direction? Haring off the wrong way would be worse than useless. He did know he wanted Copperhead under him to speed the search. Barr and Remo might be mounted on a couple of the bandits' horses—they'd found a dozen or so hobbled not far from the cave.

"Saddler, go back and see if you can find out anything at all about which way those five fellows might have gone. Barr, take a turn around the perimeter again—they might be coming back, and we want to spot them before they spot us. Remo . . . stay with me. I need you."

Whit, unassigned, tagged off after Saddler. Remo knelt beside Dag. "What do you want me to do?" he asked quietly.

"Break me out if I appear to groundlock myself. I need to do some deeper groundwork inside Chicory's poor bashed head, here."

Remo nodded gravely. Trustingly. Absent gods, did Dag *look* like he knew what he was doing? Surely Remo should know better by now. Dag sighed and dropped down into that increasingly easy, ever more familiar level of ground-awareness.

The inner world expanded to fill his horizon, as vast and complex a landscape as the Luthlian woods. No wonder that, once a fellow had done this, any other sort of making seemed trivial and dull. A calling, indeed. But his elation was short-lived. These injuries were subtler by far than Hod's knee, the groundscape deeper and much stranger. Far beyond Dag's understanding.

I don't have to understand everything. The body is wiser than I'll ever be, and will heal itself if it can. Let him just start with the obvious, mend the biggest broken vessels. He'd done that before. Maybe that would be enough. *It had better be enough.*

He continued the inner exploration. This end went with that one, ah. A little shaped reinforcement would hold them together. For a time. Another, another, another. Ah! *That* torn artery was the main source of the trouble, yes! Dag brought it back into alignment, reinforced it doubly. And then blood was leaking into the pocket more slowly than it was leaking out, and then it was hardly refilling at all. This time, when the bulge deflated, it stayed shrunken. Another push to position the shell-cracked bone. The squashed brain tissue expanded back into its proper place, still throbbing. Another ground reinforcement quelled its distress . . .

In his exacerbated sensitivity, Remo's little ground-bump felt like a blow to the side of Dag's head. He gasped and fell, disoriented, upward into the light.

"Are you all right?" asked Remo.

Dag gulped and nodded, blinking and squinting. "Thanks. That was timely."

"Seemed to me you'd been in that trance for an awful long stretch."

Had he? It had seemed like mere minutes to Dag. Whit appeared at his side; he handed Dag a cup of something, and Dag, unsuspecting, drank and nearly choked. It was nasty, sickly sweet, but it burned down his throat in a heartening way. Some sort of horrible fruit brandy, he decided, from the bandits' stores. His stomach, after a doubtful moment, elected not to heave.

Dag had done all he could think of for the skull fracture, for now.

They were into the *wait and see what happens* part. He set Chicory's head down gently, cradling it in a folded blanket, and clambered to his feet. His stiffened joints moved like chalk scraping over a slate. Bearbait reappeared—when had he gone off?—and earnestly took in Dag's brief instructions about keeping his leader warm and lying still till Dag got back. For once, Dag had no objection when Remo grabbed his arm to steady him on his feet. Weirdly, the tiny ground-rip he'd taken from Chicory seemed to be giving him a spurt of strength, even as Whit's vile liquor quickened the blood in his veins. He suspected he'd have cause to regret both later, but now . . .

"Whit, give me another drink of that skunk syrup. Barr, where's Barr . . . ?"

"Here, sir."

"Find anything outside?" Dag lifted the cup again and sipped with an effort. The fumes did clear his sinuses.

Barr shook his head. "Not yet."

"Any other word which way our missing bandits all went?"

"The first two had evidently talked about heading back toward the Beargrass," reported Whit. "Nobody knows about Crane and the Drums."

They need not have all gone the same way. Only the latter trio really concerned Dag, so that northerly hint was not too useful. It occurred to Dag suddenly that Alder had been Crane's lieutenant before the Drums, and might possess clues that were beyond the rest of the bandits. Which gave Dag an excellent excuse to ease his heart and go back to the boats first, even better than his need for his horse. Alder hadn't been very forthcoming before, but he could be made to be, Dag decided grimly. One way or another.

Supported by Remo, Barr, and Whit, Dag stumbled out of the reeking cave into chilly predawn dew. The sky had a steely cast, the stars fading, the half-moon turning sallow overhead. He could find his way through the foggy woods with his eyes alone, now. He sent Barr and Remo off to pick out mounts for themselves from the bandits' string, then made his way back up the hill behind the cave. His stride lengthened despite his exhaustion, so that Whit was pressed to keep up.

✒

Fawn had lain down fully dressed in her lonely bed nook, despairing of sleep, but she must have dozed off, because she woke dry-mouthed and grainy-eyed. Grayness in the shadows hinted of dawn. A tall shape eased past, slipping through the stores—Dag, back? Her relief was so great that she relaxed again, almost letting her exhaustion draw her once more into precious sleep. But no, she had to hear his tale. She lay a moment more, listening to faint clinks from the kitchen. Muttering. The scrape of the rings of Berry's bunk curtain being pushed back, the red flare of someone turning up the oil lantern burning low on the table. Berry's voice, sudden and shocked: "What—!"

Fawn's eyes flew fully open, and she started up in bed. Thumps, bangs, crashes, a wrenching groan—Bo?—a yelp from Hawthorn, Alder's cry: "Don't hurt her!"

A strange voice, curt and cruel: "No? How about this one?"

Fawn swung upright, uncertain which way to run. She darted toward the kitchen a pace or two, craning her neck, and skidded to a halt. Alder was loose, swinging around and onto his feet with his chains still dangling from his wrists. She saw the back of a tall man—a Lakewalker patroller, by his clothes and the dark braid down his back—but it wasn't Remo. Bo had fallen to his knees, clutching his stomach with reddened hands, and Hod crouched with him, white-faced and frozen with fear. The tall man, she saw, held the squirming Hawthorn tight to his chest. A knife blade gleamed in his other hand.

"Don't move, Berry, he'll do it to Hawthorn same as to Bo!" cried Alder desperately. "He never bluffs!"

Fawn turned and sprinted.

She banged through the front hatch, sped past the animal pens, and thumped across the gangplank, drawing breath for a scream to wake the whole row of boats. A huge shape in the clinging mist lunged at her, smacking her so hard in her gut that she was thrown backward, and her scream sputtered out half-voiced. She wrenched and bucked violently as the man-mountain pulled her off her feet and whipped her through the air. One sweaty hand grabbed her face, spanning it nearly from ear to ear; the other clamped her shoulder. The grip tightened like a vise, and she realized he was about to snap her neck. Abruptly, she went limp.

A gruff voice growled, "Huh. That's better." Her captor felt down her body as he repositioned her. "Ah, a girlie! Maybe I'll save you for Little Drum." He strode forward, holding her half by her head, half under his arm, like a wet cat carried by its scruff. Over the gangplank and past Copperhead, who laid his ears back and snaked his neck but, alas, didn't whinny or squeal.

Dag, Dag, Dag, help me! If he was within a mile, he must sense the terror in her ground. *And if he isn't, he won't.* She struggled for air against the pressing, stinking hand, thought of biting, thought better of it. The light of the lantern seeped around her blocked vision, then she was twisted upright and set on her feet, both hands held easily behind her back by just one of the big man's paws. She managed one sharp inhalation before the other paw clamped over her mouth once more. The back of her head was jammed against a warm chest—barely winded, to judge by its steady rise and fall. She peered down over her nose at a log-like arm in a frayed sleeve stained brown and red-brown, reeking of sweat and blood.

Berry, Hod, and Bo had all been forced to kneel around the post that had lately held Alder, who was securing their wrists one to another with a length of line. He had to jerk Bo's hand away from his stomach. Blood soaked the front of the old man's shirt. His face had gone gray, looking worse than any hangover Fawn had ever seen on him, and he squinted as if in bewilderment, panting for air. Berry's terrified glance jerked back and forth between him and Hawthorn, still held tight by the stranger.

The man turned half-around. He had black brows and a craggy face shadowed with beard stubble, and his eyes gleamed darkly. Fawn wondered if they would be a different color in daylight, like Dag's. "So what's this?" he inquired, nodding at Fawn.

"Two girlies!" said the man-mountain. "One for me and one for Little Drum, I figure." He grinned, gap-toothed and sour-breathed.

The Lakewalker said wearily, "Haven't you two had enough fun for one night?"

"Not the yellow-haired one!" said Alder urgently. He hesitated. "They can split the other if they want, sure." He added after a moment, "She claims to be married to one of the Lakewalkers we surprised on this boat, but she's really just a farmer."

The black stare narrowed on Fawn. What the man was thinking she could not guess. "Seems to me they surprised you, Alder," he drawled after a moment. "What happened here?"

"It was Skink's fault," said Alder, still knotting line. "We went up to check out this boat like usual, but the Lakewalkers were all inside and we didn't spot 'em, except for the odd one that didn't look like a Lakewalker, see. They got the drop on us. The odd one, he did something, some groundwork, and Skink began spewing like a waterspout. Told them everything about the cave, *everything.*"

Alder wasn't telling everything, Fawn realized; he'd left out how he had been recognized by all the folks from Clearcreek. Did he imagine he could lie to——this had to be the renegade Crane, yes. And the man-mountain was Big Drum. *So where is Little Drum?*

"Those patrollers, they stopped every boat coming down the river and got up a gang to go jump the cave. Hours ago. They could be coming back at any time."

"Only if they succeeded," murmured Crane, raising his brows. He didn't sound terribly disturbed by the news.

"They had sixty or seventy fellows. And that one-handed Lake-walker——he had to be at least a patroller captain. Acted like this was all in a day's work, he did. It's all up with us now." Alder sounded almost relieved. "We've got to cut and run." His voice went wheedling. "You told me yourself you didn't expect the Cavern Tavern to last out the year. Those Tripoint fools was the warning, you said. Best we heed it."

Crane sighed. "Well, at least it seems I get a new horse out of the deal . . ." He paused, his head turning toward the bow. His curiously chis-eled lips pinched; his eyes narrowed. Consulting his groundsense? "Aw, what's Little Drum stirred up now?" He wheeled and, quite without expression, struck Hawthorn in the face with his knife haft hard enough to knock him across the room. Hawthorn fell in a stunned heap, breath stuttering. Berry cried out; Hod whimpered. Fawn strained uselessly against the heavy grip that held her.

Crane drew a long breath. "We're about to have company. Too late to get off this boat. Alder, go cast off the rear lines. Big Drum, drop the bow lines and then get yourself up on the roof and get an oar ready. You too, Alder. We'll push out and take it down to the crook of the Elbow, instead——should give us enough of a start. Give me that spare girl."

Reluctantly, Big Drum handed Fawn over to his leader; Crane grasped one arm with bruising pressure and turned her in front of him. The knife blade rose to her neck and pressed there, most convincingly.

"What about Little Drum?" Big Drum demanded.

"That'll depend entirely on how quick he can run. We'll see if she can buy him time to get here, but we're not waiting long." Following Big Drum, Crane shoved Fawn ahead of him out onto the front deck.

∾

Dag's legs jarred like hammer blows as he bounded downhill so fast it felt like falling. Fawn's fear howled through his groundsense. He tried to make out what was happening on the *Fetch* through a cacophony of distress: Bo hurt bad, Hawthorn and Berry in terror, Hod distraught—Alder loose and moving. And two new grounds, both grossly knotted and distorted, the darker one half-veiled.

On the way back from wherever they'd gone, Crane and his lieutenants must have checked their lookout point and seen the inexplicably deserted boats tied up along the creek below. Crane's Lakewalker groundsense would have found Alder on the *Fetch*—not happy, but for all Crane knew, still hoodwinking the boatmen. If Alder was still duping his victims, Crane might want to support him; if a prisoner, maybe free him—but in either case the first thing Crane had to do was slip aboard and reach him, between groundsense and the dank mist eluding notice by the sleepy watchmen. *And then things went bad. For both sides.*

By the time he'd barged through the last of the trees and the *Fetch* came into sight, Dag was so winded he had to stop and put his hands on his knees as black patterns swarmed in his vision. He raised his head as his eyes cleared. The big fellow with the knotty ground tossed the second of the two bow ropes over the side and retreated to the roof, unshipping a broad-oar. The man with the half-veiled ground shouldered through the front hatch, coming out onto the deck. He held Fawn. A knife blade gleamed against her neck; he wiggled it to make it wink and nibble into that soft flesh, and he looked up to lock Dag's gaze, frozen not twenty feet away beyond the end of the gangplank. Whit came dashing up, his bow waving in one hand and an arrow in the other; with shaking hands, he tried to nock it.

"Your little friend can just drop that bow," said the man dryly, shoving Fawn in front of him for a shield and tightening the bite of the knife. Dag thought he saw a line of red spring along its edge.

"Drop it, Whit," said Dag, not taking his eyes off the stranger. Crane, without doubt. Whit's lips moved in protest, but he let his bow fall to his feet. Fawn's eyes shifted, and her feet; Dag prayed she would not try to break away. This one would slice her head off without a blink. A trio of boatmen, attracted at last by the ruckus, thumped down the creek bank toward the *Fetch*. Dag's fear of no help coming gave way to terror that this help's clumsy advance would crowd Crane into dreadful action.

Behind this tense tableau, Alder climbed to the roof and unshipped the second oar.

"Push off," the leader called over his shoulder.

"What about Little Drum?" asked the big man.

The strange Lakewalker glanced up the hill. "Not coming."

Alder's oar swept backward, although the other oarsman still hesitated. The gangplank creaked as the boat began to pull away under it. Dag lurched forward.

"Ah!" Crane chided, lifting his knife under Fawn's chin so she rose on her toes. "You really need to believe me." He flicked open his ground to display his cold determination to Dag.

It wasn't even a decision.

Dag raised his left arm, stretched out his ghost hand twenty feet, and ground-ripped a cross section as thick as a piece of boot leather from Crane's spinal cord, just below his neck.

The man's dark eyes opened wide, astounded, as the knife dropped from his nerveless fingers. He crumpled like a blanket folding, and his head, unsupported, hit the deck with a weird double thump. He did not cry out; it was more of a questioning grunt.

Fawn, after a gasping hesitation, leaned over, snatched up the knife, and pelted inside. The big oarsman trod forward to the edge of the roof to see what was happening. He met Whit's arrow, released from his grabbed-up bow, square on. One hand lifted to grasp the shaft half-buried in his broad gut, but as the boat shifted, he stumbled and fell over the side with a cry and a smacking splash.

Dag leaped for the gangplank, but not before he glimpsed Berry jump up from the stern to grab the short end of the steering oar, jump down again to swing on it like a tree branch, and bring the long end around in a mighty arc, smashing into Alder's hip and sweeping him over the opposite side of the roof and into the cold creek water.

21

What Dag most wanted to do was question Crane: Fawn knew this because, putting her back on her feet after grabbing her up in a breath-stopping hug and mumbling a lot of broken words into her hair, it was the first thing he said that she could actually make out. But after one glance at Bo he reordered his plan, dispatching the panting Whit to organize the boatmen who'd been drawn by the ruckus to fish Alder and Big Drum out of the water and secure them, preferably on some boat other than the *Fetch*.

"What about Crane?" Whit demanded.

"Just leave him lay. He's not going anywhere."

Dag had the queerest look on his face as he said this, but before Fawn could figure it out, she was drafted as his hands, helping to straighten out the groaning Bo atop a blanket on a hastily cleared stretch of kitchen floor, peel away his shirt, and wash around the stab wound. Dag sat cross-legged, irritably cast off his arm harness, and fell into the healing trance that was becoming increasingly familiar to Fawn—and, she thought, to him. He was in it for a long time, while the shaken Berry, cut ropes still dangling from her wrists, tended to an even more shaken Hawthorn, who was bleeding from a broken nose and crying. Hod helped everyone as best he could.

Whit took a long time to report back. The arrow-riddled Big Drum had been easy to capture, as he'd waded to shore and put up no fight when he got there. Alder had tried to swim away. Some boatmen chased him down in a skiff and wrestled him out of the water, beating him into submission. He'd almost drowned, and Fawn, glancing at Berry's stiff face, thought it was a pity he hadn't. Dragging out his existence one more miserable day seemed a great waste of time, emotion, and hemp. Both men had been tied up on the *Snapping Turtle,* the shaft in Big Drum's belly cut off but left in, lest botching its removal keep him from his hanging.

Fawn was wondering if she should shake Dag's shoulder, or send someone to find Barr or Remo to do whatever it was Lakewalkers did to break unintended groundlocks, when he at last drew a long breath and sat up, animation returning to his face. He stared around blinking, found her, and cast her the ghost of a smile. Emerging from his task, he looked much less wild and distraught, as though the effort had recentered him somehow. Except that Fawn hadn't seen him look so drained since Raintree.

Bo had been conscious throughout, but silent, watching Dag with a brow furrowed as much in wonder as in pain. "Well, Lakewalker," he breathed at last, then muffled a cough.

"That healin' o' his is a thing, ain't it?" commiserated the hunkering Hod.

"Don't try to talk," whispered Dag. His dry voice cracked, and he cleared it; Fawn hustled to retuck the blanket she'd put around his shoulders and to fetch him a drink. He raised the tin cup to his lips with a trembling hand, swallowed, and went on more easily. "I've ground-glued together the two slices through your stomach walls where the blade punched in and out, and likewise some of the bigger blood vessels in there. Crane's knife missed the biggest ones, or you'd have bled to death before I got here. Fawn'll have to stitch up your skin." Fawn nodded, carefully washing away the gory matter that Dag had drawn from the wound by ground projection. She had Dag's medicine-kit needle already threaded, and bent to the task. Bo made little *ow* noises, but endured.

Dag went on cautiously, "Biggest danger now's infection. I expect there'll be some. Got to wait and see how that plays out."

Truly. A gut-wound like this was more usually a death sentence, fever finishing what bleeding started, as Bo likely knew, because he nodded shortly. When Fawn tied off her last thread, Whit, Hod, and Berry combined to lift Bo carefully into his bunk. Dag simply lay back on the floor and stared up at the roof.

Fawn was just wondering if they should also unite to lift Dag to his bed, when Barr and Remo clumped in to apologize for killing what they sincerely hoped had been an escaping bandit up in the woods. Fawn nipped to the front hatch to peek out, and saw a couple of saddled horses beyond the gangplank. Over one was draped the body of a skinny, red-haired fellow, his sharp, contorted face pale in death.

Crane was still lying in a heap beside the animal pen; his chin moved and his eyes shifted to glare at her, and she flinched and fled back inside. *Dag, what did you do to him? That was like no making I ever seen or heard tell of . . .*

In the kitchen, Barr was frowning down at Dag and asking the very question she'd longed to: "Dag, what the *blight* did you do to that fellow out on the front deck?"

"Is that Crane?" Remo added, glancing toward the bow.

"Yes," said Dag, still staring at the roof. "I broke his neck. In effect. He won't be getting better, in case anyone was worried about tying him up."

His expression glazed, Dag watched Fawn upside down as she bent and peered at him in worry. She remembered the shock in Crane's eyes when he'd dropped the knife and collapsed like a wall falling. *In effect.*

But not in any other way? Would the patroller boys think to follow up that little flag of truth amongst Dag's laconic misdirection? Either Dag would explain in his own time, or she'd wait for a private moment to ask, she decided.

Hod and Whit took tumbling turns giving a description of the events around and aboard the *Fetch* to the two patrollers, with an occasional corroborating moan or snort from Bo. Berry added little, still holding the sniffling Hawthorn. But as their words turned his frightening experience into a tale, he seemed to revive, uncurling from his childlike clutch in his big sister's lap, slowly regaining the dignity of his eleven years, and finally adding a few flourishing, if gruesome, details of his own. By the time they'd finished, he mainly wanted to go off and inspect the corpse of Little Drum. Dubiously, Berry released him.

"I about swallowed my heart when I saw that big knife at Fawn's throat," said Whit, "but I swear she looked more mad than scared."

"I was plenty scared enough," said Fawn. And yet . . . Crane hadn't been nearly as scary as the Glassforge malice, even if she might have been equally dead at either's hands. How odd. Flying from a knife at her throat to an immediate need to pull things together for Bo's sake, maybe she just hadn't had time to fall apart yet.

Some boatmen called from outside, a troop sent back from the cave to help guard the boats—a bit belatedly, Fawn thought tartly. The two young patrollers and Whit went off to help sort out things. It was full dawn. Dag sat up.

"I have to . . . I can't . . . let me sleep for one hour. Bo can have a few sips of water, nothing else." He climbed to his hand and knees, then to his feet, making no protest when Fawn lent him a shoulder to help him lurch to their bed nook. She did insist on pulling off his boots. He was asleep by the time she flung a blanket over him.

Barr, Remo, and Whit had been grimly excited, describing their victory at the bandit cave. After they'd defeated the Glassforge malice, Fawn recalled, Dag had been wildly elated despite his weariness. There was not a trace of triumph in him now, and she wondered at the difference. In the kitchen space that still reeked of the night's terror, the floor splotched with blood, Fawn sighed and quietly started fixing breakfast.

✺

Fawn let Dag sleep for closer to three hours; he woke on his own when the *Fetch* pulled away from shore. Stumbling out to the kitchen, he ran a hand through his bent hair, and asked, "What's been happening?"

"Not much," she said, passing him a mug of tea. "Everybody decided to move their boats around to the cave landing. Berry, Whit, and Hod are topside." She gestured upward with her thumb. "I sent Hod and Remo out to clean Crane up a while back."

Dag's brows bent, whether in bewilderment or disapproval she was not sure.

She explained, "It was more for us than him. Getting paralyzed like that loosed his bowels and bladder, seemingly. He was stinkin' up Berry's boat. Besides . . . even corpses get washed before burying."

He nodded glumly. She ran him out onto the back deck to wash up, took his bloodied clothes to soak in a bucket, and handed him fresh ones. The day was turning pale blue as the weak sun climbed, not so much warming up as thinning the chill. Since his hand was still shaking, she also helped him shave, a skill she'd acquired that time his arm had been broken, just before their marriage. Hot food and a cleanup were worth at least a couple hours of the sleep he hadn't got, she figured.

Their rattling around woke Barr from his own nap; Remo had been lying in his bunk but not sleeping, and he too rose to join them.

"I have to question Crane," Dag repeated. He nodded to the patrollers. "You two had best sit in. A quorum of sorts."

"I want to hear that tale, too," said Fawn.

He shook his head. "It's like to be nasty, Spark. I would spare you if I could."

"But you can't," she pointed out, which made him wince. Feeling pressed by his dismay, she struggled to explain. "Dag . . . I'll never be a fighter. I'm too little. My legs are too short to outrun most fellows. The only equal weapon I'll ever have is my wits. But without knowing things, my wits are like a bow with no arrows. Don't leave me disarmed."

After a bleak moment, he ducked his chin in assent. When he'd finished swallowing down his breakfast and his tea, they all followed him out onto the front deck. The *Snapping Turtle* was out ahead, approaching the crook of the Elbow, and the keelboat from Silver Shoals trailed them at some distance. The *Fetch* seemed very far from any shore, running down this stretch of swollen river.

Crane was laid out—*like a funeral,* Fawn couldn't help thinking—in Remo's spare shirt, covered by a blanket and with another folded under his head. His arms lay flaccid along his sides, nerveless feet to the bow. Dag settled down cross-legged next to him. Tidying up the two men first had lent this encounter a curious formality, as though they were couriers from distant hinterlands meeting to exchange news.

Even Crane seemed to feel it, or at least he was no longer trying to bite folks as he had when he'd first been washed. Fawn wondered if his several hours of being stepped past and ignored like a pile of old laundry had felt as weird for him as it had for everyone else. And then she wondered if Dag had arranged it that way on purpose, the way he'd left Barr without food to help tame him.

Fawn dragged the bench forward a little behind Crane and settled on it out of his direct view. But however mangled his ground and groundsense, he had to know she was back there. Barr leaned against the pen fence across from Dag, overlooking the captive; Remo sat at Crane's feet.

"So what's your real name?" Dag began. "Your camp? How'd you come to be alone?"

"Did you lose your partner?" Barr asked.

"Did you desert?" asked Remo.

Dag continued, "Or were you banished?"

Crane pressed his lips together and glowered at his interrogators.

"One of the prisoners told me he was an Oleana patroller," Remo put in uncertainly.

Silence.

"If that's the case," said Dag, "and he's a banished man, then he's likely Something Crane Log Hollow." Crane's head jerked, and Dag's lips twisted in grim satisfaction. Dag went on, "Because that's the only Oleana camp I've heard tell of that's banished a patroller in the past half-dozen years, and there can hardly be two the same."

Crane looked away, as much as he could. "Crane will do," he said. His first words.

"So it will," said Dag. "So I have the start of you, and I have the end. What's in between?"

"What difference does it make?"

"To your fate? Not much, now. But if you mean to tell your own tale and not just leave others to tell it for you—or on you—you've got maybe two more hours while we go 'round the Elbow. After that you'll be out of my hand."

Crane's black brows drew down, as though this argument unexpectedly weighed with him, but he said only, "You'll look pretty funny dragging a man who can't move off to be hanged."

"I won't be laughing."

Lakewalkers, Fawn was reminded, seldom bothered trying to lie to each other. Could Crane even close his ground, in his disrupted state? Dag had to be partly open at least, and not enjoying it. Barr and Remo kept tensing, like people flinching from a scratched scab they couldn't leave well enough alone, so Fawn guessed they were partly open, too.

Crane turned his head from side to side, frowning. "What the blight did you do to me, anyway? I can't even feel most of my body. With sense *or* groundsense."

"I once saw a fellow fall from a horse," Dag answered not quite directly, "who broke his neck in about the same place as I broke yours. He lived for some months. We won't inflict that on you."

"But you never touched me! You were twenty feet off, over on the bank. It was some sort of evil groundwork you did!"

"It was," said Dag impassively, not quibbling with the modifier. Remo and Barr looked disturbed. Crane's startled gaze said, *What are you?* plain as plain, but he didn't voice it.

Crane's utter helplessness had been made clear during his cleanup. He must realize by now he was a dead man talking. Fawn knew how to feign indifference to torments one could not escape, but she'd never before seen real indifference used so. Crane seemed pained to have his mind roused from its sullen retreat.

More silence.

"So," Dag probed again, "you were a mule-headed rule-breaker, and didn't care to reform, so Log Hollow threw you out. Maybe a thief."

"That was a lie!" said Crane. But added after a moment, "Then."

"Was it?" said Dag mildly. "There was a farmer woman, I heard. Maybe youngsters. What happened to them? When your camp stripped you and booted you out, did you find your way back to her?"

"For a while," said Crane. "She didn't much care for what I brought her from hunting, compared to what I'd used to bring from patrol. Then the blighted strumpet died. I gave it all up for nothing!"

"How'd she die?"

"Fever. I was away. Came back to a blighted mess . . ."

Dag glanced at Fawn, his face set tight, and she touched the thin, drying scab on her neck left from Crane's knife. Dag had been skin-close to losing her, last night. She'd sometimes worried what might happen to her if Dag were killed; never, she suddenly realized, what would happen to Dag if she died. His first widowing had nearly destroyed him, even with all the support of his kinfolk and familiar world around him. What would it be like with *nothing* around him?

"And the youngsters?" Dag said. His voice was very level, devoid of judgment. It would have to be, Fawn thought, to keep Crane talking at all. She bit her knuckle, picturing the lost children.

"Foisted them on her sister. She didn't want half-bloods. We had an argument . . . then I left. After that I don't know."

Fawn suspected that had been an ugly argument. The death of either parent would be a disaster for young children, but the loss of a mother could be lethal for infants, even with near kin or dear friends to take up the burden. Crane had clearly owned no knack for keeping either. Dag did not pursue this, but led on. "Then what?"

"I knocked around Oleana for a while. When I got tired of living in the woods, I'd take what jobs some farmer would give me, or try the dice. Took to thieving when those didn't play out. It was so easy, with groundsense. I could walk like a ghost right through their shops or houses. I 'specially liked doing places where they'd given me the evil eye and run me off, when I'd asked honest first."

Remo said, in an outraged voice, "Oh, *that'd* make it good for the next patrol to go through, to have Lakewalkers suspected of stealing!" Dag waved him to silence. Crane's lips turned in a mockery of a smile. How old was Crane? Older than Barr or Remo, to be sure, but younger than Dag, Fawn guessed. About halfway between? Remo was looking at Barr the rule-bender in a way that made him shift uncomfortably. Barr glared back at his partner as if to say, *I would not have——!* But Fawn thought both could see, *Yes, how easy.*

Crane continued, "One night, some farmer woke up before I was done gathering, and cornered me. I had to shut him up, but I hit him too hard. That's when I decided to leave Oleana. Took myself down to the river, spent his money on passage on a farmer flatboat. I started to think—maybe if I got someplace far enough away, I could become somebody else. Shed my skin, my name, start over somehow. I was going to decide when I reached the Confluence, whether to go south to Graymouth or maybe north to Luthlia, though I'd no love of snow by then. It's said they don't ask too many questions up there, if a patroller can take the cold. But then the fool boat boss put in at the Cavern Tavern, and I met Brewer and his game."

"What was his game?" Dag's voice was curiously soft, now. Remo squinted at him in doubt. Crane's words were flowing as if he'd half-forgotten his listeners, wound up in his tale and his memories. Dag did nothing visible to disrupt the flow; Fawn couldn't tell if he was doing something invisible to channel it.

"It was how it amused Brewer to restock on bandits when he'd run low," Crane said. "When he'd taken captives alive, two or more at a time—it worked best with at least four—he'd set them to fight each other, in pairs. If they refused to fight, they'd be slain outright. The second pair almost never refused. If he had more captives, he might make the winners fight each other, too, but anyway, the prize—besides being allowed to live—was to join his gang. He said he could turn most men that way—after they'd killed their friends for him, he'd own their minds."

Alder, Fawn thought. Was that what had happened to Alder? In that case, what *exactly* had happened to Buckthorn, and Berry's papa, and the rest of their crew? She shuddered, realizing Dag wasn't keeping his voice low just for the menace of it. It was so his words would not carry to the top deck.

"His arithmetic was off, by my reckoning," Crane continued. "But I was his prize, when I showed up. To turn a Lakewalker to thievery and murder! He thought he was the game-master, he did. I didn't tell him I was ahead of him down that road."

A strange brag. If Crane couldn't be the best, he'd compete for being the baddest? *Evidently so.*

"I won my rounds, of course. It was too easy. I stayed on a few weeks, learned the trade, persuaded and beguiled a few fellows just to see what would happen. Then I took Brewer's game to its logical conclusion. From behind. I was never quite sure if he was surprised, or not."

"Once you'd won, you could have left, surely. However you were guarded before," Dag said suggestively. "If you could walk past farmers like a ghost, why not bandits?"

"Go where? Farmers still wouldn't have me, and Lakewalkers . . . would've been able to smell the blood in my ground, by then. So maybe Brewer won after all, eh?"

"Suicide?" said Dag mildly.

Crane stared at him in astonishment. "I didn't have a bonded knife! Nor any way of getting one, once I was banished. The blighted camp council stripped mine from me along with everything else." Crane turned his head away. The flow of his talk dried up for several minutes.

Fawn's face screwed up in the slow realization that Crane—even Crane!—was taken aback at Dag's suggestion not because he feared self-murder, but because he scorned to so waste a death, with no sharing knife to catch it. His response seemed quite unthinking and altogether sincere. And Remo and Barr looked as though they found nothing odd in this at all. She pounded her fist gently against her forehead. *Lakewalkers! They're all Lakewalkers!* All mad.

Dag finally spoke again. "You've kept this gang going for a long time, though, as such things go. I can see where you gave the bandits a sort of twisted leadership, which held them to you, but what held you to them?"

Crane jerked his chin—in lieu of the shrug he could no longer make, Fawn supposed. "The coin, the goods, I'd not much use for, but Brewer's game fascinated me. Besides being mad after money, I think Brewer liked running the cave because it gave him something lower than himself to despise. Me . . . It was like owning my own private fighting-dog kennel, except with much more interesting animals.

"I hardly had to do a thing, you know? They just arranged themselves around me. Drop any Lakewalker down amongst farmers, that's what happens. If he doesn't rise to the top, they'll blighted shove him up. They *want* to be ruled by their betters. They're like sheep that can't tell the difference between shepherds and wolves, I swear."

"So did you make them, or did they make you?" Dag asked quietly.

Crane's smile stretched. "You are what you eat. Any malice learns that."

This time, it was Dag's turn to twitch, and Crane didn't miss it.

Dag took a long breath, and said, "Remo, give me that knife you found."

Remo rather reluctantly pulled the sheath cord over his head. Dag weighed the knife in his hand and regarded Crane sternly. "Where'd you come by this? And that boatload of Lakewalker furs?"

Crane twisted his head. "It wasn't my doing. Just an evil chance. Pair of Lakewalker traders down from Raintree chose to pull in their narrow boat and camp practically in front of the cave. There was no holding the fellows, though I told them they were being blighted fools. I lost six of those idiots in the fight that followed."

"Did you try the game on the Lakewalkers?"

"They didn't live long enough."

Dag touched the knife sheath to his lips in that odd habitual gesture. "You're telling me half the truth, I think. This knife was bonded to a woman."

Crane's jaw compressed in exasperation. "All right! It was a string-bound couple. They both died the same."

"You murdered her, and didn't even let her *share?*" said Remo.

"She was dead before I got to her. Fought too hard, there was an unlucky blow . . . At least it saved me a tedious argument with the Drum boys. I figured it'd be a bad idea to let them learn they could play with Lakewalkers."

A rather sick silence followed this pronouncement.

Crane did not break it. Past hope, past rage, past revenge upon the world. Just waiting. Not waiting *for* anything, just . . . waiting. He spoke as if from the lip of a grave he no longer feared but wanted as a tired man wanted his bed.

Dag's hand folded tightly around the sheath. He asked, "If you had a bonded knife, would you choose to share, or to hang?"

Crane's look seemed to question his wits. "If I had a bonded knife . . . !"

"Because I think I could rededicate this one," said Dag. "To you."

Barr's mouth dropped open. "But you're a patroller!"

"Or a medicine maker," Remo put in, more doubtfully.

"I said, I *think*. It would be my first knife making, if it worked." He added dryly, "And if it didn't work, leastways no one would complain."

Crane blinked, squinted, said cautiously, "Do you fancy the justice of it? To put an end to me with that woman's own knife?"

"No, just the economy. I need a primed knife. I hate walking bare."

"Dag," said Remo uneasily, "that knife belongs to somebody.

Shouldn't we try to find the rightful heir? Or at least turn it in at the next camp?"

Dag's jaw set. "I was thinking of applying river-salvage rules, same as with the rest of the cave's treasure."

Barr said, "Should he be *allowed* to share? His own camp council didn't think so even back when he carried far fewer crimes in his saddle-bags."

"He's Crane No-camp now, I'd say. Which makes *me* his camp captain, by right of might, if nothing else. I guarantee his priming would have no lack of affinity, leastways."

His glance met Fawn's startled one; his lids fell, rose. *Yes,* she thought, *Dag would know all about affinity.* Barr and Remo were both looking at him with some misgiving after these peculiar statements. Fawn didn't blame them. An even stranger look lingered in Crane's face, as if it shocked him to find there was something still in the world for him to want—and it was in his enemy's hand to give or withhold. Wonder grew in Fawn, winding with her horror. She'd expected Crane to say, *Blight you all, and let the malices take the world.* Not *Yes, I beg for some last share in this.*

As if testing his fortune in disbelief, Crane growled blackly, "We made better sport in the cave. Would it give you a thrill, big man, to kill me with your own hand?"

Dag's gaze flicked down. "I already did. All we're doing now is debating the funeral arrangements." He leaned on his hand and pushed himself up with a tired grunt. He was finished with his questions, evidently, although Barr and Remo looked as though they wanted to ask a dozen more. Not necessarily of Crane.

"Captain No-camp?" Crane called as Dag started to turn away.

Dag looked back down.

"Bury my bones."

Dag hesitated, gave a short nod. "As you will."

Fawn followed him to the kitchen, where he drew the bone knife from its sheath and hung the cord around his neck. He made no move to hand either back to Remo.

"Scoop up a kettle of river water and put it on the fire for me, Spark. I want to boil this knife clean of its old groundwork before we reach the cave landing."

❧

After the *Fetch* moored above the mouth of the bandit cave, Crane was removed on a makeshift litter of blankets stretched between two keel-boat poles borrowed from the nearby *Snapping Turtle*. Heads turned and murmurs rose both from boatmen and roped bandits as he was carried past. He shut his eyes, possibly pretending to be unconscious, an escape of sorts; the only one, Fawn trusted, that he would have. Dag followed, but was seized on almost at once by Bearbait and one of the Raintree hunters, who dragged him off to the cave to look at the hurt men again, or maybe at more hurt men.

Wain's lieutenant, Saddler, tramped down the stony slope and hailed Berry.

"We found a slew of boats tied up behind that island over there," he told her, with a wave at the opposite shore, the same level leafless woods that lined most of the river along here, save for the weathered ridge that backed the cave and shaped the Elbow. Only the—relative—narrowness of the channel gave a clue to a river-wise eye that it was an island. "Wain wanted to know if you could pick out your papa's. Or name any of the others, for that matter."

"If the *Briar Rose* is back there, I suppose I ought to look," Berry agreed halfheartedly. She glanced at Fawn. "You come with me?"

Fawn nodded. It had to feel to Berry like being taken to look at a body dragged from the river, to see if it was a missing kinsman. You'd want a friend to go with you.

"I'll come, too . . . if you want," Whit offered cautiously.

A silent nod. Berry's mouth was strained, her eyes gray and flat. It was hard to read gratitude in her face, though Fawn thought some might be hidden there. It was hard to read anything in her face, really.

Saddler and another strong-armed keeler rowed them across in a skiff. Paths threaded between the trees and across the island, wet and squelchy underfoot, as though the river had recently overtopped the banks and left a promise to return. Fawn's shoes were soaked through before they reached the other side. This channel was narrower, choked with fallen trees and other drifted debris.

Up and down the shore, derelict boats were tied, both keels and flats. A few curious boatmen were poking around in them. Some boats in better condition looked as though they'd been in the process of having their original names scraped away and replaced by new ones, or other identifying marks altered. Others had sprung leaks and settled into the mud. The newest captures were tied at the top end, upstream, and Fawn thought she recognized a couple of the names of the Tripoint boats Cap Cutter had been seeking. Fifteen or so in all—Fawn found herself estimating the sizes of the missing crews, and shivering. And this didn't even make up the whole, because the bandits had burned some boats, as well. *As many died here as at Greenspring.* If accumulated secretly over a year or more, and not in a few dreadful days. *And there wasn't even a malice.* Malice aplenty, though.

Two flatboats at the far end of the row must have lain here since last fall, for the ice had opened their seams and buckled their boards, and what caulking hadn't given way in the winter cold had rotted out in the summer heat. They sat low in the water, weathered and ghostly, and even Fawn's eye could pick out the *Rose,* second from the last, because it was the exact same design as the *Fetch.*

Berry made her way across a sagging gray board and lowered herself carefully to the decaying deck; Fawn and Whit followed. With a creaking of rusted hinges, Berry pulled open the front hatch and peered into the shadows within. She wrinkled her nose, hiked up her skirts, and stepped down into the cold water. Fawn, deciding her shoes could get no wetter, did the same. Whit saved his trousers and waited in the hatch, watching Berry in worry.

Most of the fittings had been removed, including the glass windows in the gaping frames toward the back of the cabin. Blue daylight filtered through, reflecting off the water to give a drowned glow to the space. A lot of warped barrel staves were still left, half-floating, slowly rotting. Some kegs might once have held salt butter or lard; Fawn wasn't sure if they'd been broken open by humans or a passing bear. Wildlife had been in here, certainly. Berry waded right through water to her knees, back and forth; twice, she reached down and pulled up unidentifiable trash. It took Fawn a few minutes to realize she was looking for bodies—or skeletons maybe, by this time—and was immeasurably relieved when none were found. Berry climbed up briefly through the kitchen hatch to peer around the back deck, then, still in that same silence, made her way to the bow and onto shore where Saddler waited.

"Anything left?" he asked.

She shook her head. "It's good for nothing but firewood, now. Half of it's too waterlogged even for that."

He nodded, unsurprised. "Wain says you're to have a share from the cave. Plan is, we mean to fix up what boats here will still float, and take the goods we found piled up down to the Confluence."

"You'll see that Cap Cutter gets word of his lost boats and men? I expect you'll catch up with him about there."

Would Boss Cutter be wounded in his male pride to learn that the lowly *Fetch* had destroyed the river bandits, when all the *Tripoint Steel*'s bristling bravado had missed the mark? No, more likely by the time the tale was carried downriver by the keelers, boastful Boss Wain would feature as its hero. Well, Berry would not begrudge it to him.

"Cutter from Tripoint? Aye, we know the fellow. Will do." Saddler ducked his head. "What don't get claimed by the old owners' kin will be sold. Together with our salvage shares, it's going to add up to quite a bit."

"I don't want no share of this," said Berry.

"More for us, but that ain't right, Boss Berry. I expect Wain'll have a word or two about that."

"Wain can have as many words as he wants. They're free on the river." She scraped strands of pale hair out of her eyes.

Saddler shrugged, dropping the debate for the moment. "There's a couple other flats up the row we got more than one guess on. I'd be grateful if you'd take a look at 'em. Settle an argument, maybe."

She nodded and let herself be drawn off.

Whit stood on the muddy bank, looking from Berry's straight, re-treating back to the rotting hulk of the *Rose*. He ran a harried hand through his hair, and said to Fawn, "I had one shoulder for if her be-trothed was dead, and another for if he was run off with another gal. But I got no shoulder for this. And she's not cryin' anyhow. I dreamed of cutting out Alder, but not this way! What'll I do, Fawn? I want to hold her, but I don't dare!"

"It's too soon, Whit. I don't think she could stand having her hurts touched yet."

"But I'm afraid that soon it'll be too late!"

Fawn considered this. "Dag once told me that Lakewalkers wear their hair knotted for a year for their losses, and it's not too long a time. She's just been hit with a lot of losses. Her papa, Buckthorn—Alder, too. Alder's the worst of all, because she's lost and found and lost him twice."

"She don't cry at all."

"Maybe she's like Hawthorn, and goes off in the woods to cry private. You do wonder . . . what sort of life a girl must have had to spurn comfort even in the worst pain, as if needing help was a weakness. Maybe she figured if only she was strong enough, she could save everything. But it doesn't work that way." She frowned and went on, "After the Glassforge malice, Dag comforted me, but he had some pretty deep experience to draw on, I reckon."

"I ain't got no deep experience," Whit said, a little desperately.

"I'd say you're getting some now. Pay attention."

He rubbed the back of his wrist across his nose. "Fawn . . . I grant that malice roughed you up and scared you silly, but it wasn't as complicated as this."

She took two long breaths, and finally said: "Whit . . . when it caught me, the Glassforge malice ground-ripped the ten-weeks child I was carryin' in my womb. When I miscarried of it, I almost bled to death. Dag saved my life that night, taking care of me. Nothing could save my baby by then."

Hit on the head with a fence post about summed up the look on Whit's face. Well, she'd certainly got his attention. "Huh . . . ?" he breathed. "You never said . . ."

"Why did you *think* I ran away from home?" she asked impatiently.

"But who was the—wait, no, not Dag, couldn't have been—"

Fawn tossed her head. "No, the papa was a West Blue boy, and it doesn't matter now who, except that he made it real plain he wanted no parts of his doin'. So I walked on down that road by myself." She drew air through her nose, and went on, "Where I met Dag, so it came out all right in the end, but it wasn't—*ever*—simple."

"You never said," he repeated faintly.

"Silence doesn't mean you're not grieving. I didn't want my hurts rummaged in, either. Or to have to listen to a lot of stupid jokes about it. Or otherwise be plagued to death by my family."

"I wouldn't have made . . ." He hesitated.

"For Berry, you just be there, Whit. Be the one person in the wide green world she doesn't have to explain it to, because you were there and saw it all for yourself. Hand her a clean cloth if she cries or bleeds, and some warm thing for the pain that doubles her over. The time to hold her will come. This day isn't over yet."

"Oh," said Whit. Quietly, he followed her up the riverbank to rejoin Saddler and Berry.

22

Flanked by Remo, Dag exited the cave and dragged his hand over his numb face. The groundwork on the Silver Shoals fellow's cut neck was holding, and Chicory had opened his eyes a while ago, swallowed a mouthful of water, complained that his head hurt like fire, and pissed in a pot—all good signs—then fallen back into something more resembling sleep than blackout. In the meanwhile, however, one of the flatboat men—not the papa or his son, thankfully—had died unexpectedly when a deep knife cut his friends had thought was stanched had opened again beneath his bandages and blood had filled his lungs.

If I had been here, I might have saved him. But if Dag had been here, he wouldn't have been at the *Fetch,* and others would surely have perished. *If I were ten thousand men, everywhere at once, I could save the world all by myself, yeah.* Dag shook his aching head, grateful to Fawn for sneaking him those extra hours of sleep, because that last blow, atop his fatigue, might well have shattered him else. He had an old, deep aversion to losing those who followed him in trust. *They weren't following you. They were following Wain and Chicory.* Dag considered the argument dubiously, for who had aimed Wain and Chicory, after all? But it was bandage enough on his brain for now.

It was a bright though chilly noon; if he looked out into the distance, he could take it for a peaceful early winter day on the river, which glimmered beyond the fantail of scree that swept down from the cave to the shore. As long as he kept his eyes to the silvery-gray tree branches, and didn't let them drop to take in the mob of men scattered below. Some cook fires had been started along the edge of the woods, with men moving around to tend to them. Other men slept in bedrolls, or lay injured. Or tied up. Dag's squint at the latter was interrupted by Barr, hurrying up to him and Remo.

"Dag, you better come over here."

Another man gravely hurt? Dag let himself be dragged down the slope, stones turning under his boots. "Why haven't they hanged those fellows yet? I confess, I was hoping that part would all be over by the time we got here."

"Well, there's a problem with that," said Barr.

"Not enough rope? Not enough trees?" Berry had rope in her stores, he thought. Although if they had to lend it to hang Alder, it might be best not to tell her.

"No, there's—just listen."

"I always listen."

A circle of men sat on logs and stumps at the edge of the scree, near the line of moored boats. Wain was there, and Bearbait, and the other three boat bosses: Greenup from the big Oleana flatboat, who looked not much older than Remo; Slate from the Silver Shoals keel, a muscular man of an age with Wain; and the one named Fallowfield, the fatherly flattie from south Raintree. They seemed variously confused, worried, or angry, but all looked mortally tired after being up all night for the brutal fight. Followed by the uncovering of the cave's full history of horrors in whatever confessions they'd collected from the bandits, possibly in even more gruesome detail than what Dag had obtained from Skink, Alder, and Crane. Crane himself now lay in his blankets over on the opposite side of the scree, shadowed by the leafless scrub, walked wide around by the nervous boatmen. Whatever the debate was, it had apparently been going on for a while.

"There he is," said Slate.

An unsettling greeting. Dag nodded around the circle. "Fellows." He didn't add anything hazardously polite like *What can I do for you?* He squatted to avoid looming, and after an uncertain glance at each other, Barr and Remo copied him.

Wain, never loath to take the lead, spoke first. "There's a problem come up with the bandits and this Lakewalker of theirs."

Dag said cautiously, "We agreed that the farmers would look to the farmers, and the Lakewalkers to the Lakewalker. Luckily, we caught Crane early this morning while he was trying to get to Alder on the *Fetch*."

Gesturing at Barr, Bearbait said, "Yeah, your boy here told us that tale. I hear you got Big and Little Drum, too. Good so far, aye."

"Thing is," Wain continued, "some of these here bandits are claiming they shouldn't ought to be hanged, because they couldn't help what they did. That they were forced to it by Crane's sorcery."

Boss Fallowfield put in, "Yeah, and once one of 'em claimed it, they all took up that chorus."

"What a surprise," muttered Barr.

Dag ran his hand through his hair. "And you entertained that argument for more 'n five seconds?"

Bearbait frowned. "Are you saying they aren't none of 'em beguiled and mind-fogged? Because some of 'em seem more than a bit that way to me."

And Bearbait would have seen the real thing, in the Raintree malice war last summer. Dag bit his lip. "Some are, some aren't. Skink was beguiled, as you know." Nods from all who had helped interrogate Skink when they'd been planning the attack yesterday, which was everyone but the late arrival Slate. Dag added, "Have you all heard anything yet about that cruel recruiting game of Brewer's and Crane's?"

"Oh, aye," said Wain. Troubled nods all around seconded this, although some didn't seem as troubled as others. It occurred to Dag that the game was a bit like the rougher keeler tavern duels, in a way. And yet . . . not.

"I don't believe there was any of what you call sorcery involved with that—it worked for Brewer just the same, remember," Dag pointed out. "Besides, some men were here before Crane ever arrived. And some drifted in on their own—the Drum brothers, for instance."

Bearbait squinted at Dag. "Could you pick out which of them bandits over there was beguiled and which was lying?" He nodded toward the prisoners amongst the trees opposite.

Dag said carefully, "Do you think it should make a difference in their fates, when all of them are red to the elbows pretty much the same?"

"You're surely not thinking of letting any of these murdering thieves *go*?" said Remo in a voice of indignation. "After all the trouble we went to catching them!"

Greenup grimaced. "At least one was begging to be hanged to end it." Dag wasn't sure what the grimace meant. Did the young boat boss prefer his bandits to be stoical? Granted, hangings were much less embarrassing that way.

Bearbait dug in the ground with the stick in his hand, then looked across at Dag. "See, the way it was, I saw folks the malice had mind-slaved up in Raintree. When the spell was broken—or outrun, anyways—they would come back to themselves. Their true selves."

"With their memories intact," Dag murmured.

"That was a mixed blessing, true," sighed Bearbait.

Dag picked through his next words very carefully. "What Crane did was very different from a malice's compulsion." *Was it?* "In power, if nothing else. It's like comparing a pebble to a landslide."

Boss Fallowfield scratched his graying head. "Landslides're made of pebbles. So—are you actually saying it *is* the same?"

Dag shrugged. "You wouldn't say that if you'd ever been caught in a landslide." He *must not* be drawn into being made judge of these men, selecting some to live and some to die. But if he was the only one with knowledge enough to make the judgment . . . "Look." He leaned forward on his hook, gestured with his hand. "All here are either survivors of the game, or helped run it. They all had another choice once—and there are a lot of bodies up in that ravine or down in the river bottom to prove it was possible for some men to choose otherwise. I don't think any here were so beguiled that they couldn't have escaped, or at least tried. In fact, that's why Crane was away from the cave last night—because he was hunting down two fellows who'd chosen to walk away from the horrors. Grant you, they didn't make it."

Dag paused to contemplate the unpleasant ambiguity of that. Yet it would surely be a huge injustice to those who'd died resisting this evil to let these laggards go free. Most were ruined men by now, schooled in arcane cruelties; it would be madness to unleash them on the world. The rivermen had no way to hold them as prisoners. Such was his opinion. *But it shouldn't be my judgment.*

"If you're going to hang them all the same, it's pointless for me— or Barr or Remo"—Dag hastily stopped up that possible gap—"to pick out one from another. And if you're not—it means farmers aren't judging farmers anymore. Lakewalkers are. You'd just have to take our word blind, because you'd have no way of checking it yourselves. I don't think that's such a good idea, in the long run. If you mean to let any here go, it should be for your own reasons, on your own evidence. Farmers to farmers, the Lakewalker renegade to us." Dag thought it important to get in that word, *renegade. So who's No-camp now?*

Slate said, "Will Crane hang with the rest, then?"

Remo, unfortunately sounding up on a high horse, said, "He's chosen to die by our own rituals. Privately."

Greenup stared distrustfully. "You Lakewalker fellers aren't planning to spirit him away, are you?"

Barr rolled his eyes. "With a broken neck?"

"It could be some trick," said Slate.

Dag said, unexpectedly even to himself: "It won't be private. You'll see it all, every step."

"Dag!" cried Remo and Barr together. Remo's appalled voice tumbled on, "Dag, you can't!"

"I can and will." Could he? Dag's knife maker brother, Dar, worked in careful solitude, possibly for a reason beyond Dar's general misanthropy.

"He should hang with the rest, to be fair," said young Greenup.

"He's chosen to die by sharing knife," said Dag. "I promised to make the knife for it. To try, leastways."

Wain's eyes narrowed. "But don't Lakewalkers think that's an honorable death? That don't seem quite right, either, when hanging sure ain't. Patroller."

"It's not about honor. It's about saving something useful from all this, this river of waste," said Dag.

Slate said, scratching his chin, "I admit, it don't sound quite fair to me, either."

All the boat bosses were frowning suspiciously at the Lakewalkers now. Dag sighed. "All right, then let's talk about something you do understand. Let's talk salvage rights, which you all were divvying up in prospect a while back. I claim this knife as my salvage share." He fished the bone blade from his shirt, twisted the cord over his head, and held it up. "This knife, and its priming."

Slate's brows flicked up. "That alone?" he inquired, in a very leading tone. Quick to scent a bargain, these Silver Shoals fellows. Greenup, too, looked intrigued, as if mentally recalculating something.

Dag added hastily, as the other Lakewalkers stirred, "I don't speak for Barr and Remo, who also put their lives in the balance for this last night—as some of you may yet remember. This is just for me."

"Oh, sure," said Slate brightly. "Give the patroller his knife, if that's all he wants."

"And its priming. Its priming," Dag went on, "for any of you who don't realize what I'm talking about—although when this day is over I swear you will understand it through and through—will be Crane's mortality. Crane's heart's death, which he will pledge to it."

Faces screwed up around the circle in deep misgiving.

Breaking the silence, Bearbait drew breath. "The other patrollers can make their claims as may be, but give that medicine maker whatever due-share he asks, I say."

Boss Slate, perhaps reminded of his crewman with the cut throat, shrugged in discomfort. "Well . . . I guess it's all right. Maybe. I do say that Lakewalker bandit should die first, though. Where all those fellows he tricked can see it."

"That'll be a lifelong lesson to 'em," Barr muttered. At least a few around the circle quirked their lips in some slight sympathy to his exasperation.

"Briefly, aye," Dag agreed wearily. *Ye gods.* But it wasn't the bandits he wanted to take the lesson. It was the boatmen. And everyone else. Because tales of this day's doings would go up and down the river as fast as a boat could travel. They would inevitably end up garbled. But Dag swore that they wouldn't start out that way, not if he could help it. *So you'd better get this right, old patroller.*

❧

Dag returned to the *Fetch,* trying to remember everything he'd seen Dar do to prepare himself for his knife-bindings. Sharing knife makers generally, he reflected, were sheltered in the center of most camps, in the most protected and private of spaces. In the very heart of Lakewalker life. He would be turning that heart inside out.

He told his shadows Barr and Remo to go find something to do for half an hour, because any hint less broad would not have been taken, and led Fawn out onto the back deck as the nearest they could manage for a scrap of privacy. There, he explained what he meant to try.

She merely nodded. "Anything Dar can do, I 'spect you can do better."

He wasn't sure if all that confidence was well-placed, but he had to admit, it was warming. He gripped her strong little hand in his. "The groundwork will be up to me, but the thing is, some parts of the task are going to need two hands. Bleeding Crane, mainly, to bring his ground into the knife blank when I set up the involution. Much like the way you led your ground into my marriage cord back when we wove them. I would—could—ask Remo or Barr to help me, except that I'd really prefer to keep them clear of this task. In case there's trouble about it later."

Her brow wrinkled. "Why should there be?"

"Because I'm not just making a knife. I plan to make it a demonstration of Lakewalker groundwork for every boatman here who I can get to look and listen." He added after a moment, "You could leave before I actually, um, prime the knife. You wouldn't need to watch that part."

"Ah," she breathed. She looked up to catch his gaze square. "But, you know, it's not impossible, if I'm to be a true Lakewalker's kinswoman, that such a task might fall to me someday. It would be the worst thing to botch I can imagine. Don't you think I'd better watch and learn how it's done right?"

He swallowed, nodded, folded her in tight. "Yes," he whispered. "That, too."

At length, he let her go, and she went into the kitchen to fix him a meal with no meat, because he did remember Dar ate no flesh before a binding. When he came in after carefully washing up, she set before him a dish of potatoes, apples, and onions fried up in salt butter, took a little for herself, and passed the remainder on to Hod and Hawthorn, who would be staying in to keep watch on Bo. In an attempt to spare Dag, Remo had given a ground reinforcement to Hawthorn's swollen nose, for the pain and bruising; Dag would release the trace of beguilement later, he decided, when he had the chance to set it properly.

As Dag scraped up his last bite, Fawn set down a cup beside his right elbow. He looked over in surprise to find it piled with oats.

"There you go. You sit there and ground-rip those till my hair turns purple, you hear?"

"Um?"

She sat quietly beside him, her back to the room. "Because it seems to me that when you take in something vile that you can't hack up, next best thing for it is to take in something bland, to cushion it."

"Ah. You, um . . . realized I ground-ripped Crane."

"Pretty much straight off, yeah. So now there's a bit of him in you, isn't there? Till you break him down, at least."

"Does that . . . bother you?"

"I think it bothers you. A lot."

"True, Spark," he sighed. He took her hand and pressed the back of it briefly to his forehead. "Stay near me through this. It helps me remember who I am and what I am about, when things get too confusing."

He took up oat grains and rolled them between his fingers, tossing the ripped ones onto his dirty plate, until, indeed, the outlines of things started to look preternaturally sharp and strange.

If there was anything more he ought to do in preparation, well, he didn't know what it was. After a moment of consideration he unbuckled his arm harness, set it aside, and rolled down his sleeve, buttoning the empty cuff so it wouldn't flap. He adjusted the knife sheath on his chest, clasped Fawn's hand, and rose.

Dag had the litter-carriers position Crane in the middle of the scree just a few paces from the shore, heart-side toward the river, so that the sixty or so boatmen could sit or stand on the slope that rose toward the cave and all hear and get a clear view. Whit, Wain, and two other keelers set down the litter and retrieved Wain's poles, and Whit retreated to one side to wait with Berry. Remo and Barr sat a little way off on the other, at a deliberate distance chosen by Dag to mark them as witnesses, not participants. Dag folded a blanket for his knees and Fawn's on Crane's far side, where they would not block the boatmen's view. She knelt and looked up at him expectantly.

The boatmen crunched around on the rocks of the incline, finding positions, hunkering or sitting or standing. None crowded all that close. The half dozen or so of the *Snapping Turtle*'s keelers who'd heard his talk on Lakewalker groundwork back at Pearl Riffle were amongst those toward the front, staring with interest. At least this afternoon they were all stone-sober. So.

Dag stood up, raised his voice to carry to the edge of the crowd, and began—again: "First I have to explain about ground, and Lakewalker groundsense. Ground is in everything, underlies everything, live or inert, but live ground is brightest. You all have ground in you, but you don't sense it . . ." He'd made this explanation so many times down this valley that it felt as smoothed as stones in a streambed. Some here had heard earlier versions, but it never hurt to hammer it in again. How many hundreds of times had he repeated himself explaining patrol techniques to each year's new crop of young patrollers?

Ground. Groundsense. Malices . . . That last caught any attention still drifting loose. The youngsters took it for tale, their elders who'd seen blight for an eye-opener; the Raintree men who'd brushed up against the malice war nodded and exchanged murmurs, both amongst themselves and with their curious neighbors.

Crane was staring—glaring—up at Dag with eyes gone wide with disbelief. Dag hadn't asked Crane's permission to make him the material of this demonstration, but he felt no qualms. If Crane hadn't lost his choice with that first murdered farmer back in Oleana, he'd done so a hundred times since. His disordered life had done the wide green world a great deal of harm. Let his death do it some scrap of good.

If this is good.

Now Dag's rattling chain of words came to the secret heart of things. He pitched his voice up again. "The creation of sharing knives is considered the most demanding of Lakewalker makings, and the most"——his tongue hovered a moment on *secret,* but chose instead—"private. The knives are carved from bones, Lakewalker bones, willed as gifts. Not robbed from graves, and not ever, despite the rumors, stolen farmer bones. These are legacies from our kin. The gifting is a solemn part of our funeral customs." Also the messy part, but he wasn't going to go into that yet. Because now came the most essential, most questionable part of today's desperate lesson.

He drew the bone knife from the sheath at his neck and handed it to Fawn, who rose to take it. "My wife, Fawn, is going to go around amongst you now and show you a real sharing knife. Please touch it and hold it a moment." *But blight and absent gods, don't drop it on the rocks.* "All I ask is that you handle it carefully and with respect, because . . . because I once had such a bone blade willed to me by my first wife, and I know how I'd feel if . . ." He broke off with a gulp.

Fawn moved amongst the crowd, overseeing the knife being passed back and forth. Dag found his voice again and went on, "We found this knife lost in the cave cache with those Lakewalker furs. We figure some Lakewalker maker in Raintree made it, from the thighbone of one of his or her camp-kin. No telling whose—there was no identifying writing burned on this blade, as there sometimes is. It was bonded to a Lakewalker woman who was murdered by these river bandits just about on the spot where I'm now standing . . ."

Of all today's revelations, the knife was the one Dag was most determined the boatmen should understand, body-deep—and so through their hands as well as their ears and eyes. How much closer could he bring folks without groundsense to the feared Lakewalker so-called sorcery than to actually let them touch the cool, smooth surface of that fraught bone, weigh it in their palms, pass it one to another? Dag, who never prayed if he could help it, prayed forgiveness of the unknown donor for this use of the gift. But to his immense relief, Fawn's passage was marked not by repulsed groans, or worse, nervous laughter, but by reasonably reverent, or at least polite, quiet.

Remo's and Barr's mouths were tight, their eyes wide. They both looked ready to bolt, if only they knew where. But they held on.

Fawn at length returned, handed the blade back to Dag, and knelt attentively once more. He held it up. "The knife makers don't just shape the surface of bone when it's carved; they also shape its ground, both naturally as its nature changes from bone to knife, and through groundwork to prepare it for its next task—which is to hold a Lakewalker's mortality as if sealed in a bottle. This knife was already dedicated like that, but with some groundwork and boiling water earlier today, I cleaned out the unused bonding. This is now a bone blank, same as if it just came from the carver's hand. So the next step I have to show you is the new bonding."

He knelt by Crane's left side, his back to the muted gleam of the river. "Blood is 'specially interesting for groundwork," he called up the slope, "because it bears a person's live ground even after it leaves the body, at least till it dries and dies. In a regular bonding, the prospective heart's-death donor would bleed a little into a new greenwood bowl, but we're going to sort of skip that step."

The knife to cut open the vein would be heated, too, to prevent infection. There were several refinements that Dag recalled from the time he'd been bonded to Kauneo's knife that were just not needed, here. In a moment of wild panic, Dag wondered whether he could fake it if this didn't work—stab Crane with the useless blade before he could complain, and pretend to his audience that he'd actually made and bonded a true knife. But Remo and Barr would know, blight.

Dag found himself settling cross-legged more comfortably, as if for a healing, which was disturbing—right, let it join the yapping pack of his doubts to deal with later. This groundwork had even less room for irresolution than did patrolling. He glanced at Fawn and relieved her of one concern: "He can't feel a thing anywhere below his neck. You can't hurt him." She nodded grimly. He tipped the bone knife down below Crane's arm as Fawn, holding up the dead weight a little awkwardly, took Dag's war knife and scored a deep cut on the pale surface of skin, squeezing it to make it bleed and drip.

And then Dag dropped down into that other world, of inner essence seen from the inside, close-up. The material world—the light of the afternoon, the bare trees, the stone slope, the rustling men craning their necks—faded like a ghostly vision, present but formed of fog, and the coursing torrents of the ground beneath it all became palpable to him. The men were roiling complexities, Fawn a blazing fire. Dag *was* his ground. The knife in his hand was a knotted pattern of potential. Crane . . . Crane was a dark and furrowed mess, but his blood dripped brightly.

Dag extended his ghost hand beneath the vivid stream, casting his mind back over the involution he'd known best: the one in his own pledged knife, which he'd watched be made for him by the maker in Luthlia. He had himself unmade it again in Raintree as part of breaking the malice's deadly groundlock. The involution was the knife maker's greatest gift, the cupped hands to hold the offered mortality. He folded his ghost hand around a splash of Crane. His current unwelcome affinity with the renegade might well be rendering this easier—add that dark thought to the pack, no time for it now. He let his ground flow into the furrow along the inner edge of the blade, there to join with the knife's own waiting ground. Let it all set, solidify.

He pulled back, parting from that piece of himself he'd turned into a cup for Crane.

And gasped in astonishment. *Ah, blight! I didn't know it was going to hurt this much!* He watched in horrified fascination as his ghost hand tore away from the part of itself caught in the knife. It felt like biting off his own finger. Ye gods, and Dar went through this every time he bonded a knife? *Brother, I beg your forgiveness.*

If the curl of ground was just right . . . *I either have it now, or I don't. If I don't, I can boil the blade again and start over—many a maker's apprentice has had to do just that, their first few trials.* But beneath that was the stronger thought, mule-headed in its certainty: *I have it.*

He came back, blinking, to the surface world, trembling and cold as if from a deep healing. The bloody knife shook in his tight grip, but it was his left arm that ached, and his ghost hand felt on fire. A quick check found his groundsense down to a hundred paces. Again. *I won't be recovering from this in a day.* But the groundwork was over. Everything after this was going to be . . . he declined to finish the thought, *easy.* Everything after this was going to be as blighted bizarre as everything before, likely.

Dag swallowed and found his cracked voice. "Now, at this point in a usual knife making, the maker would clean it up and give it to its new owner, to use later on. A good binding can last a lifetime." By definition. He stuck his hand out rather blindly toward Fawn. She raised her brows at him, pried the knife from his stiffened fingers, and rubbed the spare blood from it with a cloth. Dag wasn't so sure how good this binding was—it seemed clumsier than his Luthlian knife's, not as fine. But solid, yes. Possibly overbuilt? Maybe he was only supposed to have, say, bitten off the tip of one finger? But the lifetime this binding waited on would be measured in minutes.

"Primings vary. My father put his knife through his own heart during a dire illness a dozen years ago. My first wife rolled over on hers when she was dying of wounds on a far northern battlefield. Remo had one from an elderly kinswoman who gave up the last precious months of her old age to it"—out of the corner of his eye, Dag saw Remo flinch—"and had to be helped to it by her own daughter. I've seen patrollers help each other. You understand, a sharing knife is not normally used as an instrument of execution." Or as a means of instruction to a pack of farmers, Dag had to admit. "But one way or another, this is something no farmer has ever seen, so *pay attention.*" He snapped that last to the back of the crowd in his captain's voice. They jolted upright and attended.

"You're a blighted madman, you know that?" Crane murmured up to him. He'd kept his face turned half-away from the gawkers on the hill through most of this.

"I have my reasons," Dag murmured back down. "You might even have understood them once, before you wrecked yourself."

"Me, they banished. If they have a lick of sense, you they'll burn alive."

Ignoring this, Dag sat again, and said, "Open his shirt, Spark."

Her nimble fingers undid the buttons, folded back the cloth, bared Crane's chest. Dag wondered if Remo was going to want his shirt back, after. He looked gravely into Crane's silvery eyes, and received a black-browed scowl in return.

"Ready?" *Do you assent?* Of all requirements for this making, that was the most profoundly unalterable.

"If you want my dying curse," growled Crane, "you have it."

"Figured that."

"So if my curse is as good as a blessing, is my blessing worth a curse? Blight it, take both. You can sort them out yourself. I'm done." He turned his face toward the bright river. "Let me out of this hopeless world." He added after a moment, "Don't let your blighted hand falter."

Assent enough.

Dag positioned the tip of the sharing knife under Crane's rib cage, pausing only long enough to explain softly to Fawn about the correct angle to reach the heart, and how much force to use to reach it in one swift punch without breaking the blade prematurely. Her face was taut, but her eyes were intent. She nodded understanding.

Dag extended his groundsense to be sure of Crane's heart, gripped the haft, and in an abrupt motion, forced in the blade to its full length.

Crane's lips shivered and his eyes rolled up, but all Dag's attention was back at ground level. He froze, still clasping the haft, as the dissolving mortal ground began to flow toward the knife as if sucked into a drain. Would his involution hold it all? Would it close and seal properly . . . ?

Yes.

Dag breathed again. As Crane did not.

He blinked, looked up, looked around. The hillside of watching men had gone really, really quiet.

Dag drew the primed knife from its fleshly sheathing and held it up high. "This Lakewalker"—he declined to use the terms *renegade* or *banished* at this point—"has now given his mortality into this knife, to share again, if the chance favors me, with the next malice to cross my path." Twenty-six Lakewalkers before Crane had trusted Dag not to waste their deaths, and had their trust upheld. Of all the knives and lives that had passed through his hand, this was surely the darkest. *Blight, but I came by this one the hard way.* He handed the knife to Fawn to clean and slip back into the sheath at his neck, because his hand was still too clumsy with the shakes to manage the task in one try.

"Whether Crane has paid for his crimes, I can't tell you. This is a separate tally."

23

Her face carefully held stiff to hide how her stomach shook, Fawn helped Dag rise from Crane's still body. She had prudently brought along Dag's hickory stick; with that in his hand and Fawn under his left shoulder, he made his way along the shoreline. At Fawn's nod of invitation, Berry followed, and Whit came after her. Barr and Remo were left to oversee the disposal of the corpse. The crowd of sobered boatmen, too, broke up and moved into the trees to tend to their next grim chore.

Dag headed not back to the *Fetch*, but downstream to the next creek and up its rock-strewn banks to the narrow meadow where the bandits had hobbled their horses. Some of the meadow grass was still green, especially along the creek, though most had turned from autumn gold to winter dun, a sort of standing hay. The dozen or so horses grazing there swiveled their ears at the newcomers, then put their heads down once more, except one big brown fellow who whuffled curiously as they passed near. Dag stopped to rub its poll, which made the beast droop its lip and flop its ears foolishly.

"I like horses," murmured Dag. "They're so big and bright and simple in their grounds. And best of all right now"—he sighed—"they're not people. Over there, Spark." He nodded to a lone cottonwood tree at the meadow's edge, soaring up to scratch at the sky with its bare branches, and ambled over to sit and lean his head back against the ridged gray bark, closing his eyes. Fawn sat herself beside him. Unusually, he let his left arm lie in her lap, and she stroked it gently, which made his lips move not unlike the horse's. The whuffling horse followed them in short hops of its hobbled front legs, then lowered its face to nudge him for more rubs, which he reached up and supplied without opening his eyes.

Fawn suspected that the animals—calm, warm, and nearby in his groundsense—maybe helped blot out what was going on beyond the tree-clad ridge that lay between them and the cave. If Dag had any groundsense range left after all that performance, he could furl it in, Fawn supposed, but that would leave him alone in silence. Silence was all right just now; the *alone* part, maybe not so good.

Whit wandered out amongst the horses, looking them over in expert evaluation. Berry, who had also stopped to stroke a quiet one, if more dubiously, turned her head at a faint cry. Out of sight of the cave they might be; apparently they weren't quite as far out of earshot as could have been hoped. She stepped away from the horse and stood rigid, staring back up the slope at the woods, face set. Tall. Alone. And at the next cut-off cry, trembling. She looked, Fawn thought, like an aspen tree being gnawed down, slender and doomed.

Whit watched her anxiously, then held out his open hands toward Fawn in desperate question. Fawn cast him an encouraging nod. He gulped, walked over to Berry, and, still without a word, folded her into his embrace. It wasn't a gesture of courtship, simply one of comfort offered in a bleak hour. *Something warm to wrap herself around when the pain folds her over.* Berry rested her head on Whit's shoulder, eyes closing tight. The blond head was a little higher than the dark one—Whit was a sawed-off Bluefield, after all—but with her chin bent down, their hair mingled on a level that was close enough.

Whit held her for a long time, till she stopped shaking, then led her to a more comfortable seat on a fallen log near the stony creek side. He put his arm around her and snugged her in tight as they watched the horses graze.

"Do patrollers ever hobble their horses?" Fawn asked Dag. Because she didn't think she could bear to talk about anything harder just yet. "You do wonder how well those things work to keep 'em from running off."

He fell in willingly with her lead, perhaps for similar reasons. "We use them sometimes. Because if a patroller's horse gets out of his ground-sense range, he's put to the same wheezing work of chasing it down as any farmer." Dag's lips turned up in some wry memory. He opened his eyes to stare out on the benign scene. "Hobbles don't slow a horse down much if it's seriously panicked. I imagine the habit of feeding them here does more to keep them close."

"They don't look as ill-cared-for as you'd think. I wonder how many were stolen from boats, and how many came with the bandits? Well, I suppose Wain and the boatmen will work it out."

"Yeah, it's all salvage at this point," Dag said. He tucked the knife sheath out of sight in his shirt and leaned his head against the bark once more.

After a time, Remo and Barr came over the ridge and picked their way across the creek to Dag's tree. They both looked gloomy.

Dag opened his eyes again. "Hangings finished?"

"Not quite," said Remo. "We did get Crane laid out. I'm glad we didn't have to butcher him."

Barr made a face. "Who'd want a knife from Crane's bones?"

"The boatmen dug a trench," Remo continued. "He was the first to go in it."

"It's not very deep," said Barr, "but I imagine they'll pile some river stones on top. Some of the boatmen were for making the bandits dig it themselves, but finally decided it was more trouble guarding them than it was worth."

Remo added morosely, "One of the keelers had kin on one of the boats the bandits took a month or so back. He found out just what exactly had happened to them, I guess. Wain let him cut off Big Drum's head personally. Little Drum's, too, even though he was dead already. They're going to put them up on poles in front of the cave as a warning to others."

"We left right after that," said Barr.

Healthy young men or no, to Fawn's eye both looked as shaken as she felt, and not just from the extra sensitivity lent by groundsenses possibly not closed tight enough during these proceedings. Barr wandered out into the meadow to pat a horse, too, a tidy piebald mare.

"Hey," he called back over his shoulder after a moment, "this one's in foal! Whoever takes her is going to get a bonus horse!"

Remo walked out to see, and Fawn tagged after. She was reminded of Grace, left back in West Blue, and was washed by an unexpected wave of homesickness. How could you be homesick for a *horse*? But she suddenly missed her own mare fiercely, wondering how she was getting along, and if Grace's round barrel looked any rounder yet. She stretched her hands and ran them over the black-and-white belly, speculating how far along this mare was. Dag's horse-raising tent-sister Omba could have told exactly, with her groundsense. Maybe Barr shared the talent.

Remo put his hand on the mare's withers and looked across at Barr, who had started picking burrs out of her mane. Remo pitched his voice low. "Wain said we were due a share of the salvage rights. We could take a couple of these horses. Ride back to Pearl Riffle before the snow flies."

Barr looked up in surprise. "Huh! When did you change your mind?"

"Crane . . . was pretty awful. I'm thinking now it's not such a good thing for a Lakewalker to be exiled from his kin. Even if they do badger him half to death. Maybe we should just go take our lumps."

Fawn, stroking the mare's warm flank, observed, "I don't think it's good for anyone to become outcast, Lakewalker *or* farmer. Look at all those bandits."

"Speaking of ending up in a pit of your own digging, yeah," said Barr. He picked at another brown, spiky burr, carefully separating the coarse hairs from it. "I thought you wanted to see the sea. Or else go drown yourself in it."

"Neither one, anymore." Remo's voice went lower. "The world is uglier than I'd ever dreamed. I've had enough. Let's go home."

This hopeless world, Crane had said. And Crane had certainly done more than his share to make it worse.

"Not all of it's that bad," Barr said mildly. He glanced across the meadow; Fawn followed his gaze to Dag, still leaning head-back, looking utterly spent. "Thing is . . . I think I've changed my mind, too. And even if I hadn't, I don't think it'd be so good to let *him*"—he jerked his head Dag-ward—"go walking around out there all by himself, either. In fact," he added judiciously, "I think that might be worse than the worst snag-brained thing I've ever done." He raised his eyes. "And you know I've done some champion snag-brained things."

Fawn cleared her throat. "Dag does have a partner," she pointed out. She held up her cord-wrapped left wrist, drawing their eyes and maybe groundsenses as well. "We're as roped together as any two Luthlian patrollers out on the ice. And I'm not about to let him go drown in the dark and cold, neither."

Remo rubbed his lips. Barr undid another burr. Neither argued.

I've taken everything Dag was, and thought the trade fair because he did. But he needs more than just me. She stood straighter and said, "Still, I really think having you two along has been good for him. An anchor in the old when he's straining and reaching for something so new no one has ever grasped it before. Because he's not really a patroller anymore, not in his ground. He's trying to turn into something else."

Remo nodded. "Yes, medicine maker."

"Or knife maker," said Barr more doubtfully. "And if he's going to be *that,* we sure enough have a duty to guard him. Camp or no camp!"

Fawn shook her head, though not in disagreement with that last. "First thing a new maker has to do is make himself. I think it's hard for any youngster to do that, even apprenticed to a mentor in a chosen craft, but Dag's trying to do it all on his own, somewhere in midair. I've seen him mend a busted glass bowl, and a lot of hurt people, and a lost sharing knife, and what he did in Raintree I can't begin to describe, but what he really wants to mend is the world."

Remo stared at her, appalled. "No one can do that!"

"No *one,* no. I 'spect Dag would say the world's big and we're small and I guess we all break in the end. But when all the old arguments about farmers and Lakewalkers have gone 'round and 'round 'bout sixteen times and plowed into exhaustion, the problem of Greenspring will still be sitting there." Fawn swallowed. "We may not be able to win that toss, either, but it'd sure be nice to have some company while we're losin'. That's one."

Remo's lips moved, but no sound came out. He blinked rapidly.

Fawn drew breath and went on: "Cracking that beguilement mystery open was worth your coming along all on its own. That's two. And I don't know how many more boats and lives those bandits would have destroyed before the end if we hadn't chanced along to stop them. That's three. Three good reasons are good enough for going on with, Dag says."

She glanced aside. *I could wish it was less hard on Berry.* But the boat boss was sitting on the log next to Whit, finally beginning to talk a bit. Whit was listening attentively. He had an arm around her waist in a comforting sort of way, and she was making no move to shrug it off. Berry's strength still impressed Fawn, but she was glad that maybe she didn't have to be strong so all-by-herself, now. Because that could be wearing on a woman.

"I don't know," said Remo. "I don't think I know anything anymore."

"Blight, I *never* did," said Barr. "It hasn't stopped me!" He blinked cheerily, and fell into his old, wheedling voice. "You've got to come along, Remo, to keep me from falling into the sea. Or to push me in, whichever."

Remo scratched his head, and said wryly, "Hard choices."

"Hey . . . !"

Leaving them to take up their comfortable, habitual squabbling, Fawn made her way back to Dag, satisfied.

A while after the last unnerving noises stopped drifting over the ridge, they all made their way back to the *Fetch* the long way around, back of the cave, avoiding both the woods and the new poles down by the shore. Fawn expected she'd go peek at those gruesome standards later, and then be sorry she had. She definitely wasn't going to venture into the winter-bare woods until the crop hanging there had been harvested and planted. *And maybe not even then.*

Dag thought Berry would have been glad to shove off that very afternoon, as the Fallowfield family's flatboat did, but they were all held there by the boatmen's demands on Dag for medicine work. Yet by the following morning Chicory was doing better than Dag had anticipated, sitting up and eating, if wincing at his tender skull and throbbing headache. The

Raintree men made plans to camp at the cave for a few more days, then ride home in gentle stages, taking the bandits' horses and horse gear for their salvage share. Fawn opined that it was a good idea to get Chicory back into the hands of Missus Chicory as soon as might be to finish recovering. In all, Dag thought the Raintree hunters would be trailing home with fuller bags than if they'd managed to successfully complete their original river venture, and much sooner, so Missus Chicory might forgive the broken head. If perhaps not let anyone forget it for a good long time, or so Bearbait feared.

After Dag released his Lakewalker assistants around noon, the pair disappeared and did not return till after dark. He intercepted them at the end of the gangplank as they approached the *Fetch* somewhat surreptitiously, each lugging a sack.

"What's this?" Dag asked.

"Shh," said Remo, with a glance at the boat. Dag allowed them to lead him out of earshot along the bank.

Barr said, "We decided to patrol upstream a ways, and see if we could track where Crane and the Drums caught up with his two deserters. Which we did. We buried the bodies." He grimaced, which Dag took to indicate the scene had been rather worse than just plain bodies. He did not feel any need to ask after the details.

Remo continued, "It took a bit longer to trace Crane's cache. I don't think anyone without groundsense could have found it."

"Does Wain know about this?"

"Oh, yeah," said Barr, "we took the goods to him first. He allowed as how since it was twice-stolen and wouldn't have been found at all without us, we could keep it for our salvage share. We swapped out the things we didn't want with some of the boatmen—there's a regular market going on up at the cave just now. I couldn't quite stomach the clothes and boots, but some of those keeler boys are not so finicky."

"They didn't fit us," Remo interpreted this more precisely.

"A fellow could come back someday and do some real interesting treasure-hunting within a day or so's ride of this place," Barr said, a speculative look in his eye.

"That accounts for you two missing dinner, but why the tiptoeing?" asked Dag.

Remo rubbed his mouth. "Boss Berry refused any salvage share for the *Fetch*."

Barr put in, "Which about broke poor Whit's heart, I think, but he wouldn't take any if she wouldn't."

Remo went on, "I know you said that wasn't to apply to us, sir, but I figured it might be better not to trouble her mind."

Dag, who had put his new sharing knife away deep in his saddlebags, because he flat declined to wear it around the same neck where he had kept Kauneo's in honor for so many long years, nodded understanding. "Yes," he agreed, "put those bags away discreetly, and no, don't trouble Boss Berry just now."

"Yes, sir," said Barr brightly. Both patrollers looked relieved to be freed from responsibility for this ruling, although Dag doubted Berry would say anything even if she noticed. The pair made their way quietly across the gangplank, discretion somewhat spoiled when Daisy-goat bleated curious greetings. Dag shook his head and followed.

Berry's hard quest was over, but time and the river flowed only one way, and flatboats perforce went with them. The *Fetch* left the cave landing the next dawn. Of the patients Dag was taking along, Hawthorn was recovering enough to be active, if still ouchy about his reset nose, but pleased to be let off chores for another few days. When active turned to pesky, Dag would pronounce him well. Bo was more worrisome, developing a rising fever. Dag gave up his sweep duties on the roof to sit with him and, together with Fawn, keep a close eye. Anxious for the old man, Hod proved a dab hand as an attendant, steady and careful when it came to the needed lifting and turning, and he bore up bravely even when the hurting Bo unjustly swore at him.

During the periods when Bo fell into an uneasy doze, Dag turned to another chore. Gathering up what few pieces of paper the *Fetch* harbored, he sat down at the kitchen table to pen a letter to Fairbolt Crow about the renegade Crane and his fate at the river cave. Whether as patrol leader or captain, the writing of reports had never been Dag's favorite task, and he'd ducked it whenever he could. Which still meant that he'd written more of the blighted things than he could rightly remember. The lurid events and Crane's evil history fit oddly into the well-worn forms and phrases of a patrol report, but Dag trusted Fairbolt, at least, to be able to read between the lines. Dag was not entirely satisfied with the results, but he had no more paper to do it over. Fairbolt was not, strictly speaking, Dag's camp captain anymore, but Dag could not escape the conviction that someone with his head on straight ought to have the facts.

Bo's fever grew worse that night, and Dag gave ground reinforcements till he nearly passed out. But in the mid-morning, the fever broke. Dag fell wordlessly into his own bed, awakening in the afternoon with an incipient cold, his first in years. Happily Barr and Remo were both able to help with that, a familiar task for patrollers on search patterns in all weathers, and Dag—with another cup of oats silently proffered by Fawn—fended it off with no worse effects than a sore throat and slight sniffle.

Dag had the *Fetch* stop at the last Lakewalker ferry camp on the north bank of the Grace just long enough for him to deliver his letter to the patrol courier there, turn over the effects of the murdered Lakewalker couple for possible identification, and give a very truncated account of the late doings up in Crooked Elbow to the shocked camp captain. He did not linger.

∾

They came to the Confluence in the late afternoon of the following day. Dag, Berry, and Whit were on the sweeps. Dag having now no need to beg—or attempt to beg—a knife, Berry was just as happy not to have to struggle to pull in the *Fetch* at the big Lakewalker camp that occupied the point, though Barr and Remo climbed to the roof to stare at the many tents to be seen amongst the trees, and at the wharf boats and goods-sheds maintained along the shore by the Lakewalkers themselves.

Fawn joined them as the *Fetch* swung past the point and the Gray River could at last be seen. She shaded her eyes with her hand, her lips parted in an unimpaired world-wonder that eased Dag's heart. The waters of the two great streams did not at once mingle, but ran along side by side for some miles, clear-brown and opaque.

"The Gray really is gray!" said Fawn.

"Yep," said Dag. "It drains the whole of the Western Levels. It's well-wooded along here, but about a hundred miles due west, depending, the trees fail and the blight gradually starts. It's said that after the first great malice war, the blight reached the river here, and the whole Gray was dead from the poison, but it's long since come alive again. I find that a pretty encouraging tale, myself."

The westering sun was playing hide-and-seek behind cold blue-gray clouds with glowing edges that filled the sky from horizon to horizon. "I think that's the widest sky I ever did see," Fawn said. "Is it because the land's so level out here?"

"Uh-huh," said Berry.

"And I thought Raintree was flat!" Whit marveled.

"It's beautiful. In a severe sort of way. Never seen a sky like that at home." Fawn turned completely around, drinking in all that her eyes could hold. "That's a thing to come see, all right."

In a maternal spirit, she dragged Hod outside to share the sight; he gaped gratifyingly, but, rubbing his red nose, soon went back inside to hug the hearth. Despite the chilly wind, Fawn sat at Dag's feet for the next half-hour, watching for when the two streams would at last become indistinguishable. During the stretches when they had merely to ship their oars and float on, Whit and Berry doubled up boat cloaks, guarding each other from the blustery discomfort.

Dag found himself thinking, *I'm so glad we brought Whit.* He wished the boy all good speed and fortune in his courtship, because he thought Fawn must warmly welcome such a tent-sister. *And my tent-sister too, how unexpected!* The most important thing about quests, he decided, was not in finding what you went looking for, but in finding what you never could have imagined before you ventured forth.

Keep that in mind, old patroller.

As the year slid toward its darkest turning, the late dawns and early sunsets squeezed the daylight hours down to less than a double handful. After encountering a spurt of snow flurries the morning before they'd passed the Confluence, Boss Berry took advantage of having three Lakewalker pilots aboard and reversed her ban on night running—also because she no longer needed the daylight, Fawn figured, to watch for wrecks that might be the *Briar Rose.* For five nights straight they floated down the wide channel far into the evenings, until nearly half the winding river miles between the Confluence and the Graymouth were behind them, and the cold breath of winter eased into something, if still damp, much less penetrating.

Then one afternoon the wind swung around to the south, the clouds broke up, and the air grew downright warm. Berry relented enough to tie up the *Fetch* during a spectacular sunset in the immense western sky and declare an evening of rest. After a string of nights handing out hasty meals to the off-watch crew to eat while crowding around the hearth, Fawn celebrated by fixing a bang-up sit-down supper, with everyone squeezed together around the table for once, even Bo, though she made sure his food was soft.

The meal was eaten with appetite enough, but in uncharacteristic and rather weary silence. After a glance around at the long faces, Fawn swallowed her last bite of fried potato and declared, "Well, this is no good. You're all looking as glum as a chorus of frogs with no pond. We should do something after the dishes to ginger folks up. How about archery lessons? Everybody liked those. We still have plenty of lanterns in stock. And there's hardly any wind tonight."

Hawthorn and Hod looked interested, but Whit scrubbed his hand over his face and said, "Naw. I don't think that would be so much fun anymore."

Dag's eyelids had been drooping in a combination of fatigue and food-induced mellowness; at this, they flicked open. He watched Whit, but did not at once speak.

Fawn glanced at Dag, then badgered, "Why not?"

Whit shrugged, made a face, and seemed about to fall into hunched silence, but then got out, "It feels funny to be making a game out of it, after I shot a man."

"Big Drum?" said Berry. "Whit, we're right *glad* you shot Big Drum."

"No, not him." Whit made a frustrated waving-away gesture. "Besides, I didn't kill Big Drum; that fellow who cut off his head later did that. It was the other one. The first one."

"What first one?" Fawn asked carefully.

"It was the night before, at the cave. Some fellows ran out trying to get away, which was exactly why Dag put us bowmen where he did, I guess. I was so scared and excited, I couldn't hardly see what I was doing, but . . . my first shot, my very first shot ever, went right through this bandit's eye. Killed him outright."

Fawn winced and murmured *Eew*. Hawthorn, unhelpfully, made a very impressed *Ooh*.

Whit waved again. "It wasn't the eye thing that bothered me. Well, it did, but that wasn't . . ." He drew air through his nostrils, and tried, "It was too easy."

Bo rubbed his rough chin in some sympathy, but rumbled, "Whit, some men need killin'."

Berry put in perhaps more shrewdly, "It doesn't need to be catching."

"It's not that, exactly," said Whit, his brows drawing in.

Dag spoke for the first time, so unexpectedly that Fawn gave a little jump. "No, but you're not the same person, after. It changes you in your ground, and that's a fact. Whit, Barr, and Remo all crossed that line for the first time that night at the cave, and there's no stepping back over it. You have to go on from where you are."

"I suppose you did the same, once," said Remo diffidently. "So long ago you don't remember, likely."

"Oh, I remember," said Dag.

Nods all around the table at this received wisdom.

Dag set his tankard down so hard his drink slopped out. "Absent gods, do you people have to swallow down every blighted thing I say? Don't you ever choke?"

Fawn's eyes widened, and hers were not the only ones; surprised heads turned toward Dag all around the table. Hod flinched.

"What the blight's bit you?" said Barr. Saving Fawn the trouble of composing a more tactful question to the same effect.

Dag drummed his fingers, grimaced, blurted: "I killed Crane by ground-ripping a thin little slice out of his spinal cord. That's how I dropped him on the deck. From twenty feet away, mind you. Remember that mosquito back in Lumpton Market, Whit? Just like that. But inside his body, same as I do healing groundwork."

"Oh," said Whit, his eyes growing big. "I, um, didn't realize you could do that."

"I realized. Even back then." Dag's glance darted around the table. "It was too easy."

Fawn recalled, then, where she'd heard that exact phrase before, if in a different tone of voice, and it wasn't just now from Whit: Crane's confession. But Whit hadn't been there for that. His echo of the renegade's words was accidental. *Dag's isn't,* she thought. Did Barr and Remo catch the twisted meanings, too? *Do I?*

"*That* was what you did to Crane? Ground-ripped him?" said Barr blankly.

"I didn't know any person could do that," said Remo, more warily. "I thought only malices . . . ?"

"It's a very weak version of the same thing, yes. I have reason to believe it's an advanced maker's skill as well, or some variant, but since it's come out—come back—in me I haven't had a chance to find a maker skilled enough to ask. You can easily defend against it by closing your grounds, which is why I had to wait for a moment when Crane opened his. It only worked because I took him by surprise."

"Oh," said Barr, relaxing. "That's all right, then."

"For some of us here," said Dag dryly.

Whit, at least, looked as though he caught the full implications; his mouth went round. Whatever was Dag about, to plop out this admission here, now, in this company? Was it for Whit's sake, or his own?

Fawn sat up straight. "Dag, this is morbid. You aren't no more going to turn into a malice, or even into Crane, than Whit is going to turn into Little Drum. For that matter, *I* made that arrow Whit shot in that fellow's eye, with my own hands, as strong and straight and sharp as Cattagus could teach me. And I made it for killin'—whatever needed killin'—because I figured it would be down to either the other fellow or Dag at that point, and I knew which I wanted it to be. Same goes for my brother, if you've any doubt." She drew breath. "A knife, an arrow, ground-ripping, they're all just different tools. You can kill a man with a hammer, for pity's sake."

The farmerly alarm around the table faded as folks digested this thought. Dag said nothing, though his tension eased; he cast Fawn that odd little salute of his, and a slow nod. Had he never thought of ground-ripping as a tool, before? Or only as some uncanny magical menace? Fawn loved him beyond breath, but there was no doubt his tendency to Lakewalkerish gloom could be awfully exasperating, some days.

Dag said, "So you see, Whit, if there's an answer to your trouble, I haven't found it yet either. As for the bow lessons, though I do enjoy them very much, they were never a game for me, not even when I was a tadpole Hawthorn's size. They're earnest training for earnest business." He blinked and added, "Same as ground-veiling drills, come to think, which we've also neglected for the past week. I'll see you two out on the deck tomorrow morning." He tilted his head at Barr and Remo, who did not argue.

Dag went on, "I won't invite you out to play a game, Whit—and Hod and Hawthorn, and the rest of you—but I will invite you out to continue your training. Because—as you've seen—you never know when you'll need a skill, and more lives than your own may depend on it."

"My papa used"—Berry's breath caught, broke free again—"used to say, *Nothing worth doing is fun all the time. But it's still worth doing all the time.*"

Whit gave her a crooked smile, and nodded.

The archery lessons commenced by lantern light as soon as the dishes were washed up. Fawn was pleased to see the company's mood lift, with all the exercise and interplay and stretching of legs running up and down the riverbank, which had been her whole purpose for the proposition in the first place. So that part was all right.

She was more worried for Dag, as he wrapped himself around her and fell into exhausted slumber that night. They hadn't made love since before the cave. If Fawn hadn't watched Dag convalescing after Raintree, she might have feared it meant some dwindling of his affection, but she was clear this was only profound fatigue. Yet this time he hadn't been physically injured, or blighted, or ground-ripped. He had put out ground reinforcements—and unimaginably more complex healing efforts—till he couldn't stand up, though, and the tally of the strange ground he'd taken in, directly or as part of unbeguiling, was daunting. Skink, Chicory, Bo, Hawthorn, who knew how many boatmen; most of all, that big wedge of Crane.

Yet Fawn wasn't sure but what Crane had done more damage with his poisonous tongue than his dubious ground. He'd sure tried, anyhow. Dag should have paralyzed that part of the renegade, too, she decided. Had Dag's odd outburst at dinner been some belated response to Crane, or just general accumulation?

Dag's ground had to be in the most awful mess just now, come to think. Like a house the day after some big shindig where all the neighbors and kinfolks came, and ate and danced and drank and fought till all hours and your least favorite cousin threw up on the floor. You couldn't hardly *expect* to get any work done till you'd cleaned up the place again all tidy, and you couldn't tackle that till the hangover passed off.

Upon reflection, Fawn was profoundly thankful that Dag showed no weakness for drink. Patrollers in their cups had to make the most morose drunks in the world.

She snorted and rolled over, cuddling in tight. *Please be well, beloved gloomy man.*

24

The next day the *Fetch* floated through yet more of the bleak, treeless, unpeopled country they'd been passing for the last hundred miles. Berry promised there would only be about another day of this, then the banks of the river would grow more interesting than these endless scrubby sand bars: strange new trees, still green in the dead of winter and bearded with moss, mysterious creeper–hung side channels, an abundance of birds. Fawn mainly wondered if they would see any of those scary swamp lizards of Dag's, and if Bo's tales about the snakes were true. By noon the air was warm enough to go up on the roof without a jacket or boat cloak, and Fawn joined Berry, Dag, and Whit to keep company and to soak up the pale but valiant sun. With no duty to watch ahead for hazards, she was the first to look behind them.

"Hey, is that a narrow boat comin' downstream, or—or not? If it is, that's the biggest narrow boat I ever did see."

Dag swung around. A slim vessel some thirty-five feet long was rapidly overtaking them. Paddles flashed in the hazy winter light, ten to a side; the occupants kept up a song to unite the rhythm of their strokes. Distance muffled the words, but Dag seemed to smile in recognition.

Barr, whose own watch was coming up soon, came out and stared over the stern rail, a half-eaten apple in his hand. "Isn't that a Luthlian boat?" he called up excitedly.

"Yep," said Dag. "But those aren't Luthlians paddling, exactly. Those are southern Lakewalkers, heading home from a couple of years of exchange patrol."

"How can you tell?" asked Fawn. "Their clothes? Their ages?"

The big narrow boat was already shooting past them—a quarter-mile off but still in the channel, as the river was a mile wide at this point. Even at that distance Fawn could see the mix of strong, young men and women, laughing and leaning into their work.

"That, and the enthusiasm. Though if you were outrunning the Luthlian winter, you'd paddle hard, too. That's twenty or thirty new patrol leaders over there, young veterans. See, there're areas to the south that haven't seen a malice emergence in two, three hundred years. But the rule is, you can't be a patrol leader till you've been in on at least one malice kill, preferably more. For obvious reasons."

Fawn, who had not only seen but made a malice kill, nodded perfect understanding. Barr, who hadn't, looked envious.

"So the southern Lakewalkers export all their best young patrollers up the Gray for a couple of seasons. And hope they get them back."

"Do the malices take so many?" asked Berry.

"No, actually. The biggest causes of losing young patrollers in—or to—Luthlia are accidents and the weather, and marriage. The malices are a long ways down the list. There are those who say the malices aren't nearly as scary as the Luthlian girls." Dag grinned briefly.

"Not you!" said Fawn.

"I was a much braver man, when I was young."

Whit cocked his head, watching the narrow boat pulling out of sight south around a broad curve of the great river. "Hey, Dag—it just occurred to me. I never asked. What was your name up in Luthlia when you were married to Kauneo? Because it wouldn't have been Dag Redwing Hickory Oleana, then. Dag Something Something Luthlia, right?"

Barr, about to abandon the back deck again for the kitchen, paused and glanced up over the roof edge, ears plainly pricked.

Dag cleared his throat, and recited, "Dag Wolverine Leech Luthlia, in point of fact." He added in hasty clarification, "Leech for Leech Lake, like Hickory Lake."

"So Wolverine was Kauneo's tent-name. And, er . . . Leech would have been your camp name?"

"Yep. It's a pretty well-known camp, up in those parts."

Whit scratched his chin. "Y'know, that Dag Bluefield thing is starting to make all kinds of sense, all of a sudden."

Fawn ignored him to ask, "Did the lake really have leeches?"

"Oh, yes," said Dag. "Big ones—six inches, a foot long. They were actually pretty harmless to frolic with. Kept you alert while swimming, though."

He grinned to watch her wrinkle her nose and go *Eew!* Which made her wonder if that had actually been the aim of his anecdote.

∾

Six more days brought them to Graymouth.

But not, Fawn discovered to her disappointment, to the sea; the town lay not on the shore but ten miles inland. Downstream from the bluffs on which the town stood, the river split into several channels that ran out into a broad, marshy delta. The town itself was divided into two portions, Uptown along the bluff, Downtown—sometimes called Drowntown—along the riverbank. Fawn supposed she could think of them as the two lips of the Graymouth, and smiled at the notion.

Uptown, as near as Fawn could tell from this waterside vantage, was built of substantial houses and goods-sheds and pleasant inns; Downtown, of cheap temporary shacks, rough boatmen's taverns, rickety sheds, and camps. The shore was lined with much the same sort of businesses as Silver Shoals, if not so many of them, plus long rows and double rows of flatboats—some for sale, some being used as floating shacks—and keelboats. On the southern end, the boats were of a very different shape and had tall masts sticking up; fishing boats and coasting vessels that actually dared thread the delta and put out to sea.

Downtown boasted a lively day market and trade of all sorts. Keelers looking to hire on upstream crewmen propositioned Whit and Hod within a short time of the *Fetch* tying to the bank, and another fellow tried to buy Copperhead right off the deck. Copperhead—rested, refreshed, and rowdy after his long boat ride—showed off by trying to kick out the pen slats. Dag rescued Berry's boat and the innocent bystanders by saddling the beast and taking him out for a hard gallop.

Whit and Hawthorn took off down the row of boats; Fawn snagged Berry to guide her to the market to find fresh new food for supper. Barr and Remo followed them, trying to look tall and grim, like guardsmen of some sort. Fawn thought if it weren't for the sheer embarrassment of it, they'd be clinging to each other like youngsters lost in the woods, surrounded by all these strange farmers. They stuck tight to her, anyhow, staring around warily.

"It's not as big as Silver Shoals," Remo muttered.

"Couldn't prove it by me," Barr muttered back.

Who's protecting who? Fawn didn't say aloud. Tact was a fine thing.

She did spot a pair of older Lakewalkers at the far end of the market square, a man and a woman, but they were too far away to hail, and by the time she worked around to that side, they had gone off. Were they local, or from upriver? Was there a camp near here? She would have to ask Dag. But they all returned to the *Fetch* before the Oleana boys had a chance to work each other into some sort of ground-panic.

There she discovered Whit had undermined her dinner menu by bringing in a fish the size and shape of a platter, which he said was fresh from the sea and which he'd bought off a sailboat a ways down the row.

Fawn stared at it in horror as he proudly held it out. "Whit, that fish has two eyes!"

"All fish do."

"Not on the same side! Whit, those fellows spotted you for an up-country boy and foisted off some defective fish on you."

"No, this kind is supposed to look like that"—he studied it in some doubt himself—"they said. But the *important* thing is, I got us a ride down to the shore tomorrow morning in their boat. They go out every day the weather allows to do their fishing, see. They'll drop us off on the beach in the morning and pick us up again on their way back. We can take a picnic!"

A picnic, in the heart of winter? Well, why not? In West Blue, a foot of snow would have fallen by now. Here, it was merely cloudy and chilly.

Bo vouched for the two-eyed fish, which didn't exactly reassure Fawn, especially after his tale about the rolling hoop snakes used for cart wheels, but so did Berry, so she cooked it up as best she could. Dag ate it without hesitation, but, well, patrollers. Fawn, conscious of his crinkling eyes on her, eventually broke down and nibbled. It was alarmingly delicious.

So it was she found herself packing a big basket with food and another with blankets by lantern-light the next morning, as the laggard sun would not be up for another hour. Berry and Whit undertook to bring Hawthorn; Fawn supposed she and Dag would trail Remo and Barr behind them in a not-dissimilar fashion.

Hod elected to stay with the still-convalescing Bo, and not just due to the tales about the people-eating sea fish with giant teeth and the things with tentacles sporting suckers that popped blood from your skin. The two—parentless Hod and childless Bo—seemed in a fair way to adopting each other. They'd all come a long way from Oleana, Fawn thought, but Hod especially. He'd become a competent boat hand, and more. He was not so skinny, not so shy, and was a good two inches taller, partly from her cooking but mostly from not carrying himself so S-shaped. They'd be in Graymouth some weeks yet; when Bo felt better, she would make sure Hod found his chance to visit the shore.

Fawn had never ridden in a sailboat before. The creaking of its lines and tilting of its deck as the patched and discolored sails caught the faint dawn breeze made her nervous, but Dag was watching her closely, so she raised her chin and tried to sit bravely. The four fellows who ran the boat—two brothers and a couple of their half-grown sons—did appear to know what they were doing, and were glad to show the curious Whit, too. After a bit, even Barr and Remo unbent and horned in on the deal. Dag seemed content to lean back with his arm around Fawn.

Dawn over the marshes was gold and gray, a severe winter beauty all its own. Birds swarmed up to greet the light, though their cries seemed strange and sad in the misty air. From time to time along the channel Fawn could spot the decaying remains of flatboats amongst the other wrack, wrecked and washed down in a flood, or else simply abandoned and allowed to drift out to sea. Half in fear and half in hope, Fawn made out every drowned log to be a lurking swamp lizard, but Dag said not, though he promised to find her one later, an offer for which she thanked him politely but unencouragingly.

"One good thing about this time of year," Whit called, slapping his neck. "Hardly any mosquitoes."

"True enough," Dag agreed amiably. "Come high summer, these southern mosquitoes carry off small children to feed to their young."

"They do not!" Hawthorn cried indignantly, which made the fishermen grin. "You shouldn't ought to tell such tales to Whit, he's bound to believe you 'cause on account as you're tent-brothers."

The corners of Dag's mouth tucked up. He murmured, "Ah, you never met my Luthlian tent-brothers. Those Wolverine boys trained me out of that right quick."

The boat bore left at the next split in the channel, and in a half-hour more, a line of dun-colored sand dunes rippled across the flat horizon. The ascending sun began to draw up the mist, so that the far distance seemed to be veiled by a gilded gauze curtain shifting in a gentle draft. The boat scrunched bow-first into the sandy shore just behind the dunes, and the fellows jumped out, took the baskets, carried Fawn, Hawthorn, and Berry dry-shod across the last stretch of water, and united to help give the sailboat a good shove back out into the channel.

Fawn watched it drift away. So, if the boat sank out there on the big sea, would they ever be able to get back to Graymouth? Far up the channel, a faded red sail loomed, so perhaps they would be able to hail another fisherman, and not be stranded. On that reassuring thought, she took Dag's proffered hand, warm in the cool light, and scrambled up the dune, sand shifting under her sliding feet, which made her laugh breathlessly. Dag watched her profile anxiously as she pressed to the crest, and the world's rim opened before her astonished eyes.

The vast expanse of water gleamed like steel, blending in a muted, distant, silvery-gold line with the equally vast, lavender-edged sky. It was like being inside a great bowl of liquid light. On the strand, stretching away like wool rolled for spinning, waves broke and murmured. The damp, strange-smelling air caressed Fawn's flushed cheeks as she stared and stared. The smell seemed to be some stronger cousin to that of a riverbank or creek bed, but with a tang all its own like nothing she'd smelled before. She took in a huge breath of it. "Oh. My."

Hawthorn whooped and ran down the sand dune; Berry, laughing, called him to slow down and slid after, Whit on her heels. Remo and Barr, with a wild look at each other, followed.

Dag scanned the horizon, brows pinched. "It was all warm and blue, first time I was down here," he muttered. "Which was fifty or a hundred miles west of here, though."

"That was late spring, too, you said. 'Course it was warmer," said Fawn.

He cast her a grave look, and swallowed. "This isn't . . . this wasn't the wedding trip I'd promised you, I'm afraid."

"You promised to show me the sea. That there is it, isn't it?" Most amazingly the sea. Fawn tossed her head.

"I didn't anticipate Crane, nor river bandits, nor exposing you to all those horrors." With a hesitant finger, he traced her neck where Crane's knife had lain. He added after a moment, "Nor making you cook for a boatload of folks the whole way."

Blight Crane. "I don't think we anticipated the *Fetch* at all, nor Berry, nor Bo and Hawthorn and Chicory and Wain and all those others, but I'm glad to have met them. Even Remo and Barr turned out pretty good, in the end. I've learned so many new things I've lost count, which I wouldn't want to give back nohow." She hesitated, searching for the right words to ease his misplaced fear of disappointing her, without pretending that the cave hadn't mattered. "Mama used to say to me, when I was young and pining for my birthday or some other treat to come quick, right now, *Don't go wishing your life away.*" She tightened her grip on his hand. "Don't you go wishing my life away, either."

He smiled a little, although she was afraid it was half for amusement at that *when I was young* part. "There's a point, Spark."

"You'd best believe it." Firmly, she pulled him down the slope.

Hawthorn already had his shoes and socks stripped off and trouser legs rolled up, and was prancing about in the foam that bubbled and hissed around his feet. Barr and Remo watched him rather enviously. They set down their baskets beside a likely-looking mess of driftwood and all walked up the beach together. Everyone including Dag bent to collect seashells and marvel at the strange shapes and colors. Fawn was especially taken with the round, hollow ones, like sugar cookies with flower patterns pressed in the center, trying to imagine what wondrous creatures had made them or lived in them.

Noting that no blood-sucking tentacles had yet reached out to grab Hawthorn's ankles, she took off her shoes and socks, too, gave them to Dag to carry, and walked through the tickling foam despite the chill. She scooped up a handful of the water and, not that she hadn't been warned, tasted it—salty, metallic, and vile! But for all that, not regretted. She spat it out and made a face that made Dag grin, or at least smirk.

A half-mile on, they came upon a huge dead fish washed ashore. It was even bigger than Dag's channel cat, sleek gray with a pale belly, with an ugly underslung mouth lined with far too many sharp, triangular teeth. It had teeth in *rows*. It had evidently been there awhile, because it also stank to the sky, which at least saved any argument about its edibility and whether Fawn should be made to attempt to cook it. Hawthorn, Remo, and Barr were delighted by it, especially the jaws. Dag and Fawn walked on, leaving them crouching down trying to cut out the jawbones from the smelly carcass to carry off for a souvenir, possibly to work the teeth later into some sort of Lakewalker hair ornaments. There certainly seemed to be plenty of teeth to go around. Berry and Whit wrinkled their noses at the aroma wafting up from this process and retreated as well, to walk side by side along the top of the dunes.

Fawn and Dag held hands and strolled on, though after the fish with the teeth Fawn put her shoes back on and kept her feet safely to the damp sand. You just never could tell about Bo's stories. Fawn glanced up to find Dag's brows had pinched again. She thought of shaking him out of his abstraction, or making him wade in the water to wake up, or *something*. Instead, she simply asked, "What's weighing so heavy on your mind?"

He pressed her hand, smiled too briefly. "Too much. It's all a tangle, in my head."

"Start somewhere. Doesn't matter which end." Whatever had bit him was still gnawing, that was plain.

He shook his head, but drew a long breath, so he wasn't going to go all surly-quiet, anyhow. "My healing work, for one. I saved two fellows in the cave. If there'd been three or more hurt that bad, the rest would have died all the same. How can I set myself up as a medicine maker for farmers when I know it'd be a cruel false promise for all but the first-comers?"

"Even Lakewalker medicine makers have helpers," Fawn pointed out.

He frowned thoughtfully. "I sure do understand now why they leave as much to heal on its own as they can."

"Two's still more than none. And most days they wouldn't come in mobs like that."

"But on days they did, it could sure get ugly." His frown did not lift. "There were other problems came clear to me at the cave, ones I hadn't thought of. Justice, for one. How can Lakewalkers and farmers live together if they have to have separate justice? Because there's bound to be clashes, that's what justice is all *about,* dealing with clashes folks can't settle for themselves."

Now it was Fawn's turn to say, "Hm."

"Crane said . . ." He hesitated.

"You shouldn't let Crane's lies get under your skin."

"Isn't his lies that bother me. It's his truths."

"Did he tell any?"

"A few. You are what you eat, for one."

Fawn sucked her lower lip. "All folks learn from the folks around them. Good behavior and bad behavior both. You can't hardly help it."

He ducked his head. "Lakewalkers tend to think themselves above that, when they're amongst farmers. Takes 'em by surprise to be taught anything, it does." He added after a moment, "It did me, leastways. But the other thing he said . . ."

Sudden silence. *Now we're getting down to it.* "Mm . . . ?"

"About Lakewalkers rising to the top. One way or another. Whether they want to or not. That, I'm afraid I've seen. On her own boat, Berry defers to me!"

Fawn wrinkled her nose in doubt. "You're also a man near three times her age," she pointed out. "You'd be a leader amongst Lakewalkers. You wouldn't expect to be *less* a leader amongst farmers."

"Amongst Lakewalkers, there would be others to keep me in line."

"Well . . . Wain didn't defer so easy, for one."

"Oh, yeah, Wain. I sure settled him down, didn't I?" His hand waved and clenched in a gesture of disgust—or self-disgust?

"Um . . . before the attack, you mean, when the boat bosses were all arguing?"

"You spotted that, did you? Yes, I persuaded him. What Barr tried to do to Berry but was too clumsy to bring off." His face seemed to set in a permanent grimace, contemplating this. "Though at least I didn't leave him beguiled."

"It was an emergency," Fawn offered.

"There will always be another emergency along. How long before a need becomes a habit becomes a corruption? Lordship comes too easy, for some. And it was lordship near slew the world."

His stride, scrunching through the sand, had lengthened. Fawn quickened her steps to keep up. He continued, "Unless we keep separate lives. Did we come all this way down that long river just to find out the folks we were arguing with back at Hickory Lake were right all along?"

"Slow down, Dag!" Fawn panted.

He stopped. She gripped his sleeve and turned him to face her, looking up into his troubled gold eyes. "*If* that's the truth, then that *is* what we came all this way to find, yes. And we'll need to face it square. But I can't believe it's a truth so solid that there's no cracks at all with space left for us to fit in."

"As long as malices exist, then the patrol must be maintained, and everything that backs it."

"Nobody's arguing with that. But making farmers less ignorant and Lakewalkers less obnoxious doesn't have to mean turning the whole world tail over teakettle. You made a good start on the way down here, I thought!"

"Yeah?" He dug his toe in the sand, bent, scooped up a smoothed rock lying there, swung back, and flung it out over the waves. It vanished with a faint plop. "I made a start like throwing a rock into this sea. I could stand here and throw for years and never make a difference you could tell."

Fawn straightened her spine and scowled up at him. "You're not fretting because you couldn't keep your promise to show me the sea. You're fretting because somewhere in that murky head of yours you were hoping to have the whole problem solved by now, and hand it to me tied up in a bow for my birthday present!"

His long silence after that broke in a rueful chuckle. "Oh, Spark. I'm afraid so."

"I should have thought a patroller would be more patient."

He snorted. "You should have met me at age nineteen. I was going to save the whole world that year, I was. *Patience* and *exhaustion* turn out to have a lot in common."

"Well, then, you ought to be real patient right now!"

He laughed out loud, a real laugh finally, and hugged her in tight. "You would think so, wouldn't you?"

They turned around and started walking back toward the distant carcass. Fawn was pleased to see that Barr and Remo had finally taken their boots off and were wading around in the surf with Hawthorn, even if they were only washing up after the fish-butchery. But there was a suspicious amount of splashing going on for such a practical purpose.

They collected the boys and their prizes—Fawn was fascinated to handle the sculpted teeth with their strange serrated edges, once the blood and smelly gristly bits had been cleaned off—and made their way back to their cache, where the men built a driftwood fire. Hawthorn made Dag light it while he watched closely, venting hoots of delight. Fawn was grateful for the orange heat on her face, because the breeze was still chilly and damp. Even the patrollers thought the colors licking up around the bleached wood—blues, greens, spurts of deep red— were magical.

At length, Berry and Whit came back. Only now they walked up the wet sand not just side by side, but holding hands tightly. As they came near, Fawn saw that Berry looked wistful, and Whit looked sappy. She and Dag, sharing a blanket like a cloak, glanced at each other and grinned in recognition.

As the pair came up to the fire, Dag leaned back, eyes crinkling, and called, "Congratulations!"

Whit looked faintly horrified.

"Lakewalkers," sighed Berry.

"Dag!" Fawn poked him in reproof. "At least let them say it for themselves!"

"Well, um . . ." said Whit.

Berry scraped a strand of sea-blown hair out of her eyes. "Whit's asked me to marry him."

"And she said yes!" put in Whit, in a tone of wonder.

It made the ensuing picnic properly celebratory, to be sure. Hawthorn was quite taken with the notion that he would now have a tent-brother, in the Lakewalker style. Whit glanced at Hawthorn, glanced at Dag, and looked quite thoughtful all of a sudden.

Later, handing around the food, Fawn murmured to Whit, "Good work, but you sure took a chance. You were real lucky to bring it off so soon!"

He whispered back, "Well, you said I ought to wait till I was as far from that cave as it was possible to get." He stared out at the gleaming sea. "You can't get any farther than this."

They ate, drank, rested—in some cases, napped—and watched the repeating miracle of the waves and the turning of the tide. The sun sloped down to the west, lighting distant clouds that towered peach and blue above the lavender horizon, making Fawn think of the tales of the great shining cities of the lost Lake League on a drowned shore halfway across the continent. On a lake so wide you could not see across, so it had to be something like this. *I should like to see that lake, someday.*

Dag was asleep with his head on her lap when a white speck out to sea resolved into a familiar sail. Distant figures waved at them from the deck as the fishing boat rode the tide and breeze into the estuary's mouth. She awoke him with a kiss, and they packed up and climbed the line of dunes to meet it at their landing place.

At the top, Whit turned to walk backward, then stopped. "This is the end of the world, all right."

I once said I would follow Dag to the end of the world. Well, here we are . . .

Whit continued, "Sure is impressive. But just too big. I think the river will be enough water for me, from now on." He smiled at his river lady and tried to steal a kiss, thwarted because she gave him one first. Hawthorn only wrinkled his nose a little.

"The *Fetch* won't go upstream," Berry reminded him. "We'll be walking home."

"And all uphill, too," said Whit, making a wry face.

"That'll be one long walk," said Remo, to which Barr added, "Yeah, I need to get me some new boots."

Fawn turned from the sea to look out over the flat marsh, fading into immense hidden distances, and felt dizzy for a moment, imagining the wide green world tilting up before her feet.

"You know, Whit, it all depends which way you're facing. This way around, it looks to me more like the world's beginning."

Dag's grip on her hand tightened convulsively, though he said nothing. Together, they all slid down the slope of sand to meet the boat.

Author's Note

Feeling that my memories of houseboating on the Ohio River in my youth weren't quite enough to support my tale, I turned with great reading pleasure to additional sources. I quickly found that while material on steamboating ran the length of the Mississippi, the earlier era of keel-boats, flatboats, and muscle power was much less widely documented.

Especially worth sharing with the reader curious for more are: *The Keelboat Age on Western Waters* (1941) by L.D. Baldwin; *Old Times on the Upper Mississippi: The recollections of a steamboat pilot from 1854 to 1863* (1909) by George Byron Merrick; *A-Rafting on the Mississip'* (1928) by Charles Edward Russell; *A Narrative of the Life of David Crockett, by Himself* (1834) (Bison Books facsimile reprint 1987); and, rather a prize because it was only printed in a limited edition of 750 copies, *The Adventures of T.C. Collins—Boatman: Twenty-four Years on the Western Waters, 1849–1873,* (1985) compiled and edited by Herbert L. Roush, Sr.

The Merrick, the Russell, the Crockett, and the Collins were all authentic firsthand accounts, immensely valuable for the kind of detail that cannot be found in general histories. I owe Russell for Whit's memorable phrase when falling in love at first sight with a great river because I could not sum up those feelings any more perfectly and Crockett, not only for the flatboat-sinking incident, for inspiration for the charming character of Ford Chicory—himself. I heartily recommend this autobiography, which seems to have been penned as an early political memoir; its politics have been pared away by time, but its personal aspects remain riveting to this day.